Defining Destiny: Book I

Approaching Dawn

H. K. LORE

Adventures of Azyria

This is a work of fiction. Names, characters, organizations, places, events, and incidents are products of the author's imagination. Any resemblance to real world counterparts are entirely coincidental.

Cover design by Heather Kannianen
Edited by Brittany Lindensmith and J. K. Lore

Acknowledgements

Approaching Dawn would have never reached completion if not for the love, support, and dedication of my wonderful friends and family. To all who encouraged me, uplifted me, and believed in me: *thank you.*

There are those who assisted me on my journey more than words can adequately convey, but still I will try.

Thank you to my long-time best friend Justine McCorkle for always listening and providing endless support. All those long nights of text role-playing and even longer nights of playing tabletop shaped me into the author I am today; I would not be the same if not for you. I treasure our adventures together and the experience it gifted me.

Thank you to my sister-in-law Brittany Lindensmith for your time and effort spent editing and polishing the material. Your expertise and professional eye helped whip the book into shape. That, and your feedback hoisted up my spirit when it was otherwise downtrodden. I am fortunate to have such a knowledgeable, loving pillar of support.

Thank you to my brother-in-law John Lindensmith for your thorough feedback and critique. Your input brightened my spirits on even the gloomiest of days and powered my motivation when I had otherwise run out of steam. You helped assure me that being an author was worthy of all the blood, sweat, and tears I had poured into it. Your commentary was invaluable on the final legs of writing the book, and I am incredibly blessed to have had such encouragement.

Thank you to my parents, Sherrie and Joe Dawson. You believed in me even when I had little faith in myself. You reassured me when I was despondent and spurred me on when I was zealous. You always nurtured my creative spirit throughout the years and never once trivialized my goals and dreams. Your support and acceptance of my creativity has played no small part in my development. I am forever grateful I have such loving, positive parents.

Finally, thank you to my beloved husband, Jared Kannianen. Without you, especially, this all would have never been possible. I am reminded day-in and day-out of all the ways you embolden me. It is because of your boundless love, interest, devotion, and inspiration that *Approaching Dawn* could become more than just a dream – than a collection of musings and scrambled fragments of plot. With your helping hand, it became a *reality*, a completed novel, a wish granted. You always, *always* believed in me and picked me up no matter how many times I fell. Your support, consolation, and input were the glue that cemented the project together; it would have all fallen apart if not for you. You are so very special to me; I am overjoyed to be following my dream with you at my side.

You all have my infinite appreciation. Again, *thank you.*

Table of Contents

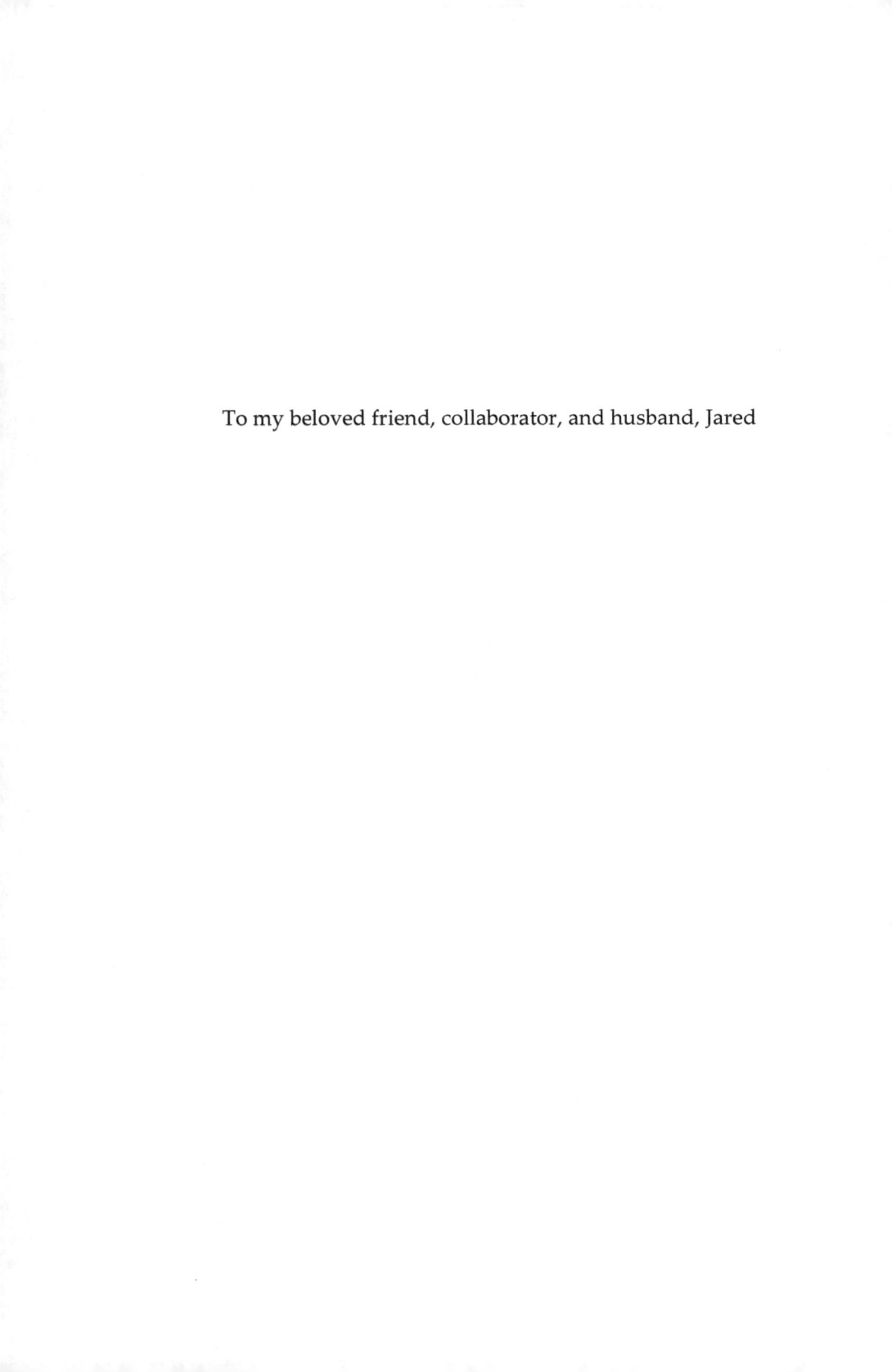

To my beloved friend, collaborator, and husband, Jared

Chapter I

Sphinx

They were *perfect*. Delightfully colorful, plump; all the qualities of a fantastic prize checked off. Of course, such a quality was to be expected from the best shipment on that corner of town. Sphinx had been waiting for the familiar sight of the rickety, old cart to come down the way, and its arrival did not disappoint. *'Right on time!'*

He stared at the barrow as it noisily teetered past, a glow in his eye as he assessed the contents of its cargo. The mass of golden pink bobbed and bounced with the effects of the cart's trek, but none came too close to rolling out onto the street. They were not stacked high enough for such, as though the stocker knew that the cart would jitter and wobble, and thus lose precious merchandise through such a bumpy journey.

It would not be a far-fetched assumption to think such of the cart owner. They pushed the ancient thing with hands older than the barrow itself, their footsteps slow but dedicated. She was Mrs. Thickett, cousin to the producer of the quality cargo she drove along. Mrs. Thickett was a sort who liked things in order, someone who would definitely hate to lose some merchandise to a bumpy cart. Sphinx knew her mannerisms well… and temper. She was passive (enough) until she lost one of his games.

He sat with crossed legs atop a stack of crates in a narrow alley near the bustle of the market ahead. The boy hopped down from his perch, the tiny thump of his landing smothered out by the noise of the market beyond. He was straightening his brilliant, red vest when a young and unfamiliar female voice called out, "Wait up, Grandma!"

Sphinx blinked before peering towards the source, and the glow of his eye found his lips in a smile. A girl, perhaps around his age, was following behind Mrs. Thickett, pushing a cart of her own in a hurried manner. This cart was much newer but considerably bumpier as it was forced along. The vehicle acted as though it were fighting her eager push as it kept snagging on the aged, uneven brick path of Old Trader Way.

She passed by him, her focus on her apparent grandmother ahead. Sphinx watched with a twitch in his lip as her youthful form left him behind. She was human and had long, chestnut hair that waved behind her as she scampered along. Her face was pleasant to look at... amongst other parts of her.

He almost didn't notice a plump, pink prize spill out of her cart and onto the road. The girl certainly didn't, as she once again cried out for her grandmother's attention.

Sphinx approached the fallen cargo and muttered a magical incantation. The merchandise shuddered before springing to life, hopping from the ground and into his hands. He gently squeezed the treasure, noting an ideal texture and firmness. *'Perfect, as always. He'll love these.'*

With that, he began to follow behind Mrs. Thickett and her supposed new apprentice, his expression shifting into a pleasant smile. He stayed a reasonable distance behind, juggling the misplaced item from hand to hand.

When they approached the heart of the market, the mildly busy road they were walking upon opened into a massive square, vendors of several trades occupying it. A bustling crowd browsed about, eager and willing to buy. It was Old Trader Square, one of the copious 'old-fashioned' trading hubs of East Akarth. Sphinx much preferred this place to any store; there was more acceptance of his antics amongst the traders who gathered here. Perhaps this young girl would be no exception; that thought spurred a chuckle.

Mrs. Thickett seemed bent on finding her past spot as they moved along the edge of the market. They finally came upon it, the area marked as reserved. Mrs. Thickett nodded to herself and mumbled something Sphinx did not catch thanks to the volume of the square. He could read that she was satisfied, however.

As the two began to prepare their stand, Sphinx hung back, standing nonchalantly against a bench.

"Have you lost half your cart, Siena? Gods, you can't be crazily shoving the thing!" he heard Mrs. Thickett scold over the commotion.

Sphinx eyed the treat in his hand.

"I'm sorry, Grandma... It just kept getting caught! I—" the girl attempted to excuse, but Mrs. Thickett was having none of it.

"You have to slow down! Your mother *insisted* you help out, and I was kind enough to accept. Don't make me regret that!"

"Okay, Grandma..."

"You're going to be a lady before long, you know! This job will do you good. Your mother worries you're too—"

"Flighty. Yeah, yeah, I know..." She took the words with tired regard.

"Cutting people off is rude! Now, help me get this banner up..."

Sphinx set his gaze back on the two of them, and he watched the girl, Siena, closely. She had a tiny frown but was focused on the task her grandmother asked of her. They were sprawling a colorful sign across a wooden stand; *'Thickett's Peach Patch'* it read.

"Isn't it called an orchard of peaches?" Siena questioned, her eyes on the sign. "Why does it say 'patch'?"

"Don't be silly! It's good business — it rolls off the tongue easier." Mrs. Thickett shook her head and squinted into the crowd, the morning sun shining brightly. "I'm going to turn in our permit. Do *not* help any customers yet, you hear?"

"Yes, Grandma..."

The elderly woman began her walk to the permit station, allowing him the window of opportunity he was waiting for.

He approached the stand with a whistle, still tossing the misplaced produce from hand to hand. Siena didn't appear to notice him, for her attention was on the hustling of the crowd, who luckily did not show interest in their stand quite yet.

"Hello, there!" Sphinx chimed, his greeting startling her.

"OH! Um! We're closed!" she spat out in a hurry, whipping around to face him. Her face bent with confusion when she saw the peach he was holding.

"I believe you dropped this earlier," he said sweetly, gesturing to the fruit. "I only imagine you want it back."

"Ummm. Yeah, yeah!" Her hand extended to take the produce from him and he handed it over, his grin wide. "Uh, thanks!" Siena stared down at the fruit, her expression a tinge perplexed. "I'm surprised you didn't just... um... you know."

"Steal it?" Sphinx guessed.

"Well... yeah." Siena shrugged and didn't meet his gaze.

"Where's the fun in that?" he inquired, flashing a toothy smile. "I'd rather earn it."

"Earn it?" Siena finally faced him, her eyes—an amber hue, Sphinx noted—wide with wonder.

"Yep! If I can manage to trick you, I win four peaches! How does that sound?" His smile held.

"Trick... me? But, no! That's not allowed; Grandma would hate it! We're— we're closed anyways!" she desperately refused.

Sphinx laughed. "Closed? Well, I'm not a typical customer, right? Your grandma doesn't have to know; she'll be gone for a while."

"But... no! You have to buy it!" she rebutted, stubborn.

"Ah... I see." His shoulders raised in a drawn-out shrug. "Well, I don't have the coin to buy them, *but* I was kind enough to return that peach anyways. Won't you just humor me?"

Siena looked conflicted. "What do you mean by 'trick', anyways? That sounds mean..." she spoke through a frown.

"Mean? Nothing mean at all! You just have to answer a riddle," Sphinx assured her.

"A riddle? That's it?" Siena now seemed intrigued. "I do like riddles..." The girl moved her eyes to the crowd, where her grandmother had left. "...You said you have no money?"

"Not a coin to spare, as it goes. Will you help me?" He did his best to channel all his charm into a smile.

...and Siena was charmed. "Well, alright! Let's hear your riddle, then."

Sphinx thought for a moment. If she liked riddles, that might mean she's good at them; it would have to be a tricky one. "Sooo... Say there are three peaches, and you take away two of them. How many do you have?"

Siena blinked before smiling wide, answering instantly. "One, of course!"

Sphinx smiled wider. "Do you? I thought I said *you* took two of them."

Siena's smile faltered as it clicked. "Aw! That was a good one!" she then laughed, and it was a lovely sound. "You win, I guess!"

"So, how many peaches does that mean *I* have?" Sphinx inquired with a smirk.

"Four," Siena giggled, turning around to grab the agreed amount. She handed him his prize, a rosy blush coloring her tan cheeks.

He accepted them with a nod before opening his pouch to store them away. "Perhaps we'll have to play again sometime," he mused, confirming the bulge that was now in his bag with a little pat.

"Maybe," Siena agreed. "My name is Siena, by the way. What's yours?"

"You can call me Sphinx, Siena," he replied, his words smooth. "It was—"

"Not *you* again! Gods help me— Listen, rascal, you better scram and leave this stand alone!" Mrs. Thickett's voice was a rude intrusion to their conversation.

Sphinx, all smiles, turned around to spot the aged women clomping over. "Hey there, Mrs. T!"

"I mean it! Go on!" she ordered, jabbing a finger away. "Siena, don't you talk to that boy! I said we were closed!"

"Yes, Grandma." Siena shared a worried look with him, but Sphinx merely winked back at her.

"I was just returning a peach that had fallen out of the cart. I'll be on my way!" Sphinx remarked, truthfully enough.

"Indeed!" Mrs. Thickett scoffed.

Sphinx straightened out his vest before beginning a confident gait away from the stand. When he reached a fair distance, he pulled a peach from his bag and bit into it, the satisfaction of his success as sweet as the flavor. *'Yep! Perfect, as always!'*

Chapter 2

Sphinx

The sun was descending by the time his errands were through, transforming the sky into a stunning display of orange and purple. The summer sunsets of Akarth were a thing of beauty, and Sphinx had the mind to watch it before the night swept in. *'I'll have to hurry.'*

He checked his bag outside the Hilltop Library entrance to assure his work was truly done for the day, and the items were all there: peaches, bread, magic books, and paper.

He sealed the satchel with a satisfied grin and skipped the last stair before landing on the sidewalk. He adjusted his bag and set off in a hasty trot, his head lifting to stare at one of the many towers ahead. It was his destination, and about a ten-minute walk away… if he didn't hustle, that is. Hustling, he could make the journey in about seven minutes. *'Let's try for six! I'm sure he's getting antsy.'*

He got there in ten anyway. A detour was needed, for not even two blocks away from the tower, he caught overly curious eyes peering from an alley. It was a younger girl who sported dirty clothes and was skittish when he glanced over. Sphinx's gut was far from thrilled at the aspect of seeing someone so close to their hideaway, and he wondered if that was selfish. *'No, I have to keep us safe.'* Even so, he wondered if he should have at least offered a piece of bread.

He took a winding way to the tower from there, cautious and watchful of any followers. By the time he snuck through the fence and slipped past the loose board in the sealed-off back entrance, he was confident that no one was watching.

A dusty, stale room was what he stepped into, the only things occupying it being a stairwell and several sloppily stacked boxes. It wasn't a very large space, and a door Sphinx knew to be on the back wall was hidden thanks to the plethora of storage. The tiny spears of light that spilled through the clasped boards did little to light up the place, but that would be no issue.

He walked towards the stairwell, whispering an incantation under his breath. A tiny orb of light manifested next to his head via the effects of the

5

spell, and he began to ascend up the stairway, the steps creaking and moaning with his weight.

The stairs delivered him into another room, this one much larger but equally cluttered. It, too, was dark, but a window welcomed in red-orange light, catching the edges of the crates in the brightness of sunset. With a swiping of his fingers, the orb left its spot by his head and traveled about the place, spotlighting the area beneath it wherever it went.

He stared at its wake, scrutinizing for anything off or different. The orb made a full circle around the room and nothing revealed to be amiss. He nodded to himself before walking towards a door on his right and heading through it, its aged hinges protesting with a croak. Another staircase met him beyond the door, this one spiral in nature. He began his way up without delay, the orb lighting his path.

It was to be a long climb up. As he went, he began to whistle. The whistling grew louder, and then even louder still with the assistance of yet another magic trick. A visible sound wave embodied from the spell and it shot up the staircase much faster than he.

Flight after flight of creaky, noisy stairs affirmed his ascent. Finally, he found himself at the end, and the stairs opened into another sizable, unlit room.

"Karreo?" Sphinx called out into the dark.

His hand again moved to order the orb around the place. This room was much cleaner, with reasonably less clutter and crates to be found. The walls around the room were decorated with several thin windows, but a heavy cloth was tacked up over them, smothering out the light from outside. In one of the corners was a blanket-laden nest, compiled out of worn cushions and sagging pillows. The boxes of the room were serving as makeshift furniture, boasting books and candles and plates on their surfaces. The unused crates were stacked up neatly against the wall behind the nest, blocking off any windows there.

In the middle of the room was a ladder that led up to a handle on the ceiling. Sphinx made his way over and nimbly climbed up, pushing the handle at the top. A square of the ceiling gave way, spilling in a wave of golden light. Sphinx winced against it and hoisted himself onto the floor of the room beyond, the orb fizzing out of existence in the process.

The whole area was awash in the colors of sundown, as massive clock-shaped windows occupied every wall. Moth-bitten drapes and sheets were pinned up against them, but they did little to contain the light pouring in. A mechanism hung from the ceiling, a system of gears that connected to every wall. They did not turn nor click, and a thick layer of dust clung to the apparatus, lit afire by the ending day. Shelves filled with tools and books were pushed up against the glass, and there was another huddle of blankets and cushions in the corner of the room. Sitting atop one of the pillows was a figure.

They turned to look at Sphinx upon his arrival. A young human child stared back at him, familiar to Sphinx, but not. They were male, with short black hair paired with round, blue eyes.

Sphinx's features burst into a thrilled smile. "Karreo?!" he cried out, his tone high with excitement.

The young human nodded ungracefully.

"You did it!" Sphinx rushed over and dropped to hug him. "You finally shifted! Look at you!" Sphinx broke the hug to stare more closely at the boy. A hand rose to Karreo's head and Sphinx's fingers felt around his scalp. "No horns!" He craned his neck to look behind the child. "No tail!" Sphinx put his hands up to Karreo's cheeks and cupped them. "You did it! Your skin isn't even a little red! And your eyes — they're blue!"

Karreo's head bobbed in a nod to all Sphinx's observations. "Yeah… But it's really, really hard," the child admitted, dropping his gaze. "I'm trying to focus, I really, really am."

"You're doing it!" Sphinx happily assured him. "I'm so proud of you!"

"I—" Karreo's eyes squeezed shut. "I can't no more; it's too hard."

"It's okay, it's okay! It'll get easier with practice! Believe me!"

Karreo's eyes opened and his irises, instead of a dark blue, now appeared a vivid yellow. The sclera of his eyes went cloudy before turning black as shadow. Karreo's lip trembled and more of him began to shift.

The olive of his skin faded away and was replaced with a brick red hue. Triangular stripes accenting his cheeks revealed, along with a bumped ridge atop his eyebrows. Tiny, bud-like horns sprouted from the sides of his head, and his ears stretched and adopted tips. The nails on his hands grew into dark claws, and a tail manifested, tipped with a barb-like shape. His black hair was the only thing that remained unchanged.

Karreo's yellow eyes were glossy with tears and the moisture spilled over. "I can't do it," he gargled with a sob.

"Hey, hey, I said it's okay." Sphinx's arms wrapped around him in a hug for a second time, squeezing tight. "It's your first time hiding everything at once! You did so well!"

Karreo had no answer other than more tears.

"I know what will cheer you up!" Sphinx suggested, unwrapping his arms from around his brother. "Here, here, look what I got!" He dug into his bag and pulled out one of the wonderful pink treasures he had earned prior that day. "It's from the best shipment, even! You love these!"

Karreo's eyes went wide and intense at the sight of the peach. His tears ceased flowing and his lip quit trembling.

His change in tune had Sphinx beaming. "Let's go get this cut up for you."

■ ■ ■

Karreo devoured his peach slices in a hurry. Sphinx sat across from him at their makeshift table, wiping clean the knife he had used to chop the fruit. They sat back in the room below, a few candles now lighting up the space modestly. The latch door had been left open, letting some golden light into the room as well.

"How come you can so easily...?" Karreo muttered eventually, breaking the silence since leaving the clock room.

"Hmm?" Sphinx hummed, glancing over.

"Transform and stuff..." Karreo elaborated.

"Lots and lots of practice, brother of mine." Sphinx smiled warmly at his sibling. "You'll get it; it just takes time."

"But I wanna now," Karreo lamented. "I wanna go outside."

Sphinx wanted to frown at that but held the urge at bay. "One day, Karri, one day soon. You just have to keep practicing." He went back to rubbing the knife. "It's for your own safety. I can't let—"

"I know, I know," the child sighed.

Sphinx's pity swelled for his younger brother. "...Hey, I know where we can get another makeup kit— the professional stuff. If you still have that big coat, we can go for walks."

"I still got it..." Karreo replied in a mutter. "I hate it; it's too big."

"That's a good thing when you have to hide a tail!" Sphinx laughed.

"I look dumb in it," Karreo whined.

"But not like a demorin!" Sphinx reminded. "It'll have to do for now. I don't like you being cooped up here, either."

"...When I can shift, do I get a cool name, too?" Karreo asked him.

"Of course! Can't be saying your real name, silly," Sphinx chuckled. "Have you thought of one?"

"Nothing as cool as 'Sphinx'," Karreo mumbled, licking his fingers free of peach juice.

"But you've thought of something?"

"...Maaaybe." Karreo's shoulders bumped in a tiny shrug.

"Well, let's hear it!" Sphinx leaned an elbow on the crate, curious.

"Nah, it's dumb..." his brother fought.

Sphinx put a hand to his chin and rubbed it in thought. "Hmm, you're right. It can't *possibly* be as good as the one I thought up for you."

"...What's that?" Karreo inquired, his eyes widening with intrigue.

Sphinx gave a toothy smile. "Peaches."

"Nooo! That's a dumb name!" Karreo objected. "It has to be cool!"

Sphinx had an amused scoff. "Well! What's yours, then?"

Karreo didn't answer at first. Then, quietly, "...Tiger."

Sphinx's grin doubled and he nodded encouragingly. "I like it! ...*Tiger*."

Karreo blushed and stared down at the table, his ears twitching. "I'unno..."

"Well, you have time to figure it out," Sphinx assured him. "For now, why don't we go catch the rest of the sunset?"

Karreo perked up. "On the balcony?"

Sphinx affirmed his guess with a nod. "Yep!"

Karreo sloppily got to his feet and hustled towards the ladder. His sibling was up in the clock room in a flash and Sphinx laughed at his enthusiasm. Part of it did bite, however. *'He's so excited because he hardly gets to be out there...'*

There was a door in the clock room that led to a narrow balcony in front of the tower faces spanning the entire distance around the building. The structure was very tall, being a clock tower.

The clock tower had long since been in its prime. The place had been abandoned for decades due to gears that always managed to break or fail altogether. Since its abandonment, tales whispered of a supernatural presence that haunted the premises. Karreo had been worried when Sphinx had chosen this location for their hideaway, but the older sibling pointed out that it would work to their advantage. "Not many people want to go to a haunted place," he had said. "And if there *is* anything here, don't worry! We're hellborn, they won't bother their own!" Thus far, Sphinx had been proven correct. Nothing had bothered them, including any ghosts or ghouls.

Karreo stared with huge eyes out onto the massive city, his height only allowing a view from between the railing. Sphinx ruffled his brother's hair before looking out to enjoy the view himself.

The sun was close to disappearing beyond the horizon, the light bathing the city stark and colorful. The twilight was beautiful to behold, a pleasant summer breeze enriching the experience.

The sky was more dark than light when Karreo finally broke the silence that had overcome them. "...Hey, Valen?"

"Hm?"

"Can we go read the magic books?"

"Of course we can. I even got some new ones today," Sphinx – rather, Valen — replied.

"Really?!"

"Really, really."

"I want to read them now!" Karreo exclaimed, elated. The child hurried back inside, his tail trailing behind him.

Valen chuckled and followed his little brother with a grin, shutting the door behind them with a click.

Karreo hurried down the ladder and plopped down on one of the pillows of the nest, gripping at a blanket in anticipation. Valen sat down next to his sibling, and Karreo scooted onto his lap.

Valen dug through his satchel and pulled out one of the new books he had picked up that day. He had an agreement with the man who ran Hilltop Library that if he could understand the books he picked out after studying them, he could keep them. He had to prove it, however, which was never difficult; a simple test of skill or understanding was all Samitri Dayas needed for proof.

Mr. Dayas was an older floraling scholar who was thrilled to see a boy of Valen's age take interest in the magical arts. "Better than what many in your situation turn to," the elf had told him once. "Use it as an outlet."

The floraling needn't remind Valen; magic had always fascinated him since he was a young child. It turned out that he had a knack for it, too. Many cantrips had come to him through innate power, but that was no surprise. "Your demorin heritage gives you a connection to the rucanic," his father had explained. "This will grant you abilities, and those abilities will grow with study. Understanding your power and then building upon it is a worthy goal."

However, the study of the rucanic was banned in Akarth, unless the mage-in-training was registered with the city and in possession of a permit. Valen was neither of those things, and never planned to be. Therefore, months ago, it had surprised the demorin to find a contact in Mr. Dayas.

Valen had acquired a fake permit, which apparently wasn't very convincing, for when the demorin had attempted to rent books with it, Mr. Dayas had noticed immediately. Yet instead of handing him off to the authorities, the scholar had brought Valen into his office and questioned why he wanted to learn the rucanic. Valen figured there was no further consequence in being transparent, and explained his innate abilities and desire to learn. When Mr. Dayas inquired why he hadn't just gone the honest, legal route, Valen explained that he lived on the streets, giving him little other choice.

The scholar had proved to be a freethinker and chose to help him despite the illegality of it. "No one is going to be blowing up any buildings at your level," the lavender-colored floraling had excused. "I don't see the harm in encouraging a youth in a tight spot who has a drive to learn."

It was a generous gesture, considering the repercussions of assisting a rogue mage. Valen hoped nothing drastic would befall Samitri Dayas, but the scholar had never shown any worry. "We all have our business. The government doesn't have to know everything."

Reading the books Mr. Dayas supplied him with made the innate power he held understandable, let alone utilizable. The anatomy of spells and how they worked was captivating; Valen adored learning how the rucanic pieced together.

Karreo held interest, too, as it turned out. The symbols fascinated him, and he enjoyed being taught what they all meant and did. His brother was already recognizing a few key runes, which, at only six years old, was impressive. '*They would be so proud of him...*'

"What's this one about?" Karreo questioned from his lap.

"Illusions," Valen answered, cracking the book open. He flipped through the pages until an illustration or runes sped by. It didn't take much searching, for a spell formula revealed itself near the start.

Valen assessed the spell, scouring for any runes that were familiar at first glance. The rucanic mark for 'shadow' was written near the middle of the formula.

10

"What's this one, Karri?" he asked, tapping a finger to the rune.

"Uuuhhmm," Karreo hummed, uncertain. "Uhhhh…"

Valen's gaze went on the candles next to them, more specifically the shadows they dropped. "What is the light casting?"

"…Ummm. Shadow! Shadow! It's the mark for shadow!" Karreo eagerly responded.

Valen grinned. "Good job!" He then searched for another familiar rune. "How about… this one?"

Chapter 3

Valen

The room was dark with the blue of night when Karreo mentioned he couldn't sleep. Valen rolled over to face his little brother, his tired eyes barely keeping open to stare at him.

"Why's that?" he wondered, groggy.

"I miss Mommy and Daddy..." Karreo muttered, his voice small and sad.

That woke Valen up. He scooted closer and wrapped his arms around Karreo, bringing him near. He couldn't find any words to say, and so he kept quiet.

"...Do you?" Karreo asked into his chest.

Valen pet his sibling's back to soothe him. "Of course I do, Karri, but Mommy and Daddy need us to be strong..."

"I know," Karreo mumbled. "I just miss them a lot..."

Valen nodded and kissed the top of his head before squeezing him tightly. "They'd be so proud of you for shifting all the way today."

"Yeah... so the bad people don't get me, too," Karreo answered grimly.

Acid of discomfort began to bubble in Valen's stomach, and the demorinkin fought a sigh. "Don't worry about the bad people, Karri... We're going to be fine, okay?" *'I promised.'*

Valen thought back to the night his father made him promise that. Their parent had been acting strange, jumpy. He had grabbed Valen's hands and squeezed them tightly. "You're growing into such a fine young gentleman, Valen," he had said.

Valen had wanted to say something snarky to that, but his father's peculiar behavior kept the words in his throat.

"Someday something terrible might happen, and your mother and I won't be there to guide you. You'll be fine, but your brother... he's so young. I can't—" He had shaken his head, and then stared at his son dead in the eye. "Promise me that if anything ever happens to us, you'll keep both of you safe."

"Of... of course, Father." Valen hadn't known what else to say; his father's words had unsettled him as if a chilling wind had slithered past. "Dad... Are you okay?"

Their father had then let go of Valen's hands and thrashed his tail through the air harshly, as though dismissing something. "I'm fine. I only worry for your future sometimes, as parents do."

For some reason, Valen had allowed that to excuse the oddity of the situation. *'I should have pried. Maybe I could have helped...'* Logic argued that it would've been a recipe to get them *all* killed; then Karreo would have had no one. It didn't take away the sting that he had done nothing to help, however.

It had been eleven months ago that it all happened. Two nights following the promise, their mother announced a surprise vacation for the two brothers. "We want you to meet your Aunt Jenane. She lives in Akarth! You've both always wanted to go, haven't you?"

They had. Valen and Karreo were thrilled to go someplace new; they hardly ever left the small town of Riverview. 'Small town' being a relative term. It was definitely not the country, and a larger settlement by all means, yet it was nothing compared to the sprawling metropolis of Akarth. Akarth sat just further down the river, a two-day carriage ride away.

"You'll get to take a vehicle!" their mother had said thrillingly. "How exciting is that?" The trip to Akarth by vehicle was shortened to only a two-hour long trip, plus wherever you were heading into the city. Valen and Karreo had only been in a vehicle a few times in their life, for the family had never owned one. In a town where you could walk everywhere, there had been little demand for something so pricey.

They were to leave in the middle of the night, and their parents were staying behind. Valen still vividly remembered packing, wondering what the largest city on the continent would be like. He had stepped into that car with a smile, eager for the events to come.

They drove through the night into the deep city, the trip totaling a four-hour car ride by the end of it. Their chauffeur escorted them into a house they had presumed to be their aunt's, but revealed to be a bed and breakfast inn when the driver checked them into a room. The chauffeur then gave Valen a letter and a package, showed them to their room, and that was the last time they ever saw him.

The room was a humble two queen suite with a country-esque vibe to the decor. Karreo was bouncing on the bed and laughing when Valen sat down at a desk in the corner, wondering what the letter could be.

He remembered his heart stopping and an impossibly heavy stone crushing his insides as he read it. The letter was from their father, and what it said is something Valen would never forget.

My dearest, dearest Valen and Karreo,

Your mother and I are so proud of you both, and no words adequately describe our love for the two of you. We have watched you grow and mature, but I fear that we can no longer be there for you.

You have lived a life of peace and safety, but forces beyond our control long to see that life shattered. There are those in this world that despise our kind, and they have narrowed their sights on our family. I will not lie to you, for you both need to understand this very, very clearly.

Demorin hunters have tracked me since my young adulthood, and while I escaped their gaze for nearly two decades, that is not the case anymore.

They have found me, and have made it clear that they intend to kill me. They know of your mother, but they do not know of you children.

It was only a matter of time before they discovered your existence unless drastic measures were taken. Please, please forgive us for the atrocities we must perform as your parents. We're sending you both away to Akarth, where you must hide and protect your identities. As demorinkin you possess the innate ability to disguise yourself through shapeshifting – you must utilize this ability for your own safety. You are not safe being what you are. I apologize for this world, for it cannot accept us for our heritage. I apologize to you, for having to bear this reality because of my own actions. I am sorry. I am sorry…

There is so much I want to say to you both. I want to continue being your father and teaching you the ways of life. I want to take you into my arms and tell you that it will be okay. But I cannot do any of these things. You must carve your own way from here.

These hunters call themselves 'The Fangs of Hellbane', and while they are not large in numbers, they are very organized. They are ruthless and unforgiving and will do anything to find you if they discover your existence.

I regret that no family can assist you. Your mother's relatives have made it very clear that they want nothing to do with our family due to your mother's choice in taking me as her mate. This world truly has little tolerance for our kind.

Akarth is the ideal place for you both. It is large and there are many places to hide. You can build a life here; I believe in you.

We have left you with our remaining wealth, and I apologize it could not be more. Within the package you will find the funds, as well as items for protection.

Resent us if you must, but do know that we love you more than anything.

Please forgive us.

-Your father

An impossible fog of disbelief had held him under siege. He reread the letter time and time again, but none of it felt real. He couldn't process it; he desperately wanted to believe it was some sort of cruel joke.

"What's it say?" Karreo had pondered out loud from the bed.

Valen hadn't replied. No tears came as shock resounded from every corner of his mind. He felt numb and empty, and could not fully grasp what had just happened.

He had checked the package, and inside was a set of dual daggers, ones Valen recognized as his father's old adventuring knives, as well as a set of his rune infused bracers. Underneath that was the money their father mentioned; it only amplified the nightmarish feeling overwhelming him.

Valen had eventually left the letter and package on the desk and went to the bed where Karreo now sat instead of bounced. "Hey, Karri," he began, the tears finally pooling. "We need to talk."

He remembered Karreo's widened eyes boring into him. "Is it bad?"

Valen's lip had trembled and he forced his head into a jerky nod. "We're not going to see Aunt Jenane, Karri."

Valen could barely recall what happened after that. There was a lot of wailing and crying, he knew, and it ended with them embracing, despairing together.

Valen had felt terrified at any possible route they had to trek from there. They remained at the inn for a week, the stay chewing through the funds they had been given like a hungry rat to flesh. Karreo wasn't allowed to leave the inn room, for he wasn't practiced enough to hold any kind of shift. Valen could disguise himself due to his own past practice, but he still hardly left the room himself.

The world was a different place. Everyone they saw was now a potential threat, and his head and heart were drowning in the hostile reality they now lived in. '*I have to keep us safe. What do I even do?!*' It was a common thought that allowed him scarce sleep at night and no moments of relaxation in the day.

Valen knew that they couldn't stay there but had not an idea where they should or even could go. He was smothered by the responsibility that now plagued him, and his very being was the epitome of overwhelmed.

He decided eventually that they had to leave the inn, and so he went to a clothing store nearby and bought a heavy, large coat and scarf. They packed that day, using the suitcases they had brought with them for their once perceived vacation.

Valen took the note with him, and equipped one of the daggers he had inherited with anxious hands. Giving the other set to Karreo was unreal, and Valen despised the look of a knife on his brother's belt. '*He's only five!*'

They left in the thick of night, Karreo crudely disguised in the clothes Valen had earlier bought, both of them miserable.

His brother didn't understand. "I want to go home," he had whimpered several times, to which Valen had no idea how to respond. He was lost concerning how to console his heartbroken sibling.

"We can't, Karri, we don't have a home anymore," is what he eventually told his brother, and those words still soured his tongue even now.

They spent the rest of the night wandering the city aimlessly, an alley being their ultimate destination. Valen's gut told him to save the little money they had left for food and water, and so inns and hotels were not an option. If the situation spared them any mercy it was in the form of the whole ordeal happening in Phettem, the heart of summer. The nights the two were forced to spend outside on the streets of Akarth would have been potentially life-threatening if not for the summer weather. Regardless, the two spent those nights huddled together as though it were the most bitter cold to befall the realm.

During their time on the streets Valen had turned to bars and inns to eavesdrop and chat up locals, attempting to find direction or a place to live. About a month after everything changed a lead finally presented itself.

Apparently, there were tales that an abandoned clock tower on the east side of Akarth was haunted. It was perfect! They headed to find the tower without delay, and although it was a couple days' journey—thanks to the utter vastness of the city—they eventually found their new hideaway.

They had broken in by tearing loose one of the boards blocking a back entryway of the tower. The dust that covered the rooms rivalled a freshly fallen snow, and there were hundreds of crates blocking any kind of path through the place, but stepping foot into that clock tower had been the most relief Valen had felt since the whole ordeal began.

Karreo didn't share the feeling. He was not only terrified of the place, but unimpressed with it. "I don't want to live here!" he had wailed. "I hate it! I hate it! I want to go home!"

"This *is* home, Karreo!" Valen had pleaded with his sibling. "I'm sorry but this is all we have!"

Accepting the place was easier when they finally stepped up into the clock room. Karreo's attitude was swayed by mystification, the view of the city hypnotizing him. Valen had to admit it was impressive, himself.

"We really gotta live here?" Karreo had questioned.

"Not forever," Valen clarified. "One day we'll have something better, Karreo. I promise."

Valen's recollection was broken as the sound of rolling thunder rumbled in the present. As he came to, he could hear Karreo's soft breathing, revealing that he was back asleep.

Valen's eyes burnt and he buried his face into Karreo's hair. Rain began to fall. "I promise."

Chapter 4

Valen

Valen stared through a forest of calcium streaks upon a mirror in their room, inspecting his reflection to the ambiance of a heavy rain. A young man with brick red skin stared back, peering with yellow eyes against a backdrop of blackened sclera.

His tail ticked from left to right as he studied his natural form. He had all the traits his younger brother did: triangular spots on his cheeks, a ridged brow, pointed ears, claws, tail, and horns, although there were differences to be noticed. The horns on Valen's own head were more developed with age, thus longer, and a dark red also colored the rims of Valen's ears, unlike Karreo.

His hand went up to touch his horns, which were an ivory color, noting the ribbed texture and how they were starting to curl up at the tips. With full development, he could expect the curve to grow more dramatic.

His focus went down to his bare torso. Ridges similar to the ones on his brow lined his shoulders, collarbone, and forearms, and they were mildly sharp to the touch. Rough patches of skin capped the length of his fingers and toes, and instead of spots, different types of markings decorated the rest of his figure.

The middle of his chest was a pinkish white, and his neck and shoulders were saddled with a reddish brown. A darker red joined the saddle on his neck and extended down to the tops of his arms, stripes of the same color stretching from the marking, coiling around his arms and chest. The bottoms of his hands and feet showed the same paleness of his chest, and his legs were similar to his arms, only the pink of his underbelly stretched past his waist and colored the insides of his thighs and calves.

He opened his mouth to inspect his fangs, which were considerably longer and sharper than human canines. The rest of his mouth proved mundane, although his saliva did have a salty taste to it. Not that he could taste it, being he knew nothing else, but his father had informed him that all demorin-types shared the trait, a byproduct of their relation to brimstone in the Nether realm

Valen couldn't help but respect how unnaturally strong demorin blood was. The siblings were not products of direct demorin breeding, and neither was their father. It was unknown how far their demorinkin heritage stretched back, but it was enough that their father's father and his father were not pure outer planar, for certain. Valen wondered if the demorin traits would ever leave the family's lineage, and his reflection suggested it was doubtful.

Valen, as well as his late father, had a longish face with a larger nose and gentle brow ridge. His eyebrows were thick, but not unruly. This all combined into something rather handsome, and puberty was in the process of blessing him with their father's defined jaw and chin. His features proved a tinge sharper than his father's, however, courtesy of the rare appearance of their mother's genetics.

Their mother, a normal human, had been keen featured with a small, pointed chin and full lips. Her skin was a dark olive, her hair a wavy black. Not many traces of her appearance were passed down to her children, most likely due to the intensity of their father's heritage.

He combed his claws through his hair, pushing it into place and encouraging it to fall more handsomely. Valen's hair matched his family's black and was currently worn at a length that stretched beyond his ears but remained a couple inches from his shoulders. The ends of his hair had a habit to flip subtly, but the humidity hanging in the tower air made the curl more dramatic. He wondered if he liked that or not.

"I'm cold…" Karreo shuddered from behind him, still entwined in their nest.

"I know, Karri. I'll get the blankets from upstairs," he told his sibling.

It had been raining for the last two days, turning the warm late spring air considerably chilly. Valen did not mind the rain, nevertheless, for the water supply it brought them.

It *did* make venturing out into the city an unappealing idea, however. He had stayed inside the tower for the last two days, reading the new books he had earned and practicing their lessons. Now they were out of bread, however, spurring him out into the wet and cold.

He reached over and grabbed his freshly cleaned clothes from where they were hung to dry the night before. Their 'clothesline' was a rope stretching between two highly stacked crates, but it did its job well enough.

He stepped into his pants, which were a faded black, and reached for his cream-colored shirt. Prior to yesterday, all the clothes he owned hadn't exuded the most pleasant smell, and dirt splatters along with other filth had clung to them. Fortunately, a quick scrub using soap he had earned weeks before and the rainwater they gathered had freshened them up just fine.

He buttoned up the shirt and adjusted the collar with a roll of his neck. Next came Valen's most prized possession: his vest, an article that boasted a marvelous, dark shade of red, his favorite color. His father had made it for Valen on his 12th birthday, the 24th of Moxtem, two months before everything had happened. Presently it was the 4th of Toffintem, the end of spring and beginning of summer.

20

His heart gave a pang as he adjusted the vest, aching over the memory of their father and a life that felt long behind them. He shook his head and worked to tuck those thoughts away. They had been more persistent lately with the flare up that had burdened him two nights past. It was not common anymore that his mind lingered on what had transpired, for he was doing his best to move on and build a life for Karreo and himself. *'It's all we can do...'*

Valen turned his attention back on the mirror and began to concentrate. His reflection began to change, first with his skin transforming into an olive color, then the markings fading, and eventually his horns disappearing. His ears shrunk, the ridges on his brow melded into his skin, and his tail vanished. His eyes were the last to shift, the yellow irises altering into a relaxed green and his black sclera brightening into white.

He studied his handiwork and smiled, no fangs showing. "Much better," he said to himself.

"Nah uh..." Karreo disagreed.

Valen turned to look at his brother, his eyebrows raising. "Nah uh? What do you mean?"

"It's not better... I like you better before..." Karreo was hiding most of his face with the blankets, so all Valen saw was his eyes. It was enough to tell he looked troubled.

Valen sighed and went over to lean down in front of the nest. "We have to hide ourselves, Karreo. It's what we need to do to stay safe."

"Why do they hate us?" Karreo sadly asked, his young eyes glittering with betrayal.

Valen bit his lip and stared towards the crates against the wall. How many times had he himself asked that question? The answer was obvious enough: people distrusted demorins and other hellborn beings. They looked different, arguably scary, and had a reputation of doing mischief and evil.

Life back in Riverview had been Valen and Karreo's first taste of prejudice. Many had trouble accepting what they were, while others outright feared them. Truth be known, it was why Valen already had experience shifting. Their father had taught him how from an early age, explaining that sometimes it was safer to hide than face the judgement of the world. Tragically, he had been correct on that.

Their father had only begun teaching Karreo how to transform before everything happened. They had been taking it slow, only concentrating on hiding one feature at a time. Therefore, Valen had never expected his sibling to completely hide his true form so early on. Valen hadn't been able until he was eight, after all, and even those transformations were sloppy and hard to maintain.

Granted, Karreo's progress should be much faster than Valen's had been, for factors drove his sibling that never burdened Valen in his own childhood. He hoped his brother would be quick to learn; he didn't like to stomach the thought of Karreo being stuck in the tower for *years*.

"Why?" Karreo nudged, still waiting for an answer to his earlier question.

"Because they think we're bad," Valen answered uncomfortably. "I don't know, Karreo. It's just the way it is."

"But we're not bad!" the child wailed. "They're the bad ones!"

Valen sighed and stood up, the instinct to tick his tail there, but no tail present to respond. He wasn't sure what else to say. "I'm going to go switch out the pails and get the blankets, okay?"

His brother sniffled loudly. "Okay…"

He grabbed a coat before going up the ladder, his limbs feeling heavy. He despised the reality Karreo was being forced to understand. Valen wished things were different, but what good did wishing do? *'I can't change the world. All we can do is accept it.'*

The clock room was grey and echoing with the sound of falling rain as he hoisted himself into it. Valen put on the coat and opened the door to the balcony. A pushy wind greeted him as he stepped outside, swirling around cold droplets of rain that felt sharp when they hit his face. He squinted against the storm, picking up pail by pail and bringing them inside. He did this gently, as not to lose any precious water. In total, there were seven large and heavy buckets he brought in.

When they were all indoors, he grabbed seven additional empty pails that were stacked up against the wall in waiting. He placed them out on the balcony and immediately they began to fill. Satisfied, he closed the door.

His brief time outside already had him soaked, and he knew it was only a sample of what that day was going to bring him.

He went into the corner and took up the blankets from the clock room nest, the bundle awkward in his hands. He tossed them through the latch door and they tumbled around the base of the ladder. He went down after them, his dampened clothes sticking to his skin with every movement.

He took the blankets back up into his arms and proceeded to dump them on top of Karreo. "Special delivery!"

Karreo didn't giggle, only continued to lay there.

Valen's features twisted with concern. "Do you want some hot water? It would help warm you up."

The six-year-old merely nodded.

Valen walked over to a large pot topped with a metal mesh they had near their makeshift table. On top of the mesh was an old kettle they had found stored away in one of the crates around the tower. They had found all sorts of useful objects buried away in storage, including the pot and mesh the kettle sat upon, the many pails they used to collect rainwater, and the blankets lining their nest. They hadn't even finished going through all the boxes yet, so it was a wonder on what other treasures awaited.

Within the pot were the makings of a fire, but the flame was dim and barely flickering. Valen had started the fire earlier that morning to heat up the kettle water, not to mention himself. They typically used crushed crates and straps of linen for wood and tinder, and Valen knew a spell that created a spark to get the flame going. He was reminded several times a day of how useful his cantrips and magical knowledge was.

He grabbed the kettle and poured some water into the cup he had used that morning. He wagered that the water shouldn't be too hot, judging by the weakened flame. With a quick sip, he ruled that it was a satisfactory temperature, indeed.

"Here you go, Karri." He delivered the cup to his sibling, and Karreo sat up to receive it. "Careful, it's hot."

Karreo raised the cup to his lips and took a ginger sip.

"What do you say?" Valen reminded.

"Thank you…" the tiny demorinkin replied.

"You're very welcome." *I sound like Mom.* "Alright, Karri. I have to go now. Stay inside, okay? I'll try and be back by sundown."

"Okay…" His brother looked troubled, and it troubled Valen in turn.

"Make sure you keep practicing shifting! You're already getting so good at it," Valen encouraged.

Karreo's head bobbed slowly in a nod, his bummed demeanor failing to let up.

Valen wrestled down a frown of his own and extended a hand to ruffle his brother's hair. "I'll be back."

■ ■ ■

Sphinx

The market was surprisingly busy for such a rainy day. *'Guess hungry bellies don't wait for sunshine.'*

He stuffed the bread he had just earned into his bag before it could be soiled by the rain.

"You doing alright in all this rain, Sphinx?" the bread stall owner, Aldras Panto, asked. "It's been coming down mighty hard. You got a place that keeps you dry enough?"

Sphinx smiled wide at the vendor. "I keep dry enough, Mr. Panto. Don't you worry."

"Well, alright. If you ever find yourself tired of it, I know the Phet temple down on Eastway has been taking in youngins like yourself during the storm. Can't have you getting sick. Who will fool me out of my bread?"

Sphinx laughed. "I'd find a way. Thank you for the information and bread, Mr. Panto. You have a good day." He began to stroll away.

"Stay out of trouble!" the bronze-colored terran called out.

Mr. Panto and Sphinx had an interesting relationship. The merchant had originally been hostile towards the sight of him, writing him off as an urchin thief come to steal his produce. Of course, that had been originally true, but then Sphinx had gotten an idea. "I'm not here to steal it," he had cheekily corrected. "I want to play a game! If I win, I get some bread. How about it?"

That had been the birth of his street namesake. Sphinx wasn't sure how he managed to get not only Mr. Panto, but many of the other merchants that gathered in Old Trader Square to play along with his trickery. Perhaps they were all just happy he was not there to steal, and willing to do what they had to keep him from trying. Regardless of why, he had formed a relationship with many of the vendors.

Mr. Panto was his favorite. The middle-aged terran was stern at first, but a fair, sincere man at heart. Being a terran, he stood tall and bulky with dwarfed proportions, showing off the biorocks that sprouted from his back in a halter he always wore. His skin was a dark bronze, while the rocks that decorated him were a brilliant green that matched his eyes. The dwarf had no hair on his scalp, but a beard woven into two braids adorned his chin.

As Sphinx walked, he thought about the temple and how a solution like that could never work for his brother and him. He was relieved that they had a home in the clock tower, no longer taunted by opportunities of the sort.

He looked up in time to spot a familiar face step in front of him.

"Hey, Sphinx!" the girl from Thickett's Peach Patch, Siena, greeted. She had no umbrella and was partly dry, but quickly growing wetter. "Out in the rain, huh?"

He smiled, pleased to see her. "A little rain couldn't keep me away." His smile shifted into a smirk.

She giggled, and Sphinx couldn't help himself from appreciating the look of her wet form.

"Well! Do you want to play a game again? I have four peaches if you win, just like last time," Siena offered.

He blinked, surprised. He had been meaning to stop by the peach stand again today, but this made his work *much* easier. While Mrs. Thickett *adored* him so, it was sometimes hard to get her to play along with his games.

He grinned away his shock. "You liked our game last time, then?"

She only giggled at that. "What do you say?"

"I say... What gets wetter and wetter the more it dries?" It was a fitting riddle for the day.

"Um... Uh... Well..." Siena pondered, a hand rising to her chin.

"Well?" Sphinx urged, confident he had her.

"A towel!" she suddenly exclaimed. "A towel gets more wet as it dries!"

Sphinx's smile was the one to falter this time. He then laughed. "Correct! I suppose that means I lose." He didn't lose his game very often, that was for certain.

"You lose, yes..." Her smile stretched further, and through the droplets on her face he could see her cheeks redden. "Buuut! You get the peaches anyways! My treat."

That surprised him. She dug into a bag slung across her shoulder and pulled out the fruit. She then held them out with a blush.

He stared at the produce, uncertain.

"Well go on! Take them!" she laughed, sounding amused at his reaction.

He did as she ordered. "If it's your treat, then."

"Yep!" Siena was all smiles as she went on to say, "We should play again sometime soon. Maybe it doesn't have to be at the market?"

Sphinx's brow raised. "Oh?" She wasn't the only one to blush.

She laughed sweetly. "There's a gazebo I like to go to on the river walk next to Eastway. Do you know of it?"

He did. He nodded with a smile, almost uneasily, but excited. "Are you asking me on a date?"

She shrugged and tucked some of her soaked hair behind an ear. "Well, if I was, would you say yes?"

Sphinx grinned stupidly, his heart beating fast. "Yes."

"I'll see you there tomorrow evening at 7:30, then?" Siena said.

Sphinx's smile was wide enough that it strained his cheeks. "It's a date," he agreed.

Chapter 5

Valen

Valen obsessively adjusted his hair to the left—no, the right—utterly unsatisfied with his appearance. Everything he did made him look silly or weird or—

"You already shifted, so why are you still staring?" Karreo interrupted Valen's fretting, his tone confused.

He turned his gaze away from the mirror and onto his little brother. Karreo was sitting on a crate, one of the magic books in his lap, his little feet dangling. His eyes were on his older sibling, his expression perplexed.

"Well, uh..." Valen's mind quickly worked to generate an excuse. "I'm... going on a secret mission tonight. I need to make sure my disguise is completely perfect."

Karreo's eyes went large with wonder. "Secret mission?" he repeated.

Valen tugged at his vest, swelling with pride. "You heard right." *'It's essentially the truth.'*

"What're you doing on the secret mission?" Karreo inquired curiously, seemingly enchanted with the idea.

"If I told you, what kind of secret would it be?" Valen winked at him.

"But we're brothers! You can tell me stuff..." Karreo protested.

Valen chuckled and shook his head. "I'm afraid not, little brother."

Karreo appeared unhappy with that response as he pouted his lip and jutted his vision away from his older brother.

Valen's face scrunched with consideration. "...Tell you what. I'll give you a hint!"

Karreo perked up and looked ready for it.

"If everything goes well..." Valen let the phrase hang in the air to build suspense. "...I *should* come home with more peaches."

"Really?!" Karreo exclaimed.

"Yep!" Valen said, his chest puffing out as his ego inflated. "But that's all I can say!"

Karreo looked the very image of excited. "Okay!"

Valen snickered and turned his attention back on the mirror, noticing that a blush was now coloring his face. A grin stretched his lips as he thought about his 'secret mission', and his insides fluttered with anticipation. He had never been on a date before; the thought of it made his chest flip with a mixture of excitement and nervousness.

He went back to primping his appearance, a byproduct of the anxiety the situation cast on him. While Valen was typically confident enough in his looks, he now couldn't shake a feeling of inadequacy.

The rain had stopped that morning, so their little rendezvous that evening would be considerably less and soggy. It wouldn't be long before he'd have to leave the tower, head towards Eastway, and meet Siena at the gazebo along the riverwalk.

...In fact, what time was it now? He looked to his watch, a gift from his mother several birthdays ago, and saw that it was 7:20.

His heart erupted into a gallop. "I have to go!" he abruptly sputtered out. He hastily grabbed his bag and raced to the stairs. "Bye, Karreo! I'll be back!"

"Bye, Valen!" he heard his brother holler out. "Bring back lots of peaches!"

. . .

Sphinx

He was late by the time he jogged up to the gazebo, sweat clinging to his brow and the hairdo he worked so hard on disheveled. He had misjudged how far away the riverwalk was from the clock tower, so he was even later than he thought he'd be. Even with running a good part of the way, it had taken a solid half an hour to get to the river due to all the traffic and bustle of the city.

Breathing hard, he leaned up against one of the four posts of the building before peering ahead, spotting Siena sitting on a bench that wrapped around the inside of the structure.

She was staring off towards the river, a striking ribbon of red accenting her hair, which was styled in a braid. She wore a rich brown blouse that stretched to her knees and a scarf around her neck that matched the ribbon in her hair. Black leggings showed off the form of her legs, her feet bearing an intricate sandal with a modest heel. The outfit complimented her tan skin and chestnut hair flawlessly.

She was beautiful to behold. His breath caught in his chest, and he gawked as his brain attempted to catch up with him.

She turned away from the river and caught sight of him.

"Sphinx! There you are!" she gasped. Her youthful features bent into a smile. "Late, I see."

He smiled awkwardly. "Sorry to keep you waiting."

She giggled, enchanting Sphinx with the sound. "Almost thought I'd have to look out onto the river all by myself."

"No need for that," Sphinx assured her. His nerves alight, he stepped up onto the platform of the gazebo and went to sit next to her. His legs subtly brushed up against hers as he sat down, filling him with a rush.

She beamed at him, her cheeks pink and her amber eyes bright. "You look very handsome."

His cheeks burned at that; he certainly didn't feel handsome at that very moment. He lifted a hand to run through his wrecked hairdo, and his mind worked to return the compliment. He felt a step behind.

"You're beautiful, yourself," the words eventually came out, not near as smooth as he intended them.

She giggled yet again. "You think so?"

The blush on his cheeks burned redder. "Yes," was his lackluster reply.

Siena tilted her head and she scrutinized him with a narrowing of her eyes. "What's wrong, Sphinx?" she questioned, cheeky. "Haven't you ever been on a date before?"

His face ranked similar in heat to the summer sun. "I..."

She gave a full-fledged laugh. "It doesn't matter." She looked towards the river behind them, her cheeks pushed up in a smile. "Look at how lovely the river is! I love just coming here and staring at it..."

Sphinx followed her gaze, and the river proved gorgeous, indeed. The yellow and blue hues of the ending day were flashing and sparkling atop the current, reflecting the sky. It wouldn't be long until the sun began to fully drop and golds and reds would be added to the pallet. Being Toffintem, the sun was now setting around eight thirty, which, Sphinx was embarrassed to realize, was growing close. A quick glance at his watch revealed it was 7:55.

They stared in silence for a beat or two, and Sphinx turned his eyes back on his date. "It's beautiful," he started, a stubborn swallow in his throat. "But you're prettier."

She blushed and wiggled her shoulders bashfully, her amber eyes catching glint of the sun as she turned to stare at him. She didn't say anything, but she did softly grin and gaze deep into his eyes.

It made Sphinx uncomfortable but mesmerized him equally. His heart was thumping hard in his chest, sending reverberations throughout his entire being. Something about the way she was staring stimulated him, and he felt a firmness in his lower abdomen respond.

"Thank you," she finally spoke, her tone sweet.

"You're welcome," he replied, again finding himself battling with the lump in his throat. He fidgeted and moved his bag more onto his lap, embarrassed at the thought of her spotting what hid underneath.

"Well, want to go for a walk?" she offered. She didn't wait for an answer as she got to her feet.

Sphinx experienced a surge of panic. "I, uh—"

"Come on, silly!" Siena insisted. Her hands grabbed his and pulled him into standing.

Sphinx's legs felt wobbly as he was forced to his feet, embarrassment pulsing with every speedy beat of his heart. Her hands stayed folded around his, and it only agitated the stimulation overcoming him.

She began to lead him, dropping one of his hands as she dragged him along. His face ablaze, he complied, completely uncomfortable. '*Snap out of it!*'

"What's wrong?" she giggled, looking back at him with amusement. "Come on!"

He nodded ungracefully and desperately gripped his satchel with his free hand. He strategically walked with it hanging in front of him, and, to his relief, the problem began to fade away with every forced step.

When they reached the walkway, he was getting to a point where he could relax. Her hand around his still had the power to make his heart flutter, however.

"Do you like walks, Sphinx?" she questioned. She quit leading him, but did not drop his hand.

"I, ah, yeah! I like them," he replied, internally cringing as he stuttered.

"I like them, too. My mom thinks I take too many, though..." Siena sighed, focused on the path ahead. "She says now that I'm fifteen, I have to stop being so 'flighty' and grow up."

"You're fifteen?" Sphinx commented, surprised. That was two years older than him!

"Um, yeah. How old are you?" Siena said, blinking at his apparent shock.

"Ah..." Sphinx was back to blushing. "I'm, uh," he hesitated. "...thirteen."

"You're only thirteen?!" Siena exclaimed. "I thought you were older!"

"Is... that bad?" Sphinx frowned, worried.

"Well, no—" Siena stammered. "I just, I figured... You seem older."

That managed to put a twitch in Sphinx's lip. "Do I?" He began to walk them forward, their hands still entwined.

"Yes..." Siena answered, her voice smaller. She was blushing, Sphinx noted.

"Well... I don't think taking walks is a flighty thing to do." Sphinx guided the conversation back to the former topic. "Why does your mother think that?"

"Because she thinks it's childish," Siena explained, frowning. "She thinks I spend all my time doing things that don't matter..."

"What kinds of things do you do other than take walks?"

"I like to paint and write stories," Siena gushed, a large smile overtaking her prior frown. It faded quickly, however. "Dad says I have a great imagination, but Mom says I need to stop wasting time..."

"Art isn't a waste of time," Sphinx argued. "Without art, the world would be awfully boring."

"Exactly!" Siena agreed, passionate. "I'm so glad someone understands! Everybody thinks it's so silly..."

Sphinx wondered how often she was badgered for her interests. "It's not silly, Siena," he told her, honest.

She set her eyes on him and held them there. The way she was staring had him feeling shy and excited all over again. His focus shifted to the river.

"What do you like to do, Sphinx?" she asked before long.

"Well..." What hobbies could he share with her? It wasn't the longest list. "I do like to make music," he said.

"Music? You can play?" She sounded delighted.

Sphinx nodded and faced her once more. "I used to have a guitar, but I don't..." His eyes fell to the masonry below. "I don't have it anymore." Memories flashed by of his sorely missed possession, and he had a brief wonder of what ever happened to all the things in their old home.

"Oh! Why not?" Siena pried.

"...It got lost." Sphinx elaborated, fighting to keep his tone neutral.

"Oh... Well, one day you'll get another one!" she said hopefully. "Maybe your parents will get you one for your birthday or something!"

A jolt shot through his chest, and his head dipped in a short nod. "Maybe..."

"...You alright?" Siena inquired.

"I also like riddles." Sphinx veered the conversation away from the topic with a bluffed smile.

"Of course!" Siena laughed. "Speaking of riddles! I have one for you."

"Do you?" Sphinx's brow raised, his curiosity piqued. His mind was willing for the distraction.

"Yep! If you guess right, you get a prize!"

"A prize? Well, let's hear it then." He wondered what the prize could be, intrigued.

"Okay!" She paused for a moment. "If I have it, I don't share it. If I share it, I don't have it. What is it?"

Sphinx thought for a moment. What was something that if you share it, you no longer had it? The answer popped into his mind relatively quickly, for it proved relevant to his current situation.

"A secret," he answered, confident.

"That was fast!" she laughed. "You are really good at riddles."

"So, what's my prize?" he spurred, eager to sate his wonder.

She laughed again and then was suddenly kissing his cheek. It made Sphinx halt his footsteps as he was taken off guard. The gesture ignited his entire being in warmth and slowed his mind.

"Bet that's the first time you've gotten that kind of prize," Siena giggled.

"I, uh..." Sphinx began, still wooed by the kiss. He summoned his wit as a last defense against her charm. "You're right. The vendors don't usually hand out that kind of prize."

Siena found that funny. "Well, I have a more familiar prize if you can guess right again."

Sphinx smirked as the heat from the last prize burned on. "I'm game."

"What has hands but cannot clap?" she tested.

That was a familiar riddle for him; it was one he had enjoyed telling Karreo in the past. The image of the clock room filled his mind, the mighty hands of the faces stuck forever in the time they were discharged.

He pretended to think, and had that drag on until she likely thought that she had him. Then, "A clock."

"Aw! Almost had you!" she hooted. "You win! Again!" She reached into her pouch and awarded him four peaches.

He was all smiles as he received them. He transferred them into his own bag, relieved he had been right in assuming she would bring peaches for him to win on their date.

"Always a pleasure," Sphinx remarked, satisfied.

Siena giggled playfully, beaming.

A silence followed their game, and they proceeded their stroll down the riverwalk, still hand in hand. The lack of talking made Sphinx feel more shy, but Siena didn't appear to mind.

"So, what else do you like to do?" Siena eventually went back to their prior discussion.

"I like to cook," he mentioned. It had been months and months since he last cooked, however, back before his life had… changed. When curiosity in the culinary arts had first struck him, he had been only a child, but that had not hampered his desire to learn. He had spent countless hours in the kitchen, experimenting with different flavors and constantly trying new recipes. He had flipped through many books and eagerly watched chefs on television, sponging up tips and valuable techniques. When he was only ten it had become habit to prepare meals for his family, to the relief of his parents. While they were not terrible at cooking, it was no passion of theirs. He had become more than willing to pick up responsibility for the chore.

"Wow! You're a chef, then?" Siena wondered.

Sphinx chuckled. "I like to think so."

"That's so great! I'm no good at cooking – don't have the patience."

"That is rather important," Sphinx agreed. "I also like to sing," he added after some more consideration. Flashbacks from his old life stirred, memories of sitting on the porch of their modest little home, strumming his guitar and singing songs for his mother. A seasoned vocalist herself, she would give him advice and teach him the ways of music. She always loved to hear him sing...

"Ooh! You do?!" Siena said, and the flashback dissipated.

Sphinx nodded and faked another grin.

"Show me!" Siena urged, giving his hand a squeeze.

Sphinx felt unprepared. He hadn't sung as much since everything changed; It was all too quiet without his guitar.

"Pleeease?" Siena pleaded.

He appeased her wishes.

"Here's to a heart so brave and bold,
A story to tell the young and old.
A hero that faced the utmost quest,
Who challenged the monster and passed the test."

The song was an old, *old* favorite of the Akarthi area. He sang the song in a gaudy, exaggerated voice, but he delivered it well.

"She marched with haste to slay the beast,
Promised, of course, the finest feast!
The battle was long, the stakes were high,
But with the dawn came her victorious cry."

Siena giggled as he sang, entertained.

"Victory, victory!
Sweet victory!
Victory for the noble lass.
Victory, victory!
Sweet victory!
The monster is slain, gone at last.
The monster is slain, gone at last!"

She clapped as he finished. "You're good!"

He gave a half bow and she laughed.

The red of sunset was beginning to drench the city, and it showed brilliantly upon the river. It was an impressive backdrop for their walk.

"Mother wants me home before dark..." Siena pointed out. "My house isn't far from here. If we keep walking, we'll hit it soon."

"Does she know about this?" Sphinx asked.

"...No." Siena shifted, looking uncomfortable. "If you don't mind... Maybe—"

Sphinx caught her drift. "I can drop you off a block away."

Siena looked relieved. "She hates me dating – says I'm too young! What happened to wanting me to become a lady?"

"I think you're a fine lady," Sphinx flattered. "Not too flighty at all."

Siena smiled at him, warm and humbled. "Thanks, Sphinx..." She stared down at the ground. "So... no offense... but Sphinx is an awfully strange name."

Sphinx snickered at that.

"It's not your real name, is it?" Siena pushed, her honey eyes too curious.

Sphinx looked at her, smirking. "Of course not," he answered bluntly.

Siena frowned. "Would you tell me your real name, then?"

Sphinx shook his head. "Sphinx is as good as my real name, Siena."

"Well, fine then..." she pouted, having the appearance of someone offended.

Sphinx shrugged his shoulders. "It's no offense. It's not just you."

She didn't reply.

"Honest, Siena," he assured.

She looked back towards him. "Why did you change your name?"

"I'm someone different than who I was," he explained. "That's all."

Siena's expression went sideways. "What does that mean?"

Sphinx shrugged yet again, and he had no more words to offer her.

"...Well, I guess that's your business, then," she gave up, to Sphinx's relief.

He only nodded in response.

"Well, 'Sphinx' is a fitting name," Siena said after a rather awkward silence. "Being you like riddles so much."

Sphinx grinned. "I picked it for a reason."

Sphinxes, feline-esque beasts from the netherworld, had a habit of ensnaring victims with puzzles, most famously riddles. Those unfortunate enough to fail the riddle were subject to whatever the sphinx had in store, which was typically handing over valuables and riches. More extreme versions of the mythos suggested the sphinx would devour their victim or even steal their soul. However, as a hellborn subjected to nasty stereotypes, Sphinx couldn't help but wonder if those particular claims were equitable or not.

Even so, he couldn't help himself from cracking a joke. "Luckily, I don't plan on eating anyone for failing my riddles."

Siena snorted. "Just our produce, hopefully!"

Their giggling transitioned into silence, and soon Siena was telling them to stop.

"Well," she began with a deep blush, her hand letting go of his. "I had a good time today, Sphinx."

Sphinx blushed in turn and nodded. "Me too."

"Maybe we can do it again sometime?" she offered.

Sphinx smiled at her. "Perhaps. What did you have in mind?"

"Same time on Sundae?" she suggested, twirling her hair in a cute display.

"Sounds good to me."

"Great!"

Before he could react, she was kissing him on the cheek yet again. Following that, she began to run off, giggling.

"Bye, Sphinx!"

He watched her form take down the street, the stun of her kiss stubborn to fade.

"Bye..." he said softly, a hand raising to caress where she pecked.

Sphinx turned heel and walked home with a smile.

Chapter 6

Valen

Valen sucked in a deep breath, the world around him dark as his eyes were closed, the sound of the city a faint murmur. He sat in the clock room with his hands on his knees, his father's enchanted bracers laid out in front of him, waiting to be activated.

The demorinkin exhaled and focused within himself, searching for the flow of his runa, the very energy behind spells and all magical power. It took several minutes before he could pin down the soft trickle of his reserves, coursing within him like a modest stream through a forest.

"To activate an enchantment, you must awaken the runes by applying pure rucanic energy," his father's advice echoed in his memory. "This is accomplished by finding your inner current of runa and directing the flow out of yourself and onto the runes. It is a tricky process; runa is stubborn to bend without the guide of a spell. It will take much practice and a lot of patience, but I think you can manage it."

Thus far, his father had been wrong on that. Despite his many, many attempts over the last several months, Valen had never managed to direct his runa flow out of himself. Although he could pin the current down, controlling it was another matter entirely.

"You can't force it," his father had warned him once. "You have to redirect it, rather."

Valen attempted to adhere to that pointer, but it was no use; his flow was ever loath to accept his influence no matter which angle he tried.

He sighed and cracked his eyes open, still honed onto the steady pulse of his reserves. He stared down at the bracers and placed his hands atop them, their reinforced fiber smooth to the touch. He bit his lip and for the umpteenth time attempted to concentrate his current towards his fingertips, motivated.

His heart skipped a beat when he managed to catch the stream, the sensation vibrating his insides with a deep hum. He gasped as the current began to run along his appointed course, but in his excitement, he shepherded it far too quickly. Thus, his hold failed, the hum within him levelling out.

He groaned and hung his head, upset with himself. It had been a *week* since he last managed to get a hold on his current, but he had blown it yet again.

With a huff of defeat, he stood up and decided his time was better spent doing something else.

. . .

"You have to focus, Karreo," Valen prodded his sibling. "What's five plus two? Come on, you know this."

"I don't wanna do math today..." Karreo dismissed, staring out of the clock window and into the city beyond.

Valen sighed and followed his brother's gaze. It looked to be a nice afternoon. Karreo's mind was likely distracted with scenarios of running about and playing, activities children were *supposed* to be free to do. Their situation was a cruel one.

Valen had been attempting to teach Karreo a basic education since a few months ago, after the shock of the tragedy had mostly faded. While he was successful at first, it had been growing harder and harder to get Karreo interested in studying as of late. He was a bright child who enjoyed learning, but was distracted and stir crazy from their predicament. *'Dad could always get him willing to learn. Ugh, Dad... I don't know what to do.'*

Before everything changed, their father had been tutoring them both for their education instead of enrolling them in public school. Looking back on it now, Valen was very thankful of that choice, and wondered if their parents had the worst in mind when making that decision. Their father had merely claimed it was so they could learn at a faster rate than any public school could teach them, and perhaps that was true, but was it the full reason?

Their dad had only just started with Karreo before tragedy struck but had been teaching Valen for years. Being a patient, smart man, he had been a fantastic teacher, and many of his lessons had stuck with Valen. The demorinkin hoped he could transfer those teachings onto his sibling well enough.

Their father had had plenty of time to devote to tutoring them for his right leg had been permanently handicapped due to a healing potion that had gone awry. The injury was a consequence from his adventuring days back before Valen was born. He had spent his days schooling his children and furthering his sewing business, crafting and enchanting specialty items for adventurers. It had been lucrative enough, and with their mother's added support in working at the town hall, they had lived a comfortable life. The money they had left behind for their children had dwindled significantly, but Valen had kept a fair amount of it and hidden it away within the tower for saving. If there was ever an emergency, they had at least some coin to spare.

Valen knew he would one day have to work if they ever planned on living somewhere other than the clock tower, but it was an overwhelming idea. It would have to be under the table for any other job required citizenship records and all kinds of legal documents they did not have. Acquiring them would be a death sentence; they had to remain hidden and unknown, lest their parent's murderers have a trail to follow. They simply could not risk earning a legal identity.

Let alone, who knew what the government would attempt to do with them if they were aware of their existence? The thought of being separated from Karreo scared him more than the demorin hunters did.

Being a street urchin, the privilege to work was a scarce one. Even employers that were willing to hire illegals were not desperate enough to employ children. Perhaps in a few years, or if Valen could master shifting into another older-looking form. It all felt ages away.

Not to mention that the unregistered jobs sometimes called for becoming involved with a crowd Valen did not wish to find himself in. He was trying to keep his family safe, not entwine them in syndicates and other illegal practices that came with many enemies and risks.

'*We're comfortable anyways, aren't we*?' A voice whispered that it would not be forever so. That, and he had promised his brother something better.

The brothers continued staring out of the clock window. Valen wrapped an arm around his little brother and squeezed him. "What do you want to do, then?"

"I wanna go outside…" Karreo muttered.

"Well…" Valen started with another squeeze. "Let's practice shifting, then. We can—"

"I don't wanna!" Karreo objected with a shove. "I hate it! It's stupid! I wanna go outside!"

"You can't unless you can shift, Karreo." Valen desperately called upon his father's patience. "I can't let you go out there – it's not safe!" he stressed his words with a hint of pleading.

"It's stupid!" Karreo screeched and got to his feet. He glared at Valen, his eyes pooling with frustrated tears. "I hate shifting! I hate it here! I hate the bad people!" he hiccupped with a sob.

Valen sighed as his brother threw his fit. He couldn't blame the child's anger and indignation; it all did make him feel very guilty, however.

When was the last time Karreo had even left the tower? It had been at least a month ago, when Valen had covered him in makeup and had him wear that oversized coat. They had taken a walk to the river, and even that short time outside had Valen on edge. Despite his brother's yearning, and the pity it filled Valen with, he could not risk anyone spotting his little brother. He had to keep him safe and away from prying eyes.

"I'm sorry, Karreo," Valen said. "It's the way it has to be."

"*I hate it!*" Karreo wailed. The child stomped his way to the ladder and went down it with loud thumps. "I hate *you!*"

The words inflicted Valen with hurt, even with knowing they were only a product of his sibling's torture. He let Karreo slip down the ladder into their living room, and then put his face into his hands, fighting tears of his own.

He barely heard Karreo sobbing downstairs, the sound muffled by what Valen assumed to be blankets or pillows.

"I don't know what to do," Valen whispered out loud softly. His lip trembled and he released a shuddering breath before stuffing his head into his knees. "I'm trying… *I'm trying…*"

■ ■ ■

Valen waited about an hour before heading down the ladder with the intent to fix them dinner. It would be the usual toasted bread, with the added treat of the peaches he earned last night on his date. He hoped it would help remedy Karreo's sullen mood.

He arrived downstairs to find Karreo entangled in the nest, sleeping. Valen had been wondering if he was getting enough sleep at night lately, and Karreo's snoozing form augmented the question. '*It would explain his behavior lately…*' Ugly situations became even uglier with the stain of little sleep. '*Then again, he might just be fed up with everything… which might lead to less sleep.*' It was a vicious cycle.

Valen started a small fire in the metal pot and placed the wire mesh over it. When it began to heat up, he placed four slices of bread on top. He removed Karreo's early; his brother hated it when they were too toasted.

When all the bread was cooked, he smothered out the fire by placing a fitted lid on top of the pot. He never poured water within their 'fire pit' for it was a waste of the precious resource and soiled any unburnt supplies that could still be used in future fires.

He cut up a peach for Karreo and placed his meal on one of their mismatched plates. He set it on their makeshift crate table and went to wake his sleeping sibling.

Valen shook Karreo gently, and after a few moments his brother responded by shifting awake. He sat up, his eyes still puffy and red from his earlier episode.

"There's some dinner for you on the table," Valen gently said.

Karreo avoided eye contact with him. The child looked exhausted and more bummed than angry. His yellow eyes stared down at the huddle of blankets enveloping him, and he nodded. He did not move, however.

"Come on, I bet you're hungry," Valen encouraged.

The boy nodded again, yet still failed to move from his spot.

Valen stared before looking down himself, biting his lip. "Karreo, I—"

"I don't hate you, Valen..." Karreo cut him off in a mumble, emotional. "I-I'm sorry..."

Valen wrapped his arms around his brother and held him tight. "I know, Karri. I know."

Karreo was back to crying, and Valen rubbed his back to soothe him.

"It's okay, it's okay..." he tenderly whispered with a squeeze. "It's all going to be okay..."

That went on for a few minutes or so before Valen broke the hug and looked into his distressed sibling's eyes. "Let's get some food in you, huh?"

Karreo tearfully nodded.

■ ■ ■

Valen managed to convince his brother to practice shifting for the rest of the afternoon. The older of the two siblings helped the younger along, offering tips and providing encouragement.

Karreo had hidden all the features on his face with success by the end of the session. Valen had been thrilled, especially when he held the shift for a whole twenty minutes! It was a promising show of progress, and Valen made sure his brother understood that. "You're not going to hide all of it right away, every time," he had said. "You're doing so well! Just keeping practicing!"

They now sat on the balcony to watch the sun go down, and the sight of the sunset summoned the memory of Valen's date from the night before. He thought about the evening to follow, and a rush of excitement filled him. Apprehension tailed it, however.

He was uncomfortable with having to lie and not be upfront with Siena, but it was necessary. He couldn't be spilling secrets to a girl he hardly knew. Even if the sight of her disappointment was a stirring one, Valen had to keep some, well, *most* aspects of his life a secret.

It didn't help that she could be a prying sort, even if she didn't necessarily mean to be. Valen sighed at remembering some of her questions and comments. What would happen if he accidentally revealed too much?

He wondered if these dates were such a good idea, after all. The teenager in him said yes, but the adult he had to be said no. It became a conflict in his heart and he leaned forward against the railing. Why did anything good have to be riddled with risk and uncertainty? Surely he'd eventually be driven crazy if he didn't welcome *any* type of zest in his life?

She was so *pretty*. He pictured her chestnut hair and honey eyes and felt a stirring within him. Spending time with her was unlike anything Valen had experienced before, and he was sore to put an end to it.

He was a good enough liar, so he didn't have to worry with her finding anything out, right? He wanted to feel assured by that, but a brick in his gut prevented him.

If he *did* stop seeing her, what would he even tell her? He couldn't wreck the relationship they were building, not if she was going to be working for Mrs. Thickett from that point on. It sounded so selfish, but how would be get his hands on the stand's quality peaches?

He sighed yet again as the struggle surged within him, souring his stomach.

Karreo set his attention on Valen and tilted his head. "Valen?"

Valen faced him and weakly grinned. "Hmmm?"

"What's wrong? Is it my fault?" Karreo questioned, his voice small and his lips in a frown.

Valen shook his head. "No, no, it's nothing to do with you, bud. Just... thinking about my secret missions..."

Karreo scooted closer at the mention of the secret missions. "Really?"

"Yep..." Valen scratched the back of his neck and debated how to phrase things to his younger sibling. "The missions... they're pretty risky..." He paused. "But if I don't go on them... I can't get peaches anymore."

Karreo's eyes went large with terror. "But you gotta get the peaches!"

What did he expect from the mouth of a six-year-old when threatening access to his favorite fruit? Part of Valen accused himself of wording it that way on purpose to back himself into a corner of seeing Siena. '*Real mature, Valen...*'

"I know, I know. I will..." Valen settled. He looked out into the city and his expression twisted with nerves. "I just... have to be careful."

■ ■ ■

Sphinx

He made certain he was early to the date the next evening. He arrived a whole half hour before seven and sat by himself at the gazebo, anxious for his date to arrive. His hair was considerably less sloppy than it had been last time, and he wore a black shirt instead of his cream one with his scarlet vest. He tied the outfit together with a pair of gray pants, which were still fresh and clean from washing them prior.

He was fussing over some wrinkles in his pants when Siena's voice hit his ears. "You're early!"

He glanced up to see her making her way over, a light blue dress hugging and stretching over her form as she walked. The look of it hypnotized him, and he fell into a stare.

It was a sleeved dress that hung barely above her knees, accented by a white belt that wrapped around her waist. The remainder of her legs showed off opaque, white tights. Her hair had been curled and primped to bouncy perfection, and a white headband peeked through her brunette locks.

He set his attention back on her face as she stepped up onto the platform. Her amber eyes flickered with excitement as she smiled at him. It made him smile himself, albeit nervously.

"You clean up nice!" Siena giggled, looking him up and down. "Black suits you well!"

Sphinx blushed from the compliment along with the reminder of his appearance during their last date. "Why, thank you." His gaze dropped subtly. "Blue is definitely your color."

She laughed and plopped down next to him. She scooted close, and Sphinx's body flared with titillation. "Thanks!" she chimed.

He, somewhat uneasily, nodded. "You're welcome," he finished the pleasantry, distracted by her legs touching his.

"How was your day?" Siena asked pleasantly. "Mine was great! I had the day off from the peach stand, and my father bought me a new set of paintbrushes! I can't wait to use them!"

"That's great!" Sphinx agreed. His day had been relatively uneventful. He had taught Karreo math and science in the morning and then studied magic until preparing for their date. "My day was fine. Can't complain."

"What counts as 'fine' to you?" Siena questioned, tilting her head. "Tell me about a typical day!"

Sphinx hid the unease the question riled with a smile. "Well, I get up in the morning and eat—"

"What kinds of things do you like to eat?" Siena cut him off.

Sphinx smirked and dove at the opportunity to drive the question off its trail. "Peaches, of course. Why do you think I go to the stand so much?"

Siena giggled. "Well, I'm glad you like peaches, otherwise we wouldn't've met."

Sphinx nodded. "That would be a shame."

"Wouldn't it?! I thought I'd make no friends since moving here..." Siena gazed off towards the river. "We moved earlier in the month, and Mom says we're staying here. I don't mind the city too much. It's different, for sure, though."

Sphinx had thought he pinned a slight accent in her voice. "Where do you come from, then?"

"Littlewood, just north of Riverview," she answered.

Sphinx blinked. He had been to Littlewood several times growing up. After Karreo was born, the family would take a carriage ride there at the start of summer and stay for the day, spending time at a festival that rolled in every year. The rides and treats and attractions had always been a delight, especially the ice cream their father always bought for them at the end of the day. Valen always ordered a stacked chocolate-strawberry with nuts, and he—

"Do you know of it?" Siena chased off the memory.

"Yeah, I've heard of it. Never been there, though." The words of the fib tasted sour.

"It's a lovely place. I miss our homestead there..." She sighed in remembrance. "We lived just a little ways out of town. Our backyard had a huuuge field with a pond where I'd catch frogs every spring." She laughed and beamed at him. "Ever catch frogs, Sphinx?"

"Can't say I have," he chuckled. "Being in a city, you find more toads..." That was another lie. He'd been frog hunting plenty of times, snake hunting too. The garter snakes that lived by the river were always a blast to capture. His mother always stressed to let them go, so they could go make babies for him to catch the next year.

"Toads are great too! You still find those out in the country," Siena said. "I miss those days... Mother says it's childish to do, though."

Somehow, that didn't surprise Sphinx. "So, you got new paintbrushes?" He was eager to get the subject off Littlewood.

"Yes! I'm so happy! My old ones were from when I was six, so..." she snickered. "They were definitely old."

Sphinx nodded at that. "I'd say. What do you plan to paint first?"

"I don't know yet..." She squinted off into the distance. "I guess I'll know when I start painting!"

He smiled. "A true artist."

She liked that. She scooted even closer still, so now their arms were touching. She scrunched her shoulders, and it perked up her chest. "I'm glad you think so," she told him.

Sphinx tried not to stare downwards, and he fought the sensation that threatened him even farther down. He couldn't prevent the blush that accumulated, however. It burned all the way to his ear tips.

Siena was blushing as well. One of her fingers twirled her already curly hair. She leaned even farther in.

Sphinx's nerves peaked. "Want to go on a walk?" he asked, standing up abruptly.

"Well, alright," she answered, almost a tinge upset.

He grabbed her hand and led her to the path they had taken last time, his heart still abuzz. Siena's hand was soft and fit snugly into his, but he tried not to think about that. He instead thought of things that would discourage the surge of hormones pumping through him.

Siena dropped his hand and then wrapped her grasp around his arm. She giggled in the process, and Sphinx felt even more overwhelmed. He must have accidentally tensed up, for Siena gave him a look.

"What's wrong, silly?" she laughed.

"...You're just really pretty," he admitted, flushing.

"Aww!" she gushed. "You're adorable, Sphinx!" More laughter followed that, and he didn't add to it.

He guided them along, and she was silent following her guffawing. The change in social scenery had him calming down within a minute or two, to his relief.

He broke the quiet. "So what made you move to Akarth?" He was nervous to potentially bring up Littlewood again, but his curiosity got the best of him.

"My mother always wanted to live in the deep city..." Siena answered with a shrug. "Sooo, one day she decided we were going to. My father used to live in Akarth, and had always missed it himself, so he didn't mind."

"How is she liking it, then?" Sphinx wondered.

"As much as my mother likes things." Siena giggled. "She doesn't please easily, but she's like that with everything."

"I would have never guessed." Sphinx chuckled. He felt a kick of pity for Siena, however. It must not be easy having such a picky, judgmental mother.

"So what about your mother?" Siena asked him.

Sphinx's head dipped with the question and a knot formed in his stomach. "...She was a very nice woman. Pretty headstrong, but kind." He didn't want to lie again, what were the consequences of her knowing that simple fact?

"...*Was?*" Siena's features froze as she realized what he meant. "Oh! You— I'm sorry! I didn't know..."

"It's alright, Siena," he dismissed. "You had no way to." He contemplated if it would be best to tell her about his father's death, and decided there was no harm in it. "I'm an orphan." He had never spoken those words out loud before; he despised the sound of them.

"You— you're—" Siena frowned heftily. "I'm so sorry, Sphinx... I..."

"Don't worry about it," Sphinx said. "It's fine, you don't have to say anything."

"...Okay."

Another wave of silence overcame them.

Sphinx's heart was aching with a dull throb, but then Siena nuzzled into his shoulder. Her touch managed to comfort him, and he ever-so-slightly leaned into her, his mind fighting off the negativity that had been riled.

"...Is that why you have no money?" she whispered after a few minutes.

"Yes," Sphinx replied simply.

"Oh..." Siena mumbled.

"Nothing a good riddle can't fix," Sphinx said, sounding upbeat despite his true emotion.

"Want to play now?" she asked him, lifting her head from his shoulder.

"Why not?" he grinned at her.

"Okay, you try and fool me," she suggested.

He had prepared a few riddles for the occasion. "I'm tall when I'm young, and I'm short when I'm old. What am I?"

"Ummm..." Siena looked to consider it. She had thought a good twenty seconds or so when she shrugged. "I don't have a clue!"

He smirked at her. "A candle," he revealed.

"Ohh! That makes sense!" Siena softly giggled. "That was clever."

"Glad you think so."

"Well," her hands left his arm and reached into her pouch. Four peaches were pulled out, just like every other time before. "Here's your prize!"

Sphinx took them and stored them away. He smiled warmly at her. "Thank you, Siena."

"No problem, Sphinx." She mirrored the warmth of his grin. "Glad I can help."

The rest of their date ticked by in silence, and it didn't take long before they were a block from her house.

"Well..." Siena stared at him, seeming uncertain. "I guess I'll... I'll..."

"See me again, same time, same place on Terradae?" Sphinx finished.

Siena blinked before smiling wide. "Yes! Yes!" She went in for a peck on the cheek, and Sphinx was ready for it this time. It didn't stop the flux it cast on him, however.

"Bye, Sphinx!"

He watched her go just like last time, his hand up to cradle where she kissed him.

"See you later..." he quietly said, unsure if he should have done that. The fluttering of his heart told him 'yes'.

And so, he listened.

Chapter 7

Sphinx

Come that Terradae, Sphinx left the tower early to finish some errands before his date. A quick run to the market to fetch more bread and then a visit to Hilltop Library was the plan.

Picking up bread was uneventful. Siena did not pop in front of him that time, and when he looked over at the stand, only Mrs. Thickett manned it. *'She must have the day off again.'*

Hilltop Library was modestly filled with a patron or two when Sphinx walked into the doors. Mr. Dayas was at his desk, wearing large spectacles as he gazed down at a document. He had a tightness in his face that suggested concentration, and his lengthy, silver hair was smoothly tied back in a ponytail.

Samitri Dayas was a floraling, and thus had natural markings on his face along with elongated ears that stretched along the sides of his head. The light blue markings stood out against his lavender skin and were shaped in curved lines and dots. They decorated his cheeks and above his eyes while gradients of the same shade of blue brightened his brow, nearly drowning out the markings there. He wore a tight gray suit coat embroidered fancily with a white, shining thread and dress pants of the same hue of gray. His somewhat lavish appearance contrasted with the rest of the library, which was run-down and declaring its age as no secret. Wallpaper peeled from the walls, most shelves had a slant in them, and the furniture of the place smelt of dust and rotting paper.

Sphinx walked up to Mr. Dayas' desk with a smile, and the floraling heard his arrival despite his concentration. He peered upwards from his document and nodded, his thin lips in a grin. "Hello there, Sphinx," he greeted quietly.

"Hey, Mr. Dayas," Sphinx returned.

"Have you already figured out those books?" Mr. Dayas pulled his spectacles off and sized Sphinx with a puzzled look. "Hasn't it only been a week?"

"Nine days, actually," Sphinx corrected. "But, yes. The first one was easy; it was a lot of stuff I already could do, it just explained how."

"Well, let's have you prove it, then," Mr. Dayas challenged.

Sphinx glanced down at the paper on Mr. Dayas' desk, which looked to be library records, and muttered an incantation on his breath. "What are you looking at, Mr. Dayas?" he then asked, snark in his tone.

"Book lease and return dates," Mr. Dayas answered, squinting at Sphinx before glancing down at his paper. The aging scholar gave a single chuckle at what he now saw. "Ah, no, my mistake. This appears to be a picture of myself, actually."

"A very dashing one!" Sphinx complimented, leaning over the desk to stare down at the photo himself. Sphinx then dispelled the trick, and the 'picture' faded back into records.

Mr. Dayas gave another short chuckle. "Well, what else have you learned?"

Sphinx set his gaze on the large picture windows behind Mr. Dayas' desk. He muttered another string of rucanic cue words, and the sound of music began to play from outside.

Mr. Dayas turned to look at the source of the sound and saw none. "Very good, Sphinx," the scholar commented. "One last spell, and you've earned yourself another book."

"Well, alright, Mr. Dayas. But... I have to ask first."

"Hm?"

"Has your skin always been red?"

Mr. Dayas blinked before staring down at his once purple hand, the color now boasting a red. "Very good! Very good, indeed!"

Sphinx dismissed the spell, proud he could impress the scholar. "I haven't finished the other book yet," he explained.

"That's alright." Mr. Dayas scooted out of his chair and began to stand up. "Let's find you another book."

They walked past a few aisles before coming across the rucanic section.

"I know just the one," Mr. Dayas said. He scanned the shelving before pulling out a book titled *Enchanting Enchantments*. Sphinx spotted that the author was Miniwink Twinkle Spunk, and his face lit up. He loved the gnome's work; she was always a humorous read.

Mr. Dayas began to carry the book back to his desk. "I'll just stamp this, and you can be on your way."

"Great!" Sphinx chimed.

Mr. Dayas did as he said and gave the book to the disguised human. "Happy learning."

"Thank you!" Sphinx said. He put the book in his bag and waved Mr. Dayas goodbye. "Have a good day, Mr. Dayas!"

. . .

He was walking back to the tower to freshen up for his date when he noticed a figure moving in an alley. When he glanced over, it revealed to be the same girl he spotted the other week, the day he first met Siena. She was in the same place he noticed her before, which was uncomfortably close to their clock tower.

She cowered and dove for cover in a hurry, but from what he saw of her, she was considerably dirty and frail.

Sphinx's conscience flared, but his survival instincts accompanied it. On one hand, he wished to help her, but the other hand warned that it was too risky. *'What harm would just a piece of bread do?'*

He stared at the crate she had hidden behind. He then reached into his bag and pulled a slice from the loaf he had picked up earlier.

He approached the crate warily. "Hey… Are you hungry?" he asked gently.

The girl peeked from behind the crate. She had dirty, pale white skin and matted black hair. She peered at him wearily, looking ready to bolt yet curious of what he held out.

He placed the bread on the crate and slowly backed up.

The girl kept her eyes intently on him. She then swiped up the bread in a flash and ducked behind the crate without a word or sound.

Sphinx gave a crooked smile and nodded his head, wondering if that was the right thing to do. *'She looked like she needed it...'*

When he began to walk, he took a winding way back to the tower like he had before, just to be safe. Like last time, she did not appear to follow.

He arrived at the fence spanning around the property and double-checked his surroundings. The clock tower sat in a business district that had fallen into little usage and popularity, and thus did not receive much funding from the city. Not many people walked these streets, so it made sneaking in much easier.

Sphinx slipped inside and went to get ready for his date.

■ ■ ■

Siena was an hour late.

Sphinx had been sitting in the gazebo anxiously when he heard crying announcing her entrance. He jerked his head up to see her rushing towards him, distraught.

He got to his feet and she ran up, throwing her arms around him. She sobbed into his chest, and he hesitantly returned her embrace.

"Siena, what's wrong?" he questioned, his tone worried.

"It's horrible!" Siena cried. "I hate my mother! I hate her!"

Sphinx frowned and gently lowered them both down on the bench. He broke the hug to stare at her. "What happened?"

"She found out about you! Grandma told her!" Siena bawled. "She said I couldn't see you anymore!"

Sphinx's guts flipped at the news, namely her grandmother knowing. "How did—"

"Grandma asked about you when we running the stand yesterday!" Siena explained. "And then she just assumed! I couldn't convince her, she just knew!" Siena sniffled.

"...Your grandma is unhappy about it, then?" Sphinx questioned. He wondered what tipped her grandmother off. Perhaps Siena had been scanning the crowd for him too much or mentioned him in a passing comment one too many times.

"She says I'm too young – so she told my mother!"

That didn't mean it was him *personally* she had a problem with, then? *'Good ol' Mrs. Thickett. I knew you liked me.'*

"...So how are you here then?" Sphinx questioned.

"I... Well... I just left," Siena elaborated. "Mom was leaving on a date with my dad. I don't think she thought I would disobey..."

"...Should you have?" Sphinx wondered, concerned.

"If she wants me to be a lady so bad then I have to make my own decisions!" Siena said, bristled with frustration towards her parent.

Sphinx shrugged mildly at that. He wasn't sure what to think of it.

"...You don't think I should be here, then?" Siena accused, sounding hurt.

"Well—I... I don't want to come between your mother and you, Siena." Sphinx said.

"You don't want to see me anymore?" Siena croaked, her face flooded with tears.

"No! I never said that—" Sphinx defended.

"Do you really like me Sphinx?" Siena inquired, her sad eyes focused on him. *"Really?"*

"I—I do," Sphinx answered desperately. "I—"

Siena suddenly leaned forward and pressed her lips against his in a kiss.

Sphinx's whole being jolted with surprise, stunned. For a moment that felt impossibly long, he was frozen.

Then, everything clicked.

He cupped her cheeks and kissed her back. He indulged in the embrace, both of their eyes closed, the wetness of her mouth and softness of her cheeks the only thing he knew in that moment. It was unlike anything he had ever experienced. It invigorated every fiber in him and conquered his inhibitions with arousal.

They kissed for a few more moments before Siena began to part, slowly. They both opened their eyes in unison, gazing deeply at each other.

But then Siena jerked away, as though frightened. "Sphinx! Your eyes!"

Sphinx blinked, the comment confusing him momentarily.

"They're yellow! And your skin is —"

Sphinx's stomach plummeted and adrenaline lit him afire. He scurried off the bench, panic coursing through him. As he became aware of his failing shift, keeping control of it grew more futile. He could feel it fading, his disorientation fueling its breakdown.

"Sphinx! Are you alright?!" Siena cried out, scared.

"S-stay away! I'm sick!" Sphinx sputtered out before launching into a run. He ran away from the gazebo as Siena shouted at his back.

"Sphinx! Wait!" She began to hurry after him.

"I said STAY AWAY!" he shouted without turning around. He heard Siena's footsteps cease after that.

He frantically fled, desperate to get back to the clock tower. He could feel the shift slipping away, his efforts to stop it in vain despite his years of practice.

Every set of eyes he passed seemed like they were boring into him, gawking at his demorin traits as they leaked through his disguise. Sphinx felt overthrown with disarray and terror. *'I screwed up! Shit! Shit!'*

After what felt like forever, he stumbled into the district where their clock tower was, still wrestling with completely letting his shift crumble into ruin. He passed Hilltop Library, and as he hurried along, a figure in the alley caught his eye yet again.

It was the girl. He pushed onwards, too driven by his panic to do much else.

He did not take a winding way to the clock tower.

. . .

Karreo

Karreo sat in anticipation for Valen's whistle to come blaring up the steps, but the tower remained quiet.

The child sighed, twiddling his thumbs in anxiety. He always hated it when Valen left... even if he was going to get peaches. The tower was a lonely and scary place when left all alone. Any creaks and bumps of the aging building sounded much louder than what they truly were, and shadows tended to move in the corners and along the walls. Daytime wasn't so bad, but the black of the main room still had the power to scare him even then.

The clock room was much brighter and considerably less spooky, but now it was getting dark. The purple sky offered little light into the massive clock windows, and Karreo was growing more anxious by the moment. Valen typically got back before twilight was spent, so where was he?

Fretful thoughts sped through the six-year-old's head of what could possibly be holding his sibling up. *'Maybe the bad people got him'* was the most common, horrendous scenario that lapped his mind. Tears burned in Karreo's eyes, blurring the room around him. He stuffed his face into his knees, miserable with worry.

"Valen... where are you?" he muttered pitifully into the growing dark. "I'm scared..." Announcing his fear only amplified it; the ghosts and monsters that thrived in the shadows couldn't compare to the thought of his sibling being captured, or worse.

He was sitting there crying, too paralyzed by his fear to move, when the whistle finally shot up the steps, through the open latch door, and into the clock room. The whistle sounded almost sloppy and distorted, but Karreo didn't pay much attention to that. *'He's home!'* He perked up instantly and ungracefully got to his feet.

"Valen!" he shouted out, relief evident in his tone. He hustled down the ladder and watched the top of the steps, his demorinkin eyes allowing him some vision in the dark.

Karreo could hear his footsteps coming, and they proved to be much quicker than what the child was used to hearing. Finally, the image of his brother shot into the room from the staircase, but something proved strange.

He was in his natural form.

"Val...en?" Karreo muttered, perplexed. Why wasn't he disguised?

As Karreo studied his brother, his appearance wasn't the only thing that was strange. Valen looked terribly distraught, and when he set his gaze on Karreo, the younger sibling spotted tears wetting his cheeks.

"Karreo! I—" Valen rushed to pick up and hug his little brother, choking out a sob. "Oh, gods, Karreo, I—I—I screwed up! I screwed up! Shit!"

'He used a bad word.' Tears began to bottle at the sight of his distressed brother, who had apparently made a mistake. It did nothing but encourage the fear that had been holding Karreo under siege.

"What do you mean?" he begged for an elaboration.

"Gods, Karreo, I— My shift failed. I— I just—" Valen cried and squeezed his little sibling.

"What do you mean?" Karreo asked yet again, the alarm in his brother's demeanor overwhelming him.

"My secret mission failed— I— She kissed me and I—" Valen couldn't deliver a full sentence without jittering. His older brother coughed out another sob. "Shit! Shit!"

"What's gonna happen?" Karreo wailed, terrified.

"I don't know, Karreo! I don't know!"

Unbearably long seconds passed by in consternation. Valen held him as they both cried and were overcome with fear. Karreo was still incredibly confused. Someone kissed Valen? His secret mission failed? Nothing made sense!

50

"Look… alright… everything… everything is—" Valen lowered Karreo down and approached one of the crates of the room. "It's going to be—" Brightness flickered to life, born from a flame at Valen's fingertip. His brother set the fire on a wick of a candle and lit it. "It's going to be…" his brother again stammered. He collapsed into the nest and beckoned his little brother over with open arms.

Karreo ran over and nestled himself there, desperate for comfort.

"It's going to be fine…" Valen finally finished as his arms wrapped around his sibling. "It's going to be fine…"

Karreo only cried as the comfort didn't come.

Chapter 8

Karreo

Valen did not leave the tower for the next several days. His brother was completely psyched out by what had happened, and refused to speak of it with Karreo. "Don't worry about it, Karri..." Valen had told him, but Karreo worried about it, regardless.

Whatever had transpired, Valen didn't get to bring back any peaches because of it. When Karreo had questioned that, Valen had only put his head into his hands and went very quiet. Karreo hated that response. "Will we ever get peaches again?" he had fearfully asked.

"...I... don't know," Valen had replied.

They now sat up in the clock tower, three days since Valen's mistake, both looking out at the morning sky. Valen appeared the very definition of crestfallen as he gazed outside, quiet. Karreo noted dark rings under his eyes that made him look more like a raccoon than a demorinkin. The younger sibling had felt the older toss and turn in their nest when they slept; both were getting mere winks of sleep throughout the night.

"...Can you make some toast?" Karreo hesitantly asked, not wanting to disturb his older brother, but making an exception for his hungry belly.

Valen's head dipped before nodding slowly. "I can do that, Karri..."

Karreo watched as Valen prepared the fire back down in the main room, his movements slow. It bothered Karreo to see his sibling so different than his typical self.

"Are you sad?" Karreo muttered quietly.

"...I'll be okay, Karri," Valen answered, monotone.

The six-year-old frowned heavily at his brother. "It's okay if we don't ever get peaches again..." Karreo assured, attempting to brighten Valen's spirits.

Valen only shook his head at that. "We'll figure everything out, Karreo. We just..." he trailed off and gave a sigh. "I don't know."

"It's okay..." Karreo attempted to soothe.

Valen bristled at that, but did not respond. Karreo set his gaze downwards, afraid he had offended.

"I'm sorry..." The child's lip jutted in a frown.

"You have nothing to be sorry for..." Valen dismissed. "This is all my fault, Karreo. *I'm* sorry..."

The conversation went quiet after that. Karreo stared at their makeshift grill as the last two pieces from the first loaf cooked. Valen always brought home two loaves from the market, and they together lasted about a week between the two of them. It always felt shorter than that.

Valen delivered Karreo's share on to a plate and handed it over, no peaches decorating the sides. That sight made Karreo's heart and tummy pang.

Valen put the lid on the fire pit and daintily chewed at his own slice. Karreo ate a tad faster, but the melancholy mood of his sibling slowed him down some.

After Valen finished he stood up and walked over to the mirror. He intently stared at himself, spurring Karreo into a frown. The child knew what was coming next.

Valen began to attempt a shift. At first he was successful; parts of him altered or disappeared entirely. But then traits would morph back into his natural form and the disguise would be undone.

This was not the first time for that to happen. Since the accident, Valen had stood in front of the mirror many times with the intent of completing a shift. He hadn't succeeded yet.

Valen's face crinkled with frustration and Karreo looked away, stressed. *'Valen could always shift before... Why can't he now?'*

Valen kept trying for the next half hour or so, and by the end of it he let out an angry holler and kicked at a crate nearby. Karreo winced and gazed down at the magic book he had retrieved during his brother's practice. It was the new one Valen had received the day of his failed mission, and the brothers had yet to flip through its pages.

"...Do you want to read the magic books?" Karreo tried.

"No! No I don't!" Valen shot back angrily. He climbed up the ladder to the clock room, his tail thrashing.

Karreo's eyes turned glossy as his brother stormed off. *'He always likes to read the magic books...'* A tear fell onto the book, and Karreo squeezed the tome to his chest.

■ ■ ■

It was the middle of that night when Valen asked if he was sleeping. Karreo shook his head, and heard his brother sigh next to him.

"I don't know what to do, Karreo..." Valen confessed. "If I can't shift... I..."

"You can do it!" Karreo encouraged. "You're really, really good at shifting..."

54

"I don't even know if we can stay here…" Valen pressed on.

Karreo's stomach dropped. "…What …what do you mean?"

"People probably saw me, Karreo… and the market I go to… I can't— I can't go back." Valen explained. "I don't know if we're safe here…"

"I don't want to move!" Karreo protested. "I like it here!"

"I like it here too, Karreo…" Valen sounded sad. "But… I…"

Karreo began to tear up. Everything was wrong; he was so sick and tired of it!

"Hey, hey, don't cry, Karri…" Valen's own voice sounded thick with emotion. "We'll find someplace else. It's fine. It's…"

His older brother began to sniffle and so Karreo lifted his head up to look at him. Tears streamed down Valen's face.

"I'm so sorry, Karreo… I'm so sorry…" he whimpered out.

Karreo snuggled into his brother as sobs rocked both of their shoulders. Valen did not move, only lay there.

"I'm so sorry," Valen repeated. "I'm so sorry…"

■ ■ ■

"We won't start packing until we find something," Valen explained over breakfast the next morning. "I can't start looking until I can shift again…" His eyes went over to the mirror. "Which is hopefully… soon."

"I don't wanna go…" Karreo muttered, bummed. The notion of leaving the clock tower was an upsetting one. Karreo had grown to like it well enough in the eleven months they had been there. He thought about the clock room and their nest and their makeshift tables and felt deeply saddened at the idea of leaving it all behind.

"…I know, Karreo." Valen sighed. "This place is perfect… I don't want to leave it, either. But I don't want—" He shook his head and didn't pull his eyes from the mirror. "I have to keep us safe."

After the meal, Karreo went to go sit alone in the clock room as Valen practiced, his heart swelled with sadness. He mourned their home and the life they had built there, wanting nothing more than to stay. He regretted every moment he had cursed the shadows of the corners and noises of the walls.

He could hear Valen growing frustrated downstairs, and Karreo eventually peeked through the latch door to watch his sibling. Valen still could not hold a shift, from what he could gather.

"Maybe you're trying too hard…" Karreo suggested, his voice small.

Valen jerked his head up to glare at his brother. He opened his mouth to say something before turning his back to Karreo, his tail showing his disposition.

Karreo only frowned before slinking away from the ladder. He sat in the middle of the clock room floor, overwhelmed with grief and feeling empty.

'Stupid secret missions...' An ache in his chest refused to let up and he gazed out the window. *'Stupid peaches...'*

■ ■ ■

"Karreo... you know I love you, right?" Valen said as they got ready for bed that night.

Karreo stared over at his sibling and hurriedly nodded.

"I do everything I do because I love you." Valen was looking straight at him. "Nothing matters more than keeping you safe. I'm only doing what I have to..."

"I know, Valen..." Karreo replied, his vision dropping to the mess of blankets huddled around them.

"...Can I have a hug?"

Karreo appeased his request and hugged his older brother. Valen squeezed him tightly and kissed his head.

"I love you, too, Valen..." Karreo spoke into the embrace.

Valen stroked his back. "Thanks, Karri..." He went quiet for a few moments before saying, "We're going to be alright. Don't worry."

With that, his older brother blew out the candles, and the room went dark.

Chapter 9

Karreo

Karreo was awoken by rough hands grabbing him abruptly. The young demorinkin let out a startled yelp, but a cloth wrapped around his mouth in an instant, choking out the sound.

He was then being yanked out of the nest and his arms were painfully pinned behind his back. Disorientated, Karreo couldn't process what was happening.

"Karre-*ffom!*" Valen started in a panic, but was cut off.

Karreo swung his head to where his brother's voice had come from. He saw two men clad in black forcing Valen to his feet, barely visible in the darkness of the room. Valen had a cloth around his mouth and his arms pressed to his back as well.

"Ha! Didn't expect two of them! We hit the jackpot, boys!" one of the men holding Karreo laughed.

Karreo's eyes were huge with confusion and fear. Valen mirrored his look and then sought to break free from the men.

Valen let out a stifled cry as his efforts were answered with force. The men twisted his arms further and shoved him brutally against the crates bordering their nest.

Adrenaline pumped through Karreo with every terrified heartbeat. He called out for his brother, but the sound was reduced to desperate muffling. He had the urge to kick and pry himself free, but fear paralyzed him.

Valen didn't cease fighting the men. He wrestled and fought against them in a frenzy, but they only kept slamming him against the crates. Karreo gawked at the sight in horror.

The top box fell over and toppled to the ground as they shoved him yet again.

"Careful, idiots! You can't harm it!" one of the men holding Karreo scolded. "We need them in good condition!"

"A bit of blood won't kill him. Come off it," a voice shot back, coming from one of the men who handled Valen.

"Come on!" the first voice then ordered.

Karreo was suddenly jerked forward with force. He and Valen locked eyes, and Karreo could spot a large cut above Valen's forehead, spilling blood down his face. He continued to struggle, but the men had too much leverage for his endeavor to make any difference. Valen kept muffling something out frantically, his eyes boring into Karreo.

The way they fastened Karreo's arms against his back hurt terribly, and tears born from horror and pain wetted his cheeks as they were pushed along. They carried them down the steps in a hurry and then out of the tower completely. Night greeted them outside, and a vehicle waited beyond the fence, a large van colored in black.

Valen's struggling worsened, and Karreo's adrenaline finally allowed him a burst of effort to attempt breaking free himself. Being much smaller, his squirming did not amount to much, and one of the men holding him gave a chilling laugh.

They drew closer and closer to the van. Karreo's chest was ready to burst as his heart raced unbearably fast.

Suddenly, both the men holding him hollered out in pain, and the firm grasp they had on Karreo lessened. Karreo wiggled free and tumbled to the ground.

He jerked his head up to stare at the men. They stood frozen in place, their limbs and heads twitching and convulsing as though in anguish.

Karreo switched his gaze to the men holding Valen, who stood there agape, confusion in their eyes as they gawked at Karreo's once-captors.

Karreo then looked to his brother. Valen was jerking his head to the side, his glossy eyes never leaving Karreo.

"Hey! Hey! Get him!" a new voice called out, belonging to another man who emerged from the van.

Valen desperately shouted something, and although it was muffled from the cloth, Karreo still understood. "RUN!"

Karreo sloppily pushed himself off the ground and stumbled a few steps. He then ran, his little feet blazing against the pavement as he fled.

■ ■ ■

Valen

Valen's handle on the spell grew harder and harder to hold. As Karreo launched into a run, he held on for a few seconds longer before it became too much. He released the siege on his brother's captors, the exertion the spell demanded leaving him exhausted.

The spell had come to him in the heat of the moment, and he had no knowledge of what it was. Whatever it had been, the effort certainly enervated him more than any other spell he had ever cast before.

"What the hell?! Get after him!" the man who left the vehicle ordered the men as they came to. They did as they were told, and Valen's guts churned as they began to pursue his sibling.

He was yanked forward abruptly and pushed towards the black van. The doors of the back opened and another man jumped out, rope in his hands. He began to tie up the demorinkin with the coarse material, Valen complacent as worry for his brother and exhaustion from his magic plagued him.

He was then tossed into the trunk of the vehicle, landing with a harsh thump. The doors of the van slammed shut.

. . .

Karreo

Shouting came from behind him, but Karreo did not look back. He continued charging forward, propelled by fear and adrenaline.

It didn't take long before the sounds of more hurried footsteps joined his own, and a chase was underway.

Karreo ran and ran, unsure of where to go. He cut into alleys and raced down back streets, never slowing down. He could hear his pursuers gaining, and the terror of them catching him spurred him onwards.

A block ahead revealed an abandoned construction site, and Karreo turned into it hoping to lose the men there. He fled into an unfinished building, and to his horror, the men followed him inside, hot on his trail.

Karreo weaved through skeletons of hallways and up fragile flights of stairs, the men following his path perfectly, growing closer and closer.

Panic spiked as he found himself on the roof after several stories, no other path in sight.

He turned around to face the men, the very spirit of panic. They were rushing towards him, their evil hands stretching out to grab him; to *kill* him.

Fear and desperation collided within Karreo's mind. He burst into motion yet again, headed straight for the edge of the building.

"Fuck! Kid! Stop!" one of the men barked.

Karreo did not listen.

. . .

Valen

Valen lay there, swamped with disorientation and pain. Fatigue gripped him from his earlier spell, slowing his mind. He felt trapped in a terrible nightmare. *'What the hell is going on?!'*

Who were these people?! Valen's first thought was the Fangs of Hellbane, but that didn't add up. One of the men had mentioned they needed them unharmed, which wouldn't be the case if they were the demorin hunters. Were they bounty hunters working for the organization? Valen was frightened to realize whatever the truth was.

'How did they even find us?!' Valen knew the answer to that, however painfully. His failed shift must have alerted someone. *'This is all my fault!'*

He thought of Karreo and his eyes shimmered with anxious tears. He tasted bile inching up his throat and into his mouth as nausea bullied his gut. He wanted to believe that he had done all he could to ensure his brother a chance at escaping, but would it be enough?

It was quiet for a torturous amount of time, but then there was commotion outside the van. Valen strained his ears to hear what was going on over the thumping on his heart.

"He got away!" one of the men shouted.

Valen let out a sob of relief over the news. *'Oh, thank the gods!'*

"What do you mean he *got away*?!" another yelled.

"He just jumped off the side of a building!" the other pursuer said. "Fucking maniac! No way he survived that fall!"

Valen's relief was shattered as shock usurped it.

"You have to be kidding me! Do you know how much money we just lost?! Shit! *Shit!*"

Shock reverberated from every corner of Valen's mind. *'No... No...'* He shook his head, desperate to deny what he just heard. *'No! No!'*

"Bah, screw it! We were only expecting one, anyways. Get in the van! We're leaving!"

Valen felt the car dip with the weight of people entering it before the vehicle shot forward, sending him into the back of the trunk. He thudded against the doors, yet he barely processed what was happening around him.

Nothing felt real. It had to be some horrible, hellish dream. He would jolt awake any second now; Karreo would be there next to him, sleeping soundly. He would wallow in the horror of it until his heartbeat settled back down, and then he would attempt to get more sleep. The morning would come, he would finally be able to shift again, and he would go find them a new place to live, a safe place where nothing like this would ever, ever happen.

He waited and waited to wake up, but as the van traveled along and thin lines of morning light began to border the covered van window, he never did.

He was not dreaming. The nightmare was real.

Despair and remorse overthrew the denial he longed to linger in. He began to sob, his heart breaking as reality forced itself upon him.

It was all his fault. If he hadn't gone on the date, if he had listened to his gut and done what he knew to be responsible, if he hadn't been selfish and immature, if he had decided to be the adult his brother needed him to be...

Valen wept and wailed with agony, the sound of his sorrow distorted from the cloth around his mouth.

Karreo, his baby brother, the one who he promised his father to protect, the person who meant everything in the world to him... was dead.

It was all his fault; he had failed.

Chapter 10

Valen

The vehicle came to a stop after a few hours had gone by in despair. Valen's eyes were tightly closed, shutting out the reality he now lived in. He hoped the bounty hunters would deliver him to the Fangs of Hellbane soon so it could all be over and he wouldn't have to be alone, suffocating from his shame.

The doors opened and he tensed up with dread, his eyes still refusing to open. He was roughly grabbed and pulled out of the trunk before being plopped down on the pavement feet first.

They began to lead him somewhere, his legs dragging as they forced him along in haste.

There was a salty smell in the air that Valen had never experienced before. The demorinkin pinned that it must be the ocean, judging from what he had heard about it. He had been excited to finally experience the ocean, once...

He remained with his eyes closed. He was forced up some steps before hearing a door open and then shut. They must have entered a building, for a stench of cigar smoke and herb overpowered the salt of the ocean. Valen wished the cloth went around his nose as well as his mouth.

They continued to lead him wherever, the path turning into stairs yet again. This time, they were heading down. The steps ended and the smell of mold replaced the stink of weed and tobacco.

The sound of iron moaning hit Valen's ears and then he was abruptly being thrown through the air. He crashed onto a dirt floor, his body flaring in pain. The iron groaned yet again and a loud clang followed it.

Valen finally summoned the will to open his eyes.

He found himself in a cramped, dirt-clad cell, a rusted iron door sealing him off from a grime-covered tile hallway. The lighting was poor, and more cells lay across from his. They were empty.

Valen rolled onto his back before adjusting himself into sitting. He shuddered from both a chill in the air and fear. He wasn't sure why he was so afraid; the sooner the end came, the sooner he would be reunited with his family in the outer realms.

The padded sound of bare feet approaching made his ears twitch. He forced his vision over to his cell door and spotted a familiar sight standing in front of it.

It was the girl from the alley, and she was holding a piece of bread.

He gawked at her. Where had she come from? Was she there to rescue him? Was she—

She suddenly became awash in a glow that silhouetted her figure in white, and her tiny body grew considerably larger. The glow ceased, and an adult woman stood in her place, bearing the same matted black hair and pasty skin.

She smirked deviously and ripped out a bite of the bread in her hands. She then tossed the rest into the cell with a laugh and walked away, still snickering.

Valen stared wide-eyed at the bread. His mind flashed back to seeing the girl when he was rushing home after Siena's kiss. The regret consuming him worsened tenfold. *'Why didn't I make sure she wasn't following?!'* He groaned audibly in remorse, loathing himself. *'Karreo! Karreo, I'm so sorry!'*

He kicked the bread away, regretting ever offering the 'girl' food. He felt not only deceived, but dangerously foolish.

As he sat there, shivering and broken, he looked up to the dirt ceiling and wondered how his life had come to this. He thought of the night he promised his father he'd look after Karreo and felt smothered by despair and guilt. *'Dad... Dad I'm so sorry... I—'* He leaned forward into his knees, his arms still painfully tied behind his back, wanting to bawl but having no tears left.

He didn't feel deserving of the vest he still wore on his back. Before he had gone to bed that night, he had kept the article on, longing for solace and advice from his departed father. Valen had lain there in the nest, missing him greatly, yearning for a time where he could consult him and commit his wisdom to mind and heart. Wearing the vest to bed had filled him with the closest feeling to comfort he had achieved in days, and he had fallen asleep in it. Thus, he had been kidnapped in it as well.

Karreo entered his mind, an image of his brother sitting out on the balcony and staring out into the city with hope and curiosity in his eyes. Valen's heart ached and contorted within his chest. Karreo was too young for the life that had plagued him; it pained Valen endlessly to realize that his brother would never know a life beyond the nightmare it had become. *'I promised!'*

Valen dry sobbed as he remembered bringing home his brother's favorite treat, watching as it would brighten up his mood no matter what. He recalled all the sunsets they had enjoyed out on the balcony together, admiring the city and hoping for something better. He thought back to snuggling as they studied rucanic books in the nest, Valen pointing out runes to his curious sibling. The memories tore him up and fragmented what remained of his spirit. He heard Karreo ask "do you want to read the magic books?" within his mind, and his heart convulsed with sorrow. *'I do, Karri, I do… More than anything...'*

It broke Valen's heart to know that their last days spent together were tense and fearful. *'I'm so sorry… I'm so sorry...'* He knew no apology would ever be enough; there was no way to fix anything.

His shame continued to punctuate every defeated thought as time began to tick by in the cell. He mourned a life he was torn from yet again, but this time… he was alone.

■ ■ ■

He must have fallen asleep, for the next thing he knew was the loud screech of his cell door opening, jolting him awake. He jumped with surprise and cowered away from a figure walking into his cell.

"Get up!" the figure boomed. It looked to be a male, green skinned terran who sprouted sharp, red biorocks in spots Valen had never seen in their race before. The rocks protruded randomly from his head and chest, puncturing his clothing and distorting his face, rendering him grotesque.

Valen didn't move as terror froze him in place.

The dwarf extended out a hand and menacingly yanked Valen's tied arms upwards, spurring out a cry from the demorinkin. He was forced to his feet, and the man pushed him out the cell door and into the hallway beyond.

The terran's relentless grip on his arm aggravated the pain already alive in Valen's body. Upon sleeping, he felt tremendously sore and stiff, and every step brought agony.

They didn't walk for long. The dwarf brought him down the tiled hall and to a door at the end, which he proceeded to open. The terran then shoved Valen in before shutting it. The force of his push had Valen stumbling and falling, worsening the anguish burdening him.

The room was well lit compared to the rest of the basement, and a desk lay in a corner, a human man sitting behind it. He stood up at Valen's arrival, and something about the way he stared filled Valen with dread.

He was a very thin man with a long face and crooked nose. He reminded Valen of a villain from a storybook, and he wondered if he were staring at one of his father's murderers.

The man approached Valen and the demorinkin's instincts had him crawling backwards. He eventually hit the wall, and the man closed the gap between them, his dull eyes boring into Valen.

He knelt and grabbed at Valen's arms as the terran had. His touch was like acid, spurring the demorinkin to yelp out in fear and pain.

He was forced to his feet and then pulled to where the desk was. Valen's heart thumped impossibly loud and fast in his chest. What was going to happen to him?

They stood in front of the desk and the man pushed Valen up against the wall. Valen winced from a mixture of fear and pain as the man forced him into... standing straighter?

The man stared at something on the wall above Valen's head before leaning over the desk and scribbling something down in a book. He then pulled out what looked to be scissors, and put the tool to the end of Valen's shirt.

His heart leapt into his throat as the man began to cut upwards.

"NO!" Valen screeched through the cloth covering his mouth, jerking away. Alarm spiked within him at the thought of the vest his father made him being ruined.

A whip-like slap struck across Valen's face, causing stars to dot his vision. Valen stood stunned, still recovering from the impact.

He heard the snipping of scissors and looked down in time to witness them deliver their first cut into his prized vest. The fabric gave an instantaneous flash of white before blinking back to its scarlet color. Valen didn't have the mind to wonder what that could have been.

To Valen's horror, the man snipped onwards, uncaring. He watched with tears in his eyes as the cloth, his late father's gift to him, was ruined.

When the man had finished cutting, he forced open Valen's sliced garments, exposing the demorinkin's bare chest. Valen breathed hard in consternation, wondering what the point of the man's actions were.

The man began to feel his chest and abdomen, his hands cold and rough. The human gave a nod or two at what he felt, and again scribbled something into the book on the desk.

The man then pulled out what appeared to be measuring tape from a pocket on his shirt, and began to measure Valen's torso. He put down whatever number the tape read into his book, nodding to himself.

The man's hands then went to Valen's waist, and the demorinkin felt a surge of surprise as the human roughly pulled down his trousers and undergarments in a single yank. His pants fell to his knees, exposing his naked crotch.

Immediately, the man's hands began to touch and feel his privates in the same manner he had touched his chest. Valen stood there, feeling utterly violated and confused, his breaths shallow.

The man wasn't gentle as he stretched and squeezed him. It hurt the demorinkin, and tears wetted his cheeks as he winced from the discomfort.

The human then took measurements of the teen's waist, crotch, and legs before standing to jot them down in the book.

Valen's knees wobbled as he stood there, naked and afraid. He felt completely vulnerable, and desperately wished for whatever was happening to end.

The man then grabbed at Valen's face and forced his head to the right, and then the left. He brought him back to center and the human proceeded to narrow his eyes at the demorinkin. Valen's own eyes were wide as the man squinted at him.

His hands then went up to Valen's horns, and the teen felt the man tug hard on them. He did the same to his ears, and then the demorinkin was suddenly being spun around to face the wall. Valen experienced similar yanks on his tail, and what remained of his shirt was lifted to study the ridge that travelled up his spine.

The man took a few measurements of his tail and horns and then wrote more information into the book. With that, he lifted a bell on his desk and rung it, the beautiful chime utterly contrasting with the situation.

The door burst open, and the same terran from before stomped in. He grabbed at Valen's arms and began to drag him away, the demorinkin's trousers still nestled around his ankles, his nakedness visible.

Valen's face burnt hot as he was drug back to his cell. He was tossed in as he was before, the moan and clang of iron sounding as the door swung closed.

"You're a pretty one there, demorin. You're going to make us all rich," the dwarf wickedly laughed and left him on that regard.

Valen laid there in a muddled heap, his clothes ripped and his pants down. The terran's words repeated in his mind.

Had he just been… assessed?

…For what?

Valen began to doubt that his captors were bounty hunters.

Chapter II

Valen

He was left in the cell for what felt to be hours, his vest in two and his spirit in shambles. He had studied the damaged article as tears pooled, finding it a metaphor for his broken promise.

His mind fretted over the intent of his captors. What did they mean to do with him? He had a theory, but it made his skin crawl and the despair welling in him worsen. He kept wishing to wake up, even though he knew he wasn't dreaming.

His bladder became too hard to ignore as time continued, and he was eventually forced to relieve himself on the dirt floor. In a backwards sort of way, he was thankful for his pants already being down for that.

He was sitting in the opposing corner of where he made water when the sounds of people walking down the way filled the hall.

"He's right in here," a man said, stopping in front of Valen's cell. He was a dark green skinned floraling with cropped, jet black hair. His pressed shirt and tie suggested that he was dressed for business.

A lavish looking human woman was next to him. She wore a form-fitting purple suit coat with matching pants and a yellow scarf that was tucked into her shirt. She had curled blonde hair that smelt of hairspray and her eyes were spruced with vivid makeup that matched the color of her suit.

The woman's eyes stared right at Valen, and he shifted in distress. His whole body was aflame with mortification as he sat inches away from his own waste, his pants around his ankles and his intimates exposed. He felt more like a dog in a cage than a humanoid.

Her eyes dropped to scrutinize below his waist, and Valen's ears dipped with discomfort and shame. He hated the way she was studying him; he was humiliated to his very core.

"We'll take him," the woman said finally, and she handed over a bag to the floraling.

He smiled, looking thrilled with her choice. "Very glad to do business with you," he responded with a peek into the bag. "We'll have him loaded on the boat immediately." With that, he slung the case on his forearm and gave two short claps.

Valen looked between the two of them, hesitant to understand what had just transpired. *'Was I just... sold?'*

An earthy brown female orc that smelt of salt and sweat approached the cell. The demorinkin tensed up as she swung open the door and stomped up to him.

She fixed his pants before hoisting him over her broad shoulders and heading out into the hall. Valen wondered if he should struggle, but what good would it do? He felt hopeless and dispirited.

She carried him down the hall the opposite way the dwarf had taken him prior. At the other end were spiral stairs heading upwards and a door adjacent to the steps. They headed through there and into another hallway. At the end of the passage lay another door, and when they went through it they found themselves outside.

It was dark out, and the sounds of splashing water and dock bells told of the ocean's presence. Valen's guts knotted as she hurriedly carried him along. What was going to happen now? Was he that blonde lady's *property*? If so, why was he being loaded onto a boat?

She led him onto a narrow dock and then onto a ship plank, arriving on a small motorized vessel. She ultimately brought them into a room found at the very bottom of the ship, underneath the cargo bay. The space was hidden beyond a secret door and was so cramped that her hulking form could barely stand in it. Four doors occupied the wall of the room, and she opened one of them, revealing an even smaller space that was about the size of a cell. A chain that was attached to the wall ended in a clasp.

She took up the clasp and fastened it around his ankle, Valen too downtrodden to fight it. She set him down more gently than he had been handled yet, and untied the rope around his wrists, the skin there revealing raw and scraped.

With that, she slammed the door. Valen sat there alone, his body and heart utterly sore. *'What's going to happen to me?'*

■ ■ ■

Valen could eventually feel the rocking of the boat, leading him to assume they were underway to... wherever they were going.

He spent the first few hours yearning for the blackness of slumber, but it did not come despite his exhaustion. He was kept awake by torturous thoughts and realizations concerning his nightmarish situation, not to mention the painful stimuli that burdened his body.

Valen had never been so empty and without drive. He could find no reason to carry on as he sat there awaiting slavery and gods knew what else. He cried out for his deceased family, longing for comfort they could never again provide in the living realm. He wondered why the Fangs of Hellbane hadn't tracked him down and put an end to it all yet.

Sleep did eventually find him, but it was shallow and came with no relief. He was often startled awake by disturbing imagery from his dreams or the sounds of Karreo shouting or crying. Although a product of his own imagination, he could swear it was real for a few moments upon waking. He desperately pleaded his brother to not haunt him; to forgive him. *'I'm so sorry... I'm so sorry...'*

He had no way of knowing what time of day it was, but hours after they seemingly left port, the female orc came down to the room to feed him. Valen guessed that it was breakfast, thus morning, and decided to track time by that assumption.

When the orc had come down to deliver his meal, which was a tiny serving of jerky, she had also given him a bucket. "Piss and shit goes in here, NOT on the floor!" she had firmly made clear. "Get any on the floor and it gets dumped on your head." Whenever she came to feed him she would take the bucket and leave a new one behind.

According to his perception of time, it was now the third day of their voyage. The mental burdens weighing him down had only grown heavier as time stretched on, nothing but his thoughts to keep him company. The room was dark other than a thin line of brightness from underneath the door, present because of a dim light out in the secret room that was always kept on. The bleakness within him shouted louder in the dark.

He was attempting to rest when the door barged open. The female orc stood there, no jerky or bucket in her possession.

"Won't be taking the boat no more," she began, her orcish accent thick. "Seems someone wanted ya mighty, mighty bad. Already paid for ya without getting a looksey-looksey first." She grunted and bared her tusks in a twisted sort of smile. "Offered to pay for air transport and all. Rich prick. Didn't even let ya go to auction."

Valen stared at her, his mind failing to follow. Paid for? Hadn't he *already* been paid for?

"But I was already... the lady at the... the cell?" the words slurred out of him.

The orc squinted at him. "The lady at the cell? Nah, she's the trafficker. She sold ya, hellborn. Made a lot of money – more than she paid."

Valen's stomach didn't take the idea of being treated as a product with acceptance. His guts cramped and twisted within him, the disturbing reality of the situation an unpleasant one to digest.

"We'll reach Falinfire with nightfall. We'll get ya on a plane from there and that'll be that." She laughed and it unsettled Valen to his core. "Yer a special one. We never ship brats from Akarth by the air. Ya know how pricey that is?"

Valen could only look down, too bothered to face her any longer. He didn't move as nausea set in and labored his breathing.

The orc laughed again as she shut the door, smothering out the light of the room as she went.

■ ■ ■

The orc returned after a few hours had passed. Valen was again gagged with a cloth around his mouth, and his wrists, which had only just begun to heal from before, were bound with coarse rope. His ankles were also tied this time around, disallowing him any mobility. He could not muster incentive to fight being bound, and so he allowed it to happen without a struggle.

He was then placed into a box that was taller than him, tiny specks of holes allowing a dense bit of air into the container. The demorinkin's heart thumped fast with anxiety as she sealed the lid on the crate. He felt positively trapped and about to suffocate as he was lifted from the cargo bay and onto the deck. He was then wheeled off to gods knew where, the tiny holes of the box doing nothing to provide scenery of the world outside.

Breathing did not get any easier as he was transported around. The cloth on his mouth only added to the challenge, and before long he could not escape a sense of panic. He wanted to struggle, to put up as much of a ruckus as he could, but he was packed within the box tightly and could barely move any of his limbs. Any shouting was reduced to muffling, so screaming for help would be an effort gone unnoticed.

Frightened tears dripped down his cheeks and wetted the cloth gagging him. He could barely hear the noise of the world beyond the crate as it all began to muddle and distort. He squeezed his eyes shut, the darkness of his mind offering no solace.

He could feel the box being hoisted after some time of being wheeled around, and then placed down horizontally, so he was on his back. It only added to his unease.

It remained like that for a minute or so, and then it was being picked up again, this time placed down on the side. This was at least a tad more comfortable for the terrified demorinkin.

As he laid there, his panic began to wane but not his nerves. He was hesitant to wonder what awaited him, and wanted nothing more than to never find out.

■ ■ ■

Hours passed in the crate, Valen hearing nothing but what he assumed to be the humming of a rucanic engine somewhere nearby. Earlier there had been a point where he felt a pull on his innards and a sensation of moving upwards. He had pondered if that was the infamous 'taking off' associated with aircrafts.

Hours continued to tick by, and Valen eventually found himself blinking awake after an immeasurable amount of time. The compactness of the crate had created a surge of panic upon waking, but that had mostly diminished as he became reacquainted with his predicament. He noticed in disgust that he had soiled himself in his sleep, rendering the crate even more uncomfortable.

More time passed even beyond that, but then, abruptly, Valen felt a similar sensation to 'taking off'; it was a dipping feeling this time.

Minutes following that, he felt his box being handled again. The dread within him erupted at whatever was to happen next, and he closed his eyes, picturing his parents with Karreo happily sitting between them, laughing joyfully. '*You were spared this, at least… Oh, Karreo…*'

"Geez! This thing reeks!" a man's voice exclaimed.

Valen's face burned with humiliation.

"Just move her steady. We're delivering this to… R-69, it looks like. Let's get it to the car," another said.

Valen was terrified to move, but his instincts demanded he do *something* to help himself.

In a sudden burst, he began wiggling around as much as he could, screaming against the muffle of the cloth, desperate for them to notice him.

"...Donald? Do you hear th—"

"Shh! We're not supposed to ask questions, remember?" the other replied in a scold.

"...Right."

Valen's shoulders rocked with dry sobs as his efforts were noticed, but ignored. He was utterly helpless, doomed to whatever fate he had unfortunately been entwined in. He felt denied of an existence worth living; he just wanted to die and see it all end.

He was placed down almost gingerly before hearing a vehicle starting up. He felt a shift as the car began to move.

It wasn't a long drive, and the men who carried him placed the crate down with the same delicateness as before.

"Oh, hey there, Francine! Didn't expect to see you here yet!" the first voice called out.

"Apparently this one is a rush job! They're paying the company extra to get it delivered now," a new voice responded, this one female.

"Well, we'll get it loaded now, then!"

"Please do, boys!"

Valen felt nauseous from all the moving. The crate was hoisted and dropped off somewhere else yet again, Valen still unable to see what was occurring around him as he tried peeking through the holes.

With that, he heard a loud clang and the sounds of talking outside whatever Valen was loaded onto. It was too muffled to understand. There was another shift of movement, and Valen's journey continued.

■ ■ ■

It was only about another half hour before Valen's box was being handled yet again. There was no conversation this time, and his handlers moved with precision and haste.

He was wheeled somewhere and then put down with little force.

Valen's heart leapt into his throat as a crowbar suddenly began working at the nails sealing the box, surprising him. It startled him with enough intensity that he lost hold on his bladder. Valen cowered in fear as the box lid lifted and he shut his eyes, too scared to look.

"Ahaha! He's a beauty, he really is!" a feminine voice said, trilling with laughter.

"Worth the rush! Lookit those horns! Ah, get him out of there!" another voice said, also sounding female.

Valen felt his shoulders being grabbed at and he cried out in terror. He resisted, but it had little impact.

"Don't be shy, demorin boy! Awww, I see you had a little accident or two! Don't worry your handsome head none! We'll get you cleaned up before getting you to your new home!" the woman spoke mockingly. She gave another trill of a laugh.

"Cleaned up indeed! We'll see if you were worth the price, yes," the other added.

He was dragged along at a hurried pace, and Valen finally forced open his eyes to see the world around him.

Two women handled him, both bearing skin that looked too tight for their gaunt faces and hair that was sloppily resting in an up-do. They were not old, but the effect of their skin was deceiving. They carried him down an empty, dim hallway with wiry arms.

They arrived in what looked to be some sort of washroom, as it had a shower, sink, and many cabinets. One of the women gave a cackle and shut the door. She locked it with a key, causing Valen's horror to spike.

"Let's get you washed up, hellchild!"

They cut away his clothes with daggers they pulled from their hips, the kiss of the blades cold and sobering as they slid close to Valen's skin. They tossed away his outfit into a trash bin, and the last of Valen's hope shattered as his prized vest fell into the garbage.

The women laughed at his apparent dismay and lowered him into the shower. They turned on the water, and Valen yelped as icy cold water began to drench him.

"Must be cold, huh?!" one of the woman hooted. Valen felt her grab at his privates painfully.

"You've all but disappeared down there! Don't tell me our client bought a dickless twerp," the other laughed, her voice high with amusement.

He closed his eyes as the woman proceeded to mock and tug at him, all while being bombarded with frigid water. A sharp finger then slipped inside him, causing him to shriek in surprise and pain.

"Can't even take a finger?! Ha, you're in for a rough time, then!" one of the woman sneered as the finger probed and scraped.

The demorinkin coughed out a sob, helpless as he was assaulted.

"Mind his TAIL!" one gushed as they finally began to scrub his body.

"It's so THICK!" the other hollered. "Worth the price for just the tail, I'd say!"

It felt impossibly long before they were finished. He was shuddering and nauseous by the end of it, and they roughly removed him from the tub to dry him off.

"What a good demorin you were!" one cooed.

"Such good behavior! You'll do just fine!" the other chimed.

After they finished drying him off, they took out a loincloth-like article from one of the cabinets. It was a drab brown material that hardly stretched past his intimates. They wrapped it around his waist and buttoned it.

"There! Now you're ready," the first said.

"Such a charming hellchild you'll be," the second added. "Worth every copper!"

With that, they unlocked the door and began to drag him out. Valen's eyes kept on the bin where they had tossed his vest, his eyes moist with tears. It was like saying goodbye to his father all over again.

They took him down the hall and into another room before heading out a door. It revealed to lead outside, a night-time sky he had not witnessed for days greeting them. The area looked to be some sort of back alley, and a gray van was waiting.

The women opened the trunk doors and Valen's survival instincts begged him to struggle. He tried, but the effort was pitiful and they only laughed at him.

They loaded him into the van and slammed the doors closed. "Bye, bye, hellchild!"

"Fare thee well, demorin spawn!" the second chortled.

Valen could only bawl as the vehicle began to drive away.

Chapter 12

Valen

The van drove along, every second having the weight of an hour. Valen could not fathom what awaited him, even after the constant conditioning of the last few days. His face was flooded with tears as the van drew closer and closer to delivering him to the reality his life had become.

Memories of his past two lives teased him from afar, reminding him of what he would never again have. He pined for his family and the wholeness he had felt before tragedy struck. He thought of his vest, his late-father's gift, the last thing that brought Valen any semblance of comfort, sitting in the trash bin of the washroom.

He never imagined he could feel so miserable; he was positive he could stare into death unblinkingly, perhaps even welcome it with open arms. He imagined he would come to with his family embracing him, hopefully having forgiven him. *'What if they haven't? What if they hate me for what I've done? What if they —'*

The vehicle violently jerked, interrupting his anxious fretting. The car wiggled to an ungraceful stop, and then he heard shouting beyond the wall that separated the trunk from the rest of the car. Following that were gasps and hollers of pain, and Valen's mind raced with confusion. *'What the hell is —'*

The back doors of the trunk flew open, and Valen jolted back in surprise.

Through the blue of the night he could spot a figure reaching an arm into the car, and Valen fearfully flinched away from it as much as his binds would allow.

It was no use. The figure connected with his tied ankles and sharply tugged. Valen yelled out against the cloth gag as he was forcefully pulled from the vehicle.

His body was yanked out and fell onto stone pavement. Adrenaline allowed him no time to linger on pain as he turned his attention up to his new kidnapper.

They revealed to be a woman wearing a thick, hooded cloak and brown fiber armor studded with silver stars. The cloak's striking white stood out against the darkness. Yet, what stood out even further still was a gold trim shaped into stars bordering the hood. The glossy and sheen fabric gave the impression of a faint glow.

She was glaring at him, and Valen noted that her striking gold eyes had a faint aura to them. Her skin had a similar radiant effect, highlighting her white complexion.

She was beautiful, but Valen hardly noticed that detail, for she unsheathed a longsword from her belt and raised it high, a glint catching along its length in the moonlight.

"You perish now, hellspawn!" she bellowed, her eyes searing into his.

Thus, he found himself staring at death after all. He stared back unblinkingly, but it was not from acceptance, rather terror. He did not welcome it with open arms like he imagined he might. Instead, he pushed it away in a desperate rally for survival.

Her blade began to fall rapidly, aimed for his neck. Valen felt something burst within him, something primal and ancient within his blood. It was an energy directly linked to his instincts, born via his heritage.

It was a spell, and it was not the first time he had experienced its power erupt.

His attacker's body went still as she shrieked, the blade in her hands freezing along with her. She shuddered and convulsed as Karreo's captors had, and Valen glared at her, defiant. His grip on the spell was becoming arduous, however, and he found it slipping away alarmingly fast.

Suddenly, a dart zoomed through the air and struck straight onto her neck, just as the control of Valen's spell escaped him. He desperately tried to roll away, but then something was tackling into his assailant, toppling her over. In the same moment, he felt himself being pulled off the ground and picked up.

He looked up at whoever was handling him now, and saw a young man smiling at him, bearing feline-like features.

"That was a close one!" he said in a laugh, hoisting the demorinkin.

Valen gawked at him as his mind attempted to catch up.

Shouting then came from in front of the van. Two more people wearing the same uniform of Valen's attacker emerged. They had bloodied swords, Valen noted with a churn of his innards.

They began to rush Valen and the stranger, but their necks were hit with darts and their legs were struck with bolos, causing them to stumble to the ground. Valen proceeded to gape, his mind cluttered and slow from the effects of his spell. Exhaustion was seeping through him, lulling him into a fog.

Valen's vision moved to his attacker, and he saw another young man who appeared identical to the one who held him, searching her unconscious body. He had a furry, striped tail that ticked as he dug through her belongings, and was clad in snug-fitting fiber armor. He took notice of Valen staring and looked over with a wink.

Judging from the feline features and tail, Valen assumed they were both felidaren. He had seen their kind before, but had never personally dealt with any.

Valen noticed on the corner of his eye that two other alike-looking men were searching the other bodies now. The man holding him said something in a strange tongue that Valen did not recognize, and each of the identical felidaren jerked their head in a nod.

A feminine voice called something out from on top of the van, and Valen craned his neck upwards to see another felidaren, this one appearing older. She was crouched and staring at the one who was carrying Valen, her green, feline eyes shining.

The young man holding him laughed and seemed to assure her of something. She gave a firm nod at whatever he told her.

With that, the felidaren carrying Valen burst into a sprint. As they moved, the demorinkin felt far away from the action, and the exhaustion burdening him continued to intensify.

He didn't have the power to fend it off any longer; his eyes closed as fatigue overcame him.

■　■　■

Valen blinked awake and was greeted with a warm light. There was a softness underneath him, and no bounds restricted his limbs. He pushed himself into sitting up, his body feeling heavy, but practicing a freedom it had been without for days.

He looked down at himself and noticed he was not wearing the loincloth, but a clean set of clothes instead. The outfit consisted of a black short-sleeved shirt and gray sweatpants.

His attention went to his surroundings, his mind still fuzzy with sleep. He was in some sort of bedroom. He laid atop a bed that neighbored a nightstand and tall dresser.

...A bed? When was the last time he had even slept in a real bed? It had been at the inn in Akarth, when his life had dramatically changed... for the first time.

Valen's heart harrowingly pushed those memories away, but they persisted in the back of his mind, an eternal reminder. He proceeded to study the space to help make sense of his current situation.

Upon the nightstand was a glass of water and a bread roll sitting on a white plate. Valen's stressed being rejected the idea of food, despite the empty pit in his stomach that demanded sustenance.

As he sat there, confusion multiplied within him. What in all the realms of existence had *happened*?

He recalled the van and the people who had attempted to murder him. His skin crawled as the words the woman shrieked when she raised her sword repeated in his mind. Had she been a member of the Fangs of Hellbane, his parent's murderers? *'Who else could it have been?'*

If so, they had finally found him. However, their efforts to finish the job had not succeeded, partly because of his spell, and partly from his mysterious rescuers.

He was wary to call them that. Why had they chosen to save him? Did they work for the person who bought him? Why else would they have been there to help? A jolt of panic surged through him at the possibility of wherever he was being his 'new home'.

Valen couldn't shake a burden of grogginess as his mind attempted to make sense of it all. Exhaustion punctuated everything he did and thought, and his stomach growled within him, sour and cramping with hunger.

He eyed the glass of water and plate of food on the bed stand. He could at least drink the water; he had last had a drink on the boat, however long ago that even was. His throat burned with thirst, eager for him to follow through with the decision to drink.

He took up the glass with a tired hand, frowning down at the liquid as nausea hounded his guts. Paranoia worried if it was drugged or poisoned.

He decided it was worth the risk and took a gulp, the coolness of the liquid a privilege his throat had long been denied. The water on the ship that been warm and sour tasting, yet this water was refreshing and cold.

It was a small victory for his spirits. The sip was the first pleasant experience he could remember before —

He suddenly noticed something on the corner of his eye. The door of the room was ever-so-slightly cracked open, and stark green eyes peered from outside, peering right at him.

It startled Valen so much that he jumped and dropped the glass, the contents splashing onto his lap and then the floor as the cup landed with a thud.

The door closed in a snap, and Valen heard footsteps scurry off.

"Mooom! He's awaaake!" a younger voice called out from beyond the door.

Valen sat there in waning shock, his heart beating fast. The eyes reminded him of the felidaren from the night before; they had all shared the same vividness of green.

He looked down at the spilt water and frowned, his parched throat craving for what now soaked his pants and the floor. *'Of course...'*

The door opening made him jump for a second time, and he cowered against the wall as a figure walked in.

It was the female felidaren from on top of the van. Several details about her that Valen had not noted before were revealed in the light of the room. She had tortoiseshell fur and straight, brown hair that was tied in a loose bun. There was a pronounced bump in her belly, leading Valen to wonder if she was pregnant.

Valen sat there in apprehension, afraid the worst was about to ensue.

"How are you feeling?" the felidaren began, her voice gentle.

Valen shifted uncomfortably as he was unable to meet her gaze, a lump in his throat from fright.

"...You must be very confused," the woman went on in the same tone. "It's alright, you're safe here. You can relax."

Valen wanted to believe her, but felt plagued with suspicion and uncertainty. He finally faced her, his ears dipped, hesitation showing all over his face.

She slowly nodded at him, her expression as warm as her voice. As he stared, he wondered if what she said could possibly be the truth. *'They did... rescue me...'* But *why*; *how*?

"If you'll come with me, there's someone who would like to talk with you. They don't mean any harm. We're here to help," the felidaren suggested.

He felt a spike of nerves and dropped his stare. A sense of timidness that was instilled in him from recent events rendered him wary of interaction. What did this person want? Who were they? The idea of conversation made him feel vulnerable and only upset his insides further.

He could sense her staring at him, waiting. Valen didn't know what to do or say; he felt ill with stress.

"Come on, kit. It won't take long. After we're done you can get some more rest. How about it?" the felidaren encouraged.

Valen nervously set his gaze back on her. He could not detect any dishonesty or mischief in her demeanor, but still, he worried.

Regardless, he scooted off the bed and stood up with wobbly knees, a mixture of exhaustion and anxiety.

"There you go," the woman smiled warmly. "Follow me."

She opened the door and they both walked out, Valen's steps slow and taxing. His legs were heavy and sluggish as he went, the motion of walking on his own will striking as unfamiliar after all that had happened. He kept expecting to trip on binds or experience a flare of pain in his arms from them being pinned against his back.

Neither happened as they exited into a hall and then through another door. Another hallway waited beyond, and they turned a corner before she guided him through an archway. The appearance of the place thus far was paneled with wood on both the floor and ceiling, and lamps sprouted from the walls to modestly light up the area.

They passed another archway as they moved along, but Valen had no time to glance through it. The felidaren led him through another door and they found themselves in a small room, a staircase lying in the back of the space and another door straight ahead.

They did not go up the stairs, rather through the door.

They entered a room that contained a large, long table. All seats of the furniture were empty, save for one. A human woman was sitting at the opposing end, her hands folded neatly on top of the table. She wore a calm expression as they walked in, nodding at Valen as though she were expecting him.

Valen kept his focus off the woman. The felidaren guiding him pulled out the chair at the other end of the table, and offered it to the demorinkin. Valen sat down, apprehensive. His eyes fell to the table and stayed there.

The felidaren was sitting down in a chair adjacent to him when the woman began.

"It is good to know you are alright, young man," she said. "Especially with the additional trouble we did not foresee in your rescue."

Valen did not lift his gaze nor respond.

"You must be eager for an explanation," she went on. "My group and myself strive to rescue those who have been tragically affected by the humanoid trafficking industry within this city, like yourself."

Valen squirmed at the words 'like yourself'. The nightmare he had lived being a product of humanoid trafficking was a difficult fact to swallow. None of it had sunken in yet, and her words forced the concept down.

"I am relieved we can count you as a success story, despite the... turn your rescue took," the lady continued.

Valen closed his eyes, images of his assailant and her readied sword sending a chill down his spine. In his gut, he knew that his attackers were the Fangs of Hellbane.

"Your heritage obviously... had the power to distress the ones who attacked you."

Valen winced and became glaringly conscious of his exposed natural form. The long eleven months spent keeping his true self a secret had conditioned him into feeling utterly uncomfortable in his genuine skin. He felt naked and vulnerable to these strangers who knew of what he was and could use that information against him.

"Do you know who assaulted you?" the woman asked, her tone even.

Valen's eyes kept shut as his emotions swirled around within him. He did not answer her as the room slipped into silence.

"...Is there any reason someone would be after you? Have you done anything to provoke someone?"

Valen did not reply. He did not want to speak of it, especially to a stranger. '*Why do they even care?*'

"...We're only trying to help you. If you are not honest with us, there's nothing we can do to help."

'*There isn't anything you can do!*' He only thought the words rather than spoke them.

"...Let's back up, yes?" the lady decided. "Did you have a family back in Akarth?"

Valen tensed up, her question summoning the cruel reminders he sought to keep in the back of his mind forward. The weight of his situation crushed him, and he did not respond.

"...Is there anywhere you can go back to?"

The despair within him proceeded to smother him. He bit down hard on his lip, one of his fangs cutting it open with ease.

"...What's your name?"

His instinct was to answer 'Sphinx', but that identity had died with the gracing of Siena's lips. That knowledge tore at him.

He did not reply, his true name something he was loath to share. As far as they were concerned, he was nameless.

"...We're trying to help. If you don't answer me, how can we?"

He answered her prying with silence.

"...I am going to assume you have no family and that you are homeless. If that is incorrect, stop me."

Valen didn't.

"...We will do everything within our power to give you back a life. I promise you that. But if we are to do that, we must get down to the mystery of your attackers first. We do not want to place anybody into any unneeded danger."

Valen eyes threatened to burn at her words, but the tears did not manifest, likely due to them running out. There was no life for him ahead. The Fangs of Hellbane had found him. And even if they hadn't, what was left? He wondered why he hadn't allowed his attacker to slice his neck; why he had pushed death away in the name of survival. *'What's the point anymore?'*

The lady sighed when he did not answer yet again. "...Perhaps you are still very tired and in need of more rest. If you are ever ready to talk, just let us know." She then faced the felidaren and nodded her head.

The felidaren stood up and weakly grinned at Valen. "Come on, kit. Let's get you back to your room."

Valen sat there a few moments longer before slowly getting to his feet. He followed the felidaren as she led him out, sparing the lady who asked him the questions no glance.

The felidaren guided him back to the same room he woke up in, the walk uneventful and quiet.

When they finally arrived, she opened the door and let him walk in. Valen's eyes found the nightstand, and he realized that there was a new glass of water there.

"You were brave," the felidaren commented. "Take your time, kit. Understand you're safe now. Whoever attacked you won't be finding you here."

He doubted that. He approached the bed and sat on it, the feel of the mattress an unfamiliar sensation.

"If you need anything, I'll be nearby. There is a restroom out the hall doors and to the left, the first door. There's showers there, too. Feel free to use them."

Valen scrunched his brow as she talked, perplexed. He wasn't going to be trapped in the room?

"Did you get all that, cub?" she smiled at him, and something about it reminded him of his own mother.

He replied for the first time in the form of a nod.

"Great. My name is Kyla, by the way. Kyla Cattiaikin." She flashed her fangs in a smile. "Again, that's Catty-eye-kin. It's a bit of a mouthful, so most just call me Mrs. Catty."

A bit of a mouthful, indeed! 'Catty-ay-kine? Catty-en-ken? Catty—' Mrs. Catty it was, then. Valen couldn't help but find her name ironic, considering her felidaren heritage.

Mrs. Catty looked ready to leave, but then hesitated. She pointed to the door. "Open or closed?"

Valen blinked at the question. He considered it before answering in a small voice, "Closed."

"Will do," Mrs. Catty replied. With that, she shut the door.

Chapter 13

Kyla

"If he won't talk, we're at an impasse…" Avalene Porte lamented, her brow scrunched and her hands steepled. "His attackers have been uncooperative in our interrogation— the demorinkin is the best lead we have this very instant."

"The boy will come around," Kyla assured her old friend. They both sat in the room where they had questioned the boy minutes earlier. "We just have to be patient with him."

The demorinkin's refusal to talk did not surprise the tortoiseshell felidaren; the horrors of what he'd likely been through as well as the shock of nearly having his head lopped off didn't make for a very chatty youngster. His assailants' lack of cooperation was even less shocking.

"We need answers *now*, Kyla. How are we supposed to help if he doesn't talk? We don't have that much time; Bartholomew Sniver was found beheaded in his *own living room*." Avalene let the words hang for effect.

Bartholomew Sniver was an esteemed and respected collector within the scholarly community, so it was surely troubling to learn that artifacts and priceless ornaments were not the only rarity he had a passion for collecting. Apparently, young, living samples from exotic races and breeds were amongst his prized possessions. Avalene had explained that his collection was, to put it delicately, 'interactable'.

This had been a secret, of course, for such a thing would certainly stain his reputation, let alone require massive payoffs to the authorities if they knew of it. Her group had been tracking the immoral collector for some time, so when he had purchased the young demorinkin, they had devised a plan to finally bring him to justice.

However, as they found out earlier that day, someone else had beaten them to it. A sword left in the headless collector's chest was identical to the weapons of the attackers from two nights past: a white blade adorned with a gold-colored hilt that was carved into the shape of a star sporting two fang-esque extensions.

This led them to believe the two attacks were connected. While their reasons for killing the demorinkin's purchaser were debatable, it could be assumed that they meant to finish what they had started the night Kyla and her family had intervened, at least.

The demorinkin's attackers assisted in proving that assumption. Although they had been uncooperative and cryptic in the few answers they revealed thus far, they had made one thing crystal clear: they despised demorinkin and other hellborn beings, and those who would strive to help them. This had led them to verbally swear Avalene and her group as enemies, which, by extension, would include Kyla and her family.

Avalene continued. "They are not to be underestimated. He is not safe until they are dealt with."

"He's safe here. Do you really doubt that?" Kyla almost felt slightly offended! The Den was *the* place to hide, if ever one. They had brought the demorinkin there following his attack for a reason.

Avalene shook her head. "I do not doubt that, but it's not like he'll be here much longer."

Kyla tilted her head. "He won't? Why is that?"

Avalene squinted her eyes at her, and Kyla couldn't contain a grin.

"What are you suggesting?" the vigilante asked.

"I don't see why he can't stay here as we figure everything out," Kyla clarified. "You're right, these people are not to be underestimated. He needs a safe place to stay as he recovers."

"...And you are fine with taking up that responsibility?" Avalene challenged. "*Niem* is alright with it?"

"Don't worry about Niem," Kyla dismissed. "I am fine with it. He will be, too."

Avalene's eyes remained in a squint. "I cannot ask this of you, Kyla..."

"You aren't," the felidaren said. "I'm *offering*. There's a difference. Is there a problem with it?"

"Well... I..." Avalene sighed, having the look of someone troubled. "I am uncomfortable with this resting on your shoulders. You were only hired to intercept the boy, that is all. You've already involved yourself more than needed by bringing him here. It's not your place to worry with this part of the process."

"But I *am* worrying," the felidaren replied. "I *want* to help, Avalene. Is paying me more what you're *really* worried about?" The felidaren put her cheek into a hand, smirking.

Avalene gave her a sideways look before rolling her eyes. "Payment is not the issue."

Kyla chuckled.

"I just don't want your family put in danger."

"In case you haven't noticed, dear friend, danger is not a stranger to our family. It's why you hired us, is it not?"

"This is *much* different than pulling heists and bamboozling guards," Avalene stressed.

"Is it? It all boils down to the same formula. Besides, whoever these people are, they have no lead! No one saw us leave with him – I made sure of it. And! Even if anyone had, he's safe here of all places. If this was not a safe place, Avalene, I would not be sitting here with you now." Kyla was convinced keeping the demorinkin there was the right thing to do; she wasn't about to let Avalene walk up the stairs doubting it.

Avalene held Kyla's eyes in a stare. "...Talk with your family first. Make sure they all understand what is being agreed to. Until you do, I cannot accept."

Kyla's lips shifted into a smile. "Fine then. And when they agree, what's your decision?"

"Talk to them, Kyla," Avalene pressed. She scooted out of her chair, a hand cradling her head. "Gods, I have a headache. This has been one stressful case..."

"We'll give you one less thing to worry about. Trust me."

Avalene waved her off and the room went quiet for a beat or two. "When are you due again, Kyla?" she asked.

'*Is this because I'm pregnant?*' "Early Unatem. Is that what this is about?"

"I was just curious," Avalene shot down. "Do you have a name picked out for him?"

"Aylan." Kyla smiled warmly. The felidaren gave a quick glance down at her bulging belly and rested a hand on it.

"He'll be your... what? Twentieth?" Avalene gave her one of her rare smirks.

"Seventh," Kyla corrected.

"...And how has your health been? I know that —"

"My health has been *just fine*," Kyla stopped her there. "Honestly, is that why you're worrying?"

"To be truthful, no. I was merely curious. What I'm worried with is —" the human cut off and snapped her tongue. "Just talk to your family, Kyla. Make sure you're all on the same page."

"Alright, I will," Kyla promised. She looked down at her baby bump again. "Do I have to convince the baby, too?"

Avalene rolled her eyes at that. "I have your payment, by the way. I'm sorry for the holdup."

Kyla perked up at the mention of compensation. "No hard feelings there! I knew you'd pay us when you got the chance." Truthfully, these particular missions were never about the paycheck to Kyla, anyhow. It was still a lovely bonus, however.

Avalene reached into her bag and pulled out a purse that looked plump and jingled with a promise of coin.

"Toss it here," Kyla urged.

Avalene didn't listen. She walked up and gently held it out instead, spurring Kyla into laughing.

"There's extra in there for... the trouble you ran into," the ex-government worker mentioned. "I do still apologize for that... We had no way of —"

"It all comes with the territory," Kyla excused, taking the pouch. "It's appreciated, though. Thank you." She recalled the unexpected turn the rescue took with a shake of her head. Her family had been tracking the van and waiting for it to reach their planned trap when the vehicle suddenly had the tires blown out. Her sons and she had barely reacted in time as three figures suddenly rushed the vehicle, doing away with the drivers and breaking into the trunk to remove the boy. Luckily, through quick thinking and teamwork, the murder attempt had been a thwarted one and the attackers had been captured.

Avalene nodded her head in multiple little bounces. "Well, I have to get back to the warehouse and figure out how we're to handle future interrogations with our… guests. I'll be back tomorrow. May the shadows guide and protect you."

"Let Nocturna smile on you," Kyla returned the farewell. "We'll see you tomorrow."

■ ■ ■

"He gets to stay here?!" her youngest son Talis exclaimed, his tail frizzing in excitement.

Following her meeting with Avalene, she had tracked down all her boys for a quick family meeting. All six of them sat around the living room, listening to what she had to say. Talis wasn't the only one to brighten up at what she suggested; the rest of her sons looked intrigued with the idea.

"As we figure out what's going on, yes." Kyla explained. "Would you all be alright with that?"

A reception of hurriedly bobbing heads answered her. All her children looked remarkably similar to one another, as they all shared a similar gray tabby coat, green eyes, lithe form, and brown hair. Their facial features and markings offered little assistance in telling them apart, but, being their mother, Kyla had an easy enough time.

"What about Dad, though?" her oldest, Gavin, questioned. Gavin was aged at seventeen and the most responsible of them, so his question was only fitting.

"I'll handle your father," Kyla brushed off. "However, there's some things that need to be made clear."

They all waited.

"You are *not* to bother him while he's here. Give him some distance; he's been through things you boys couldn't even imagine." The mother in her ached at the idea of them enduring what the demorinkin had likely dealt with. "Is that understood?"

"When you say… bother…" Rorrik, the fourth oldest, pondered. "What does that mean exactly?" Rorrik had freshly turned thirteen only days earlier. The job to rescue the demorinkin had been his first 'official' mission, so to say, and he had done Kyla proud. He had been the one to tackle the boy's attacker.

"It means not playing pranks on him or stressing him out even further." Kyla gave her offspring a sideways look. "You are all *not* the easiest to deal with. Just keep your distance for now."

"You offend us, Mother," Jate, the second oldest at sixteen years old, laughed. He had been the one to carry the demorinkin to safety, and his frame proved more muscular than his other siblings due to the extra conditioning and training he placed his body through.

"Darn. I was looking forward to a test subject…" Quinn, the third of her children, aged at fifteen, teased. Quinn proved to be the most eccentric of the bunch—which was saying something. Not that it was a trait Kyla frowned upon; Quinn's curiosity and cleverness made his hobby of tinkering and inventing a lucrative one.

"So we can't even talk to him?" Calvin, the fifth oldest at ten years old, complained. Calvin, like Talis, was too young to go on official missions. Not that he didn't beg to.

"Not for now. Let him relax first," Kyla answered.

"That's boring, though!" Talis whined. The youngest had just turned eight last month, and was learning the ropes of their family's business with ease. Talis had a habit of mimicking his older brothers' antics, as younger siblings are wont to do; thus, keeping him in line could be a struggle.

"So you just want us to *ignore* him?" Rorrik inquired, his tone incredulous.

"I want you to avoid being seen by him in the first place." Kyla made clear.

"So if he spots us… we don't have to ignore him?" Rorrik went on, perking up slightly.

Kyla caught on to what he was getting at. "Don't let it happen," she stressed. "I love you boys, but you… come on a bit strong."

"We love you too, Mom," Jate laughed.

"I mean it. Do you all understand me?" Kyla spoke with a hint of sternness.

"Yes…" her sons chorused.

"Good." Kyla smiled at all of them. "You all know what to do, then."

■ ■ ■

"Absolutely not!" Niem hissed. "He is NOT staying here any longer. He should have never been brought here in the first place!"

Kyla frowned at her mate as she laid on their bed, a revealing nightgown showing off her pregnant curves. "Where else could we have brought him, Niem? People wanted him dead."

"That is *not* our business nor responsibility," the black-furred felidaren rebutted. "It was foolish to bring him here, Kyla. *Foolish.*"

"If you expect me to regret it, I don't," Kyla said. "I wasn't about to let him fall right back into danger. And I don't plan to change that."

"I said no!" Niem fought. "If someone wants him dead, they become our own enemies by protecting him, Kyla! We do not need to involve ourselves in this. It's unnecessary!"

"You think his life is unnecessary?"

"It is not our responsibility!" he barked. "Your clients can handle it from here. It's *their* job, not ours!"

"He won't talk, Niem. He's traumatized and won't open up until he can calm down. He might not have the luxury to do that anywhere else. He's safe here."

"Is that supposed to convince me?" Niem growled. "It is not our problem. I will not risk my home to this stranger. Forget it."

Kyla didn't want to have to resort to her next tactic, but her mate wasn't budging. "I don't ask for much, Niem. I want to help him. Can't you do this for me? *Please?*"

"This is too much to ask for, Kyla! No!"

"He's already been brought here! The damage is done, isn't it?"

"The longer he stays the more the risk grows. No!"

"Why are you suddenly doubting our hideout now, Niem? It's safe here! They have no lead to find him. What are the chances of them tracking him down while he's here? Even if they somehow did, we have the resources to hold them back!"

Niem didn't reply to that. His tail thrashed back and forth, his eyes on the wall rather than her. His silence was a good sign.

Kyla moved off the bed and went to wrap her arms around her mate. "Do this for me. *Please*," she pleaded into his neck.

The felidaren gave a long growl and then a hiss. "He won't be here a second longer than he *has* to be. Do you understand me?"

Kyla kissed his neck before nibbling on it softly. "I understand." She began to lick him, and the tension in Niem's shoulders lessened a tad. "Thank you..."

He sighed as a response.

Kyla's arms around him tightened, and she nuzzled him lovingly. She began to pull her mate to their bed, eager to convey her gratitude.

"Come here, you. I've been needing a good lay all day," she purred.

Niem didn't argue with that.

Chapter 14

Rorrik

"So is he actually a real demorin?" Talis asked, leaning over the island in their kitchen with large, curious eyes. The eight-year-old's feet dangled inches from the floor as he hung across the table.

"Not fully," Gavin replied as he iced a cupcake with a butter knife. "He's demorin*kin*, meaning he's not a purebred demorin."

"How do you know that?" Calvin wondered from next to Talis. Rorrik's younger brother held a sprinkle jar in his paws, ready to douse any freshly iced cupcakes.

The oldest shrugged and adopted a mischievous look in his eye. "I may have heard Mom talking about it with Miss Porte..."

"Ooooh, someone was *eavesdropping*," Jate chuckled, pulling a fresh batch of pastries from the oven as a timer dinged.

Gavin shrugged yet again, but offered a knowing smirk. The end of his tail gave a flick. "His papers say he's early teen, five foot, and from Akarth."

"Whoooa!" Talis exclaimed. "That's really far!"

"His papers?" Quinn questioned. He was also busy frosting the sugary treats.

"Miss Porte shouldn't have left them unattended before the meeting," Gavin said, his tail flicking yet again.

Quinn laughed and remarked, "You're pretty good at that informant thing!"

That spurred a grin out of the oldest brother. Gavin had been training to be an 'official' informant for the last few months. It had been coming naturally to him; Gavin always managed to understand any situation. If he didn't, he had a way to find out. Combine that with the stealth they had all been honing since their childhood, and you had one gifted informant-in-training.

"You've been awfully quiet, Rorrik," Jate derailed the conversation. "Lazy, too."

Rorrik looked over at his older sibling with an unfrosted cupcake in his hands. It had remained without icing for the last minute or so, his focus having run off with distracting thoughts.

He took up some frosting with a butter knife and began to cover the cupcake. "Happy now?" he asked.

Rorrik's mind wasn't exactly on cupcakes. Instead, he found himself wondering about their mysterious guest. The demorinkin's presence intrigued the young felidaren greatly.

It was the morning following the stranger's awakening. The demorinkin had first woken up yesterday afternoon, having slept for hours since they saved him, which was two nights ago now.

"What's on your mind, brother dear?" Quinn inquired, setting down the cupcake he had just covered in sugary goodness. Calvin attacked it with sprinkles instantly.

Rorrik shrugged. "Mom is a buzzkill…"

His older siblings chuckled at that, but the younger ones nodded in agreement.

"Yeah! It's stupid how we can't talk to him…" Calvin pouted.

"It makes sense. He doesn't need your ugly faces scaring him even more," Jate teased.

"I'm better looking than you!" Calvin disagreed.

"He finally ate that roll Mom put in there for him," Gavin pointed out, coming between the teasing.

"Well, the guy had to be hungry," Jate said. "Doesn't surprise me."

"Stressed bellies aren't always eager bellies," Quinn contributed. "It's a good sign!"

Gavin nodded. "When he's not so stressed, maybe Mom will lighten up."

"Maybe…" Rorrik said. How long would *that* take, though?

He finished frosting the cupcake and placed it down. Talis beat Calvin to sprinkling this time.

"So what are you all up to today?" Jate asked.

"Picking pockets at Jadison," Calvin answered.

"Me, too!" Talis added.

"Scrounging for parts," Quinn responded, setting down another frosted cupcake.

"Training," Gavin took his turn in replying.

"I'm going for a run over by Rovester," Jate revealed. "Then I'll probably be keeping watch by Farpoint – whatever Dad wants me to do."

His siblings turned to look at him, waiting for his own response.

Rorrik hadn't planned anything for the day. Well, plans he could admit, at least. He scrounged his mind for an answer.

"Probably just studying the new packet Mr. Wachest gave me," he replied.

"But it's *Runedae*!" Calvin challenged incredulously. "Why would you study today? We don't have to."

"That does seem unlike you…" Gavin commented. The way he looked at Rorrik suggested he suspected him of something.

"Hey, I like learning," Rorrik argued.

"Could've fooled me," Jate laughed.

Rorrik whacked him with his tail, and it only added to his brother's laughter.

"Well, that's your choice then." Gavin grabbed a bag sitting on top of the dining table and slung it on his shoulder. "I'll see you all later."

"I'm going to head out, too!" Jate declared. He swiped up a finished cupcake and took a large bite out of it.

"Great choice in pre-run tasties," Quinn sassed, amused.

"Sugar gets the blood going!" Jate agreed with a wink. "Alright! See ya, kits!" He began to follow Gavin out.

"I'm not a kit anymore!" Calvin called out after his departing sibling, annoyed.

"Yeah!" Talis added with a pout. "We're not!"

Jate only chuckled in response as the two eldest left the kitchen and beyond.

"Well, we'll put frosting on these later," Quinn chuckled before stashing the fresh batch onto a shelf in the fridge. "Come on, you two. Let's head out," he said to the two youngest. He then eyed Rorrik and smirked. "Have fun with your *studying*, Rorrik."

"I will," Rorrik confirmed. '*I will...*'

■ ■ ■

Rorrik sat down at the dining table, giving a quick glance through the packet. If he was going to lie about studying, he needed to have a basic understanding of what it was teaching. His brothers and mother were sure to ask what he had learned, after all. Luckily, he was a hasty reader and had a knack for absorbing information.

The packet described a brief history of their city: Sengard. Being the Wesvarln capital, it had a rich history behind it, one that would certainly take more than one packet to get through. Rorrik wasn't very enchanted with the lesson. He normally didn't mind learning, but his mind was elsewhere.

He continued a speedy glance-through, his ears perked for any movement throughout the basement. The place remained quiet, his mother and father having left much earlier in the day, and now all his siblings being gone as well. There were currently no other guests at the hideout save for the demorinkin, which made his job easier.

When he had a reasonable idea of what the first pages of the packet were discussing, he moved out of his chair silently, his tail in a tick. He returned the packet to its place in his tutoring box and approached the collection of cupcakes they had been working on that morning. He picked one up to eventually munch on and set down the hall in a tiptoe.

His mother had specifically said that they only had to remain unseen when it came to their guest. Therefore, so long as he was, what was the harm in taking a peek at what the demorinkin was doing?

He approached the section of the hideout dedicated to guests and snuck down the hallway, his tail twitching. He went through the doors of the first wing, moving them open with practiced quietness, and went up to the door he knew the demorinkin to be behind.

He sat there for a few seconds gaining his bearings with a silent intake of breath. He had to be exceptionally quiet, lest he be spotted. He crouched down and put his hand on the knob before gingerly turning it. He began to inch the door open...

...Only to hear another door open in the same instant.

He snapped his head to the source of the sound and saw the wing doors open, the demorinkin standing there surprised.

They stared at one another as awkwardness took the situation, the apparentness of what Rorrik had been doing no doubt understood between the two of them. The demorinkin looked remarkably wary and uncomfortable.

"Aheheh..." Rorrik chuckled awkwardly, slowly getting to his feet. "Uhh..." His mind worked to produce a suitable excuse. *'That's it!'* He held out the pastry he carried, a smile stretching his features. "Want a cupcake?"

The demorinkin didn't look at the sweet at first, but then he slowly moved his eyes down on it.

Rorrik continued to offer it, channeling as much friendliness as he could into the gesture.

The boy switched his gaze back to Rorrik, and a slight ripple of confusion traveled across his face.

"You don't want it, then?" Rorrik asked.

The demorinkin frowned and then dropped his gaze on the sweet yet again.

"If you don't want it, I can—"

He shook his head and reached a shaky hand out to take it, to Rorrik's surprise. The felidaren let it happen.

The demorinkin stared down at the cupcake that was now in his own hands, and Rorrik noticed that the boy's eyes were growing shiny with threatening tears.

Rorrik awkwardly looked to the wall and then the ground. He peeked into the demorinkin's room and saw that the glass of water on his nightstand was empty.

"I'll, ah, get you some more water," he offered. He slipped into the narrowly opened door and fetched the glass. When he popped back out, the demorinkin had moved out of the wing doorway so he could walk past him.

Rorrik scurried off to do what he said. He filled the glass in the kitchen, nervous his mother would randomly come travelling down the steps and question what he was doing. She never did.

He returned to find the door to the stranger's room still open, the demorinkin sitting on the bed, his eyes on the treat. It was untouched.

Rorrik entered the room feeling a tinge bashful, which was an unfamiliar sensation. The demorinkin glanced up when he arrived, but returned his eyes to the cupcake.

The felidaren placed the glass on the nightstand, and no bread roll sat on the plate there, as Gavin had mentioned.

"Th...Thank you..." the demorinkin suddenly spoke quietly.

Rorrik slightly jumped and perked his ears. He faced the demorinkin, but the teen did not return his gaze.

"Ah... You're welcome!" Rorrik found himself unable to contain a grin.

"I... I haven't had a cupcake in..." The boy shook his head, and Rorrik noticed the tears building in his eyes were still threatening to break free. "Gods... it's been awhile."

"Well, there's more where that came from, if you want." Rorrik gestured to the door. "We made a whole batch of them earlier."

The demorinkin finally looked up at him, and Rorrik was stunned to see a weak grin grace his lips.

"I'll get through one first..." the teen decided, setting his attention back on the cupcake in his lap. "Thanks, though..."

"No problem! Hopefully you like chocolate!"

The demorinkin nodded. "I love chocolate..."

"You'll love those, then," Rorrik grinned. He waited for the demorinkin to try the pastry, curious to see what his reaction would be.

The teen unwrapped the cupcake before bringing it up to his mouth, hesitating before taking a tentative sample. He perked up and gave an 'mmm', seeming to enjoy what he tasted.

Rorrik's grin became a fledged smile. "See?"

The demorinkin nodded. He took another bite, and then another.

Rorrik leaned up against the wall as the other teen finished the treat.

"That was... really good," the demorinkin complimented, licking vanilla frosting from his fingers.

"...Want another one?" Rorrik asked, pushing off the wall.

The demorinkin looked to the open door of his room and gave a subtle nod.

Rorrik smiled and hopped out of the room much faster than the demorinkin did. He waited in the threshold as the other teen inched off the bed and stood up slowly, wariness apparent in his body language.

He didn't meet Rorrik's eyes as they set out into the hall and then out the wing doors.

"I might as well show you around while we're at it," Rorrik suggested.

The demorinkin didn't reply, but didn't appear to protest the plan, either.

"Your room is part of one of the guest wings. All the rooms are pretty much the same, even the ones in the other wing." He pointed to the doorway right next to the one they had just left. "If you go through there, there's three more rooms." In the wing the demorinkin's room was in, there were six.

He began to lead them to the left. They passed by a door. "That's the guest bathrooms, but I'm guessing you already knew that."

The demorinkin nodded simply.

They crossed through the arch that led into the entryway. "This is the entry hall. If you go through that door," he pointed to the only door in the space, which lay further down and was adjacent to a dresser, "it leads you to the stairs and meeting room. The stairs lead upstairs, which is still our hideout, but it's much safer down here." Rorrik wasn't even sure if the demorinkin was allowed to leave the basement; he hoped it was alright to tell him about the stairs.

"If you go through here," he crossed into the archway that led into the living area, "you find yourself in the living room! We call it 'the den.'"

The same wood paneling of the floors and ceilings carried into the space. The den hosted a seating area composed of multiple couches and chairs, enough to seat nine total (or more if you were a creative sort). Across from the seating area in a smaller extension of the room was a card table. He directed his guest's attention to a door on the wall. "That door leads to a bathroom."

On the far side of the room, the wall was partially knocked out to reveal a view into the kitchen, their next stop. "In there is the kitchen!" He guided him in, a bounce in his step. It wasn't very often that *he* got to give the guests tours.

The kitchen was home to a long table that could comfortably seat eight, found in the bottom section of the room close to the den archway. Counters lined all along the back walls, joined by a fridge, oven, and sink. A table serving as a kitchen island sat in the middle of the counters, bordered by two wooden pillars, the cupcakes his brothers and he had decorated earlier occupying the table's surface. The icing glistened in the lighting of the room, which was lit by lamps that hugged the ceiling. Above the table was a hanging light fixture.

Rorrik looked over at the guest with a smile. The demorinkin was gaping at what he was seeing. Rorrik pinned him as impressed, judging by his round eyes and slightly parted mouth; it filled the felidaren with a sense of pride.

"Pretty nice, huh?" He pointed to another archway to their left. Looking down it, one could spot double doors on a distant wall. "Through there is the hallway we were in before, and the doors lead to where my family's bedrooms are. We can't go in there, though." Guests were never allowed in that section of the basement.

"That's pretty much it!" Rorrik finished, beaming. "What do you think?!"

The demorinkin was looking around with the same look from before. "It's... wow..." he mumbled, his shock translating into tone.

"Isn't it? It's great here!" It was certainly home; he had grown up in these walls along with his siblings.

"Why... don't you have windows?" the demorinkin questioned with a hint of confusion.

"We're underground! *And* this place is a secret! Not too smart to have windows," Rorrik answered. "Upstairs has windows, but that part is the inn. Like I said, it's still our hideout, but not as safe as down here."

The demorinkin took that with a stunned nod. "This is a... hideout?"

"Yep!" Rorrik chimed. "My family does a lot of secretive things, so we need a hideout so we don't get caught or found by anybody. Isn't that cool?"

The guest nodded yet again. He looked everywhere but at Rorrik.

"Well! Here are the cupcakes!" Rorrik sprung over to the island and took up one of the treats. They were all chocolate cake with vanilla frosting, a family favorite. The sprinkles on top were multicolored and crunchy.

The demorinkin followed, eyeing the sweets with yearning.

"Go ahead and have as many as you want!" Rorrik offered, unwrapping the cupcake before taking a bite out of it. He didn't chew fully before finishing, "We have even more in the fridge, but they aren't frosted yet."

The demorinkin picked up one of the sweets and unwrapped it carefully. He then bit into it, perking up as he had before.

They munched on their cupcakes in silence. Rorrik finished before the guest did.

"...Sooo, want to frost the rest with me?" Rorrik offered, gesturing a claw to the fridge. "It's fun! You can put the sprinkles on them, even."

"Uhhh," the demorinkin blinked as he processed the offer, half of his cupcake still in his hands. "Um, sure!" The last of his words were delivered with more enthusiasm than Rorrik had heard him use yet.

"Okay!" Rorrik fetched the batch from the fridge and placed it down on the counters behind the table. He took up a knife and began to wiggle each of the pastries out of the pan and onto the counter.

The demorinkin looked on, still getting through his own cupcake. He finished it as Rorrik worked.

"There we go," Rorrik said as the last of the cupcakes plopped onto the counter. "You can use this." He gave the teen a butter knife, and the demorinkin received it rather cautiously.

Rorrik fetched the leftover frosting from the fridge and put it between them on the island table. He dipped the knife he had been using into the icing and slabbed some on a bare cupcake. "Do you know how to do it?" he asked.

The demorinkin nodded before dipping his own knife into the icing container. Rorrik watched as the teen slathered frosting onto a fresh cupcake and began to spread it. The way he worked the knife and icing suggested that he had done it before.

He finished icing it and picked up the sprinkle jar before neatly dusting the pastry. The end result revealed to be a very pretty cupcake, much less sloppy than the ones Rorrik's brothers and he had made.

"That's really good!" Rorrik complimented.

The demorinkin's lips twitched into a slight grin. "I like cake decorating…" he spoke more certainly than ever before.

"Us, too! We like to make a lot of pastries," Rorrik replied. He shook some sprinkles onto his own cupcake and placed it down next to the demorinkin's. He laughed at how they compared.

The two dipped their knives into the frosting and started on the next two cupcakes. Rorrik noticed on the corner of his eye that the demorinkin was glancing over at his progress.

"If you arc the knife upwards and move it in a swirl, it raises the frosting into shape," the demorinkin offered advice.

Rorrik stopped what he was doing and blinked before grinning mischievously. "Oh, *really*? I thought you did it like this…" He flicked the knife, flinging a glop of frosting into the air and towards the demorinkin. It landed right on the other teen's nose.

The demorinkin stood there in surprise, obviously not having expected frosting to suddenly fly off the cupcake and hit him square in the face.

Rorrik laughed loudly, amused. He then felt frosting hit his own face, to his shock.

He faced the demorinkin and found him staring intently at his cupcake, looking innocent enough. He then pretended to notice Rorrik staring. "What's that on your face?" he asked, feigning puzzlement.

Rorrik laughed and flung more frosting at the demorinkin, to which the other teen returned fire. The guest began to laugh along with him, and it was a great sound to hear.

That continued for a time, both hooting with laughter and having fun. They were sticky and covered in frosting when Rorrik suddenly spotted someone standing in the kitchen archway.

His frosting-covered ears went back as he noticed it was his mother.

■ ■ ■

Kyla

'What did I tell him?!' At first, Kyla was offended. Her son had deliberately disobeyed her. She didn't expect such blatant disrespect out of her child!

But then, as she witnessed the two of them playing and laughing, she felt foolish. There the demorinkin was, the one who had been too stressed to say more than a word or two to anyone, settled down enough to have a *frosting fight*. She was wrong to doubt her son's charisma.

Regardless, it did not change the fact that Rorrik hadn't followed orders. She'd have to handle that... later.

Rorrik's ears drew back when he finally noticed her standing there. The demorinkin tilted his head at Rorrik's reaction and then took note of her presence himself. His ears dipped as his eyes bore into her, horrified.

Kyla put a hand on her hip and smothered down any remaining frustrations. The two of them gawked at her in terror, both no doubt waiting for her anger to flare.

"Well, boys... I suppose that's one way to frost a cupcake," she finally said, smirking subtly.

Rorrik blinked, as did the demorinkin, her comment obviously not what they expected.

"Last I checked, you're supposed to put the frosting on the pastry itself, not one another," Kyla observed.

"We'd... thought we'd try something different?" Rorrik tried, grinning nervously.

"Different indeed." The mother faced the demorinkin. "Do you remember where the showers are, young man?"

He nodded, the same terrified look never leaving him.

"Why don't you go wash up?" she suggested in a kind voice. "There are more clothes for you in the dresser of your room. Just leave the dirty clothes in the basket of the shower room."

The demorinkin nodded again before sharing a look with Rorrik. Seeming ashamed, he dipped his head and started to walk out of the kitchen, Kyla moving out of the archway so he could pass.

As he went into the living room and beyond, Kyla's kind demeanor turned considerably more sour as she looked upon her son.

His ears shot back again.

"What did I tell you?" she began in the feline tongue, her tone stern.

"It was an accident!" Rorrik cried, matching the language. "I didn't mean to be spotted!"

She squinted her eyes at him. "And did you put yourself in a situation where you *could* be spotted?"

"I—" her son cut off and faced the floor, his sugary coated ears flat. "...I was just real curious and I— I wanted to... I'm sorry..."

"Are you? Honestly?"

"Yes..." her son mumbled, his vision on the floor

Kyla let him wallow in his shame for a few more moments. "Well… You shouldn't have done that." A few more seconds… "But… I'm glad you did."

Rorrik jerked his head up, seeming stunned. "What?"

"I… shouldn't have doubted you… You were able to get him to open up." She smiled softly. "I'm proud of you."

Rorrik merely blinked, speechless.

"But! That does not mean you're off the hook," Kyla made clear. "You are *not* to lick *any* of that off. Go take a water shower. *Now*."

Rorrik pouted and turned to walk to one of the family bathrooms, his tail dragging on the ground.

"And you will be studying for the rest of the day!" Kyla called out after him. "Which is what you were planning anyways, right?"

She heard him groan as he opened the doors to the family hall and went through.

She shook her head. Hearing from Jate that Rorrik had stayed home to study had filled her with expectations of finding her son spying on the demorinkin, not what she had walked in on. It had been a surprise, for certain.

Kyla shrugged it off and approached the counter to pick up a cupcake. After removing the foil, she bit into the pastry with a sideways grin. *'Whatever works, I suppose.'*

Chapter 15

Valen

The rush of hot water splashing down from the shower made him cry out briefly. He had been bracing for it to be freezing, a repercussion of his prior trauma. It wasn't until a few moments of tension passed that he finally allowed himself to understand the water was favorable, and he shakily sighed away the memory of ice and pain.

Valen leaned into the wall as the water rolled down his back and sung to his aching muscles. The liquid soaked his naked form, the warmth of the water as it streamed over him something he had not experienced in months. Even when he would heat up buckets of water back at the clock tower to give himself sponge baths, bathing was not the same. His last real shower had been before his parents' murder, two lives ago.

He wasn't sure how to feel or what to think of anything; confusion punctuated every experience since his rescue. His life had just been ripped to shreds by the tragedy that had befallen him, but then he was delivered into a place with better living conditions than what he left? It was difficult to realize that the situation he found himself in showed promise of comfort. Part of him just wanted to remain miserable, and that part often won.

The night before had been awash in anxiety and fear with little solace to be found despite what he had been told by his rescuers. He could call them that now; he found himself hesitantly believing that they meant to help him. What they had told him added up, even if Valen had trouble coming to terms with it. He was a demorinkin; the world was wary at best towards their kind. The notion of anyone jeopardizing their own safety to help him struck as unlikely.

Yet, these felidaren had. Perhaps they were right when they mentioned he could relax. After all, he had woken up that morning safe as they said he would be despite the fear and dread of the Fangs of Hellbane pulling him from his bed as he slept. The brunt of his paranoia lessened like an idea that had the power to scare in the night becoming underwhelming with the help of the sun. He allowed himself to feel a shred of solace, his being too exhausted from all the negativity to fight it.

The female felidaren, Mrs. Catty, had come to talk with him briefly at the start of the day. She had mentioned that he was going to be staying there as they worked 'everything' out, which left Valen wondering what that entailed. She had told him to get plenty of rest, food, and water and to feel at home. She then left with a warm smile before closing the door, and she had again reminded Valen of his own mother.

It was a bittersweet sensation. In one sense, it filled Valen with a comfort he had long been without, but in another, it was a reminder of his mother's death. Regardless, it made him moderately less wary of the felidaren, and he could relax a tad more when she was around.

As he stood in the stream, the frosting that clung to his hair and face rinsed away with the pressure of the water. His stomach was in knots over what had happened; it was strange to look back on it.

He hadn't known what to think at first when he found the felidaren sneaking into his room. Valen had left just minutes earlier to relieve himself at the guest restrooms, a decision that had long been delayed out of anxiety. It became apparent that the felidaren was there to deliver more food onto his plate, the item this time being a cupcake instead of a roll.

The pastry had stirred something within Valen; old memories of him baking at the house in Riverview summoned instantly at the sight of the treat. It had been almost a year since his last cupcake; Karreo and he had not had the luxury of sweets when they were out on the streets. A nostalgia and yearning for the pastry had rendered him unable to refuse.

From there, things had just felt... easier. At least, for a brief amount of time. The anguish and despair crushing him had lessened as the sweetness of the cupcake danced about his taste buds.

It helped that the tabby felidaren was springy and friendly; Valen had enjoyed interacting with someone else around his age. He hadn't made any true friends in months, the pressure of his predicament and nervousness to interact with the world labeling it a bad idea to form any. He hadn't realized how desperately he craved interaction of the sort. Goofing off had been easy. Natural, even.

Mrs. Catty intervening had been sobering. Not only did her entrance embarrass him, but it pronounced a reminder of what exactly was happening. The miserable part of him was betrayed that he'd even *dare* to enjoy himself in the wake of his brother's death; he didn't deserve to. It was all his fault.

He had slunk off to the restroom, barely overhearing as Mrs. Catty scolded the felidaren sternly as he reached the entry hall. His regret amplified; he hadn't wanted the felidaren to get in trouble. The fact he had only added to his remorse.

The guest restroom was akin to a public toilet. There were stalls that contained toilets along a wall and counters that sported sinks along another. A mirror hung above the counters and next to them was an archway. Beyond the opening were the showers. There were four in total, each closed off with a curtain, and a bench lay across from them on the opposing wall. Next to the bench was the basket she had mentioned as well as a series of shelving stocked with towels.

He had grabbed a towel in shame and slipped into one of the showers, still clothed. He battled with apprehension over the idea of stripping down, despite being shielded by a curtain. No one else was even around, but still he was anxious. He had eventually summoned the courage and slung his sticky clothes over the bar along with his towel.

He decided it was time to scrub in the present. A selection of soaps was up on a rack, one revealing to be shampoo, another conditioner, and the other body wash. Such a variety joined the privileges that he had been without for over a year. The only soap he had access to at the clock tower was an all-purpose bottle that had dried out his skin and hair; the idea of shampoo was one long forgotten.

Should he take advantage of it? The desire to remain miserable shouted no, and so he only grabbed the body soap. He scrubbed his scalp thoroughly before washing the product out of his hair, the stickiness of the frosting stubborn to succumb.

His scrubbing spread down to his body, the knots in his stomach tightening as his hands travelled along his torso. He found himself apprehensive to scrub beyond his waist, the memories of his molestation still fresh and burning within him. Despite the negative connotation, he gingerly began to scrub his privates, wincing in memory of the trauma. He made quick work of it and never looked down, a relative of shame preventing him.

He stood there as the soap washed away, but not the memories. He shuddered and felt cold despite the heat of the shower. He just wanted to finish and get dressed.

He turned off the tap and wrapped himself in the towel he grabbed. He dropped off the dirtied clothes in the basket and set off towards his room with a hustle in his step.

■ ■ ■

He had found fresh clothes in the dresser as Mrs. Catty said he would. The outfit he compiled consisted of a blue shirt and similar sweatpants to before, these ones black. Valen was appreciative of the tail cut in the pants, even if it was snug fitting around the larger base of his own tail.

Now he lay on the bed, the foil of his earlier cupcake sitting on the plate of the nightstand. The taste of chocolate and frosting still haunted his taste buds. Unfortunately, it also haunted his guts.

He was suffering from a cramping stomach, no doubt from eating such a rich treat after days of low quality to no food. His innards churned and roiled within him, leaving him completely uncomfortable.

A knock at his door surprised him.

"Can I come in?" Mrs. Catty's voice asked softly.

Valen's voice felt far away from him as he tried to summon it. "Yes," the word eventually came out, choked and tiny.

The door opened slowly and in she walked, a cup in her hands.

"My son mentioned you had a cupcake... or two," she said as she studied him. "I imagine you're not receiving that well."

He didn't look up at her as he lay there, figuring it was obvious enough.

"Drink this. It'll help," she offered. "Sit up first. Can't have you choking."

He pushed himself up, wincing as he received the glass. He inspected it, seeing a clear liquid that smelled of lemon and mint.

"It'll help relieve some of the pain and get rid of gas build up," she explained. "It's lemon water with mint. It's helped my boys through plenty of stomach aches."

He took a meager sip. The sweetness of lemon and freshness of mint was an unfamiliar combination to him, but not a bad one.

"Make sure to drink the whole glass," Mrs. Catty advised. "I'll be in the kitchen. If you need anything, just ask."

He nodded, still sipping. She smiled at him and took her leave, her tail swishing behind her. She closed the door as she went.

He got through the entire glass before lying back down, waiting for the effects of it to kick in. To his relief, it began to help some. Then, it helped a lot.

The memory of earlier looped his mind, the image of the springy felidaren holding out a cupcake refusing to leave him. He closed his eyes, tired and perplexed. *'What a weird day...'*

■ ■ ■

The next morning, Valen finally allowed himself a look in the mirror since his capture. His heart contorted as he examined his reflection, recognizing with a pang that he would never again appreciate his vest's vivid red. It struck him with insurmountable sorrow; he felt empty and alone without the vest, and now he was to forever be without it.

He continued studying himself. The brick red of his skin seemed duller, his black hair shaggier. There were bags under his sunken eyes, and a cut above his brow that was having trouble healing. He realized immediately that it was from when he was kidnapped, when he had attempted to pry himself free.

He squeezed his eyes closed as the memory of his capture seared through his mind, disintegrating away any comfort he'd built up over the last couple of days. He was disconsolate and nauseous at the reminder of his baby brother being gone, to be forever denied a life worth living beyond his parent's death. *'It's all my fault. It's all my fault...'*

Disturbingly, a realization struck him. If he hadn't done his spell – if he hadn't tried giving his brother an opening to run – Karreo would have been captured and thus saved. If he hadn't attempted to be the hero, if he hadn't – *if he hadn't—*

He kicked at the wall as frustration with himself peaked, yet again overcome with self-hatred and remorse. It was yet another mistake that had cost his brother's well-being.

It explained why he felt so *guilty* at enjoying what his rescuer's hideout had to offer. Karreo never got to enjoy it, even though he should have. There were so many things Karreo *should have*, but never got to do. *'Oh, Karreo, I'm so sorry!'*

He set his attention back on the mirror, his lip trembling and his eyes shimmering with tears. It was all because his shift had failed; all because of the demorin face that stared back at him. His brow narrowed with determination. He never wanted to see that face again!

He began to shift, his focus honed with anger. The horns melded into his head, and the ridges on his brow disappeared. The sclera of his eyes went from black to white, his yellow irises altered into green. His skin turned olive, his teeth lost their fangs; his tail disappeared, his claws became nails. All his demorin traits fell away, revealing the Valen that should have been there for his brother, the Valen that shouldn't have failed.

He glared at Sphinx as more tears left the rim of his eyes. *'You failed... you failed...'*

"Whoa..." a voice suddenly said.

He yelped out in surprise, and his focus was dashed. His form blinked back into its natural one as he swung his head towards the voice.

The springy felidaren from yesterday stood in the doorway, the door half open, his green eyes wide. He was gawking at Valen, and Valen gawked back in turn.

Valen felt a whip of anger thrash. "Can't you knock?!" he spat.

The felidaren gave him the same wide-eyed stare. "You can transform?!"

"Not when I actually need to!" he growled out, sinking in his shame. "Go away!"

"Can you transform into anything?"

"No! *Leave!*" Valen barked. He stomped over to the door and slammed it shut, the felidaren hopping back to avoid being crushed.

Valen collapsed onto his bed. He was back to wishing the Fangs of Hellbane would track him down after all. The grief was suffocating him. *'Everything is wrong! I can't do this!'* He sobbed and sobbed, discovering an ocean of tears in him yet.

As time passed, his anger eroded into sadness. He was entirely alone and hollow, miserable through and through. He longed for the embrace of his vest and the confirmation of Karreo snuggled up next to him. He wondered what the city of Akarth looked like from the mighty clock tower windows and what Siena was doing at that very moment. What did she think about what happened? Did she look for him? Did she fear him?

What about Mr. Panto? Would he grow worried when Valen failed to show up day after day? Was Simitri Dayas confident he would walk into the library any time now, ready to show the floraling what he learned, only to begin to doubt he would ever return? Did Mrs. Thickettt wonder where he ran off to, what mischief he was weaving? Would he ever be back to pester her and fool her out of her peaches?

It all amplified his despair, and the ache within him was far worse than the stomach cramps of yesterday. There wasn't a tonic out there to help him this time.

Valen began to regret yelling at the felidaren. He hadn't meant to, but his turbulent emotions had been easily riled. The demorinkin worried that he had scared away a potential friend.

Perhaps not, for a knock came at the door. Valen was too downtrodden to answer; his voice had been robbed by his melancholy.

"Um… I'm sorry about earlier," a voice began apologetically, Valen pinning it as the felidaren. "My mom made some soup… I… have some here if you want any…"

Valen forced himself out of bed and to his feet, his head pounding as he stood up. He walked up to the door and opened it, the felidaren seeming surprised as he came into view.

The tabby was holding a bowl in his hands. Valen stared at that rather than the felidaren, too embarrassed to do differently.

Valen held out his hands for the bowl, and the felidaren handed it over gingerly. Valen proceed to gaze down at the soup, his ears dipped.

"…Thanks," he mumbled out, finally finding his voice. "I'm… I'm sorry, too… I hadn't meant to yell…"

The felidaren perked up. "That's okay!"

Valen nodded awkwardly before going to sit on the bed, leaving the door ajar. The felidaren waited in the threshold, seeming uncertain.

"I can transform because I'm demorinkin…" Valen began, still keeping his eyes on the soup. "In case… you were wondering."

"That's really cool!' the felidaren gushed, finally deciding to walk in. "But why were you transforming now?"

Valen shut his puffy eyes as he winced from the question. "I… I was…" He wasn't sure what to say. "It's a long story…"

"Alright, if you don't want to tell me, it's okay," the felidaren said, his tone friendly.

Valen couldn't deny that he *did* want to tell someone. He was drowning in the aftermath of the tragedy; the bombardment of his guilt was too much to bear. When was the last time he even could share his problems with someone? He had been denied solace for so long; he was desperate for any type of affirmation.

"I had to shift – transform – back in Akarth... to protect myself." 'A*nd Karreo...*' He didn't want to talk about Karreo – not quite yet. It was too painful.

"Why?" the felidaren questioned.

"...People don't like – people *hate* – demorinkin... It wasn't safe to have people see me as what I truly am..." The words tasted bitter as he spoke them. Although it wasn't the full truth, it was still a reality he had to face.

"Well, *we* like you!" the felidaren insisted.

"...Why?" Valen pressed. "Why do you like me?"

"...Well, ah..." The felidaren blinked. "Why wouldn't we?"

"I'm demorinkin," Valen answered simply.

"...So?" the other teen shrugged. "I don't see why that matters."

"People think we're bad – that our heritage is evil."

"Well you aren't either of those things."

"How do you know that?! You don't know anything about me!" Valen cried, lifting his head to stare at the felidaren.

The felidaren gawked at him, taken aback by his sudden outburst. His expression then went sideways, and he shrugged yet again. "So you think I should just think that about you? Because of what you are?"

"It's what everybody else does..." Valen muttered, his gaze dropping yet again. '*People are so convinced that they'll track us down to* murder *us...*'

"Well, that's stupid."

"...You aren't scared of me?" Valen challenged.

The felidaren offered yet another shrug. "I think you look cool..."

It didn't seem likely that he was telling the truth, and yet all the felidaren's behavior thus far testified to his words. His mother and all the others appeared to reflect the same opinion. Valen wasn't sure what to make of any of it, so he decided to just press on with his tale.

"Well... Akarth wasn't like you," he wrote off. "I had to hide. And one day I... I..."

On the corner of Valen's vision, he spotted the felidaren's eyes grow wide in curiosity, but he didn't interrupt as the demorinkin searched for words.

"My shift failed and... I was spotted. Then... these bad people found me and... they took me away from my home... and took my vest..." His eyes were red from the salt of past and developing tears.

"Vest?" the felidaren asked, sounding confused by the random mention of that detail.

"A gift from my father... He... he made it for me. I... I don't... It meant so much to me, and they... they cut it up... threw it away... before you all saved me..." The words started to blur along with his vision. Valen's shoulders jumped, and he hung his head. "It was all I had left from him... and they... they just threw it out..."

"Oh..." the felidaren replied, saddened.

Valen's lip shuddered, and he shook his head. "It's all my fault... I should have... I should have..." He could go no further without explaining more, which was a conversation he would never feel ready for. "I was shifting earlier because I have to. I... I have to practice... make sure I never fail again..."

"...Well... it's okay if you look like that here. You don't have to hide."

"I'll always have to hide..." Valen mumbled somberly. The image of his attacker raising her sword to slice his neck flashed through his mind.

"Well... we already know what you are... It seems silly to disguise yourself now..."

"It's not disguising myself from you I have to worry about..." Valen sighed.

"...From who then?"

'The Fangs of Hellbane.' "Everybody else..."

"Maybe Sengard will be different than Akarth?" the felidaren mused.

'Sengard?' He was all the way in Sengard, the capital of Wesvarln? That was on the other side of the globe!

Valen shook off that surprise. "You just don't understand."

The felidaren went quiet. "Is that why those people wanted to kill you?" he eventually started up again.

Valen's innards gave a kick. "I don't want to talk about it..."

"...Okay," the felidaren accepted. "Sorry..."

Valen shook his head, emotional. He wanted to say that it was okay, but things certainly didn't feel that way.

"Well, that soup is really good..." the felidaren changed the subject with an awkward fidget. "Sorry that the cupcake upset your stomach..."

That was the least of Valen's current worries. "It's okay..."

"Um... I gotta go..." the felidaren said. He looked like he wanted to add something else, but his ears pressed back and he left without saying it.

Valen sighed as the door clicked closed with his leaving. He didn't feel any solace or comfort from sharing, only pain. 'It's all my fault... It's all my fault...'

. . .

Kyla

"He took the soup…" Rorrik announced as he came back into the kitchen, crestfallen. The rest of his siblings had already left by then.

"He did? What's with that face then?" Kyla inquired, washing the dishes that had been dirtied with cooking.

"I just feel really bad for him…" Rorrik answered in a mumble.

Kyla rinsed her hands and went to sit down at the table, patting the chair next to her. Rorrik sat down, his ears in a droop.

"Why's that, cub?"

Rorrik sighed. "I'unno… He said everybody hated what he is back in Akarth… and that he was captured because he…" Rorrik stopped talking, and Kyla tilted her head.

"Because he what?"

Her son looked to be weighing something. "He can transform… make him himself look different… He said he messed up one day and that's why he got captured…"

"Oh?" They hadn't known the demorinkin could transform. "What brought this up?"

"…I caught him transforming earlier…" Rorrik mumbled, sinking in his chair. "He got mad… but I said I was sorry, and he doesn't seem mad anymore…"

Kyla had given her son permission to interact with the demorinkin, so his earlier actions had not been disobeying this time around. She had figured if they had established a connection with one another, then there was no harm in them interacting. She had also figured it would only continue to help the demorinkin open up, which turned out to be true judging by Rorrik's story.

"So what did he say, exactly? That he was captured because he didn't transform?" Kyla asked for clarification.

Rorrik nodded. "He said he was spotted and then people came and took him from his home…"

Kyla felt a swelling of pity towards the demorinkin. He hadn't deserved anything that had befallen him – no child did. The ones who captured him no doubt took note of his exotic race and figured it'd fetch them a cute copper. They had been correct on that assumption…

"They even took a vest his dad made for him…" Rorrik added.

"…A vest?" Kyla echoed.

"Yeah. He almost cried when he said that… It meant a lot to him. He says they threw it out."

Kyla's interest was piqued. "…Did he say *where* they threw it out?"

Rorrik shook his head. "No…"

Kyla steepled her hands in thought. Avalene Porte's group was to be scoping out the building the boy was delivered to soon. She wondered if possibly… '*It's so unlikely… but…*'

"Mom?" Rorrik spurred.

It wasn't *impossible* that the vest was still around. If they had thrown it out at the building where they delivered him, it could potentially still be there. Garbage wasn't picked up for another day or so, after all.

"...We might be able to get it back," she theorized. If the vest meant so much to the boy, it would mean a lot to have it returned. It would surely help earn his trust and make him comfortable enough to talk.

"Really?!" Rorrik brightened up.

"Miss Porte plans to send a group to scope the place," Kyla started.

"I wanna go!" Rorrik intervened, his tail frizzing in excitement as he leapt out of his chair.

"What— no!" Kyla shot down. "It's too dangerous! I meant—"

"I want to get the vest back! Please, Mom! I did so well on the last mission – *Please!*"

"I'm not even sure it's there," Kyla pointed out.

"I'll look everywhere! Please! I want to do this!" Her son's eyes bore into her, sparking with determination.

"...Rorrik, are you even ready for something like this?" the mother in Kyla worried.

"I am! I helped rescue him, didn't I? You said I did really good!"

It was true... He had done exceptionally well on his first real mission.

Kyla sighed. What were the risks? Nothing should be life-threatening... She trusted Avalene's people to rein him in... It *would* be great experience...

"...Let me discuss it with Miss Porte, okay? Don't get your hopes up even if you end up going, kit. It's just a hunch that it might be there."

"Okay!" Rorrik looked ready to burst from anticipation.

Kyla weakly smiled at him. "You really want to help him, huh?"

Rorrik nodded zealously, motivated.

Kyla's smile held. "I'll see what I can do."

Chapter 16

Rorrik

"You're going on a job?!" Talis said excitedly, his young eyes full of intrigue.

"No fair! Why don't we get to go?!" Calvin whined.

Rorrik gave an exaggerated shrug and smirked. "Guess I'm just more *special.*"

"Nah uh!" Calvin disagreed. "You're not!'"

Rorrik snickered. "Why do I have this job then, and nobody else?"

The three brothers sat in the den, Rorrik having just walked into the room announcing the news. His mother had settled it with Miss Porte; he was to join the mission to scope out the bad guys' old hideout that very night!

Calvin pouted. "It's not fair... Mom never lets *me* go on any jobs..."

"You're still a little young, kit," Jate contributed from the kitchen, spreading some peanut butter on a slice of toast.

"I'm not a kit!" their younger brother objected.

Rorrik and Jate shared a chuckle at that. The memories of being told he himself was too young were all too fresh in his mind. The felidaren felt a swelling of pride that he was finally old enough to head on real missions.

"So what are you gonna do on the mission?" Talis questioned, leaning over the chair he sat on and towards Rorrik.

"I'm going to scope out the bad guys' old hideout," Rorrik elaborated. "Go through all their things, find clues, you know... really cool stuff."

"Oooh," Talis ogled.

"So why did Mom pick you, anyway?" Calvin muttered.

"I was the best to go, obviously," Rorrik boasted.

"Probably because he begged and pleaded to go," Jate butted in, still chewing, his mouth sticky with peanut butter.

Rorrik's fur went hot on his cheeks, but he smiled regardless, a fang poking out. "Either way, I'm the only one she picked. Not even Gavin is going."

"Hope you're ready for this, brother," Jate said from the kitchen as he continued munching on his toast.

"Of course I am. I did really well on the last mission," Rorrik pointed out.

"True, true!" Jate laughed. He finished his toast, having cleared it in a series of huge bites. He licked his fingers. "Hard to believe you're already old enough. Makes me feel old!"

Rorrik rolled his eyes, but his smile didn't falter.

Jate gulped down a glass of water that was on the counter. "Well, good luck on that. I've gotta run." He hopped the half wall from the kitchen and landed on Calvin, spurring out a yowl from the younger sibling.

"Get off!" Calvin hissed, much to Jate's laughter.

Talis jumped up on Jate, creating a cat pile.

"Oooh no! However, will I leave when I've been captured?" Jate bemoaned, dramatic.

Talis giggled. "I've got you!"

Rorrik looked on, still beaming from sharing his news. *'Finally not being a kit is great!'*

■ ■ ■

"I don't want to babysit some kid!" the brevin spat, his displeasure evident. "What the hell were they thinking sending some brat with us?!"

Rorrik's tail lashed in annoyance. He wasn't just 'some kid' — he was old enough to go on any mission! He was opening his mouth to hiss something at the brevin when the floraling sitting next to him piped up instead.

"That 'kid' helped intercept the demorinkin. You shouldn't be so quick to doubt him," she spoke from the darkness of her hood. The floraling boasted a dark charcoal skin color, accented with blue and white lines on her cheeks. From what little Rorrik saw of her hair, it was a blueish gray.

They were sitting in the back of a van, being carried to their waypoint.

"I don't see why he had to come for *this*!" the brevin disagreed, sitting across from them. The brevin was white in complexion and sported unruly, dirty blonde hair that waved at the ends. Being a brevin, he was not very tall, below five foot for certain. "He's going to slow us down!"

Rorrik wanted to make a quip on how he'd move faster than him, already being taller than the brevin but held his tongue. His tail didn't hold in the same manner; it lashed yet again.

"Just stuff it, Tommik." The floraling shook her head. "You always have something to whine about."

"Well, I think this is worth whining over!" Tommik, apparently, said. "You're telling me you don't think this is even slightly an issue?"

"Porte said he can follow orders fine. That, and he's Panther's kid, I doubt he'll slow us down much. Quit bellyaching."

The brevin grunted. "This is a two-person job. It doesn't need a third wheel..."

Rorrik couldn't rein in another quip. "...Well good thing I showed up, then. Wasn't it only a person and a half before?" the tabby grumbled sourly.

The floraling snorted and the brevin turned on him, his face scrunching with offense.

"What'd you say, punk?!" the brevin demanded.

"Relax, Tommik!" the floraling eased, chuckling. "Easy there, cat. Brevins don't care for jokes about their height."

"Felidaren don't care for their stealth being doubted, either..." Rorrik remarked with an eye roll.

The floraling chuckled yet again. "He's sassier than Panther, isn't he?"

"He should mind his place..." Tommik growled. "You better keep in line, kitten. I'm no babysitter..."

"Of course not," Rorrik agreed. "Hard to be when you're still the size of a kid."

Tommik went to smack him, and the floraling caught his hand.

"Enough. Both of you. Gods, Tommik. Way to let him goad you on."

"I won't be disrespected by some over-confident twerp! Fuck, Shannine, why the hell are you so okay with this?!"

"You were young once too, needing experience. This is an easy enough job. You're making this a bigger deal than it has to be," Shannine replied, ever calm.

Rorrik nodded, his ears twitching in annoyance.

"Whatever. When he messes up, don't say I didn't warn you," Tommik snarled.

The car came to a stop. "We're here," Shannine said. "Both of you, enough now. Hoods up. Let shadows guide us."

Rorrik put his hood up, as she ordered. His heart thumped fast with a mixture of excitement and anticipation as the floraling opened the door and ushered them both out with a hand gesture. He hopped out in a dexterous display, cutting off the brevin before he could leave the vehicle. He could sense Tommik glaring into his back as the other two left the vehicle.

"Let's move. It's two blocks from here," Shannine urged, slipping into an alleyway. The two of them followed.

"Lead the way, oh *wise* one..." Tommik snarked.

"I said *enough*," Shannine pointed a finger at the brevin, the shadow her hood cast on her face amplified in the night. "I swear, *you're* acting like the child here."

"What —" Tommik started.

Shannine shushed him. "Quiet." She set her eyes on the path ahead. "Now, let's go."

■ ■ ■

The building stood dark and black, foreboding. Rorrik wasn't scared, rather determined. Well, perhaps just a tad scared…

They had said the place would be abandoned, but was it fully? His mother had explained that when their family intercepted the demorinkin, it had created unrest in the organization and caused a hasty move of shop. Such haste was sure to leave behind clues and gods knew what else, which is what they were there to scrounge around for. Rorrik hoped against hope that their trash wasn't too important to take with them…

They slipped in the building through taking an alleyway and picking a lock on the back door. Tommik had made quick work of it.

Rorrik watched, figuring it was a task he could have done himself. All his family played with locks as kits rather than toy blocks. He had a knack for 'feeling' the lock, at least that's what his family told him. He was wont to agree.

The place was pitch black, but Rorrik's feline eyes offered a view of the room they walked into. It was a short hallway lined with three doors, one on the very end, two on the sides.

"Porte mentioned you're looking for something in particular?" Shannine whispered into the gloom.

Rorrik nodded. "A cut-up vest."

"A what?" Tommik hissed incredulously.

"Your ears must be tiny, too…" Rorrik muttered.

"Don't you start again," Shannine scolded them, suppressing her voice into a whisper. "A cut-up vest? Any idea where it would be?"

"…A garbage, probably."

"…We're literally looking through *garbage* for this thing?" Tommik whined under his breath. When Rorrik shot him a peeved look, he noticed some brand of goggles on his face.

"It's not like we weren't searching garbage already. We'll keep an eye out. Let's head forward."

The three tiptoed down the hall, their steps mute. They came across the first door and Shannine tried the handle, finding it locked. There was no keyhole to be jimmied.

Shannine looked to Tommik who was already kneeling, a prying tool his hands. He began to challenge the integrity of the door by shoving the tool into the narrow crevice between the frame and the knob. He began to wiggle the bar; the door was forced open before long.

"You can check in here," Shannine said to Rorrik. "We'll check the other two doors. When you're done, report out to the hallway. Understood?"

Rorrik nodded, the directions easy enough to follow. He peeked in, spotting a layout akin to a doctor's checkup room. A sink joined with counters lined a wall. Across from that was a bed pushed up against the wall, no sheets or covers adorning it. The place smelt of rubbing alcohol and medicines.

Rorrik slipped into the room, the sound of Tommik's tool working on another door coming from the hallway. The felidaren gagged at the strong scent of doctor supplies, his nose scrunching up in disgust.

His eyes scanned for a garbage, finding one in a corner. He slid up to it and peeked in, finding it... empty. His ears drew back. *'It's only one room.'*

His attention went to the counters. When he tried to open them, he found them all locked. It was fortunate he brought his lock picking supplies; he was loath to go ask for Tommik's assistance. *'I can prove I'm not just a kitten!'*

The locks were elementary and gave way easily; Rorrik barely had to work at them. The counter doors protested not when he tried them this time.

Rorrik glanced through the cabinets, finding jars of typical supplies one would expect to find in a checkup room. Gauze, cotton balls, swabs, syringes... Certainly no cut-up vests.

He proceeded to dig, knowing that the vest wasn't the only thing he was to look for. Any sign that could be considered a clue was on his checklist.

Nothing of the sort revealed itself as he finished glancing through the counters.

Tommik's head poked in the room doorway. "Hurry up in there!"

Rorrik's tail thrashed to wave him off. He stood up, his eyes glancing over the room to make sure there was nothing else worth checking. A bio-hazard bin revealed to be on the wall.

Curious, Rorrik went over to give it a snappy look. He used a dagger to pry open the slot, and the smell of old blood hit him immediately. The sight of brick red bandages accompanied it, the cluster of cloth packed in the bin too tightly.

Rorrik's ears went flat and he withdrew his dagger immediately. *'Whose blood is that?!'* Hopefully not the demorinkin's...

Checking off the room as searched, he returned to the hallway finding neither Tommik nor Shannine there yet. *'He rushed me for nothing?'* Rorrik's ears showed his displeasure with that.

They eventually both revealed themselves. Shannine was holding an envelope, and Tommik was stuffing a stack of papers into his bag.

"Find anything?" Shannine questioned Rorrik in a whisper.

Rorrik was embarrassed when they both seemed to have found something, but not he. "Just medical supplies. And... bloodied bandages..."

Shannine nodded. "Let's move on. There's another hallway through here." She went through the door at the end of the hallway, and they followed. Beyond was just what she said, this hallway having more doors to explore.

"I found an office here." She pointed to a door straight ahead. "Most was cleared out, but I found a few things that could prove relevant."

"Just storage back there," Tommik said. "Lots of supplies left behind. Rope, gags, binds, stationery... Took some of that. It's the fancy kind they've used to mail clients."

Shannine nodded. "Let's keep looking."

■ ■ ■

Room after room revealed no vest. From washrooms, to offices, to bedrooms, all the garbages were empty and void of any cut-up articles. Rorrik's hope dwindled further and further, his excitement eroded to disappointment by the time they scoured the final room of the building, the vest still yet to be found.

"Well, that should be everything," Shannine said with a tiny frown as they left the final room. Total, they hadn't found much beyond what the first three rooms revealed other than a wax seal and a coat with a custom tag sewn on the neck.

Rorrik didn't meet either of their gazes. He stared down at his bare feet, trying not to look too disappointed, but failing.

"Honestly, why are you looking for that thing, anyways?" Tommik questioned, annoyed as usual.

Rorrik didn't answer.

"Well, let's get going, then," Shannine said. She led the way down the steps to the first floor. "Sorry we didn't find it."

Rorrik remained quiet. He just wanted to get out of the stupid place...

They made it downstairs and went out the way they came. When they arrived outside and began to follow the alleyways, Rorrik froze in his tracks.

He jutted his head to look behind him, spotting dumpsters along the outside of the building.

He rushed towards them, a slither of hope driving him.

"Hey! What the hell, kid?" Tommik snapped after him.

Rorrik ignored the brevin, reaching the dumpsters. He hoisted up the lid and looked inside, finding *bags*!

"Fucking alley cat, going through dumpsters..." Tommik grumbled from afar.

Rorrik heard Shannine come up next to him. "We should really be heading back..."

"Let me just look!" Rorrik began to lift garbage bags from the containers.

"We don't have time for this!" Tommik protested. "Tell him, Shannine!"

"Be quick..." Shannine told him instead.

Tommik gave an undignified sound.

Rorrik tore through the bags, a plethora of repulsive smells and unsightly objects greeting his zealous effort. One bag after another proved to be vest-less, but still he pressed on. Most bags were filled with rotting foodstuffs, but he held on to hope.

"We need to go…" Shannine pressed.

Rorrik reached into the bin to pull out a final bag. "It's the last one!"

Shannine waited as he ripped into it. A smell much worse than the rotting food overcame Rorrik's senses, but he strived on, determined.

Miraculously, an article of a vivid red presented itself, one that matched the form of a vest. It was cut up and barely hanging together, but it was a vest, indeed!

"Is that it?" Shannine asked, plugging her nose. The floraling looked as though she were trying not to gag.

"It is!"

A flashlight then showed on them, and they whipped their heads in unison to see a figure clad in a guard's uniform come down the way.

"Hey!" the figure yelled. "What are you doing?!" The guard began to head towards them in a hurry.

"Fuck!" Tommik spat from his spot. "I told you! Stupid kid!" The brevin scurried off.

"Meet at the waypoint," Shannine whispered to Rorrik. With that, she zoomed down after Tommik before hoisting herself up onto an emergency escape ladder and making towards the roofs.

Rorrik's adrenaline pumped as he took off in the same route the other two had. He darted through the alleyways, his natural agility already spreading distance between the guard and him.

"Stop! In the name of the law!" the guard bellowed. It seemed the officer had chosen to follow him.

Rorrik had a wish to make the guard regret that decision.

Storage bins finally revealed themselves, giving him a potential route up onto the roof. He leapt onto the crates, never losing momentum as he jumped yet again to reach the roof. His fingers briefly cried out in pain as he grabbed hold of the edge before hoisting himself up in a hurry.

He could hear the guard shouting behind him as he slipped over the side and ran to the opposite edge to make his way down. Beyond that, the guard's shouts quieted into nothing.

'*That was easy.*' Rorrik had had much hairier escapes while training, that was for certain

He smiled down at the vest in his grasp, the sight wonderful to behold despite its trashed appearance and smell. '*I did it!*'

He set towards their waypoint, a smile never leaving his face.

■ ■ ■

The first thing his mother did when he returned home was suggest that they wash the garment. Rorrik wasn't about to argue with that; the smell of the article was rank.

She mentioned to him that they'd give it to the demorinkin tomorrow morning, and Rorrik found his mind dodging sleep in anticipation as he lay in bed. He was unendingly curious over what the demorinkin's reaction would be. If it meant so much to him, he would surely be overjoyed to get it back!

He was finally drifting off into slumber when he felt a body plop next to him.

"You're back!" Talis said excitingly. "How did it go?! Tell me, tell me!"

Rorrik chuckled as he cracked his eyes open. "I found what we were looking for."

"Really?! What was it?"

"It was a very important vest," Rorrik said, glowing with pride.

"Whoooa," Talis replied, always easy to impress. "Is it magical?"

"Of course," Rorrik lied. He really didn't have the slightest clue.

"That's sooo cool..." Talis gushed. He snuggled into Rorrik and began a purr. "I can't wait to go on missions..." he sighed dreamily.

Rorrik closed his eyes again, starting a purr of his own. He was satisfied and proud of his performance that day.

With that, he began to drift off yet again as he lay curled up with his brother, both purring. Dreams of the demorinkin smiling filled his mind. Morning couldn't come quickly enough.

Chapter 17

Valen

A knock at his door came in the morning. Valen's mind was heavy with exhaustion as he forced himself awake. The prior night had been tough emotionally and allowed him little sleep.

"Come in…" he groaned, his voice thick with grogginess.

Unlike Mrs. Catty, who normally was the one to stop by in the mornings, the springy felidaren peeked in, the door only opening an inch or two.

"'Morning!" the tabby greeted, chipper.

'So it is actually morning…' Valen blinked at him, wondering why he wasn't fully opening the door.

"So, um, I was out and about last night," the felidaren went on. "And, I found this *really neat* vest!" The door opened, and in he walked, wearing—

Valen's world screeched to a halt. What he was seeing didn't add up. The felidaren was wearing *his* vest — his father's gift to him! 'That— that can't be right!'

Valen gawked at the sight, his mind snagged on the idea of it. It was the same vivid red, cut in the exact spots his had been. 'But— how?!'

Valen adjusted his attention up to the felidaren's face, seeing that he was beaming at him. The tabby began to shrug off the article, and then held it out for the demorinkin, his smile only widening.

Valen held out his hands to take it, and as soon as his fingers graced the fabric he knew it was really his vest. Happiness exploded within him, and he let out an emotional, dry sob.

"I found it at the place they brought you to before we rescued you," the felidaren explained. "I figured… it meant a lot to you, so I—"

He cut off the felidaren by leaping up to hug him. He embraced him as tightly as he could, another sob leaving him, this one wet.

"Thank you!" the demorinkin choked out. "Thank you!"

The felidaren returned the hug and they stood there embracing, Valen growing more emotional by the moment.

"If you're going to be wearing it, it might need a little fixing up," Mrs. Catty's voice said from the doorway. "If you're willing to part with it again for a short time, we can do that for you."

Valen was utterly floored; he didn't even know what to say! He broke the hug to stare over at Mrs. Catty, his vision blurred with tears. He rushed over to hug her.

"Thank you! How can I—" The words cut off; he couldn't think of how to convey his gratitude well enough. "How can I make it up to you?"

The tortoiseshell patted his back and warmly gazed down at him with the expression that always reminded him of his mother. "I know a good start."

Valen blinked, not catching on.

"I don't believe we ever got your name..."

Valen's euphoria didn't allow him to hesitate in the slightest as he replied, "Valen. Valen Vaaskiir."

"Well, Valen," Mrs. Catty said. "Let's go get some food in you, and we can chat some more."

■ ■ ■

Valen sat at the kitchen table, Mrs. Catty preparing eggs at the stove. The springy felidaren was next to him, his demeanor still just as bright since delivering the vest.

"Valen, huh?" the felidaren questioned.

Part of Valen felt strange at them knowing his name, but his happiness didn't allow that sensation to linger. He nodded with a little grin.

"I'm Rorrik!" the tabby, Rorrik, replied. "It's great to finally know your name!"

Valen blushed lightly. "Likewise."

Mrs. Catty chuckled as she cooked. "It's great that you boys are getting along."

Rorrik looked to Valen with a toothy grin and offered him a wink, the sight summoning the memory of Valen's rescue.

The demorinkin blinked as a realization hit him. "You were the one to tackle that lady with the sword?"

Rorrik sat straighter. "Yep!"

Valen rubbed at the back of his neck. "Well... thanks for that, too, then."

His rescue was still bizarre to look back on. Although, quite frankly, his life had turned into one bizarre event after another. At least this time the oddity of the situation was a positive one, concerning his vest.

"My boys can be hard to tell apart," Mrs. Catty contributed.

"I noticed..." Valen agreed. "I had thought I was just really out of it..."

That made Rorrik laugh. "We do that to people!"

Valen nodded, feeling rather sheepish. *'How many are 'we'?'*

"It takes some time to learn their differences, let alone all their names," the tortoiseshell told him, transplanting the scrambled eggs from the pan onto a plate. It was the meal she had typically made for Valen lately; the fluffy texture and mellow taste were easy enough to digest for his recovering stomach. This was the first time not eating it within his room, however.

She dropped the plate off in front of him.

"Thank you," Valen said.

"Anytime, kit." She took a seat across from them.

Valen almost felt too excited to eat, but lifted a fork full of eggs to his mouth, regardless. As he chewed, the table fell into silence.

Something about it alerted Valen to what they meant to discuss. His stomach gave a sour churn and he swallowed the eggs in his mouth down hard. '*I can trust these people...*' It didn't make any of the subjects easier to talk about, merely possible.

"So... speaking of your rescue," Mrs. Catty began when he was close to done with his plate.

'*Here we go...*' Valen waited, the contents of his last bite having difficulty slipping down his throat.

"...Do you know who attacked you?" She didn't seem to enjoy asking the question.

Valen looked down at the table, apprehension a blaring horn in his thoughts. He did his best to ignore it, summoning courage to be upfront.

"I... I think so..." Valen mumbled, his voice hardly reaching above a whisper.

The mother gave an encouraging nod, waiting for the rest of his reply.

"...My... my parents... they..." He winced as the words he had to say burned his tongue. "They were... murdered... about eleven months ago... My father left me a note explaining that it was demorin hunters..." He let go a shuddery breath. "They are called the Fangs of Hellbane."

Mrs. Catty gazed at him, intent but gentle. "Did they know of you?"

"I'm... not sure. My father said no at first, but said they'd probably find out. So, he had us hide out in Akarth."

The mother tilted her head. "...Us?"

It was a spear through Valen's chest. He coaxed the food in his belly to stay there as nausea tormented his stomach.

"I..." Valen's eyes pooled rapidly with tears, as though a tap had been turned. He shook his head as sorrow overwhelmed him.

It still didn't feel real. Oftentimes he woke up expecting his baby brother to be lying there next to him, or that he was somewhere nearby, reading a tome or practicing his shifting. It consumed Valen with a crippling emptiness that those things would never be true again.

"I... had... a brother..." the demorinkin stuttered out. "My father... my father asked me to take care of him... but I... gods, it's all my fault..." He squeezed his eyes shut and a few salty tears splashed onto the remainder of his food.

Mrs. Catty didn't speak, only waited. Rorrik stared down at the table, having had gone incredibly quiet during his explanation.

"To stay safe… we had to shift… transform… I know how, but Karreo was still learning… He had to stay in the clock tower — where we lived — because it was unsafe for him to leave…" His voice was garbled from the tears. "Everything was fine… I had… I had built up an okay life for us… but I screwed it all up… I screwed it all up…"

Should he mention Siena? He felt too ashamed to. "My shift failed when I was out of the tower one day, and I was spotted. Because of that… these… these people… found me… found us…"

"They captured us when we were sleeping. They began to drag us out, and when I saw them carrying Karreo away something in me just… snapped… I… I… I did some kind of spell, and they froze in pain — Karreo was able to get away… but they chased him… They…"

Valen sucked in a shuddery inhale before pressing on, a rock in his guts crushing him.

"They chased him… and Karreo… he… he *jumped*…" He'd never had to say it out loud; it sounded so twisted and horrible and untrue. "It's all my fault…" the demorinkin croaked as a sob rocked his shoulders, the guilt corroding him. "It's all my fault…"

Valen felt a hand move on top of his. He glanced over to see Mrs. Catty reaching out to comfort him, her own eyes glossy with tears.

"What happened next?" she pressed.

"They… they put me in a van… and we drove for… gods know how long. A few hours? They had gagged me and tied me up…" Valen's wrists harrowingly recalled the scraping of rope. "Then I was put in a cell… and then I was taken to a room… and they… he…" His face went hot with shame and embarrassment; he didn't know how to say it.

Mrs. Catty nodded. "They assessed you."

He couldn't meet her eyes as he confirmed. "Then this lady came by my cell and… she…" The way she looked at him still haunted him, how it made him feel like a product instead of a person. "She bought me. Apparently, she was the trafficker, though…"

The mother hissed at that. "Jonissa Bolvur. She's the wife to the head of the business here in Sengard. She keeps tabs on things over in Akarth, makes… purchases." The felidaren spat again. "Gods, kit… Sorry. Continue."

"From there they put me on a boat… but then they said I wasn't going to be on the boat anymore. Someone… purchased me… So, they put me in a crate and…" The claustrophobia that being stuck in the crate had instilled in him reverberated in his mind, chilling him. "They shipped me by air… and then I landed… and I tried to cry for help but they… they ignored me. Said they were supposed to keep quiet.

"Then I was put on another vehicle and delivered… These horrible women took me out… and threw away my clothes… and they…" A flashback of the bath burdened his mind and his whole being became alive in heat. "They… cleaned me up… with really cold water and —" He winced, wondering how something so cold could *burn* so badly.

He left out the other details, too ashamed to admit them. "They... they put me in new clothes... and then they stuffed me into another van... and then... the van was attacked. I heard... I heard screams in the front seat, and then the doors of the trunk were opening... I was pulled out... and..."

"We saw that part," the tortoiseshell intervened.

Rorrik nodded, his gaze never lifting from the table.

"You know the rest, then..." Valen put it simply. He was numb from explaining everything, but a tinge relieved to spill it out.

"So. You believe your attackers were your parent's murderers?" Mrs. Catty inquired.

Valen nodded. "I don't know who else it could be."

"It would add up," the mother said, rubbing her chin. "We confiscated some items off their bodies, including their weapons. The hilt's shape has me thinking you're right – it's a star with two fang-like extensions."

Valen frowned as the description did sound fitting.

"Whoever they were, they murdered who purchased you. They beheaded the man in his own living room; left the sword as a calling card."

Valen's nausea wasn't improved by that information as his guts violently swirled from the mental imagery.

"His name was Bartholomew Sniver. And he won't be taking advantage of children anymore."

Valen wasn't sure what to think. He should feel happy, relieved, but all he felt was sick. The scrambled eggs inched up his throat, threatening to spew.

"...I'm sorry. I shouldn't be so distant about it," Mrs. Catty apologized before standing up. "You look like you need to lie down. You were very, very brave, kit. Come on, let's get you back to a bed."

Valen stood with wobbly legs, Rorrik watching him with a troubled look. The tabby got up to help him along, acting as a brace to lean into.

They arrived back in his room, Valen not remembering the walk.

He lay down in the bed, his mind stubborn to dismiss his conjured image of a beheaded person. It disturbed him to know that had happened because of him.

Mrs. Catty stood at his bedside looking down at him as Rorrik lingered in the doorway. "Do you want us to fix your vest?"

His spirit harked back on the excitement of his vest being back and it managed to chase away part of his inner turmoil. He nodded before sitting up to pull off the fragmented article.

She received it gingerly and grinned down at the cloth. "It'll be as good as new by the time Mr. Jollyswish is done with it. He's put together articles even worse off than this." She set her attention back on him. "Get some rest. You did very well today, Valen."

It was still a strange sensation to be called by his name, but not a negative one he realized.

She nodded in farewell and walked out of the room. Rorrik continued to wait in the threshold, his ears drooped as he stared. He then followed his mother, the door closing behind him

It was about to click closed, but then it opened again to have Mrs. Catty poke her head into the room. "Open or closed?"

Valen considered it. "Open."

. . .

Kyla

"You were finally able to speak with him?" Avalene seemed pleased. The human had just arrived for a quick meeting to discuss what happened that morning. It was now in the evening, Kyla having spent the other part of her day getting ahold of Mr. Jollyswish so that he might work on the vest. The gnome had seemed thrilled to take on the job, and promised it to be done 'in a jiffy swishy'. He was an odd, eccentric man, but that's what Kyla liked about him.

"He had quite the story to tell..." Kyla's heart still ached for the demorinkin; he was too young for all the things that had happened, all the responsibilities that had plagued him.

"Well, the sooner I know it the sooner we can help."

Kyla recanted everything she had been told that morning. Avalene took notes all the while, never interrupting.

When Kyla finished, the ex-government worker sat there, seeming deep in thought.

"It's troubling these 'Fangs of Hellbane' were able to find him," she said. "It means they have connections if they were able to get a look into human trafficking movements..."

Kyla gave a grim nod. "They've shown they know how to get things done..."

"Well, I'll get my people on it. You recovered quite a bit from his attackers before, and now we have a name to go off, too. It won't be easy to get to the bottom of this, but every child is worth it," Avalene said, determined. "When do you want us to come get him, by the way?"

Kyla experienced a surge of desperation. "You're not taking him until we have a good idea of who we're dealing with! If they're as dangerous as they seem— I don't want—"

Avalene raised her eyebrows. "Kyla, it was agreed—"

"I know what was agreed," Kyla hissed. "It doesn't matter. He's not leaving here! It's too dangerous."

124

They stared at one another for several moments, Kyla firm.

Avalene then shook her head and sighed. "I don't want to fight you on this, Kyla. If this is what you want to do to…"

"He needs a safe place. If I can give him that, I will."

"…You're very emotional over this case."

Kyla jerked her head in a nod, unashamed.

"Well, alright." The vigilante got to her feet, adjusting the strap of her satchel. "He'll be staying here, then."

Relief splashed over Kyla. "Good to have that settled."

"Indeed. Oh, I have your son's payment, by the way."

Kyla smiled, pride over her son's job brightening her mood reasonably. "He'll be glad to get his paws on that."

Avalene reached into her bag to pull out a coin purse before handing it over to Kyla. "Make sure he gets that."

"No can do. He's still living off me, so it all goes to Mama," Kyla jested.

Avalene rolled her eyes but still grinned. "I'll be off. May shadows guide you."

"And Nocturna smile on you, friend. Good luck on the research."

■　■　■

She found Rorrik sitting by his lonesome in the den, curled up tight on a chair. He was melancholy judging by his demeanor and the way his cheek was pressed up against the fabric.

"What's going on, son of mine?" Kyla asked, sitting down on the couch neighboring his chair.

The young felidaren's shoulders bumped in a shrug. "I just want him to feel better…"

"That takes time after the kind of things he's been through," Kyla assured her son. "He's not going to wake up one day completely healed. It takes steps."

"I just don't want him to be sad…" Rorrik sighed.

It seemed she wasn't the only one emotional over the case. She respected her son's empathy, seeing herself within him. The two of them were a lot alike, thus, she had a closer bond with Rorrik than the rest of her children. Not that she loved any of them any less or more, but the two of them were often on the same page, easing their relationship.

"He won't be sad forever. You have to help him along, be a friend to him."

Rorrik nodded somberly.

"I know what will cheer you up." She tossed the money bag over, and Rorrik raised a hand to catch it.

His face lit up as he realized what it was, proving Kyla right.

"It's your first paycheck all to yourself," she remarked. "That's a very special thing."

Rorrik sat up and dumped the bag into his palm. A hundred Pines poured out into his hand, shiny and well-deserved.

"I'm proud of you, kit. You did very well." Avalene *had* mentioned that their trio was spotted by the authorities, but that had led to no real consequence. The guard had been on a typical patrol and happened to spot dumpster diving, nothing too substantial. Kyla was happy Rorrik had fought to find the vest. Without it, who knew where the demorinkin— Valen— would be in spirits.

"Thanks, Mom," Rorrik replied, all smiles.

"Don't gloat to your siblings too much," Kyla told him. She stood up to ruffle his hair, and got a good look at his face in the process. She noticed a few hairs on his chin growing longer than the rest of his fur.

"Are you trying to grow a beard?" she asked him through an amused smirk. He was awfully young to be starting a mane.

He seemed almost sheepish at the question and responded with a quick shrug.

Kyla laughed. "You boys are growing up too fast." She looked down to her pregnant belly and gave a rub. "Luckily I have your baby brother on the way to tide me over."

Rorrik's gaze followed hers with a smile. He, like the rest of his brothers, were excited for a new family member. Niem didn't exactly share the excitement, but that was...

...She pushed that thought away.

"You should get out of the inn and go do something," she spurred him. "You've been here an awful lot lately."

Rorrik only had more shrugs to offer at that. He did get to his feet, however. His eyes then flickered like an idea had struck him.

"Okay! I'll be back later!" he chimed. He set towards the exit, his tail waving goodbye.

"Well, alright," Kyla called after him. "Be safe!"

. . .

Valen

He was sitting in the room reflecting on earlier that day, his stomach in knots. He didn't exactly regret finally telling his story, but felt nervous that he had, regardless. Did they think less of him after knowing the dark truth of his mistake? He had spent the day feeling uncertain and bothered.

He then heard footsteps coming down the hall, approaching quickly. Rorrik popped into the doorway, excited. A bag was slung on his arm, boasting a logo of a coat that was surrounded by flowing lines near the tail.

"I got you a present!" the tabby announced.

Valen perked up, curious. *'Present?'* What could he have bought for him?

Rorrik bounced up to the bed and handed over the bag. Valen received it, taking note of how the bag itself was even stuffed in true present stature.

"Open it!"

The felidaren's enthusiasm managed a grin out the demorinkin. "Alright, alright!"

He removed the stuffing paper and a set of clothes revealed itself.

Surprise had a smile stretching Valen's face. He pulled out the set, which contained a charcoal shirt and rich, brown pants. The clothes were freshly pressed and new smelling.

"Mr. Jollyswish said that if anything doesn't fit right he can resize it," Rorrik said. "Do you like them?!"

"I— yes—" Valen's smile kept. He hadn't had new clothes in *months*! It filled him with an excitement that had gone long undisturbed within him.

"It'll match your vest!" Rorrik added. "Much better than my clothes ever would."

Valen processed that comment before looking down to the clothes he was currently wearing. "These are yours?"

"Yep. Mom said my clothes would fit you the best. Don't worry. I have a lot extra."

"Oh, well, thanks for letting me borrow them!"

Rorrik gave a hurried nod. "Anyway, you should try them on!" He bounced out of the room and closed the door, failing to give Valen a choice in the matter.

It wasn't a problem; he was definitely planning to try them on, regardless. He eyed the door to make certain it was truly closed before hesitantly undressing. He quickly stepped into the new pants, the virgin embrace of new clothes wonderful to behold. He buttoned them up, finding they fit just fine, no adjustments needed. Next came the new shirt, another perfect fit.

He went to stand in front of the mirror, his reflection meeting him with much more life this time. In his new clothes, his skin didn't look quite as faded and his hair not as shaggy. It fed the smile still stretching his lips. While he missed his vest, that wouldn't be the case for much longer!

"Are you dressed?" Rorrik asked from behind the door.

"Yep! You can come back in."

The felidaren returned, immediately beaming as he caught sight of Valen. "Check you out!" He scanned him up and down several times. "Much better than sweatpants!"

Valen chuckled at that as he proceeded to admire his reflection. "Agreed." He then pulled his gaze away to Rorrik. "Thank you, so much."

"My pleasure!" Rorrik replied, springy as ever. "I'm so glad you like them!"

Valen looked back to the mirror. He most definitely did.

A massive hurdle felt behind Valen as he stared at his reflection. Discussing his story had been hard, but it had been a necessary step in coming to terms with what happened. He was far from healed, but with some help, perhaps he could rebuild a life worth living.

He adjusted his collar and offered Rorrik a grin. For the first time since his capture, he allowed himself to feel a shred of hope.

Chapter 18

Kyla

Kyla stood waiting for Mr. Jollyswish to emerge from the back room of his little boutique. He had called her hurriedly on her corresponder claiming there was something they must discuss immediately. He had sounded exceptionally chipper, so Kyla assumed it was only good news. Her best guess was the vest was done and ready to be picked up, which would prove impressive if it were true. She had dropped off the vest that morning, only a few hours earlier.

She had been waiting for a few minutes when the little gnome scurried out of the back door and hopped up on his stool, his magenta eyes vivid.

"It's magical!" he cried. "Magical! Magical!"

"What's magical?" Kyla asked her old friend through an amused smile. She wasn't sure what he meant exactly, if something was magical in the sense that it had rucanic properties or that something was very good or remarkable.

"The vest, dear kitty! It's enchanted! Come look, come look!" He nimbly hopped off the stool and hastily hobbled toward the back door. He opened it for her, dancing in anticipation.

Kyla followed along, her curiosity piqued. Valen's vest was enchanted? The demorinkin hadn't mentioned that detail.

"I was stitching it up, you see!" the gnome explained as they walked. "When I then noticed in between the fabrics there was a peculiar tag sewn in! I wondered if it could be a rucanic battery, and right I was!"

They arrived in his workshop and he giddily gestured to a mannequin wearing Valen's vest. It was partly sewed back together but was yet a finished project.

"Hurry, hurry! Look!" He pulled away a section of the article's back and the tag the gnome described came into view.

The tag was about four inches on each side and made from a thick, silvery thread that boasted a sheen, reminding Kyla of woven precious metal. A thin, square-shaped stone was lying in the middle of it, pale blue in color.

"You say it's a battery?" she asked. The felidaren had not seen many batteries used on clothing enchantments; typically, they were out of view and within the fabric itself, just as this one had been.

"Indeed!" Mr. Jollyswish giggled. He pointed a bony finger at the metallic thread. "That there is rucandum, an extraordinary metal and a fantastic conductor for rucanic energy! The gem is moonstone, a typical host for pure runa. The rucandum draws out the power stored within the moonstone and thus powers the enchantment!"

"I'm not seeing any runes or an anchor," Kyla noted, her eyes scanning. The queen did not find that surprising considering the battery itself was hidden; why make the enchantment visible if the enchanter was aiming for secrecy?

Mr. Jollyswish reached into his shirt pocket and held out a pair of spectacles for the felidaren. "Here, put these on, I will show you the runes!"

Kyla received the glasses without any question or hesitation, a common reaction to the gnome's antics. She equipped the spectacles and the colors of the room went drab and desaturated, all except for the vest, its vivid red still showing. A faint glow was coming from the article, and when she peered at the tag she noticed there was writing now bordering it; a signature, it looked like.

"There is your anchor," Mr. Jollyswish pointed out. He put his hand on the writing and giggled a quick incantation. With that, a plethora of luminous runes abruptly appeared in front of them floating midair, Kyla recognizing the display as a spell formula.

"And here is the spell," the gnome verified with a clap, his vibrant eyes scanning along the runes. "Good magic, charming magic; very nice for charisma. Helps you converse more precisely — get away with a lot. Makes one generally likable, irresistible."

Kyla squinted at the runes, their meaning and complexity lost on her. The tortoiseshell didn't know too much about magic, but Mr. Jollyswish sure did. "I'll take your word for it." She proceeded to look over the abundance of rucanic marks, intrigued.

"Fascinating, isn't it? You say it was a gift made by the boy's father?" Mr. Jollyswish wondered.

Kyla nodded, thoughtful over the enchantment's secrecy. Had the enchantment been a secret even to Valen, or was he aware of its power? *'I'll have to ask him...'*

"Father was a magical sort, then!"

'Seems to run in the family...' Kyla was reminded of the spell they had seen Valen perform to save his own life.

"Well, magic or no magic, still the vest I fix! See, look, I'm almost finished," Mr. Jollyswish said. "You come back... say... before closing. I'll have it done then, probably."

"Sounds great!" Kyla answered. "I'll hold you to it."

The gnome gave another trill of a laugh. "It'll be done in a swishy-jiffy!"

Valen

Following a night that had bestowed the most solid sleep since his rescue, the demorinkin decided to spend the day out of the bedroom for the first time. Rorrik had suggested he come study with him, and Valen had been intrigued by that plan. He hadn't had the time nor resources to further his own mundane education for a long while.

Rorrik's lesson revolved around the history of the city of Sengard. Valen remembered learning about the mighty capital of Wesvarln in his own curriculum years and years ago. It was fascinating to know that he was in Sengard at that very moment, oceans away from his home continent.

He had asked Rorrik if he had lived in Sengard all his life, and Rorrik answered yes. Valen explained that he had grown up on the outskirts of the most magnificent city in the realm, Akarth, and had only moved *into* the city following the tragedy of their family.

Rorrik mentioned that their family had connections back in Akarth, but he'd never been there himself. He had always been curious, but a trip to the city was not easily orchestrated. Valen couldn't say he had any desire to go back there himself, and that had tainted the conversation with an awkward quiet.

Rorrik was quick to break it. He mentioned that he'd have to show him around the city sometime, and Valen hesitantly agreed, doubting he should leave the safety of the hideout. He tried not to think about the Fangs of Hellbane, but they were an eyesore in every thought.

Rorrik's next lesson was about math, and Valen had enjoyed that. He recognized the formulas thanks to his father's solid teaching and was even able to assist the tabby a tad.

Beyond that, the felidaren said they were done for the day. Valen, somewhat awkwardly, asked if he still had any of his old lessons around, and Rorrik had laughed and dug them up for him. Valen was thankful to have something to busy his mind in the future.

They sat now in the den, Valen looking through one of Rorrik's old language books.

"Whoooa!" a young voice suddenly called out. "He's finally out of the room!"

Valen jerked his head up to see a young mini-Rorrik gawking in front of him, sporting the same green eyes. Valen smiled uncertainly at the child, embarrassed.

"Talis, that's not very polite," an older Rorrik said from the kitchen. Valen noticed that the tabby fur on him was a darker gray.

"Yeah, kit," another alike looking felidaren said from next to the darker one. "Nice to see you, by the way! Glad you're feeling better."

Valen wondered where they all had come from; he hadn't heard or seen anybody come in.

Rorrik watched all his siblings before smirking over at Valen. "Want introductions?"

"Well, sure." He might as well.

"That's Talis in front of you," Rorrik pointed. "About to drool over your book."

"Am not!" Talis objected. He crawled up on the arm of the chair Valen sat in and crossed his arms. "See?"

"He's the youngest." Rorrik gestured to the darker tabby in the kitchen. "That in there is Gavin." His hand moved to the one next to him. "And that's Jate. They're the oldest."

"We doing introductions?" Another Rorrik lookalike popped his head in from the entry hall.

"That's Quinn. He's crazy, and third oldest."

"Crazy and proud!" Quinn laughed. He smiled over at Valen. "Pleased to meet you! We'll chat more later. I should probably get this to stop leaking first." With that, the felidaren ran off.

"Don't forget about me!" *another* voice called out, belonging to a younger felidaren who stood cross-armed in the kitchen.

"Oh, sorry, didn't see you there," Rorrik said. "You're just too tiny!"

"I'm not!"

"That there is Calvin," Rorrik chortled. "He is *not* a kit, and don't you forget it."

"Yeah!" Calvin agreed. "Don't!"

"He's the second youngest," Rorrik explained. "Aaand, that's everyone."

"Is it?" Valen asked, waiting for another to pop out.

Rorrik had a loud laugh. "There will be a quiz tomorrow!"

"No study guide!" one of the brothers called out from the kitchen. Valen had already lost track of whom. He wasn't bad with names, but the family was an uncannily similar bunch.

"Well, my name is Valen," the demorinkin introduced, the action of introducing himself with his actual name still a strange one.

"Nice to meet you, Valen!" one of the older ones flattered, the other eldest brother giving a nod of his own.

"Vaaalen! Ha ha! You talk funny!" the smallest Rorrik said. "Is it because you're from Akarth?"

Valen grinned awkwardly. "Uh, well—"

"Talis! Don't be rude," an older brother scolded.

Talis, apparently, giggled before leaning in for a closer look. "Whatcha reading, Vaaalen?" The little tabby then scrunched his face. "Schoool?! But we're done for the day!"

Valen chuckled with a pinch of embarrassment, his cheeks hot. "It's never a bad time to learn." They were words his father had liked to say.

"But it's so boooring! You should come play!" He scrambled off the chair and hopped up and down. "Oh! Oh! We can play tag!"

"Well, I—" Valen started.

He wasn't able to finish as a tiny paw shot out to bop him on the arm. "You're it! You're it!" The young feline shrieked out before scurrying towards the hallway, giggling wildly.

One of the older brothers laughed from the kitchen. "You don't have to humor him, it's fine."

Valen left his chair, a slightly uncertain but willing smile on his face. He placed the book down on a coffee table. "I'm it, though."

"Yeah, Jate!" the kitten said from the archway of the living room, his tiny tongue poking out in a teasing display. "He's it! You guys better run, too!"

"Oh, is everyone playing?" Rorrik asked from his chair, a twinkle finding his eye. "In that case—" He was on his feet in a flash and slipping past Valen nimbly, laughing all the while. "Good luck catching any of us!"

"Heeey! I wanna play, too!" the second youngest chimed in. He burst from his spot in the kitchen and out of view.

Valen blinked, his mind still reacting to what had just transpired. Finally, his legs began to move and he set after the way Rorrik went, the weight and soreness of his muscles fighting him, but the eagerness to goof off spurring him on.

By the time Valen cleared the archway both Rorrik and his youngest brother were already turning the corner, their tails flopping behind them. Valen arrived at the turn and sped on from behind, not nearly matching their agility.

The youngest turned around to see if the demorinkin was following and gave a hyper shout before zooming forward in a burst of speed. Valen had never seen a child run so fast before – he was beginning to wonder if he even had a chance in this game of tag!

Valen recognized they were en route for the guestrooms he was staying in, which gave him a smidgen of hope. '*Where are they going to go? It's all dead ends!*'

The brothers once again turned the corner and out of view. By the time Valen caught up, neither was anywhere to be seen. The door to the first guest hallway was open, however, and so Valen bounded through that, his eyes hoping to catch a tail slipping into one of the bedrooms. All doors were closed save for his own room.

He slid to a halt and poked his head in, finding Rorrik... casually lying on the bed, examining his claws? The sight muddled Valen's intensity and he blinked at the tabby in confusion.

"There you are, slowpoke," the tabby winked, cheeky. "I thought we were playing tag?"

Valen flushed from a mixture of exertion and embarrassment before flashing a smirk. *'I'll show him!'*

The demorinkin lunged towards the bed in an effort of speed his recovering body had not yet allowed. He grasped for clothes and fur, but instead found sheets as Rorrik deftly moved out of reach with seemingly no effort. *'Geez, how is he so fast?!'*

"No, no, *tag*, silly!" Rorrik taunted. "Not pounce and miss!"

Valen swung around in a hurry, finding Rorrik already in the doorway, the felidaren's face showing off joyful mischief. From beyond him Valen spotted a brief flash of tabby fur disappear into the room across from them. Perhaps one of the younger ones would be an easier target?

Valen started off again, Rorrik slipping into the hall in the same instant. Valen paid the older sibling no mind and dove for the door he saw the other one disappear into.

The door opened to reveal... nothing? Valen's brow crinkled with perplexity. He *knew* he saw one slip into the room!

He walked past the threshold, his eyes drilling into the furniture, searching. He was kneeling to look under the bed when a trill of laughter sounded from directly behind him.

"Forgot to check behind the door, silly!" the youngest child said in a fit of laughter.

Valen hurriedly stood up, but the kitten was far quicker. Still giggling, the felidaren shut the door in his face before he could catch him.

Frustration flared within Valen, but it cooled quickly into determination. *'If they're that much quicker, I have to use something different than my speed!'*

He opened the door, spotting a flash of stripes turn the corner and back into the main hallway. He followed behind, his mind grasping for a strategy.

When he arrived, the second youngest was standing right next to the door, looking unaware of his presence. *'Or this works, too!'* Valen reached out hastily to grab him, but, perhaps not surprisingly, the felidaren ducked and spun out of the way.

"Too slow, Ha ha!" the child laughed gaudily. "You're a really bad guard, ha ha!"

'Guard?' Valen thought that to be odd wording, but chose not to linger on it as the kid rocketed down the hallway towards the living room, leaving him in the dust. Valen began to follow behind but then slowed down, an idea striking him. *'I need to stay by the doors!'*

He went back to look down the hall he had just left, hoping to spot a trace of anyone, and his wish was granted. He witnessed a brief flash of brown hair and tabby fur dart back into one of the bedrooms, setting up the opportunity Valen needed. '*Perfect!*'

Valen burst into the bedroom, a smile involuntarily stretching his face as he found Rorrik sitting cockily on top of a chair in the corner.

"Oh no! I've been found!" The felidaren feigned alarm both in tone and body language.

This only riled Valen's grin further and he shut the door, his hand lingering on the handle, a brief surge of magic rushing through his fingertips.

"*Finally* you do something smart," Rorrik teased.

"Oh yeah?" Valen challenged, his smile finding room to grow.

"Yeah!" Rorrik laughed, confident.

The two stared at each other briefly before Valen jumped towards the chair. As expected, Rorrik twirled out of the way and toward the dresser, giggling. Valen played chase but not with as much vigor as previously invested. '*He wants an opportunity to try and bolt, so I'll give him one!*'

Rorrik hopped onto the bed and Valen flailed after him, purposely tumbling into the sheets as Rorrik once again dodged.

"If you're gonna take a nap I'll just be on my way, then!" Rorrik hooted out.

"You can try!" Valen said, turning his head just in time to see Rorrik rushing towards the door.

The felidaren was chortling at his comment before his laughter was snuffed out, replaced instead by the jiggling of a door handle that refused to budge. Valen spared not a second and hurriedly pushed off the bed, his arm stretching out.

Rorrik spun around with a look of honest confusion, Valen's hand connecting with the felidaren's arm in the same instant.

"...You're it," the demorinkin panted out through a smirk, satisfaction and pride swelling within him.

Rorrik's stupefaction didn't wear off as the tabby dropped his gaze to look at Valen's hand on his arm. The felidaren raised his vision back onto Valen, his emerald eyes wide and full of surprise.

Valen couldn't help but start to laugh. "I got you! I did it!"

It took a second, but then Rorrik began to laugh, too. "What did you do to the door?" he inquired, confusion still apparent in his tone.

"Seems it jammed or something!" Valen guffawed out, the force of laughter aggravating his swollen ribs.

"No, really! It won't open! I didn't see you jam it!"

Valen wiggled his fingers, still laughing. "Weren't expecting a spell, were you?"

"So you really can do magic!" Rorrik gasped.

Valen's laughter began to subside. "A little here and there," the demorinkin answered, all smiles. "A lot of cantrips, mostly, but... I know a thing or two!" The pride within him continued to swell.

"That's so cool!" Rorrik gushed. "Do another one!"

"Ummm," Valen looked around the room, searching for something to influence with the rucanic. The messy bed sheets should be an easy subject.

Valen spoke out an incantation and swiped his fingers in a simple hand gesture. The bed replied to the persuasion of his spell and the sheets unwrinkled, seemingly by their own will.

"Whooa! Making the bed must be so easy for you! Lucky!" Rorrik said, impressed. The felidaren's face then went puzzled. "Hey, wait a second, I never *heard* you say any spell before!"

"Some spells are easier than others," Valen clarified. "Some just... happen, while others I don't know as well and need to say the words."

"Ooh," Rorrik nodded, satisfied with that response. "That's super cool!"

"Thanks! I'm glad you—" Suddenly, a fuzziness began to drape over the demorinkin, quick and effective. It stole all concentration and energy as it spread, and within it the bodily soreness he had been ignoring found its voice. Before he knew it, he was dizzy and fighting off exhaustion.

"I... I think I need to..." Valen slurred out, straining for the energy to talk.

"...Valen? Are you okay?"

"I... need to lie down..." Valen didn't recall the steps over to the bed, but found himself lying down in it, regardless. "I feel... I feel..."

He closed his eyes and the world went dark.

. . .

Kyla

"You boys have to be more responsible than this!" Kyla stressed, an ashamed audience of her youngest children in front of her in the living room. "He's still recovering – a game of tag is the last thing he needs!"

The mother had hurried home from a meeting with Avalene Porte after receiving a call from Jate that Valen had passed out following a game of tag. She had rounded up her children immediately and demanded an explanation. Apparently, Talis had started a game of chase and Valen ultimately passed out after casting some magic.

"I-it was fun, though!" Talis objected, his eyes large and glossy with nervous tears. "We didn't make him play, h-he wanted to!"

"You should have not given him that idea in the first place!" Kyla scolded. She turned her attention on Rorrik, her eyes narrowing. "You *especially* should have known better, young man."

"He was fine until he did the magic!" Rorrik shot back defensively, though worry clouded his voice.

"Magic should be the last thing he's performing right now!" Kyla said. The demorinkin barely had any physical strength to spare; his rucanic reservoirs had to be even worse off, especially after the intense rucana he had pulled during his rescue.

Rorrik pressed his ears back and looked to the floor, shame punctuating his frown. "We didn't mean to..."

"Of course not, but I need you boys to practice better judgment! He needs rest and peace, not your antics!"

"It was Talis' idea! Why are we all in trouble?" Calvin sorely questioned.

"Because you went along with it!" Kyla sighed and placed a hand on her brow to massage some stress away. She didn't enjoy being stern with her children, but the situation called for it. "Calvin, Talis, go work on one of your school packets until dinner."

"But, Mooom!" Talis objected, the tears in his eyes pooling over.

"That's no fair! We're done with school today!" Calvin whined with a stomp of his foot.

"You *were*, yes. But after what you pulled you're not. Now, go." She jutted a finger towards the kitchen.

"What about Rorrik?!" Calvin challenged. "He played, too!"

"Don't worry about your brother. Shoo!"

Calvin glared at his older sibling in indignation before obeying. Talis followed, sniffling and whimpering loudly through a gaudy flow of tears. Kyla watched them head through the archway and into the kitchen, her eyes keeping on them as they retrieved their packets and slunk to the table, their feet and tails dragging all the while.

Satisfied, she turned her attention back on Rorrik. He had his head dipped and his eyes on the floor, shame still evident in his demeanor.

"Is he going to be okay?" her son sadly mumbled, his voice thick.

Kyla's frustration softened. "The spells likely used up most of his energy. He just needs rest, kit." She started to head towards the guest bedrooms. "Let's walk."

Rorrik did as he was told, his head never lifting.

"So what happened exactly? What spells did he do?" Kyla asked after achieving a certain distance from the living room. She checked behind them to make sure her other children were not tagging along.

"We were in a bedroom and he locked the door with magic so I couldn't get out," Rorrik said quietly. "After he caught me, I... I asked him to do another trick and so he made the bed with a spell."

"That's it, then? Just those two spells?"

Rorrik merely nodded, his body language suggesting no fib.

Kyla was relieved it was nothing more strenuous than that. "He probably didn't have much rucanic energy to spare and pushed himself to the limit, especially after all that running around. He should be fine after some rest."

"Okay..." Rorrik sighed. "I really didn't mean to hurt him..."

Kyla fought a sigh of her own. "I believe you, Rorrik, but you have to understand his limits right now."

"I know..."

Kyla was thoughtful over what had happened. It surprised her that the demorinkin had complied with a game of tag, considering his physical and emotional condition. It gave her hope that his recovery was underway.

There was a pinch of worry as a realization hit her. If the demorinkin was making strides in overcoming his trauma, Niem would be quick to shove him out the door. The mother in her was loath to send him off.

They still knew nothing about his attackers, but hopefully that would soon change. In her earlier meeting with Avalene, Kyla had given the vigilante permission to use the information learned from Valen's story in the interrogations of his attackers, in hope to generate some type of response or answers. That, and Avalene had her people working on recon assignments that would hopefully unveil some additional answers. *'But who knows how long it will be until we get a lead?'*

She had to believe she could influence Niem enough to let Valen stay. He would be annoyed—mad even—but she wasn't about to let her stubborn mate stand in the way of something she truly believed in. *'He has to understand that, right...?'*

She looked down to her pregnant abdomen and felt a rush of confidence in her abilities. *'He hasn't stopped me before; he won't stand in my way now.'* That didn't mean Niem wouldn't make his frustration and disapproval evident, however. Her mate always had the mind to make his viewpoint clear whenever he could.

"Well, Rorrik," Kyla broke the quiet as they arrived in front of the demorinkin's door. "It's time for your punishment."

Rorrik flinched and finally met her eyes, looking pitiful.

"You are to work on a packet until dinner," she started before gesturing to the door. "But, I want you to do it here. Someone should keep an eye on him."

Rorrik didn't seem near as broken up about that compared to his siblings.

"Run and go get it, then," she ordered and he did what he was told.

As he scampered off, Kyla softly walked into the room, spotting Valen sleeping soundly on the bed. He had zonked out in a different room than the one he had been sleeping in, but that was no issue. *'Just have to wash an extra pair of sheets.'*

She approached the bed and studied his sleeping form. His brick red skin was a tinge flushed, but a quick temperature check with her hand hinted at no fever. Her hand moved to brush some hair out of his face, tucking it behind one of his ivory horns.

In doing so she felt a rush of affection akin to what her own children filled her with. She wasn't sure what it was exactly, but she felt bonded to this young man, responsible for his safety. *'Perhaps it is the pregnancy hormones.'* Whatever it was, she was committed to keeping him safe. *'He has no one else left, does he?'*

She was still staring when she noticed a buzzing from her pocket, her corresponder. She retrieved the device and read on its display that Mr. Jollyswish was calling.

She put the communicator to her ear. "Hello, Kyla speaking."

"It is finished, dear kitty! Done and better than new! I even recharged the enchantment!" the jovial gnome said. "You come and pick it up, see for yourself!"

"Quick as you said you'd be," Kyla complimented with a light chuckle.

"Work flies when the project is exciting! When can I expect you?"

"I'll be by within the hour. Thank you, Mr. Jollyswish."

"It was my pleasure! Hurry, hurry!" With that, the call went dead.

Kyla slipped the corresponder back into her pocket just in time to have Rorrik hustle back into the room, not only a packet but one of his language books in hand.

"Who was that?" her son wondered.

Kyla offered him a smile. "It's done."

Rorrik mirrored her smile. "The vest?!"

She nodded.

Rorrik's mood considerably brightened at the news. "He's going to flip!"

"I'm sure he'll be overjoyed, yes," Kyla agreed. "But, before he can get it back, I have to go pick it up first."

"Go, go, go!" Rorrik encouraged with a bounce.

Kyla laughed at her son's enthusiasm. "Alright, alright." She gave Valen one last look before heading out the door. "I'll be back."

Chapter 19

Rorrik

Rorrik had been studying for about an hour or two when his ears twitched to the sound of cloth shifting. He peeked over towards the bed and saw Valen beginning to sit up with a groan, his hand on his head.

"You're awake!" The felidaren placed his packet down on the ground before hurrying up to the bed. "Feeling any better?"

Valen winced and rubbed at his eyes. "I don't know what happened, I just—"

"My mom said it's because you have so little magic left right now," Rorrik cut off to inform him. "And you're still really tired."

Valen faced him, suddenly seeming worried. "Your mom knows about my magic?"

Rorrik blinked. "Well, yeah! We saw you do that spell when we rescued you, and I told her what happened earlier..." He frowned. "Is that bad?"

Valen looked down at the bed, his ears dipping. "She's not going to tell anyone, right?"

Rorrik tilted his head. "Why?"

"Well..." Valen started, shifting uncomfortably. "I... I don't have any kind of permit..."

Rorrik processed that comment and was unable to hold back a huge bout of laughter.

Valen looked confused. "What's so funny?"

"That's okay! We don't have permits for looots of things!" Rorrik hooted, his chest still bouncing with laughter. He tried to stifle it, but the thought was just too rich! Valen was worried about something as silly as a *permit*!

Valen didn't reply as Rorrik finished his guffawing.

"Don't worry about it, really!" Rorrik assured with a wink, his laughter finally subsiding. "We won't tell anybody."

Valen stared at him, skeptical, before weakly grinning. "Well, if you say so..." He set his gaze back down on the bed, still looking tired as he yawned.

The plopping of hurried footsteps suddenly sounded and the two of them turned to look at the threshold, Talis skidding into view, smiling wide. "Dinner is ready! Mom got take-out!"

Rorrik perked up. "Really?!" He turned to Valen in excitement. "Let's go eat!"

Valen nodded slowly, his grin growing a tad, but still weak.

❖

Dinner was grilled chicken with an assortment of sides, including mashed potatoes, green beans, pasta with cheese, and corn. Their mother required that they all take a vegetable side, to which Rorrik happily picked corn. Green beans were okay, but corn was definitely tastier!

The whole family except for their father sat around the table, all happily munching away... until Rorrik looked over at Valen and realized he wasn't touching his food.

"Don't like chicken?" Rorrik asked him quietly.

"That's not it..." Valen mumbled, his eyes boring into his plate. "I just... I don't know... It's been a long time since I've had something like this..."

Rorrik's mother took note of their exchange. "Would you prefer something else, cub?"

"It's not that I don't like it," Valen clarified, awkward. "That's not the problem at all, it's..." He sighed and looked uncomfortable.

"Well, kit, it's alright if you eat it and alright if you don't. But know that it's not wrong to do."

That seemed to pile onto whatever was bothering Valen. The demorinkin frowned and scooted out of his chair before standing up. "May I be excused?"

"Of course, cub."

Rorrik frowned at Valen as he walked out of the room, wondering what was so wrong.

"What's his problem?" Calvin spoke the wonder out loud, perhaps too early, for Valen was likely still in earshot.

"He had been used to a rough life," their mother began, shifting into the feline tongue. "He's still learning how to cope. Just give him time."

"But he should be happy he can eat chicken now!" Talis replied in feline. "Shouldn't he?"

"It's complicated, love. You don't have to understand, just be patient with him."

Rorrik frowned down at his plate, its contents suddenly not tasting as delicious.

"Well, he has a surprise waiting for him after dinner," their mother reminded. "That should help him feel better."

▪ ▪ ▪

Valen was lying on his bed when Rorrik peeked his head into his bedroom after dinner. He looked awfully melancholy; his body was scrunched up and facing the wall, his shoulders blocking out a view of his face.

"Hey, Valeeen," Rorrik started, a smile already threatening to break loose on his face. "We got something for youuu."

Valen looked over his shoulder and Rorrik's smile broke free as the demorinkin spotted the Jollyswish bag the felidaren was carrying.

"Rorrik... I can't accept anything else..." Valen rejected, a heavy frown weighing down his face.

That didn't chase off Rorrik's grin. "I think you'll reconsider. Just look inside first."

The demorinkin sighed and pushed himself into sitting up. Rorrik hopped over, excitement building within him over the moment to come.

He handed the bag to Valen and the demorinkin gingerly received it. Valen glanced inside the bag, the tissue paper adorning the gift blocking out any kind of view of what awaited inside.

"Just open it!"

Valen obeyed, albeit slowly. He moved some of the stuffing out of the way and the article revealed itself, realization striking the demorinkin as his yellow eyes went large.

"The vest!" He grabbed it from the bag, spilling out tissue paper in the process. "I can't believe it! It— it doesn't even look damaged! It—" Tears began to pool in the demorinkin's eyes as he studied the article, shaking his head. "I can't believe it! I—"

"Sooo you like it?" Rorrik questioned, his tone mockingly inquisitive.

Valen's reply was a tight hug. "Thank you!" the demorinkin cried, emotional. "Thank you!"

Rorrik returned the embrace with a laugh, his heart giving a flip at seeing his new friend so overjoyed. "Put it on already!"

"Alright, alright!" Valen said through a weak chuckle of his own. He broke the hug to wipe at his eyes and stood up off the bed, the vest in hand. He approached the mirror and began to shrug on the article at a pace that drove Rorrik crazy.

Finally, the vest found its way on the demorinkin's torso, and Valen began to button it, his eyes still misty. The last button was finally clasped, and Valen slowly turned around.

Rorrik found himself staring in awe, his jaw dropping. The vest was a perfect fit; it accentuated Valen's torso wonderfully and the color, a brilliant red, brought out the handsomeness of his skin. The felidaren couldn't help but admire, his eyes glued to the way the article folded across the demorinkin's form.

"So, how do I look?" Valen struck a modest pose.

Rorrik's mind slowed and he looked up to Valen's face, his cheeks warm.

"That bad, huh?" Valen teased.

"No! You look — you look great!" Rorrik stammered out. He shut his mouth, his face hot. *'Why am I so embarrassed?'*

"Indeed, you do," Rorrik's mother contributed suddenly, revealing herself in the doorway. "You're quite the handsome young man!"

Valen turned to look at her arrival and smiled before stepping up to give her a hug. "Thank you so much! I can't ever repay you both enough!"

"No repayment is needed, cub. Enjoy it."

"I most certainly will!" Valen broke the hug to stare at himself in the mirror, beaming.

Rorrik watched Valen check out his reflection for a few moments longer before dropping his gaze to the ground, the aftermath of his earlier awe rendering him almost awkward for staring.

"So, Mr. Jollyswish, the gnome who fixed that for you, made a very interesting observation as he patched it up..." Rorrik's mother began. "He found a rucanic battery and the runes for an enchantment."

Rorrik jerked his head back up in confusion at his mother's words.

Valen froze in the pose he was making. He turned to her, an eyebrow rising. "Enchantment?"

The parent nodded. "Did your father ever mention any enchantments?"

Valen blinked before shaking his head. "No, never."

"Hm... interesting..."

"Wait, so it's actually magical?!" Rorrik asked in disbelief, his conversation with Talis entering his memory. He had been fibbing when he mentioned to his younger brother that the vest is magical, but apparently, he was right?!

"That's right. Mr. Jollyswish was able to identify the spell. Do you want to know?"

"I— yes! What is it?"

"Apparently, the enchantment is charisma-based — makes the wearer charming and irresistible, according to Mr. Jollyswish."

Rorrik processed that information, his cheeks warming yet again. *'Charming and irresistible?'* Perhaps that was why...

"...Wait. So..." Valen's brow furrowed. "What does that mean exactly?"

"It means you can 'get away with a lot more', he said. Influence people better, connect with others more seamlessly — that kind of thing."

Valen looked to be wrestling a frown. "...Oh." He went back to staring at himself in the mirror, his face going crooked.

"...What's wrong?" his mother asked.

"N-nothing..." Valen mumbled. "He just... never told me he enchanted it..." He dipped his head and rubbed at the back of his neck. "I just... I don't know what to say." The demorinkin's mood seemed to be quickly plummeting as the frown finally won.

"...Do you want some alone time?" the parent asked with a frown.

Valen didn't lift his head as he slowly nodded.

Rorrik's mother set her attention on her son. She motioned towards the door and they both made their way out, leaving Valen with his thoughts.

They arrived out in the hallway and Rorrik looked back at Valen one last time before shutting the door.

■ ■ ■

Avalene

Avalene Porte stood with her arms crossed and her brow furrowed, adrenaline alive in her blood. A lump sat in her throat as she faced the wall behind her temporary desk at the country warehouse, her eyes on the papers and reports pinned up there. They showed as nothing but blurry text and pictures as her brain was elsewhere, psyching herself up for the task that awaited her.

She heard someone approach, the steps familiar.

"Are you ready, Miss Porte?" one of her associates, Felicity Ander, asked. Felicity was a headstrong brevin who had been dedicated to Avalene's cause since its founding almost a decade ago. She was a hard worker with a sharp mind and often served as a team member in sensitive assignments such as the one at hand.

Avalene turned around stiffly and gave a firm nod. "Let's get this over with."

They began their walk to the basement, the adrenaline coursing through Avalene pumping swifter as they grew closer to where they kept their prisoners. She could not deny the unease that what they were about to do cast on her; the captives had established themselves to be bloodthirsty extremists who exhibited little to no empathy and decency. Conversing with them was off-putting at the minimum and alarming at the height of it.

"You positive you want to question them, Miss Porte?" Felicity asked, worry in her tone. "With all due respect, it's our job to handle the questioning; you don't have to trouble yourself with it."

"I will trouble myself with whatever I find necessary, Felicity," Avalene answered with a hint of sternness.

"I apologize, I shouldn't have—"

"It's no matter."

Avalene normally wouldn't conduct the interrogations herself, but this particular case had invoked a surge of personal responsibility in her. She felt a drive to handle the questions herself.

They came upon the room, a view from the reinforced glass window on the wall offering a look inside. One of the prisoners sat completely chained to a chair and table, their head dipped so that their blonde hair covered their face. Upon closer observation, Avalene recognized it as the sole female of the captives.

Hugo Arkas stood at the ready behind the prisoner, a taser in his hands and his eyes ever on her. Hugo was a terran that had joined the force around the same time Felicity had. He could be overzealous, but his intensity was a much-desired factor in grueling jobs like these.

At the door was Mindi Cross, a marble-furred vulpen who specialized in agility in all forms of conflict, both physical and mental. By comparison, she was a newer member having joined the cause about five years ago but had been quick to establish her worth and thus was a trusted teammate.

Avalene approached the metal door and paused briefly to dispel her nerves. With a deep intake of breath, she channeled all her intensity into a composed expression. She lifted a finger to press a buzzer on the wall, and Mindi swung open the door in a flash. Both Avalene and Felicity marched in, the door pronouncing closed with a heavy clang behind them.

The room was thick with tension as Avalene took her spot in the opposing chair of the prisoner, Felicity taking her own mark behind Avalene. Her other associates remained at their stations, the room suffocatingly quiet.

Avalene drilled her gaze into the captive, her gray eyes keen, the adrenaline within her hardening into resolve. She delivered her question with sharpened calm. "Who do you work for?"

The prisoner's once gorgeous blonde hair appeared desaturated and drained of its sheen as it curtained her face, hiding her expression. "Why must time be further wasted with such a foolish effort? There is nothing to be said to *filth* like you," the captive spat out, her voice coarse.

She was right; it *was* a waste of time to run through the same old inquiry. Avalene contemplated her next question for a long second before asking, "Does the name 'Vaaskiir' mean anything to you?"

Abruptly, the prisoner jerked up her head, her dirty hair framing her stark gold eyes, a glow in them. "How in all the realms do you know of that name?!"

Avalene had anticipated something much subtler out of the prisoners if the name meant anything to them: a tick in body language or a change in tone, perhaps. Definitely not shock and animation.

"…It is the name of the boy you attacked," she answered coolly.

The golden eyes of the prisoner went even wider as shock completely usurped her expression. "The boy from the van?!"

Avalene merely nodded, endeavoring to hide the perplexity the captive's response instilled in her. It was almost like they had not known the demorinkin's identity… Had they?

Overjoyed laughter out of the captive answered that wonder. "Xerstelle above smiles on us for our cause is true! We are blessed! *BLESSED!*" The prisoner went on laughing, it striking Avalene as maniacal. "What glorious luck and fortune! How could this not mean we are righteous?"

"Elaborate, prisoner!" Avalene demanded, her demeanor roughening with both unease and disgust.

"Vaaskiir! The cursed bloodline! The wretched family that declared they were worthy amongst celestelles!" The captive had no trouble in answering, her voice high with emotion. "They cast a blemish on the righteous deeds of celestelles in a gross attempt at salvation! Demorins belong in the pits of hell, and yet Vaaskiir challenged that which should not be challenged!"

Avalene had no words, but they were unneeded as the prisoner rattled on.

"How unlikely that we find Vaaskiir's spawn by chance! Our great search is finished!" Tears began to flow out of the woman, draining her radiant cheeks.

"...By chance?" Avalene pressed.

"Yes, yes! A cold trail we had, but now no longer! His father will roll in his unholy grave to know his hell child has been found!"

Apprehension thunked hard in Avalene's gut. Perhaps revealing the boy's name was a misstep.

"Tell me! Where is the other child?!"

The apprehension in Avalene worsened still. She fought against it as she answered, "Dead. Killed by the ones who kidnapped them."

The woman threw back her head and laughed once more. "Is it so?! What gross irony that it was not our fangs to bloody him! No matter! The hell spawn has perished!"

Avalene narrowed her eyes. "Who do you work for?"

The prisoner grinned in a crazed display, the tears in her eyes shining bright, matching the glow of her irises. "The glowing light of Korinthis, the piercing sword of Nathalia, the guardians of the righteous and worthy, *the Fangs of Hellbane!*"

Chapter 20

Sphinx

Sphinx was heading down the streets of Akarth toward the market. He was hurrying because Karreo expected him home soon; he had already taken way too long at the library.

"Sphiiinx! Sphinx, wait up! Hey!" Siena's pretty voice suddenly called out, freezing him in his tracks.

He turned around to see her running up to him, spurring a warm smile out of the disguised human. "Siena! How are you?"

"Hehe! You're so adorable, Sphinx!" She closed the distance between them, Sphinx watching her body all the while, the way her curves moved hypnotizing him.

"What are you staring at, silly?" she giggled upon arriving, twirling her hair.

"You're so pretty…" Sphinx admitted, blushing hard.

She laughed joyously at that. "Oh! You're so charming!"

Her compliments aroused him, causing the red on his face to deepen and pressure to build in his lower abdomen.

Suddenly, Siena was crying. She grabbed onto him in a desperate hug, her shoulders rocking with a sob. "Don't you like me, Sphinx?!"

"I— of course I do!" Sphinx was overwhelmed at the abrupt shift in emotion.

"You left me! You hate me!" Siena bawled, soaking his shirt.

"I don't! Honest!"

She was suddenly kissing him, to which Sphinx did not resist. He melted into her, the tightness in his pants pressing as they embraced.

Siena's hands then traveled downwards and towards his erection, summoning a jolt of panic within him.

"Wait!" he cried, terror spiking. He looked down to notice his pants were gone, his privates exposed.

She didn't listen as she grabbed him tightly, spurring Sphinx into yelping out.

"Stop!" He tried to push her away, but noticed his hands were bound.

She answered by twisting and yanking painfully. With that, she began to laugh.

Sphinx looked back up at her face, realizing in disgust that it was not Siena at all, but one of the women from the shower, her bony face sneering at him.

"Demorin spawn, demorin spawn!" she jeered in a singsong, laughing coldly. "What a good hellchild you'll be!"

"Stop!" His skin burnt horribly from the cold water. "Stop! *STOP!*"

Valen's eyes opened in an instant and his body shot into sitting up, his heart pounding hard in his chest.

"You finally woke up!" Rorrik's alarmed voice came from next to him on the bed.

Valen turned to look at the felidaren, heavily disoriented from his nightmare.

"You were talking and shaking in your sleep! I tried to wake you up, but you wouldn't!" The felidaren looked the picture of worried as he sat on the edge of the bed, his tail frizzed and his eyes double in size.

Valen could only stare at him, his mind still recovering from his dreams. The illusion of burning cold water was still faintly present, haunting him. He put a hand to his face and lay back down, his heart still mid gallop.

"...Are you okay?" Rorrik asked in a small voice.

"I..." Valen shifted so his back was to the tabby, and his shoulders scrunched up to hide his head. A sob shook him as tears came on suddenly. He couldn't stop himself from crying.

"I-it's okay!" Rorrik tried.

That only worsened Valen's fit.

"What's going on; you called for me?!" Mrs. Catty's voice suddenly said.

"He was having a nightmare!"

Mrs. Catty's footsteps hustled over and the edge of the bed dipped with her weight. He felt her hands begin to rub at his shoulders, her touch encouraging more tears.

"It's over now," she soothed, her voice gentle and motherly. "You're alright. Breathe..."

Valen could only bawl, too shaken up to do much else. He shook and sputtered as his nightmare refused to leave him, unsettling him to his core.

It was not the first nightmare he had had, far from it, but they never got easier. Sometimes, it even felt like they were getting worse.

As Mrs. Catty rubbed his back and began to hum to him, however, he felt thankful for someone else being there. The impossibly long nights he had spent by himself were relentless when he woke up from his nightmares, the terrible imagery of his dreams having more power to distress him in his solitude. His loneliness was always augmented when he would reach out for Karreo, the reminder that he was gone forever always a jagged spear to his heart and spirit. Sometimes he woke to himself mumbling things to his younger brother in sleepy disorientation, him swearing he could feel the presence of Karreo's sleeping form next to him, a phantom sensation.

The panic from his nightmare began to ebb away as Mrs. Catty provided solace, but his heart still ached in pain from the cruel reminders of his dream, fueling more tears. He wanted to hole himself up and forget about everything that had happened, to be free from the torment that was never far off, even when he felt rare doses of happiness.

Mrs. Catty never left him as time passed, her gentle touch rubbing his shoulders and tickling his hair. She hummed quietly to him, generating solace Valen had not felt since his own mother consoled him long, long ago. It hurt to be reminded of her, but the comparison also brought him respite, his brokenness too desperate to be choosy.

Eventually the tears dried up, reduced to dry sobs that occasionally rocked the demorinkin's shoulders. It wasn't long after that that his sobbing finally finished its course.

Embarrassment and shame from others witnessing his grief settled in as Valen lay there in the aftermath of his crying.

Mrs. Catty tucked some of his hair behind his ear. "Do you have nightmares often?" she delicately asked.

Valen felt like shrinking as his cheeks flushed with embarrassment. He nodded, unwilling to speak.

"...Would it help to not be by yourself?"

Valen's cheeks burned hotter as he nodded once more. The idea of not spending his nights alone was a welcomed one.

"We'll see what we can do. For now, how about some breakfast?"

So, it was morning, then. Valen's stomach was empty from skipping dinner the night before and desired sustenance, but his emotional state did little to incite an appetite.

He gave a tiny nod and began to sit up, regardless, Mrs. Catty's hand pulling back as he did so. He rubbed at his puffy eyes, the salt from his tears stinging them.

"Well, get dressed and head down to the kitchen, then." With that, the mother stood up. "Ready to make those pancakes, Rorrik?"

Valen had forgotten about Rorrik being there. He turned to look at the felidaren, who was sitting on the chair in the corner, appearing droopy. He slowly nodded at his mother's question, his vision on the floor. He then got up and headed out the door, sparing Valen a look on the way out.

Valen glanced down before they could lock eyes, still embarrassed from his episode.

Mrs. Catty followed her son out the room and closed the door, leaving Valen alone to get dressed out of his pajamas.

Anxiety and hurt jabbed at Valen as he glanced over to the top of the dresser, where his vest sat neatly folded. The shock of yesterday's discovery had thrown him for a loop and left a very unsettling doubt in his mind. If his father had enchanted the garment with charisma, did that mean all the charisma Valen had was due to the vest?

He thought of Siena and how charmed she was, as well as Aldras Panto, Simitri Dayas and all the others he had supposedly befriended. Valen had been proud of his charisma after swaying the contacts he had made in Akarth, but was that even his own doing? What had been the vest and what wasn't? Was he even *likable* without the vest?

Valen couldn't help himself from feeling deceived over it all; he felt like a fool.

'Dad… why did you do it?' the demorinkin wondered, his lips jutted in a frown as he picked up the article and examined it. *'Why didn't you at least tell me?'* The demorinkin sighed, wishing his father was still around to offer an answer.

He studied the garment, hesitant to put it on. After some consideration, he refolded the vest and replaced it back on top of the dresser.

■ ■ ■

Rorrik

Rorrik stirred at the pancake batter with a small frown, feeling troubled. His plan to wake Valen up early to help make pancakes had utterly flopped. He couldn't shake the picture of Valen sobbing from his mind. The nightmare Valen had, whatever it was, had definitely shaken him up. The way the demorinkin had mumbled and thrashed before jolting awake made the felidaren shudder.

"All mixed?" his mother asked in reference to the batter.

Rorrik nodded slowly.

"So…" his mom began in the feline language. "I know you just got your own room, but how would you feel if Valen stayed with you while he's here?"

Rorrik looked up to his mother, his somberness quickly lessening. "Really?! I wouldn't mind!" he replied back in feline, his voice high with excitement.

"You're sure?" his parent questioned, serious. "You can handle his nightmares?"

"Calvin and Talis had nightmares all the time!"

"Yes, but these are different. You saw that firsthand."

The imagery hounding Rorrik's mind was summoned back. He had to admit that it scared him, but the idea of having sleepovers with the demorinkin proved more convincing. "I'll be able to help him! I don't mind, honest!"

"Well… I have to run it by your father first. We'll see."

Rorrik was too excited to entertain the idea of his dad saying no. *'I can't wait!'*

"Well, if that's all mixed up," his mother switched back to common, pointing at the batter, "then go ahead and pour it in this cup. Try not to spill." His mother handed him a measuring cup and Rorrik took it with eager hands before doing what he was told. He spilt, but only a tiny bit!

He was handing the cup to his mother when Valen walked into the kitchen, still in the clothes Rorrik had been lending him as pajamas.

"Didn't feel like getting dressed?" his mother wondered.

"Well, I—" the demorinkin looked uncomfortable. "I'm going to be taking a shower, so I figure I'll get dressed after that."

"Whatever works, kit. Go ahead and take a seat at the table, it'll be done shortly."

The demorinkin did just that, his movements slow. He sat with his back to them, his demeanor seeming like it hadn't improved much.

Rorrik gave a frown, hoping Valen would feel better soon.

"Good morning!" Jate's chipper voice suddenly greeted. Rorrik looked to see his older brother enter the kitchen and walk up to their mother, giving her a kiss on the cheek.

"'Morning, son of mine," she greeted back with a chuckle.

His brother turned his attention on Rorrik. "You're up early, Rorrik! That excited for our watch today, eh?"

Rorrik smirked at that. "If pancakes are a part of our watch…"

Jate laughed. He then noticed Valen sitting at the table. "Hey there, Valen!"

The demorinkin peeked over his shoulder and nodded in return, weakly grinning. He then turned back around, putting his chin in his hand.

"Any way I can help, Mom?" Jate offered.

"Go ahead and get some eggs cooking. Rorrik, can you butter some bread?"

Rorrik nodded and got to work. He kept peeking over at Valen, hoping the demorinkin would show curiosity in what they were doing, but he never did.

They were close to done with breakfast when two of his other brothers wandered in, Gavin and Quinn. They greeted their mother in the same manner Jate had, a kiss on the cheek.

"Are the youngest up yet?" their mother asked them.

Gavin nodded. "I got them up."

"Good, good," the tortoiseshell said. "Go ahead and tell them breakfast is ready, will you?"

Gavin headed down the hall to do what she asked.

Their mom fetched a plate from the cupboard. "Just eggs for you, Valen?"

"Yes, ma'am," he softly replied.

She prepared his helping and delivered it in front of the demorinkin. "There you go, kit."

"Thank you…" Valen said.

"No problem, cub," she smiled. "Eat up!"

■ ■ ■

Breakfast had passed by drama free. Valen had eaten his eggs slowly and silently, while Rorrik and his brothers boisterously finished their own syrup-soaked plates. Plans for the day were discussed, none of the brothers due to work on school but instead complete business-related jobs. Jate and Rorrik had been assigned to keep watch at Farpoint, which Rorrik looked forward to. Keeping watch meant lots of people-watching and eavesdropping, which the felidaren excelled at. Not to mention it was fun!

Jate and he currently sat on an awning, their eyes on the streets below. They were overlooking a populated shopping plaza, a fountain sitting in the middle of the circular street.

Jate was wrapping some bands on his shins, humming to himself. "So! How is your new friend doing?"

Rorrik's expression went sideways. "Sometimes he's okay, but most of the time… not so good."

"That's to be expected, I suppose," Jate shrugged. "He's been through a lot."

"He had a pretty bad nightmare this morning…"

Jate gave a frown that mirrored the one pulling at his younger brother's lips. "Poor kid… Must be tough…"

"Yeah…" Rorrik mumbled, painstakingly aware of Valen's troubles. Right when it seemed the demorinkin might be feeling better, something always wrecked his mood and stole any of his happiness away.

The tabby perked up a tad to share some exciting news with his brother. "Mom wants him to sleep in my room now, to help with his nightmares."

"Oh, really?" his brother chuckled. "Good luck getting Dad to agree to that."

"Why would he say no?" Rorrik's sudden smile fled just as quickly, his denial over his father's strictness finally shaken.

"Well, it's one thing having him down in our private hideout, another entirely to keep him where *we* sleep."

"He isn't a threat, though!"

"I'm not the one you have to convince," Jate laughed. "Mom has her ways, though. We'll see."

They fell into silence after that, both directing their attention on the plaza below, nothing too interesting or promising presenting itself as patrons walked about.

Jate suddenly nudged him. "Ooh, check out the fountain!"

Rorrik's eyes found the fountain, spotting nothing at first, but then catching sight of three teenage girls, a floraling and two humans.

"They're pretty cute, aren't they? Or, I forget, are you old enough to be into girls yet?"

"Of course I am!" Rorrik said, blushing hard.

Jate laughed and slapped his knee. "Sorry, just wasn't sure!"

Rorrik flicked him with his tail before getting a better look at the group of girls.

The floraling was a sunny yellow hue, her markings a reddish orange that stood out vividly. She had shining black hair that was braided in the back, long enough that she could drape it over her front comfortably. She was wearing a purple halter top and knee-high shorts, an outfit that presented her slender figure wonderfully.

The humans looked to be related, the older one having blonde hair that was tied into a high ponytail and the younger sporting dirty blonde hair that remained down. They both wore sleeveless dresses that allowed a sightly peek at their cleavage, which Rorrik found himself especially appreciating. Their outfits did well to flatter their curvier bodies.

They were all very pretty as they sat there chatting and laughing. Rorrik's blush held as he admired them.

"Might as well take a closer look!" Jate said, getting to his feet.

Rorrik didn't argue with that plan.

They climbed down from the awning with expertise that had been honed all their lives, the two brothers agile in their movements. Their bare feet found the pavement and they made their way casually towards the fountain. Well, Jate did, at least; Rorrik couldn't shake some awkwardness as they passed by the girls and sat a few seats down on the fountain edge.

Rorrik glanced over after being seated for a few moments and spotted that the girls were the ones staring at them now. He quickly looked away, his blush returning.

He looked at his brother and noticed Jate was confidently looking over at them, smiling. The girls giggled as the older felidaren gave them a nod.

Rorrik summoned his courage and peeked over yet again, catching the floraling staring directly at him, sending a flutter through his system. He didn't look away this time but instead smiled, the floraling smiling back.

He had the mind to go talk to her when Jate's hand landed on his knee.

"Someone is awfully interested in us," his brother said in the feline tongue, his voice low.

"Well, yeah, those girls!" Rorrik hissed in reply, matching the language.

"They're not the only curious ones..." Jate's eyes gazed about the plaza, seemingly aimless.

"What... what do you mean?"

"We're being watched. A man followed us to the plaza and has been bumming around since; he's kept an eye on us the whole time."

Rorrik hadn't spotted anybody follow them. His instinct was to look around, but his training told him to not be obvious.

"Uhhmm... Hi there!" a feminine voice then called out. The brothers looked over and recognized one of the girls as the speaker, the floraling.

"'Morning!" Jate greeted with a smile, his voice chipper.

"What are you guys up to?" the blonde human wondered, her voice flirtatious.

Jate stood up. "Sadly, we have to get going, but you girls have a lovely day!"

That confused the girls as well as Rorrik. '*Come on, Jate!*'

His brother began to walk off and he hesitantly followed, glancing back at the girls one last time. They were watching them go, their eyes offended.

"What was even the point of that?" Rorrik grumbled in feline.

"I wanted to check if he was still watching us," Jate excused, mirroring the language.

"And?"

"He is. He's the fellow with curly black hair wearing the striped brown shirt over by Emil's Trinket's."

Rorrik moved his head to glance around the plaza as though he were naturally looking around, hoping to catch sight of the man with his peripherals.

It took him a moment, but the felidaren finally did. The man was staring at them, just as Jate said. The man put down the ornament he had been glancing at and began to walk in the direction the brothers were heading in.

"What should we do?" Rorrik asked in feline.

"You needed a new shirt, right?" Jate questioned in common, glancing back at Rorrik.

Rorrik almost said 'no' before he caught Jate's drift. "Yeah."

"I know the perfect place!" Jate began to guide them towards one of the many boutiques that lined the street. The building boasted large windows in the front, mannequins that adorned clothing of various styles posing there, a view of the shop beyond them. A couple racks of clothes were displayed outside the store, shirts to be found on their hangers, but they ignored them as they passed.

Instead, they walked into the building, a bell strung on the door announcing their entrance. Jate walked towards one of the racks by the window, standing so he was in line with a mannequin. Rorrik did similarly.

They both glanced out the window and saw the man eventually approach, gravitating right towards one of the clothing racks outside the store. He began to browse there.

"Any ideas, Rorrik?" Jate asked quietly in feline.

Rorrik thought about it, summoning what his training had taught him. "Well, he expects us to come out the door eventually, right? Looks like we need to leave another way..."

Jate offered him a large smile. "Great thinking!"

156

"Can I help you boys at all?" the shop keep then asked, approaching them. She was an older woman, perhaps in her seventies, a polite smile stretching her aged features.

"We're just browsing for now, ma'am, thank you!" Jate answered kindly.

"Well, if you need anything, just let me know." She began to head back towards the till, her steps slow.

Jate began to wander around the store, Rorrik following along. No other customers currently seemed to be browsing about, which would make their escape easier.

"Looks like the changing rooms are really close to a door back there," Jate eventually said quietly, his language disguised. "We can ask to try on some clothes and then suggest a different size. While she's getting that, we can sneak out the door. Make sure to grab an extra shirt to wear on the way out to help disguise yourself."

Rorrik jerked his head in a nod, seeing no error in that plan.

The two brothers each picked out a handful of shirts before walking up to the clerk.

"We'd like to try these on, if you don't mind," Jate asked.

"Alright then, let me get those doors unlocked for you." The aged woman headed towards the changing rooms, her pace steady and slow. Rorrik didn't mind her speed for it meant there would be a larger time window to sneak out.

The shop keep unlocked two of the rooms. "There you are. Let me know if anything doesn't fit right."

"Will do! Thank you!" Jate smiled. With that, he shut himself into one of the stalls, Rorrik taking the other.

Rorrik slipped one of the shirts over the top of his clothes and waited for Jate to speak up, which took a few minutes.

"Excuse me, ma'am!" Rorrik heard his brother say. "Would you mind getting me this shirt, but in a size up?" The sound of clothing draping the door joined his question.

"Uh, I actually need a size bigger in this, too!" Rorrik added, draping one of the shirts he had picked out on his own door.

"Of course. Let me just fetch that for you, boys." Rorrik's shirt disappeared from the door.

The tabby waited a few moments so the woman could turn her back and begin her trek away. He knelt down and poked his head from underneath the stall, spotting her walking off.

Stealthily, he began to weasel out from underneath the door, his movements quiet and coordinated. He emerged out of the stall the same moment Jate snuck out of his own. Without skipping a beat, the brothers headed right for the door.

There was no need to break out the lock picks as the door proved unlocked. The hinges creaked slightly as Jate inched it open. The tabby nimbly slipped through the narrow opening, Rorrik following right after, the door clicking closed behind them.

They stepped into a small hallway, two doors presenting themselves on the left while a final door stood at the end of the hall.

Jate hastily tiptoed up to the one at the end of the hallway. When he tried the handle, it did not turn. He nodded to his brother and gestured to the lock. Rorrik smirked, excited his brother was letting him do the honors.

The felidaren leaned down and retrieved his lock picks before going to work on the door. Jate kept his eyes on the way they had come, his ears perked.

The lock succumbed after a minute or two of persuasion and Rorrik turned the handle, feeling smug over his quick work.

"Quick, go, go, go!" Jate suddenly muttered on his breath, alarmed.

Rorrik squeezed through the door, Jate right on his tail. They found themselves in a storage room, yet another door on the back wall. When they hustled up to it they noticed a deadbolt lock on the door, to which Jate eagerly flipped. They slipped out in a hurry and shut the door behind them, Rorrik's fur frazzling as a feeling of narrowly dodging detection wavered down his spine. It excited him, in turn.

The door had led them into an alley. The brothers didn't linger as they scurried off, a new shirt on their backs as they left the boutique behind.

Chapter 21

Rorrik

"You for sure shook him?" Gavin asked them, serious.

Jate nodded. "We ditched him after taking the back door out of a shop. When we found Calvin and Talis no one seemed to be keeping an eye on them, but I figure it was best to bring them back, anyways."

"It's good that you did," their older sibling agreed.

Five of the brothers sat around the table found within The Den's employee break room. The Den was an inn that the family business ran and was what laid above their secret hideout. Jate and Rorrik had hurriedly gathered everyone there after they had lost the man following them. The two brothers had raced to pick up Calvin and Talis in person and sent a coded alert via corresponder to the rest of the family. Gavin was already at the inn when they arrived, but Quinn had not shown up yet.

Gavin continued, "Someone is definitely poking around. When I was shadowing Blue today a client started asking about any well-known felidaren in the city. Of course, she didn't reveal anything, but the fact someone has been asking could spell trouble."

Bluebird was Gavin's mentor for his informant training. She had been working for the family for quite some time (before Rorrik was born, for sure) and had been complacent enough to take Gavin on as an apprentice. Rorrik admittedly didn't know too much about Blue; the brevin kept to herself and wasn't very chatty when Rorrik had tried talking with her in the past.

"Good thing Dad has all the credible informants paid off, then, huh?" Jate said with a nervous chuckle. "Why do you think people are wondering?"

"Blue is looking into it, but she suspects that someone has been looking into police witness reports that match the attack on the van and noticed the mention of furred tails. If that's true—and it probably is—then any felidaren is under scrutiny right now."

"What's scrutiny mean?" Talis piped up from his chair, his eyes large with curiosity.

"It means you're being closely watched," Gavin explained to his younger sibling. He turned his attention on Jate and Rorrik. "Did you mention anything about our guest when you were out?"

Jate and Rorrik looked to each other, Jate wincing.

"J-just vague stuff!" Rorrik answered worriedly, desperately trying to remember their conversation. "We never mentioned any names, or even specifics. Just that he's having a rough time."

"We were all the way up on an awning; no one should have been able to hear us up there," Jate excused, less worried than Rorrik.

"Better safe than sorry right now," Gavin said.

"Well, at least we're bug free!" Jate pointed out. "We checked everywhere on us and didn't find anything. Sooo, unless he's got super hearing, our conversation should've been safe."

They all turned to look as the door opened and in walked Quinn, gesturing to his communicator. "You say we've got stalkers now?" the felidaren inquired.

"Someone was definitely following us," Rorrik answered his sibling.

"And someone was pressing Bluebird for information on any felidaren in the city earlier," Gavin added.

"You don't say! Good think I was cooped up in the shop all day," Quinn chuckled as he took a seat, his dirtied shirt and fur verifying his whereabouts. "I'm guessing this has something to do with the demorinkin?"

"That seems the most likely," Jate answered. "I mean, it could be the typical curiosity about us, but the timing says otherwise."

Gavin nodded at that before flipping open his notebook. "So, what did the man look like?"

"He was a human male, middle aged. Curly black hair, white skin, wore a typical brown, striped shirt. He looked pretty underwhelming, really."

"I'm sure that was intentional," Gavin said, jotting down some notes. "Where did it happen?"

"Farpoint Plaza," Rorrik said this time.

"Well, he actually began following us before then," Jate corrected.

'Oh, right...' Rorrik blushed.

"I first noticed him on Wayshine Street. Around 11am."

"Did he appear to be alone?" Gavin asked, his eyes on his notebook.

"He didn't seem to have any buddies."

There was some scratching of Gavin's pen, then he flipped the writing pad closed. "Well, perhaps it's best if Rorrik, Calvin, and Talis hang around here for the day until we get more information on what's going on."

Rorrik frowned as his name was included. Was he not trusted to watch his own back?! He then reminded himself of the fact that he had not spotted their stalker and flushed with shame.

"What?! So now *we* can't go outside?"

"It's safer for now, kit," Jate said, ruffling the Calvin's hair.

"I'm not a kit! And stop messing up my hair!" Calvin pushed Jate's hand away. "This is stupid! I was having a really good day, too; I got three whole wallets already!"

"Three? Wow! That's impressive!" Quinn congratulated with a little clap. "But, your brothers are right. You three should probably stay here for now."

"Awww," Talis whined. "But its *sooo* boring here!"

"I'm sure you'll find a way to entertain yourselves." Gavin stood up as he stuffed his notebook into a pocket on his fiber chest piece. Gavin often wore his gear when he shadowed for Bluebird, giving him the look of a professional.

The rest of the older brothers, Rorrik included, didn't typically wear their armor unless they were heading out on a job. Rorrik couldn't help but envy Gavin's success but knew he would get that far himself one day. *'Just have to keep training!'*

Gavin pushed in his chair. "I take it you already alerted Mom?"

"Yep, I sent her a writ," Jate confirmed.

The oldest nodded at that. "Good." He then sighed. "Dad isn't going to be happy about this..."

■ ■ ■

Valen

The demorinkin lay curled up in bed, miserable. He wore the same pajamas from the night before, the shower he had claimed to be planning at breakfast something that had never happened. The fright of his nightmare had been stubborn to leave him, the memory of burning cold water rendering the thought of a shower distressing. That, and he was hesitant to strip down, being exposed an unwelcome idea even in solitude.

Part of him argued that a shower would help improve his morale, considering a few days of filth clung to him, and Valen had never liked to feel dirty. The rest of him rejected the notion of helping himself, demanding he do naught but wallow in his despair.

It was the same when it came to distracting his mind. Valen knew he should be reading one of the packets Rorrik gave him to busy himself, but any motivation to do so escaped him. It was like he *had* to feel miserable; that he was not allowed to feel relief. *'I deserve as much...'*

All the negativity was made worse by the fact that he was completely alone in the hideout. His paranoia over the Fangs of Hellbane was always amplified when he was by himself, and now he was more alone than he had ever been before. With the whole family gone for the day he felt exposed and unprotected. At least in the past someone had always been nearby, even if it was in a completely different part of the hideout. The fact that no one was there spooked and chilled the demorinkin, having the power to turn the simplest sound into a potential threat. He was left cursing every creak and groan of the walls, growing further and further bothered as his mind ran off with explanations for the tiniest of disturbances.

He was sick with worry when suddenly a distant thump and scrambled footsteps hit his ears. His stomach leapt into his throat and a fire of adrenaline awoke within him, cooking his body with heat. The footsteps continued, slower this time, and his paranoia bucked with dread. His fears had been realized – the Fangs of Hellbane had found him!

He noticed with terror that the footfalls were growing closer and so he scrambled out of bed, a spell readying on his hands to lock the door. He touched the knob and the rucanic energy seized the passage; the spell doing little to make him feel protected.

He was desperately searching for a place to hide when the door handle jiggled, slowly at first and then harder, sending his panic over the edge.

"Go away!" he screamed, his voice shrill as his emotions skyrocketed. "*Go away!*"

"Valen? Are you okay?!" Rorrik's voice frantically asked from behind the door.

His fear was replaced with confusion. "...Rorrik?"

"Yeah, it's me!" The door handle again shook. "What's going on? Why did you lock the door?"

Much of the intensity of Valen's panic was robbed by Rorrik's arrival, but still his heart thumped loud in his chest. "I thought you were going to be gone today?!"

"Something came up," the felidaren explained, trying the handle yet again. "Are you okay? Can you unlock the door?"

Valen hesitated, the very real repercussions of his scare marking him wary. Still, he released his hold on the spell in time for Rorrik to try the knob again, the door finally free to open. In walked the tabby without delay.

Valen didn't meet the felidaren's eyes and went to sit on the bed, his head falling into his hands, the effect of his adrenaline still overwhelming him as he visibly shook. He knew logically that he was safe for the time, but was unable to overcome the ghost of his terror.

Rorrik hurried over and took a seat next to him. "What's wrong?!"

Valen didn't want to cry; he already felt foolish enough. "I didn't know it was you..."

"...Who did you think I was?"

The question made his shoulders jump, betraying his efforts.

"...Oh," Rorrik said in a small voice, understanding. "It's okay, you're safe..."

Valen's shoulders jumped yet again as he found himself unable to fully believe that. The tears broke free. "They're going to find me..."

"No, our hideout is really secretive! They can't find you here."

Valen remained unconvinced. "They found my father," the demorinkin sobbed. "They'll find me!"

At first there was only silence to that. Then, Valen felt Rorrik's arm drape across his shoulders and was pulled in close to the felidaren.

"You don't have to worry... You're safe..." the tabby's voice was gentle.

Valen's lip shuddered and another sob rocked his shoulders. "You don't know that..."

Rorrik gave him a squeeze. "Just relax..."

Valen began to feel a faint rumbling coming from the felidaren's chest. Then, he began to hear it, too. It was a purr.

Valen fixated on the sound, discovering that it ushered away his anxieties. The tension in his body loosened its coil around him and he closed his eyes, finding himself calming down, able to relax as his panic attack ebbed away.

He sat there for a time, the rare feeling of serenity captivating him. Then, realization settled in and embarrassment usurped his solace. Awkwardness heated his cheeks and he broke the embrace by gingerly pulling away, Rorrik taking the hint as he took his arm back, the purr fading.

Valen searched his mind for words, his mind clogged with various emotions. "Sorry about that," was all he could think to say.

"Don't be sorry, it's okay!"

Valen didn't dare meet his gaze as he felt shy. Silence followed, Valen's embarrassment stubborn to fade. He felt ridiculous from both his episode and the fact that he had lingered in Rorrik's embrace, hypnotized by his purring. He couldn't shake a feeling of silliness.

"...Did you not take a shower?" Rorrik suddenly broke the quiet.

That added to Valen's blush; it must have been pretty obvious. "I never got around to it... I was trying to catch up on some sleep." That was mostly a fib.

"Oh, okay," Rorrik accepted. "...Any luck?"

Valen felt ashamed as he shook his head.

"Well, I can leave you alone if you want to try some more," Rorrik offered, standing up.

"No!" Valen cried, perhaps too desperately. He didn't want to be left alone anymore. "It's okay! I don't think I'm going to get any more..."

"You're going to take a shower, then?"

Valen's shame was punctuated and he hung his head, feeling broken.

"...What's wrong?"

Valen didn't know how to explain himself. Then again, even if he did, he wouldn't want to. The concoction of turmoil the whole kidnapping ordeal had left him with was a burden to understand and reduced him into feeling ashamed and dirty.

"I... I don't want to talk about it," Valen mumbled through a wince.

"...But you've gotta get clean eventually, right?" Rorrik said with a touch of awkwardness.

Valen's stomach twisted with discomfort. He knew the felidaren was right, but the wall of his problems was a daunting one to scale.

However, Rorrik's point was used as a rallying cry for the part of him that desired the morale boost of a shower. He *would* feel a lot better to get it over with, even if the riling of memories was an unpleasant experience. He had to tell himself that it was not the tub from before, that the despicable women that had harassed and assaulted him were not there to hurt him any longer. He had to; he couldn't avoid his hygiene forever.

Besides, he had taken a shower once, he could do it again!

Despite the logic of it all, the shadow of his nightmare and memories still daunted him.

"You're right," the demorinkin said regardless, standing up to approach the dresser to grab a fresh pair of pajamas, ignoring the folded clothes that sat on top of it, his vest included.

"…You're not going to change into your new clothes?"

"It's more comfortable this way…" The reminder of his vest gnawed at him, adding to his distress.

"Oh…"

Valen briefly wondered why Rorrik seemed disappointed until the reminder of the felidaren's endeavors to get the vest back answered the question. Rorrik had gone through a lot to salvage it, and *this* was how Valen repaid that gesture? The guilt the realization induced was another log onto the fire of his troubles.

The least he could do was excuse himself. "I just," Valen started, his eyes falling onto the vest. "I… I can't believe he did that."

"Who did what?"

"My dad… why did he enchant it and not tell me?"

"The vest? I don't know… At least it's not a bad enchantment?"

Valen disagreed as his confidence issues raced to the forefront of his mind. "I don't know…"

Rorrik waited, Valen unable to see his face as the demorinkin's back was to him.

"I mean, how do… how do I even know what was the vest and what wasn't? I always wore it when I went out, and I thought I had made friends but… for all I know I'm… I'm not even likable."

"Pff, you're plenty likable!" Rorrik jumped in. "That's a silly worry, Valen!"

"No, it's not!" Valen swung around to glare at him. "You don't understand! How would you even know, huh?!"

Rorrik looked away, sheepishness spreading across his features. "Well, I—*we* all thought you were likable even without the vest…"

Valen's argument sputtered to an abrupt halt; the demorinkin couldn't help but blush at the gaping hole in his logic.

"Well—! You guys… you… it's different. Back in Akarth I had to use my charisma to form contacts with people. I probably only succeeded because of the vest…" It bit at his pride to confess it out loud.

"...Like, what kind of contacts?" Rorrik pressed.

"For instance, I would play a riddle game to earn things at the market. It was likely because of the vest that I could do that!"

Rorrik blinked at that before shrugging. "Well, maybe your dad was just trying to help you?"

"Help me?! How was that *helping me*? Now I'm doubting myself and it's all his fault!" Moisture welled up in Valen's eyes, the betrayal still fresh.

Rorrik frowned heavily. "I don't think he meant it like that..."

"Well, the damage is done!" He stormed past Rorrik with pajamas in hand and set off to take his shower, leaving the felidaren behind.

■ ■ ■

Valen stared warily at the water raining down from the shower head, his guts churning with apprehension. He could feel a spatter of moisture as it poured down, the droplets cold on his skin. His nightmare lapped his mind, taunting him with memories he longed to never remember.

He put a hand out to test the stream, the water having the illusion of cold before fading into its actual temperature, lukewarm. Valen swallowed hard and adjusted the temperature to heat it up. Lukewarm turned to hot all too instantly and he retracted his hand, his nerves flaring.

He turned the dial back slightly and once again tested the water, finding it an ideal temperature. He sucked in a deep breath, summoning courage before stepping into the stream.

At first, the same illusion his hand underwent plagued the rest of his body, the water feeling frigid as it collided with his skin. Then, after forcing himself to stand there, the trickery vanished, the true temperature of the water proving comfortable.

He breathed a shaky exhale and leaned against the shower wall, his mind a storm of emotion. His feelings were still riled from his prior conversation with Rorrik, his self-confidence raw and bleeding from the demorinkin admitting his doubts. He winced as the uncertainties pestered him, aggravating the sting even further.

He stood there at the mercy of the storm within him, tears joining the shower's stream. The day had been nothing but stressful, from peril, to sadness, to terror and now finally anger. He wasn't sure how much more he could take; everything felt impossibly overwhelming.

He tried to focus on the warmth of the water, hoping to find comfort there. It did not come easily as he still felt bombarded by his turmoil, but the effort was not completely in vain. He did manage to experience a fraction of peace, the warm water acting as a remedy as it slipped down his body, working at the grime that clung there.

He knew the water would not do the job well enough on its own, however. Hesitantly, he reached for the soap, wanting to get the scrubbing over with quickly. He lathered his hair and then his upper torso, his hands wary to travel down further. He eventually forced them to, even his own hands touching his intimates striking as uncomfortable, the sensation of being touched summoning flashbacks of pain and humiliation.

Following that he was wont to get dressed and end his nakedness. He felt dirty regardless of the fact he had just rinsed himself clean.

He flipped the shower off after washing away the soap and reached for his towel, patting himself dry without delay. He grabbed Rorrik's clothes and got dressed into them, this shirt red and the sweatpants blue. He felt a ping of remorse over not grabbing the gifted clothes Rorrik had given him, but the fact they had been bought to coordinate with his vest was a sour reminder. Still, it wasn't his intention to offend the felidaren...

Valen began to regret yelling at Rorrik. The demorinkin didn't want the felidaren feeling like he was at fault for anything; Valen knew he was only trying to help.

The demorinkin sighed and pushed out of the stall. He tossed the used towel into the basket and began to walk out of the restroom, his mind fogging further and further with guilt.

He reached the hallway and headed back to his room. When he arrived, Rorrik was nowhere to be seen.

The demorinkin frowned and sat on the bed. He was alone yet again.

■ ■ ■

Avalene

Avalene sat waiting in the HQ meeting room, her brow wrinkled with stress. The past night had been a draining one; they had interrogated each of the three prisoners, all delivering the same shock and intensity when asked if the name 'Vaaskiir' meant anything to them. Each captive was kept in a different place of confinement, which meant they could not have planned such a reaction. It was all very troubling.

Now, she was waiting for Kyla to arrive. The ex-government worker had given the felidaren a call that afternoon to arrange a meeting to discuss news concerning the investigation. Avalene had suggested the meeting be at HQ, which Kyla had accepted without question.

The tortoiseshell was due to arrive any minute. Avalene waited, her mind unable to stop itself from replaying the sight of the crazed prisoners and their bloodthirsty eyes. She shook her head, disturbed.

The sight of the door opening disrupted the imagery, and in walked Kyla.

"Thank you for coming here," Avalene greeted. "We have much to discuss."

"It's no problem. We can't always be hosting the party," Kyla laughed. She sat down without delay. "Can I ask why, though?"

"It feels safer this way. The boy is there, not here."

"Fair enough. Especially since my sons ran into some curious eyes earlier."

Avalene raised her brow. "Oh...?"

"They were able to shake them, but Gavin also mentioned that there was some curiosity over felidaren with a client of Bluebird's. She suspects someone got a hold of the witness reports and is trying to find a trail. But, we'll figure that all out, don't worry about it! It wouldn't be the first time someone has tried to track down the family."

Avalene stiffly nodded. "I trust you."

"But! That's not why I'm here! What have you found out?" Kyla redirected the conversation.

Avalene gathered her thoughts for a moment. "The boy's suspicions were right. His attackers are the Fangs of Hellbane, the prisoners themselves confirmed it."

Kyla's face tightened at the reveal. "I was afraid of that..."

"That is not all. Apparently, his family name means... a lot to the organization."

"What do you mean?"

Avalene retrieved a stack of papers from a file on the table and slid them across the surface to Kyla as a way of explanation. "These are the transcripts for each interrogation."

Kyla read them over, her green eyes fast and concentrated. The felidaren's face grew even tighter at what she read. "There... definitely seems to be a grudge."

"At the minimum, yes," Avalene replied, the *joy* the prisoners displayed over hunting down the child a chilling reminder. "I have my people looking into the name 'Vaaskiir', but nothing has come up yet in their research. Granted, it is early..." The human sized Kyla with a serious stare. "You've made strides with the boy, correct? Perhaps he can tell us more."

The felidaren looked up from the files, concern in her eyes. "I'll see what he knows..." She looked back down to the papers, her ears pressing back.

"The prisoner's... zeal was unsettling, but luckily they are trapped under our supervision. Since they had not known the boy's identity, we can assume the rest of their organization is unaware. However, I admit that I feel uncomfortable with them remaining where they are. Thus, I have arranged plans with the warden to have them locked up in his prison."

"You still can pull strings there, right?" Kyla questioned, concern in her voice.

"I made plans with the warden, didn't I? He will allow me to question them further and do whatever is needed in the rest of the investigation."

"Did you fill him in on details?"

"I let him know that they are members of an extremist group that had involved themselves with my work, that is all."

Kyla nodded, seemingly satisfied with that answer.

Avalene couldn't fight back a sigh, her anger and stress over the situation spilling out in a long, drawn out exhale before admitting, "I did not anticipate something like this. We've never dealt with anything of this... intensity before."

"None of us saw it coming. Believe me."

"At this point we should already be trying to find the boy a new family, not hunting down his would-be murderers!" Avalene said, her tone rising with frustration. Then, much more quietly, she said, "I sometimes wonder if this is all beyond our expertise."

"It's not beyond you, just different than your typical case."

Avalene shook her head, unconvinced. "This group is extremist and has shown to be organized if they had an eye on the human trafficking of this city." The human looked away, her nerves pulsing. "I worry we are making very determined enemies. Gods, I already have enough on my plate, and this—"

"You can't just abandon him! Besides! The damage has been done, hasn't it? If you've come this far, you might as well see it through!"

Avalene narrowed her eyes at her old friend. "How do we know the boy is even innocent, Kyla?!"

"This sounds like nothing he personally did wrong! Should he have to pay for his family's mistakes? That hardly seems fair!" Kyla slapped the paper in front of her. "Besides, it says here that whatever happened with the Vaaskiir family was an 'attempt at salvation' – hardly sounds criminalizing!"

Avalene exhaled at the heat of Kyla's fire; the felidaren brought up good points. "You're right," she admitted. "Forgive me."

Kyla stared at her long and hard before stiffly nodding.

Silence took the room, and so Avalene thought it appropriate to bring up the next topic. "I cannot imagine Niem is happy the boy is still staying there."

"He's been out of town, actually," Kyla said, her tone returning to normal. "Visiting his sisters for a quarterly report in Denbrook."

"Hard to believe it's already been about six months into the year..."

Kyla weakly grinned. "I hear you there."

"Well..." Avalene started, standing up. "I have compensation for safe-housing the boy, a week's worth of pay." She pulled out a bag of money from her jacket, the purse heavy.

"Has it already been a week since we rescued him?" Kyla marveled.

"It has been, yes. A very stressful one at that." She walked over to where Kyla sat and offered the payment.

"Well…" Kyla took the money and grinned down at it crookedly. "Niem is often swayed by the jingling of a coin purse. If there's some reward to the risk, he'll come around. We'll be able to keep the demorinkin safe for as long as needed."

"It's a good thing that is double pay, then. Makes it doubly convincing."

"You know the family well, Avalene," Kyla chuckled. She then sobered up, her smile fading. "I'll see what information I can find out. Luckily, Valen has been cooperative." She put the purse into a pouch on her belt before setting her gaze back on Avalene. "Is there any other way I can help?"

"You're already doing much more than you should, Kyla," Avalene dismissed.

"But let me know if there's anything else I can do."

"I will, if something arises." The vigilante's eyes fell onto Kyla's pregnant belly. "By the way, how did your doctor's appointment go earlier?"

Kyla smiled. "Baby is still healthy!"

Avalene nodded. "That is good news." She hesitated before continuing, "…and how about yourself?"

Kyla's smile faltered for a second before returning. "Well, I'm not dying," the felidaren chuckled.

Avalene frowned. "So your condition has not improved?"

"I'm fine, Avalene. Pregnancy is always a burden on the body — it's nothing unexpected."

"Yes, this is especially true when you are already ill…" Avalene couldn't help but narrow her eyes. She hoped Kyla's decision to keep her surprise pregnancy would not have the repercussions she feared.

"Don't you start sounding like Niem, now!" Kyla laughed, the vigilante pinning it as forced. "Don't let it concern you, Avalene." There was some bite to the words; hidden, but there.

"Alright, Kyla. If you insist."

"I do," Kyla replied bluntly.

Silence followed their tension. Kyla was the one to break it. "I'll update you with whatever I find out. May the shadows guide and protect you."

"And let Nocturna smile on you. May her luck bless your efforts."

Chapter 22

Kyla

Kyla sat in her bedroom that evening, her eyes on her corresponder as nerves fizzed in her gut. Niem's contact page shone on the surface, a button push away from being called. She expelled her hesitation and hit the button, lifting the device to her ear.

It rang a few times before Niem's voice curtly answered, "Kyla."

"There's my mate. How has it been going?" Kyla spoke cheerfully into the corresponder.

"I don't have much time to talk, and you're calling for a reason, so what is it?"

"A couple reasons, actually. One, we were paid today for housing the boy. I think you'll like the amount." It was better to soften him up with some good news before springing the bad.

"He's still there?" Niem grunted.

"Of course he is. We're still figuring everything out, and you agreed —"

"I know what I agreed to." She heard him give an agitated sigh. "How much?"

"Double pay on top of an already generous compensation. You can't help but admit that's a nice price, can you?"

Niem was quiet for a few seconds. "Well, what else?"

She knew her mate well enough to recognize his approval. She continued. "Two, I'm letting you know that the boy will be sleeping in Rorrik's room for the rest of his stay." She figured that if she delivered it as more of a statement than a question then it would be harder to resist.

"He'll what—" Niem stammered. "No, Kyla! First you bring him into our hideout without approval and now this?!"

Kyla made sure to remain calm. "It's not like the boy himself is a threat, Niem. He's already staying here, so what's the harm?"

"I do not understand why you are making it your job to take care of him!" Niem growled. "It's not like you're short on children to look after — why are you so invested in this?!"

"I have my reasons, Niem," Kyla answered firmly. "It's not important to this conversation."

"Of course it is important! I need to understand why this job has made you put our family in unneeded danger!"

Kyla sighed, her own frustration building. "Our family will be *fine*, Niem. The boy, however, would not have been."

"It was not our responsibility! Porte can handle her own rescued brats!"

"We're getting paid plenty, Niem! How is this so different from all the other jobs we do?!" Kyla shot back, her cool leaving her.

"The boy has hunters, Kyla! You're earning us new enemies!"

"It's nothing we aren't used to! It's too late to turn back — we've already been over this!"

"But now you want him in *our home* — where *your son* sleeps! It's never enough for you, is it?!"

"He *needs* this, Niem!" Desperation slipped into Kyla's voice. "Just *please*, let me help him!"

Niem went quiet for several drawn-out moments. "I don't see why it's even necessary! Why does he 'need' this?" Her mate's voice was lowering in volume; Kyla took that as a good sign.

"He has nightmares, Niem. Being alone isn't good for him," she answered in a calmer tone, her voice pleading.

Niem hissed. "Gods! And what does Rorrik think about it?!"

"He wants to help him, too," Kyla replied truthfully. "He's fine with it; excited, even."

Niem was silent.

"*Please*, Niem?"

Another hiss answered her. "I have to go. If anything happens because of this, Kyla, so help me…"

"Is that a yes, then?"

Her mate hung up, offering all the clarification she needed.

Kyla put her corresponder back in her pocket and a small, relieved grin graced her lips. Apprehension was quick to chase it off, however. She recalled what she had read in the interrogation transcripts, the words of the prisoners a sobering reminder of what she had signed her family up for. Niem was not wrong to worry; they had made enemies, indeed.

She shook her head. She could not regret anything now. As she had told Avalene, the damage was done; all they could do now was see it through.

"What did Dad say?" she then heard Rorrik's voice ask.

She looked over to the door and saw Rorrik poking his head into her bedroom, his eyes big and nervous.

Kyla couldn't help but smile at him despite her anxieties. "He agreed to it."

"Really?!" Rorrik looked excited but then the emotion quickly vanished from his expression. Her son dropped his gaze on the floor, his ears pressing back. "I don't know if Valen will want to, though."

"Hm? What do you mean?" The two boys had gotten along fine, why did Rorrik suddenly have doubts?

"He got mad at me earlier today…" Rorrik explained in a small voice. "We were talking about his vest and he got angry."

"What made him angry about that?"

"He's really upset about the enchantment," Rorrik elaborated. "He says he can't tell what was the vest and what wasn't, so now he's doubting himself and it's all his dad's fault. I told him that his dad was probably just trying to help him, but that made him really mad and he stormed off…"

Kyla nodded her head slowly, processing Rorrik's story. "So he thinks he's not charismatic?"

Rorrik moved his head in a nod. "At first he thought he wasn't even likable without the vest. I told him that was silly, though…"

"Well, it sounds like he's madder at the enchantment than you, kit. You have to understand that his emotions are heightened right now; don't take it personally."

Rorrik didn't appear all that convinced. "I… I scared him pretty bad earlier, too."

"Scared him?" Kyla echoed, raising her eyebrows.

"Since Talis, Calvin, and I had to stay here today I decided to go down and talk to him but he thought I was the Fangs of Hellbane… He got really freaked out and locked the door. When he noticed it was me he let me in, but he was still shaking and crying… I got him to calm down but I still feel pretty bad…"

"Well, at least you were able to calm him down," Kyla pointed out. Rorrik's ability to do so gave Kyla confidence that her son would be able to help the demorinkin with his nightmares after all.

"Yeah, but…" Rorrik sighed. "I don't know…"

"Well, why don't we see how he's doing and tell him the good news?"

Rorrik looked nervous at the idea. "Okay," he agreed, regardless.

Kyla walked out of the room and began heading towards the guest wing, Rorrik following along. They walked in silence, Rorrik's eyes on his feet as they went. When they finally arrived at Valen's room the door was closed.

Kyla gave a gentle knock. "Valen, it's Mrs. Cattiaikin and Rorrik. Can we come in?"

The door clicked open softly and Valen came into view, his eyes avoiding the two of them as he went to sit on the bed, his tail dragging behind him. The demorinkin wore a pair of Rorrik's clothes instead of the nicer ones her son had purchased, and no vest decorated his torso. She didn't wonder why thanks to Rorrik's earlier explanation.

Kyla stepped into the room while Rorrik waited in the threshold looking awkward.

"Hey there, cub. We've got some news for you," Kyla began softly. "We were thinking that you could sleep in Rorrik's room from here on out. What do you say to that?"

Valen's head shot up in surprise. "What?" The demorinkin's eyes darted to Rorrik before jumping back to Kyla. "Are... are you sure?"

"We are. We figure it's better than being here all by your lonesome."

Valen flushed and broke eye contact with the felidaren, his demeanor reluctant.

Kyla looked between Valen and Rorrik, the mother sensing some awkwardness between her son and the demorinkin; it was probably best for her to leave so that they could sort everything out.

"Well, I'm sure everyone is hungry. I'll go get dinner started," the mother excused herself. "If you need me, I'll be in the kitchen." With that, she slipped past Rorrik in the doorway and left the two of them alone.

．．．

Rorrik

Rorrik felt uncomfortable as he stood in the threshold, his gaze avoiding Valen. He wanted to look so that he could judge how the demorinkin was taking the news of his new sleeping arrangements, but awkwardness disallowed him.

The tabby eventually couldn't shake a feeling that his presence was unwanted. He was tempted to follow his mother into the kitchen when Valen spoke up quietly.

"I'm... I'm sorry for yelling earlier."

Rorrik's ears perked before folding back into a press, his eyes finally finding the demorinkin. The felidaren was opening his mouth to say his own apology when Valen continued.

"I was just really upset... I know you're only trying to help," the demorinkin sighed, his eyes on the bed. "It's not your fault... I just don't know how to feel about anything right now."

"It's okay!" Rorrik hurriedly forgave him, eager to make the demorinkin feel assured. "I'm sorry, too. I didn't mean to make it worse..."

Valen looked to Rorrik and shook his head. "Like I said, it's not your fault."

Rorrik didn't know what to say after that. Apparently, neither did Valen as they both were quiet. They cut eye contact.

Rorrik's vision hesitantly returned to Valen. "Well... at least you don't have to stay alone in this room anymore?" the tabby tested, watching the demorinkin's reaction closely.

Valen turned his attention back on him with a weak grin. "Are you sure you're okay with me staying with you?"

"Are you kidding?" the felidaren beamed. "It's gonna be great! It'll be like a sleepover!"

Valen blinked, seemingly surprised at Rorrik's enthusiasm. The demorinkin's grin became a tad more confident. "If you say so…"

"I know so!" He gestured for the demorinkin to follow him and hopped out into the hallway. "Come on, let me show you around!"

. . .

Valen

'*Looks like I don't have a choice.*' Not that the demorinkin was unwilling for a tour, but the aftermath of his stressful day had left him exhausted.

He pushed up from the bed to slowly follow and met Rorrik out in the hall, the felidaren appearing antsy to get the tour underway.

"Let's go!" Rorrik urged before setting down the wing with much more vigor than Valen could match.

Valen couldn't help but grin at his new friend's excitement; it touched the demorinkin that Rorrik was eager to house him. He could not stave off a feeling of anxiety, however. His nights were definitely not pleasant as nightmares haunted him regularly. It comforted Valen to know that he would have someone else around in the wake of them, yes, but he didn't want to inconvenience anybody, either. That, and his desperation for comfort embarrassed him. He thought of both of his episodes that day, and his cheeks flushed with humiliation.

They made it to the set of doors Valen had previously not been allowed to enter and his apprehension intensified. The demorinkin felt like he was intruding on the family, considering guests were not typically allowed in their private quarters.

"Are you sure this is okay?"

"Yep! It was my mom's idea, and my dad said yes!" He put a hand on one of the door handles and held it there before there was a click that reminded Valen of a key turning a lock. Rorrik then opened one of the doors and held it open, all smiles as he gestured for Valen to walk in.

Valen didn't move at first, his curiosity piqued by the doors.

Rorrik noted his fascination. "The doors have a magical lock on them," he elaborated. "Only my family and approved, close friends can open them!"

Valen's feeling of intrusion did not lessen at that information. '*They're so worried about unwanted guests that they have a fancy rucanic lock!*'

Still, Rorrik urged him on with an eager hand wave. "Come on!"

Valen obeyed and walked through the passageway, Rorrik letting go of the door so he could follow. The door slowly returned to its place in the frame, a solid click confirming its closing.

"I don't think there's a lock from this way, so you can open them fine from this side," Rorrik informed with a scratch of his chin. "Anyway, let me show you around!"

The doors had delivered them into another hallway, several more doors lining each side of the walls.

"This is where our rooms are," the tabby explained as he began to lead them forward.

As they walked down Valen counted four doors on each side as well as an archway at the end of the right wall.

"That door is my room." Rorrik pointed to the first door on the left. His finger began to jump to all the other doors on the left side. "That's Jate's, that's Quinn's, and that's Gavin's." The felidaren then gestured to the fourth door on the right side. "That's Calvin's and Talis' room. We used to share but I finally got my own room when I turned thirteen this month!"

'So he's my age.'

Rorrik gestured to the rest of the doors on the right. "Those are just empty bedrooms for now. We end up using them for storage a lot."

They arrived at the end of the hallway and it revealed to turn left and stretch onwards, a few more doors awaiting beyond.

Rorrik walked into the archway on the right wall. "This is our rec room!"

Valen followed him inside and a decent-sized room revealed. Several chairs gathered around a ping pong table that sat in the back of the space, and in the first area of the room was a desk joined by a seating area, completed with a television. Shelving adorned the walls behind the desk, several books and supplies stored there.

"We love to play ping pong in here! Do you like ping pong?"

"I, uh, I've never played," Valen answered, his eyes drifting onto the table.

"We'll have to play later! It's really fun. Anyways, moving on!"

Rorrik guided them back into the hallway and the tabby pointed to the next two doors on the back wall. "These are both bathrooms. They basically look the same inside." He knocked at the first door and waited, inciting no answer from within. With that, the tabby opened the door and flipped on the light.

Valen peeked inside, spotting a bathroom clad in soft, light blue colors. All the essentials of a complete washroom could be spotted including a toilet, tub, and sink. A full body mirror hung on the wall and a cabinet stood next to the toilet.

Rorrik nodded to the cabinet. "That's filled with towels and toilet paper and stuff." He shut off the light then closed the door.

Instead of walking down the rest of the hallway, Rorrik pointed towards the remaining two doors further down the hall. "That first door is my parent's room, and the other one is a spare bedroom."

Valen nodded as he absorbed all the information, his nerves still high.

"Come on, let me show you my room!" Rorrik hurried back down the way they came, leaving Valen behind. The demorinkin pushed himself to catch up, Rorrik already waiting by his bedroom, the door open. The felidaren disappeared inside as Valen arrived.

Valen followed him in, a medium-sized bedroom presenting itself. A queen bed covered in a simple, striped purple comforter was tucked into the left corner of the back, and a wooden dresser lined the wall the door was on. The room was sparse in decoration, but a tall mirror did sit up against the wall next to the dresser, and a nightlight was plugged into an outlet by the bed.

"I just moved in here so it's a little empty..." Rorrik excused with a weak chuckle. He perked back up. "We'll bring in another bed for you! It can go over there." The felidaren gestured to the right corner of the back wall, the space perhaps big enough for a twin bed.

Valen weakly grinned and went back to taking in the room. He wasn't sure what to be feeling as he stared at where his bed would be.

"Hmmm. Oh, oh! We have bunkbeds left over from when we were kits, maybe if we used just the top bunk we could put a desk or something underneath it! What do you think?"

Rorrik almost acted like Valen was moving in! He wasn't sure how to respond. "Whatever works," he eventually said. Valen had never slept in a bunk bed before, although the idea of a top bunk had always intrigued him.

"Great! Come on, I know where we can find one!" Rorrik scurried out of the room, once again leaving Valen behind. The demorinkin fended off a sigh of worry and moved to follow the felidaren.

Rorrik was poking his head out of the double doors that led back into the rest of the hideout when Valen walked out of the room.

"Jaaate! Gavin! Come here!"

"You could at least say please!" Valen heard an older voice answer with a laugh. "What's going on?"

"We need to move a bed!" Rorrik hollered back.

"Alright, we'll be right there," another voice replied.

Rorrik pulled his head back in before hurrying up to the first door on the right wall, heading inside, Valen close behind.

A crowded room full of various supplies and bins revealed, as well as a cluster of mattresses and bed frames against the far wall. Rorrik bounced up to an intact, taller frame, his tail ticking fast. The frame was made from a sturdy wood and looked to be the top of a bunk bed.

Valen was still studying it when he heard footsteps. He checked behind him to see two of Rorrik's older brothers walk into the room, Valen unable to tell which ones. The demorinkin stepped out of their way and bumped into one of the bins awkwardly.

"Moving a bed, eh?" one of the brothers asked. "Which one?"

"This one!" Rorrik patted the frame.

"A bunk bed? Didn't you just get a queen bed?" the same sibling pondered.

"We're going to put a desk where the bottom bed would be."

Rorrik's kin got a chuckle out of that.

"Well, let's get it moved, then," the other brother suggested.

Valen went out into the hall as they began to clear a path for the bed, his awkwardness and anxieties ever building. A long exhale left him, and he rubbed at his neck, his eyes on the ground, physically and mentally exhausted.

Shuffling and quick chatter he did not understand came from the room as he waited. There was some laughter and then some banging and then more shuffling. It did not take long for the nose of the bed frame to poke out the door, one of the older brothers there guiding it out. Then, the rest of the frame emerged from the storage room and the three siblings carried it across the hall and into the bedroom with apparent ease, their teamwork making it look effortless. Valen couldn't help but gawk; he would have guessed it to be more of a challenge to move it than that!

A few seconds passed and the brothers scurried out of the bedroom and back into the storage room. After some more shuffling and laughter they emerged carrying the mattress, their movements even quicker this time as they transported it into Rorrik's room. The entire chore was done within a matter of a minute or so.

Valen stood there impressed as the three came out to meet him in the hallway.

"Anything else?" one of the older asked.

"Well, I was thinking maybe a desk," Rorrik reminded.

"Right, right. You mentioned that," the same brother nodded. "Let's get it done, then!"

With that they disappeared into one of the other spare rooms on the right side of the hallway. Valen's curiosity had him poking his head inside to see what the new room looked like. This room was stuffed with various tables and chairs as well as some other miscellaneous furniture.

The brothers approached a smaller desk amongst the storage.

"This one alright?"

Rorrik nodded.

"Alright. Rorrik, you grab a chair, we'll carry it over," the other one said.

Out they went with the furniture and into Rorrik's room, their quickness still impressing the demorinkin. Valen listened as some scooting and adjusting of furniture came from the room and walked to the door to peer inside.

An intact bunk bed complete with a mattress now barely fit in the right corner, a desk replacing the bottom bunk. *'I suppose that would make it a loft bed, huh?'*

"It's a squeeze, but it works!" one of the unknown siblings said, amused.

"It'll work just fine," the other contributed.

He was right when he said it was a squeeze; hardly two feet or so sat in between Rorrik's bed and the new one, allowing the desk's chair very little space to scoot out, but just barely enough.

"Thanks for helping!" Rorrik said.

"Anytime, little brother." One of them ruffled his hair, to which Rorrik pushed his hand away with a laugh.

The exchange sent a pang through Valen's chest as thoughts of Karreo came flooding back. The demorinkin quit his peering into the room and leaned up against the hallway wall, the pain growing overwhelming. He tried not to be envious of the brothers, but his heart did not comply. He closed his eyes, missing Karreo terribly. *'It's all my fault...'*

His pain was interrupted as he heard someone walk out of the room. Valen opened his eyes to find the two older brothers staring at him.

"It's great you'll be staying with us! Should be a lot better than that guest bedroom!" one of them said. "I'm Jate, by the way. I know we've met, but most people need a few reminders, ha ha!" He nodded his head to his brother. "That's Gavin."

Valen pushed back his inner agony and bluffed a grin. "Uh, thank you both for helping." He quickly added, "Jate and Gavin."

Jate chuckled. "You're welcome! Dinner should be ready soon. We'll talk more then!"

The two turned to leave, and Valen forced himself to take some mental notes of the two of them. Jate's hair was longer and tied in a low ponytail, and Gavin's fur was a darker shade of gray. It seemed typical for Jate to have a happy, amused demeanor while Gavin was a tad more reserved. Valen felt confident enough that he had made some headway in telling at least those two apart.

"Come try out your bed!" Valen heard Rorrik say from inside the room.

Valen sighed quietly and pulled himself away from the wall, his body feeling heavy. He headed inside to find Rorrik up on the loft bed, grinning. When he saw Valen, the tabby jumped and landed onto the queen bed with a roll.

"That'll be fun, huh?!" Rorrik laughed, entertained.

Valen blinked, impressed at the felidaren's form during the stunt. Valen highly doubted his own jump and roll would look so graceful – not that he planned on doing anything of the sort.

"Try it!"

"Last I checked it's for sleeping..." Valen pointed out, a small smirk threatening.

Rorrik guffawed at that. "It can have various purposes!"

Valen shook his head before walking up to the loft bed. He stared up at it for a lengthy moment before hoisting himself up, his climb aided by a couple of pegs along the boards. He felt clumsy as his sore muscles made his movements awkward, but he made it up to the top, regardless.

He sat on the mattress, the softness and comfort of a real bed still an unfamiliar sensation to him. He recalled the nest back in the clock tower, and once again Karreo bled into his thoughts, spurring a frown.

"...You don't like it?" Rorrik mumbled from below.

"What? No! It — it's great!" Valen was quick to clarify. "Sorry, I... I was just thinking about something." His frown only grew at admitting it out loud.

"What's that?"

Valen set his eyes on the mattress. "It's... just still weird to be sleeping in a bed again. Considering..." He let the thought trail off, hoping the tabby would catch his drift.

To Valen's relief, he did. "Oh..."

An awkward silence followed.

"Well, what do you want to do tonight?" Rorrik broke the quiet.

Valen's anxiety flared. "Uhh..." Truthfully, he was incredibly tired in both mind and body, but he felt guilty over the aspect of crushing the felidaren's excitement. "I'm not sure. What are our options?"

"Umm. I don't know, lots of stuff!"

"Like what?"

"Like... truth or dare... or would you rather... or—"

Valen's nervousness peaked. "Maybe we could just talk or something..."

"That works!" Rorrik seemed excited enough at the prospect, relieving Valen.

"Boys! Dinner is ready!" Mrs. Catty's voice then called out.

Rorrik offered Valen a sizable grin. "You heard her!"

Chapter 23

Valen

Dinner was pork chops with a side of mashed potatoes and green beans. Valen once again felt a plethora of emotions at being offered such a rich, complete meal. The guilt within him was real and controlling as it harassed his mind and body. His thoughts already being on Karreo, he could not help but linger on the fact that his brother would never again get to enjoy a better meal than sliced bread and peaches in his mortal time. It was so unfair that Valen was dropped into an improved life while Karreo had been forever denied a better existence.

Those feelings along with the combined stress of the day did not support an appetite of any degree. He felt nauseous over the idea of eating as the shame punctuating his thoughts was unkind to his guts.

Fortunately, his lack of appetite did not seem to attract questions and concerns from the family this time. At least, not audibly. Mrs. Catty had given him a look, but it was an understanding one. Rorrik had also glanced over at his plate a few times, but the felidaren never said anything about it. Instead, he eagerly chatted away with his brothers, their conversations blurring into gibberish as Valen sat there miserably.

He wanted to ask to be excused but was loath to draw attention to himself. Thus, he kept quiet and still, his eyes on his lap as dinner passed by. Everyone else eventually cleared their plates and they were delivered into the sink.

"Rorrik, Gavin, you have kitchen duty tonight," Mrs. Catty told her children. "Help me get these dishes loaded, will you?"

Rorrik groaned and Gavin nodded.

"Ha ha! Sucks to be you!"

"I would mind what I say, Calvin. You have kitchen duty tomorrow."

"Whaaat?" Valen noted that Calvin was the ten-year-old with slight attitude. His gray fur also had a browner hue in it than his other siblings.

"At least you're in the clear for now!" another brother laughed, Valen able to recognize him as Jate thanks to the ponytail.

"Jate, can you go fetch some sheets, a pillow, and a blanket for Valen?"

"Of course!" Jate smiled before leaving the kitchen.

"Talis, Calvin, make sure you get your baths before bed!" the mother then ordered, the two youngest answering with giggles as they ran off.

Valen proceeded to make notes on the siblings. '*So Talis is the youngest one...*' Was that all of them?

"Any way I can help, Mother?" another said, answering Valen's wonder.

"Hm... Why don't you keep an eye on your brothers; make sure they get ready for bed."

"Consider it done." The unknown brother grinned and turned his attention on Valen. "I feel our introduction wasn't exactly the clearest, so to refresh your memory, I'm Quinn!" The felidaren extended a hand.

Valen took it and gave a brief shake. "I'm Valen."

That made Quinn laugh. "I knew that, but it's nice to be properly introduced! We'll have to chat more later, Valen. For now..." The felidaren began to head towards the private quarters.

Valen searched for something noteworthy of Quinn and saw that his fur seemed to be the brightest gray of them all. However, all his mental notes already seemed to be escaping him as his mind felt overloaded with information.

He sat at the table as Gavin, Rorrik, and Mrs. Catty worked, unable to chase off a perception that he should be helping in some way. '*You'd be rude to not offer!*' "Is there any way I can help?"

"Don't trouble yourself with anything, cub. You're our guest. The offer is sweet, though, thank you." Mrs. Catty glanced over her shoulder to reply.

Valen nodded, not completely convinced he should be doing nothing but not ready to challenge Mrs. Catty's point, either. He remained seated in silence as the family cleaned up the kitchen, the chore going by hastily with the help of three. The time was shortened even further by the fact that the family seemed to be a competent, focused bunch.

Rorrik came by to wipe the table, a small grin on his face as he worked around Valen. The tabby finished the job and dropped off the used rag in a bucket by the sink.

"Thank you, boys. Good work."

Both of her children nodded in response.

"Well, you know where to find me if you need anything. Goodnight!"

■ ■ ■

Rorrik was up in Valen's bed tucking a sheet onto the mattress. Valen sat in the chair at the desk, his eyes wandering about the room.

"So... Have you had any sleepovers before?" Rorrik wondered.

"A long, long time ago..." Memories of Valen's first life flashed by of friends long dropped out of contact. It all felt ages ago.

"We don't get to have them often. And never, *ever* here; you're the first!"

Valen looked up and gave a sideways grin, his sensation of intruding rearing. "Is that so?"

"Yeah! None of our friends are even allowed down here to begin with, let alone in our bedrooms!" Rorrik finished lining the bed with the sheet and began covering a pillow with a case.

A wonder that had been gnawing at Valen since his rescue grew too demanding to ignore. "So... why *am* I allowed down here? Like, in the first place?"

Rorrik blinked and looked down at him, seeming unprepared for the question. "Well, because we rescued you, duh!"

"Okay, but... *why* did you rescue me? What were you even doing there?"

"Miss Porte hired my mom to intercept you. At first we were supposed to bring you to her, but then, well... you got attacked so we brought you here so you would be safe..."

"I just... don't understand why..." Valen broke eye contact as his stomach twisted with stress. "I mean, you didn't even know who I was..."

"Miss Porte helps save lots of kids, it's her job."

"But you didn't *have* to bring me here. I'm not unthankful, I'm just confused why you..." He tried to think of how to word it.

Rorrik waited, his head tilting.

"Why you... I don't know..." The words still escaped him. "It seems risky..."

"Well, it's part of the mission. We were hired to save you, and this was the safest place."

"So you'd just do that for a stranger?"

Rorrik laughed somewhat uncomfortably. "I mean, it's not like we don't get anything out of it... It *is* a job, after all."

Valen blinked. "You're being paid to keep me here?"

"Well, yeah! I mean, well, uh..." Rorrik pressed his ears back, suddenly looking as if he wished he could snatch back the last words from his mouth.

"That actually helps it make a lot more sense..." It helped ease Valen's guilt and confusion to know that the family was being rewarded for their efforts. "Why bring me *here*, though?" He gestured around Rorrik's room. "Into your actual home? That wasn't needed, was it?"

"Because we want to help! It's not just 'cause of the money..."

"Couldn't you have just slept in the guest bedroom with me?"

"I guess, but those rooms are so tiny! There's only room for one bed. This is more comfortable for everyone." The felidaren frowned down at him. "Why, does it bother you to be here?"

"I just... I feel like I'm intruding..." Valen's face flushed. "You don't have to go through this much trouble for me..."

"We don't *have* to, sure. But we are. It's not that huge of a deal!"

"But you have those private doors! Your typical guests aren't even allowed in here, you said it yourself! So why am I so different?"

Rorrik shrugged. "You're not any kind of threat."

"What, and your typical guests are?" Valen scoffed.

"Well... We're not always completely sure, I suppose."

"...What?"

"I mean, sure, we trust them enough to work for us... But that doesn't mean we trust them where we sleep." Rorrik forced a chuckle.

"...What kind of people are your typical guests?" Valen asked, worry joining the bewilderment on his expression.

"People who work with us," Rorrik told him matter-of-factly.

Valen processed the new information, his mind swimming. What kind of work did the family do, then? *'He mentioned that Porte lady... Maybe they're vigilantes or something?'*

He shook that wonder out of his mind, still not satisfied with Rorrik's explanation. "But what if I *was* a threat? What then?"

"Then shame on us for trusting you, I guess," Rorrik laughed, amused. "It's not like you are, though. Unless you're admitting to lying?" Rorrik mockingly narrowed his eyes.

"Well, no! I just — I'm trying to understand where you're coming from!"

"It's not that hard to understand, Valen. We want to help and so we are. You need to stop overthinking it."

"Well, sorry," Valen muttered. "It's just... weird when you go from people hating you to people wanting to help..."

Rorrik went back to frowning. "We're not like Akarth, Valen..."

"It's not just Akarth, Rorrik! It's everywhere! You just don't get it!"

The tabby didn't appear to know what to say as he broke eye contact with Valen. Then, in a quiet voice, "You're right. I don't get it..."

The felidaren climbed down and walked over the queen bed to get around Valen. He approached his dresser and grabbed some clothes.

"I'll... I'll be right back," the tabby mumbled. He left the room, leaving Valen to feel bad over his outburst.

The demorinkin sighed and climbed into the loft bed. He just wanted to sleep.

■ ■ ■

Rorrik

The sleepover wasn't going quite as he planned. *'What did I expect, though?'* Sometimes the felidaren forgot that the demorinkin was still recovering from all the horrible things he had been through. His mother had said that Rorrik needed to be patient and not take things personally, but as the tabby slunk down the hallway and into the bathroom he failed at the latter. All the repeated slip-ups of upsetting Valen were weighing down on him; he sat on the closed toilet seat and put his chin into his hands, bummed.

He waited a few minutes before forcing himself to get dressed into his pajamas, the act of doing so in the bathroom strange. He knew that he should probably respect his guest and not change in front of him, however. Rorrik was not shy in that respect, but Valen might be. It was better to play it safe.

He checked himself in the mirror, the reflection he saw looking handsome as ever. At least, he hoped so. Rorrik stood barely five feet tall and wore his straight, brunette hair an inch or so above his shoulders. His fur was a dark gray with brown accents, and cream-colored markings showed above his eyes, around his mouth, and on his chin. Several black stripes decorated his cheeks, and the trademark tabby 'M' was on his brow.

Rorrik's facial features took more after his father, having inherited his long face, wider nose, and established chin. There was still some roundness to his features leftover from childhood, but puberty was taking care of that.

He adjusted his hair with his claws and checked his chin for any progress on the mane he was growing, finding the results disappointing. It was hardly obvious even with closer inspection, to his chagrin.

He flexed, a fair amount of muscle responding on his body as he did so. Due to the nature of their work, Rorrik was fairly muscular, although his lithe body type was deceiving of that fact. He stepped back and checked himself out, wondering if others liked what they saw when they looked at him.

He quit his staring to finish prepping for bed. After a speedy brush of his fangs and a quick visit to the toilet he left the bathroom and headed back to his bedroom, trying to stifle out the awkwardness that still lingered from earlier. *'I'll just be careful with what I say from now on! The night can still be fun!'*

Yet, when he walked into the bedroom he found Valen already sleeping up in his bed, his back to the rest of the room.

Rorrik frowned and flipped off the light switch. He crawled into his own bed and sighed as he wiggled under the covers. *'Or not...'*

∎ ∎ ∎

Sleep dodged Rorrik as time passed, the felidaren troubled by a sudden barrage of thoughts over the mysterious stalker from their watch. Why had they been followed; were they right to assume it dealt with Valen? Had the man been listening when Jate and Rorrik briefly talked about the demorinkin? The conversation had been vague and they were high up, so everything should be fine, right?

What if it wasn't? Had they really shaken the man? What if they hadn't and inadvertently created a trail to Valen? Rorrik could not escape a sense of worry. *'Jate didn't seem worried... so, why am I?'*

He tried desperately to trust in his brother's confidence. If it was worth worrying about then they would have surely taken extra precautions. It was not the first time someone had taken interest in the family's whereabouts; he had to stop psyching himself out and just relax.

It was easier said than done, but Rorrik did eventually talk himself out of the brunt of his worry. His family was more than competent; he couldn't let himself doubt it.

Then again, Rorrik had failed to notice the man in the first place. Perhaps his older siblings and parents were competent, but could the same be said about himself? What if Jate hadn't been on the watch with him? Would Rorrik have ever noticed his onlooker?

His insecurity didn't relent as worry in his own skill level seeped in. How could he be trusted on missions if he wasn't good enough? He rolled over to face the wall, tired of his mind harassing him. It wasn't like himself to worry so much, but worry he did, regardless.

It had been a few hours by the time Rorrik's eyes closed and stayed that way, concern still alive in his mind but the lull of tiredness too strong to further ignore.

He was freshly asleep when he suddenly felt a weight land on top of him with force, yanking him out of slumber. Whatever it was began to wrestle him, causing terror to spike within the felidaren. *'They found us!'*

He rolled expertly out of being held down and reversed the pin, his eyes snapping open to stare at his attacker.

What— *who*— he saw startled him. "Valen?!"

The demorinkin's face was angry and panicked as tears wetted his cheeks. His eyes were open, but the demorinkin did not appear to be staring at him. He thrashed and squirmed against Rorrik's hold, the felidaren barely able to contain him.

"STOP!"

Rorrik felt immense confusion but listened, releasing his grip on the pin.

Valen continued to flail and kick as though Rorrik still held him down. "STOP! STOP, STOP!"

"V-Valen?"

Valen didn't appear to hear him. His fit went on, his wide-open eyes staring all about the room, seemingly recognizing nothing.

"Valen! Hey!" Rorrik tried again. *'Is he having a nightmare? But his eyes are open!'*

When Valen did not respond yet again, Rorrik couldn't fend off panic. "Mom!" the tabby cried out, desperate for help.

His mother was there in a flash. She hurried over, Valen still struggling about on the bed.

"What's happening to him?!"

She watched as Valen proceeded his worrisome behavior. "He must be having a night terror."

Rorrik watched as Valen kicked and thrashed. "Night terror?"

His mother nodded and attempted to set a hand on Valen's shoulder. He wiggled out of it and gave another scream and a whimper. Rorrik looked on, his ears flat with horror.

"He's technically still asleep. There's not much we can do. It will pass..." She once again reached out to put a hand on Valen and he once again rolled out of it.

"Shouldn't we wake him up or something?"

She shook her head. "No, that will make it worse. He needs to calm down — trying to wake him up will only excite him."

Rorrik hated that answer but didn't argue it.

Valen continued to moan and cry and kick for another minute or so, but then, very abruptly, it stopped. The demorinkin sleepily exhaled and appeared to be fast asleep, the evidence of his fit vanished.

Rorrik gawked, hardly able to believe it was done and gone so easily.

His mother stood up and yawned. "He should be fine now. Let me know if anything else happens, alright, kit?"

"...O-okay..." Rorrik stuttered, still shaken from Valen's episode.

His mother wrapped her arms around him in a hug. "Don't worry, kit, he's fine."

Rorrik wasn't as certain, but his mother was confident enough to leave. She closed the door behind her, leaving Rorrik to dwell in the remnants of his adrenaline. He set his attention back on Valen, the demorinkin sound asleep.

...in Rorrik's bed. The tabby had to wonder how Valen had even gotten there in the first place. He glanced up to the loft bed. '*Did he roll out of bed and onto mine?*' The tabby's cheeks went hot. '*Maybe a bunk bed wasn't the best choice...*'

A trembling sigh left him. '*Well, I should probably let him sleep.*'

The felidaren nestled back into the comforter, trying not to disturb Valen in the process. It was not odd to the felidaren to share his bed with another, coming from a family of cuddlers and being a very physical person himself.

He was closing his eyes so that he might find sleep again when the demorinkin turned towards him and nuzzled into his back with a gusty sigh.

The tabby's tail frazzled as well as his heart, his breath catching in his throat. He blamed it on his jumpiness; he really, *really* needed to calm down.

Valen sleeping deeply next to him, he forced his eyes closed and tried to sleep.

Chapter 24

Valen

Valen cracked his eyes open, sleepy and disoriented. A semi-lit room revealed, one that was not the guest bedroom, he noticed. Confusion gripped him hard and he jolted into sitting up, his eyes darting around to piece together where he was.

It was slow going, but recognition eventually quelled his confusion as he realized it was Rorrik's room. The initial disorientation ebbed away, but then it came crashing back as he noticed he was not in his bed.

He was in Rorrik's.

The demorinkin looked around him, the felidaren nowhere to be seen. Evidence of his sleeping remained, however, the blanket being upturned in the spot next to the demorinkin.

Valen's mind was snagged with bewilderment. His eyes went up to the loft bed and he squinted at it, the facts not adding up. He *distinctly* remembered falling asleep up there, so why was he waking up somewhere different?

He looked back to where Rorrik had evidently slept, his cheeks flushing red. *'What in all the realms happened?! I hope I didn't do something weird and chase him off...'* The aspect that he was lying in Rorrik's bed and the felidaren was nowhere to be spotted answered the question within itself. He put his head in his hands, mortified. *'Oh, gods...'*

"You're awake!" Rorrik's voice suddenly sliced into his worries.

Valen jumped and turned to look at the doorway, finding the felidaren standing there. The tabby seemed typical enough, definitely not awkward at all, although his fur did appear to be damp, and he was holding a towel.

Valen couldn't hold any kind of look with him, his face still burning hot.

Rorrik walked in and went up to the mirror next to the dresser. He ran the towel through his hair before tossing it in a basket that now sat in front of the bed. His clothes were different than what Valen had seen him wear yesterday; the outfit consisted of a mid-sleeved, two toned brown shirt and solid, forest green cargo capris.

The felidaren began running a comb through his wet hair, his eyes finding Valen in the reflection of the mirror. "So! Uh, how did you sleep?" There was evidence of some of the awkwardness Valen feared.

"Um…" Valen began, bashful. "I… I'm not sure…"

"…Do you remember, at least?" Rorrik's brow knit together in concern.

Valen's blush and embarrassment grew. Dread overcame him as he replied, "Remember what?"

"Yeah… my mom said you probably wouldn't remember." The felidaren continued to comb his hair. "You had a night terror."

"A night terror?" Valen had heard the term before. He knew they were similar to nightmares, but that was the extent of his knowledge.

"Yeah… You rolled onto my bed kicking and thrashing…" Rorrik focused intently on his own reflection as he filled Valen in. "You were screaming and I couldn't wake you up, but then you just… stopped and went right back to sleep. I didn't want to disturb you so I just let you sleep there." The tabby turned around to face Valen and offered a weak smile. "I didn't mind, though. It's okay!"

Valen was horrified to learn of what had happened. He broke eye contact with the felidaren. "I'm so sorry!"

"Don't worry about it, Valen! Really, it's fine." The felidaren forced a chuckle. "You don't have to apologize!"

It didn't feel as fine as the felidaren claimed. Valen returned his face to his hands, foolishness still burning hot within him.

Rorrik walked over and sat on the bed next to Valen. "I'm just glad you're okay! That… it… it was pretty bad." Another forced laugh came from the felidaren. "You fell right on top of me; it was quite the wakeup call!"

Valen felt embarrassed enough to cry, but luckily tears did not threaten.

"It got me thinking, though…" Rorrik's laughter faded. "Maybe the loft bed wasn't such a good plan…"

Valen didn't say anything, his tongue held by his shame.

"Maybe… you could just sleep in my bed with me? I sleep in the same bed with my brothers all the time — it's not weird! I mean — if *you* mind I can just sleep on the loft bed! I don't care, either way!"

Valen blinked and turned to look at the felidaren, his offer still processing in his mind. '*He wants to share a bed?*' Valen's blush had room to grow, evidently.

"I'll just sleep on the loft bed," Rorrik quickly backpedaled. "It's alright!"

"Well, no— I don't want to kick you out of your own bed! I'll just sleep in my own bed, it's fine!"

"What if you fall off again, though?"

"Why don't we just move in a normal twin bed?"

Rorrik's eyes found the loft bed and then the desk underneath it. He frowned heavily. "That's probably a better idea, huh?"

Valen dropped his gaze, too frazzled to answer.

"But, you know, I miss being in a bunk bed, anyway! I'm not used to the queen bed yet; it feels too big! I don't mind sleeping up there, really!"

Valen's feeling of intrusion came reeling back. "Rorrik, I'm not kicking you out of your bed!"

"I insist, though! I like having the desk, and we can't fit it with a normal twin bed in here. It's not a big deal!"

Valen frowned at the felidaren. "I can just go back to the guest bedroom, it's fine."

"No, it's not! Not after last night! You shouldn't be alone. Seriously, the loft bed will be awesome! I like being up high; I *am* a cat!" he laughed.

Valen wasn't sure what to do or say. He moved his gaze to look down at the bed, his throat tight as he was utterly overwhelmed. "I don't know!"

"Well, I do! Like I said, I'm not even used to sleeping there, anyways. It'll be fine!"

Valen had a feeling he was going to lose the argument. "Fine... If you insist..."

"I do!"

The demorinkin shook his head, a headache finding it an apt time to announce itself.

"Well, are you hungry? My mom put away some hardboiled eggs for you in the fridge, if you want some..."

Being reminded of his hunger brought it into focus, his stomach hollow from skipping dinner the night before. He nodded and crawled to the edge of the bed, his movements slow.

Rorrik smiled at him. "Let's go eat!"

■ ■ ■

"So... my mom said she wants to talk to you at lunch," Rorrik brought up as Valen ate.

Valen froze midbite. "What? Why?"

Rorrik shrugged. "She said that Miss Porte found out some information, and so she wants to talk to you about it. That's all she said to me."

Valen wasn't sure if he should be concerned or relieved. Concern won out. "Oh..." The demorinkin looked around for a clock. "What time is it now?"

"10:30," Rorrik answered right as Valen's eyes connected with a clock on the left wall of the kitchen, the clock face agreeing with the felidaren.

"And what time will she be meeting me?" Valen asked.

"Lunchtime, so anywhere from twelve to one," Rorrik said. "Until then, I got a new school packet this morning! Want to help me study?"

Valen knew he should take him up on the offer so that he might have a distraction. Remnants of his melancholy from the day before objected, but he snuffed out the negativity. "Sure."

"Alright! Let me get it." The felidaren scooted out of his chair and hustled up to the school box on the wall. He retrieved the packet and sat back down, placing it between them on the table.

Valen studied the front cover of the packet, seeing it dealt with biology. He shoveled another bite of hard-boiled egg into his mouth, trying to coax himself into the mindset to learn.

Rorrik flipped it open. "This section is going over biorocks and chloroplastic skin."

Valen didn't say anything as the tabby began to read out loud.

"Biorocks are a marvel of biological and mineral properties meshing to create an advanced form of flesh. Biorocks are the token of terran and other aggregatental races, such as gaians and some dragonkin."

As Rorrik read on, the packet described how biorock cells are an aggregate of skin, minerals, and other various properties, the exact formula depending on the genes and type of species. Unique gemstones are eventually formed as the biorock cells mature, the crystallization accelerated by a special process that is aided by biological factors of the body. The typical biorock 'sprouting' is a process that begins at species puberty and continues until death. The main areas of concentrated growth in terran and gaians are the torso, shoulders, arms, legs, and back, but rare instances and mutations sometimes cause growth in different areas. Biorock flesh has a firm and rocky texture and is very thick, while the gemstones that are eventually created are very hard.

"Chloroplastic skin cells are a special type of cell that is very closely related to plant chloroplast cells. These cells perform a job very similar to their plant cousins, transforming sunlight into energy through the process of photosynthesis. Chloroplastic skin cells are a token of floralings, some dragonkin, and many fey."

The packet went on to explain how most floralings have chloroplastic skin all over their body, but main concentrations of the cells are found on the face, arms, back, and legs. Floralings are able to use these cells to produce energy from the sun, although the amount is rarely enough to sustain full energy requirements. Thus, an additional form of sustenance is often needed to avoid malnourishment.

The lesson eventually delved into diagrams and terms that Valen had trouble grasping, his mind feeling too foggy to take in and process any information. His eyes kept finding the clock, concern of his meeting with Mrs. Catty hogging his concentration. What news did she have to tell him? Was it good, bad? Valen's gut told him bad, and he could not think of anything that suggested that assumption to be wrong.

"What do you think, Valen?" Rorrik then asked.

Valen blinked and took his eyes off the clock to look back at the felidaren. Embarrassment seized him as he could not remember any possible context for his question.

Rorrik saw his face and offered a weak grin. "Distracted, huh?"

"Sorry..." Valen admitted in a mumble. "I just... I can't stop thinking about that meeting..."

"It's alright, I get it. I figured it was worth a shot, at least. What do you want to do, then?"

Valen's look turned hesitant. "Shouldn't you continue doing school?"

"Well, I'm almost done with this packet. I'm on the questions now." The felidaren gestured down where he had already scrawled some answers. "I can work on the rest of my stuff later!"

Valen was surprised that he was almost done with the packet. '*I guess it has been about forty-five minutes...*' He glanced to the clock again, the hands reading 11:17.

"You should come play!" a voice suddenly proposed.

Both Rorrik and Valen turned to see the youngest brother standing in the living room archway. Valen strained to remember what his name was, but all he could recall was that it started with a 'T'.

"Come on!" he urged before running back into the living room. Valen spotted him sitting on the couch through the half wall, fiddling with something in his hands.

Rorrik smirked. "That doesn't look like school, Talis," he mockingly scolded him.

'*Talis! That's his name!*'

"I'm already done!" Talis whined.

"Oh, yeah?" Rorrik tested, seeming unconvinced.

"Yeah!"

"Well then, maybe Valen will play with you while I finish this..." Rorrik glanced at the demorinkin, his eyebrows raising.

"Yeah, yeah! Come on, Valen!"

Valen wasn't sure if he was up for entertaining the child but he didn't want to be *that* person. He pushed out of his chair and dropped his plate in the sink before making his way into the living room. When Talis saw him, his green eyes doubled in size.

"Yaaay!" the kitten cheered, kicking his feet with anticipation.

Talis' enthusiasm spurred a grin out of Valen as he sat down next to him, the demorinkin's eyes falling onto what he was fiddling with in his lap. It looked like some kind of... door handle?

"This one is really, *really* hard!" Talis told him, his paws turning the object to inspect it.

"No it's not," Rorrik snickered from the kitchen.

"Is too!"

Valen didn't quite follow. He continued studying the handle, not understanding how it was a plaything. '*They don't seem poor... why don't they have actual toys?*'

"You should try!" Talis didn't wait for Valen to accept or not as he forced it into his hands.

"Uh, alright…" the demorinkin said hesitantly. *'What am I supposed to do with it?'* He wiggled at the handle, yet it was firmly in place, as though it were locked. Valen wrinkled his brow, his bewilderment growing.

Talis began to giggle. "Hehe! You can't do it without your tools, silly!" The little kit suddenly sat straighter with a gasp and his eyes went large. "Unless you can use your magic! Use your magic!"

"Use my magic?" Valen repeated, feeling more and more lost.

"You *locked* the door with magic!" Talis gave little jumps in his seat. "So you can *unlock* it, too, right?!"

'…Unlock?' Realization hit Valen full force. *'It IS locked!'* He set his vision back down on the handle, a frown turning the corners of his mouth. "Wait, why are you playing with this?"

"To unlock it, duh!"

"…But why?"

"For training, silly," Talis answered as though it were obvious. "But it's also a fun puzzle!"

"…Training?" Valen's frown furrowed deeper. *'Training for what?!'* Valen's earlier theory of the family being vigilantes popped into his mind. *'I suppose vigilantes need those kinds of skills sometimes…?'*

"Use your magic! Use your magic!" Talis egged on, still bouncing.

"I don't— I can't do that!" Valen answered uncomfortably.

"Whaaat? But you can lock it, right? Just… do it in reverse or something!"

"It doesn't work that way! Besides, why would I ever want to unlock something?"

Talis guffawed at that. "Your new friend is funny, Rorrik!"

Valen heard Rorrik laugh, too, spurring the demorinkin into blushing.

"Just try it! Pleeease?" Talis pleaded.

Valen attempted to give the handle back with a shake of his head.

Talis didn't take it. "Awww, come on! Just one try!"

The demorinkin dipped his ears and looked down to the handle. Was there really any harm in trying? It wasn't like the handle was connected to anything…

His conscience huffing with indignation, he focused his attention on the lock and called upon his rucanic reserves, the magical energy responding. He attempted to influence the lock, his mind willing it to open. His perceived vision of the locking mechanism filled his third eye as he imagined the pieces sliding into place. He held his focus, the spell straining him, the lock failing to respond.

He was ready to quit when he heard and felt a loud pop from within the handle.

"Whoa!" Talis jumped.

Valen looked at the handle excitedly. "I did it!" When he turned the handle, however, it still was jammed. He tried again and confusion scrunched his face when the lock still refused to budge.

"Did you do it? What was that noise?" Talis wondered, stealing the handle back. The kitten wiggled the handle himself, finding the same results Valen did. His ears then flicked. "Wait a second!" He brought the handle up to his ears and shook it before laughing. "You *broke* it! Listen!" He shook it by Valen's ears, the sounds of fragmented parts jingling from within.

Valen's expression turned mortified.

Rorrik's laughter joined Talis'. "You broke it?! Wow, way to go, Valen!"

"I'm so sorry! I didn't mean to—" Regret and embarrassment overtook Valen. Why had he even tried to unlock it in the first place; what had he been hoping to accomplish?

The brothers continued their laughter, seemingly unbothered that Valen had just butchered their plaything. Apparently, his mistake was something to find more amusing than be upset over.

"What's going on here?" a stiff, masculine voice suddenly demanded from nearby.

Valen jumped and directed his attention on the speaker, his eyes widening and his ears dropping as he spotted an intimidating figure in the archway. They were an adult male felidaren with stark black fur and even starker yellow eyes, and he looked far less amused than Rorrik and Talis.

"Oh! Hi, Daddy! You're home!" Talis leapt off the couch and went over to embrace the man in a hug.

'*Daddy?!*' That man was their father?!

"Hey, Dad, welcome back," Rorrik greeted from the table, still mid chuckle.

The man, Rorrik and Talis' apparent father, patted Talis on the back. His yellow eyes then fell on Valen, sharp with scrutiny.

"I asked a question," the felidaren pressed, his tone impatient, his eyes still boring into Valen.

Valen desperately searched for courage to answer him, but the man's gaze daunted him.

"Valen broke the lock with magic!" Talis spoke up in his place, punctuating with a giggle. "It was really funny!"

"Is that true?" the man asked, his gaze never leaving the demorinkin.

"I—" Valen stammered, nervous enough to sweat. "I'm sorry, sir, i-it was an accident!"

The man grunted and finally broke eye contact to look at his sons. "Why aren't you both out today?"

"Uhhh..." Rorrik sat straighter and hesitantly grinned. "That's... Um..." The tabby's gaze briefly fell on Valen, almost nervously. He looked back to his father. "Gavin could explain that better..."

The black furred felidaren scoffed at that. "I would ask him, but he is out doing his job, unlike both of you."

"We *have* to stay inside, though!" Talis defended.

"What?!" the man growled.

"Dad! Why don't you just call Gavin? He'll fill you in!" Rorrik offered, speaking fast.

"Why can't *you* just tell me?" their father's yellow eyes narrowed.

Rorrik appeared uncertain and worried. "...Can we talk in the meeting room?"

"Why is that necessary?"

Valen had to wonder that, too.

"Niem! You're back!" Mrs. Catty's voice suddenly entered the conversation. The tortoiseshell walked up to the man and gave him a peck on the cheek, the felidaren standing stiff as she did so.

"Since your son won't explain, can you tell me why these two are still here?"

"That's no way to greet your mate. Let's go catch up, shall we?" Mrs. Catty took his arm and attempted to guide him out of the room.

"What's going on, Kyla? Explain." The man stood firm.

"Let's talk in private, come on."

"Does it deal with *him*, is that why we're tiptoeing?!" A claw jabbed over in Valen's direction.

The demorinkin sat there in awkward apprehension, wanting to disappear.

"Niem. *Now*," Mrs. Catty said in a low voice, her pleasantness dissipating.

The black felidaren finally listened, and the parents walked out, leaving the room quiet and thick with tension.

Valen melted into the couch, his frantic heartbeat loud in his ears.

"Um... So... That was our dad," Rorrik was suddenly sitting down next to him; Valen hadn't heard him approach.

Valen wasn't sure how to reply, and so he kept quiet, still recovering.

"He can be mean but that's okay!" Talis contributed, plopping down on Valen's other side.

"He was... different than I expected," Valen mumbled.

"Yeah, we get that a lot," Rorrik chuckled. "Sorry if he freaked you out. If it helps, he shouldn't bother you much."

Valen nodded slowly. As he sat there he couldn't help but dwell over what had created so much drama in the exchange. His stomach churning, he asked, "You guys were supposed to be out today?"

Rorrik's chuckling ceased. "Well, yeah..." He raised his shoulders in a drawn-out shrug.

Valen swallowed hard. "...*Does* it deal with me?"

Rorrik looked as though he were backed into a corner. "I'm not really supposed to talk about it..."

Worry jumpstarted Valen's adrenaline. "Is it bad?"

Rorrik's gaze fell, and he shrugged yet again. "Nothing has really happened yet. We're here so it stays that way..."

"What do you mean?"

Rorrik seemed to consider something for a long moment. "…Jate and I were followed on one of our watches yesterday. We ditched the guy, but we think he might have been following us because of you… Don't worry about it, though!"

Both dread and guilt slammed into Valen; guilt over dragging the family into danger and dread from learning his hunters were still searching for him.

"It's okay!" Rorrik attempted to assure. "This kind of stuff happens to our family all the time; it's nothing we haven't dealt with before!"

Valen leaned forward as nausea swirled in his guts. He squeezed his eyes closed, overwhelmed and wishing it would all disappear.

Rorrik's arm reached over his shoulder and squeezed. "You're safe… relax…"

"Yeah, cheer up, Valen!" Talis joined. The young felidaren began to nuzzle into his shoulder with a bubbly purr.

Valen felt bombarded from stress, the brothers' efforts unable to diminish the power of his worry.

Rorrik squeezed yet again. "It's nothing we can't handle, Valen. Just trust us."

It was all Valen could do.

Chapter 25

Valen

Valen sat in the meeting room he had been brought to following his initial rescue, his stomach hardly calmed down from earlier. The demorinkin had spent the last forty minutes in the living room bathroom, hovering over the toilet in fear he was going to spew from stress.

When Mrs. Catty had returned at noon to get him for their meeting, she was startled to find Valen so bothered. Rorrik had frantically told her something in feline, to which the mother seemed less than pleased with him over.

She had guided him to the meeting room after he said he wouldn't be sick, but in all honestly Valen still was not so certain.

"So, Rorrik told you?" Mrs. Catty asked from her spot across from him. The mother seemed miffed with the fact.

The demorinkin nodded, his head feeling impossibly heavy.

"Well, know that we're handling it, Valen. We're using it to our advantage, even. If someone is going to follow us we're going to snoop on them right back. We *will* get to the bottom of this."

He dipped his head in a nod yet again, trying his best to believe in it.

The felidaren huffed and shook her head. "But, that's not what we're here to talk about."

Valen met her eyes with hesitant intrigue.

"Avalene Porte was able to gain some headway with your attackers we captured. But if we're going to get any more answers, we need your help."

Valen waited, his apprehension building.

"First things first…" Mrs. Catty started with a long exhale. "We were able to confirm that… you were right when you guessed they are the Fangs of Hellbane. The prisoners themselves confirmed it."

Valen's spirit plummeted. He had known it in his gut, but the fact finally being confirmed was terrifying to come to terms with.

"Your last name incited a… very strong response out of them. Did your father ever mention any prior conflict with this organization?"

Valen wished upon his father's soul for courage. "Not before his letter," he said quietly.

"And what did he say in the letter exactly?"

"That... that they had hunted him since he was a young adult..." Valen answered, feeling hollow.

"...What did your father do as a young adult?"

"He was an adventurer..."

"Did he ever say what kinds of jobs he did? Any major accomplishments?"

Valen thought back to the tales his father told him as bedtime stories. "A lot of general stuff, I guess. Treasure hunting mostly, though..."

"Hm... Did he ever mention why he settled down?"

"He hurt his leg. It was crushed and didn't heal right."

Mrs. Catty was quiet. She looked down at a paper in front of her. "I ask because the prisoners mentioned an 'attempt at salvation' and that Vaaskiir declared he was 'worthy amongst celestelles'. Does that sound like anything your father might have done?"

Valen's brow furrowed in confusion and he shook his head. "Dad never mentioned anything even slightly like that."

"Do you think it is possible he hid something from you?"

Valen's expression twisted with consideration. "I don't know why he wouldn't have mentioned it in his letter. Especially if it was important..."

"True..." Mrs. Catty once again dropped her attention to the paper in front of her. "Did he know any outerplanars or celestborn?"

Valen shook his head. "Not that he ever told me..."

Mrs. Catty kept her gaze on the paper, her eyes scanning. "Have you heard of the names 'Korinthis' or 'Nathalia'?"

Valen frowned as he once again had no answers to offer. "No..."

"Well, whoever they are, the prisoners claimed affiliation. They said they were the 'glowing light' of Korinthis and 'piercing sword' of Nathalia."

Valen looked away, the wording having the power to bother him.

"So, you believe your father would have told you more if he had done something to aggravate them?" Mrs. Catty reiterated.

"I don't know why he would have kept anything else secret..." Valen muttered. He remembered his father's words, *'I will not lie to you, for you both need to understand this very, very clearly.'* "He said we need to 'understand very clearly'."

Mrs. Catty was quiet for a few moments. "...Did your father ever talk about his parents?"

Valen slowly shook his head. "He said his dad abandoned him when he was really young so he never knew him. He didn't talk about his mom much. We never got to meet her..."

Mrs. Catty tilted her head at that. "He was abandoned?"

Valen nodded.

"...Did he ever go into detail on what drove his father away? Could it be possible it was because his father had been hunted, as well?"

Valen blinked, having never thought about it. It had been so long since he had put any thought into his grandfather. "No, he never said why he left. But... that would make sense..."

200

Mrs. Catty's head jerked in a firm nod. "I have a feeling that what The Fangs of Hellbane are talking about didn't happen with your father."

"He would have mentioned something if it did."

Mrs. Catty appeared like she was gathering her thoughts. "Was your father pure demorin?"

Valen shook his head. "No, and neither was his father. It goes back for a while..."

"I see... When you say 'a while', do you know how long, or is it up in the air?"

"Up in the air... My dad didn't seem to know." Valen felt exhausted and raw from answering all the questions.

Mrs. Catty nodded. "What was your father and mother's names?"

"Aviino and Vivianna Vaaskiir."

"And where did you live before everything happened?"

"Riverview, in the outskirts of Akarth..."

Mrs. Catty nodded yet again. "What did your mother do for a living?"

"She worked at the town hall in Riverview."

Mrs. Catty appeared thoughtful. "Well, I think that's all the questions I have for now. You were so brave, cub. Your father would be very proud of you."

Valen froze at that, his eyes immediately pooling at her words. He shook his head as all the guilt festering within him came crashing into the forefront of his mind. "No," he murmured, his voice thick with emotion. "No, he wouldn't..."

Mrs. Catty noticed his shift in emotion and scooted out of her chair. She walked across the room to sit next to him, putting an arm around the demorinkin to pull him into a hug.

"You've done the best you can, Valen. I'm sure he would understand."

"It was all my fault..." Valen sniffled, his mistakes burning painfully in his memory. "He asked me... and I... I..." Tears broke free, drenching his cheeks.

"You're so young, Valen. It was so much to ask of you, and he knew that. He would want you to forgive yourself."

"Why would I...?" Valen hiccupped. "I... I could have prevented it... But I... I did it anyway! I knew I shouldn't do it, but I-I did..."

"...Do what, kit?" Mrs. Catty asked softly.

Siena's image filled his mind, her honey eyes an agonizing memory. He did not want to keep his guilt to himself anymore; he had to tell someone. "There was this girl... I-I went on a couple dates with her even though I *knew* I shouldn't. I-it was so risky but I... I did it anyways..." His body was overheated with embarrassment and shame, his cheeks blaring hot. "One day she... she..."

Mrs. Catty waited as he paused, her arms around him tight.

Valen forced the words out. "She kissed me... and... and... I couldn't... my shift... it..." He gave a shuddering exhale as his mind flashed back to the moment, recalling the horror and regret that had encompassed him. "I couldn't hold my shift. *That's* the reason it failed... why I was found... Why everything fell apart..." He coughed out a sob. "It's all my fault... It's all my fault... I knew I shouldn't do it but I did it anyways! It's all my fault..."

"Shhh." Mrs. Catty held him tighter still. "I know it's hard, cub, I do, but we cannot forever regret what we did or did not do. There's no way to go back and change what happened. The only thing we can do is move on."

"I-it's not fair, though..." Valen bawled. "Because of me Karreo never got to have a better life..." His shoulders rocked as he wept. "I promised him... *I promised him*..."

"Oh, cub... I know... I know... Shhh..."

The conversation fell into silence as Valen cried, Mrs. Catty never letting him go. His mistake had cost him and his sibling so dearly, and he despised himself for it. His heart ached to go back, to fix his wrongs and save his little brother.

And yet, Mrs. Catty was right; there was no way to go back and change what had happened. That fact only dragged him down as he drowned in his misery.

Indeed, he very much doubted his father was proud of him at all.

Mrs. Catty put a hand on his shoulder, her eyes gentle. "Forgiving ourselves doesn't come easily. It's a choice we have to make. It may take a long time to fully accept it, but the journey will never get started until we put a foot forward. I know it's hard, kit, but you have to move on."

Valen could not meet her eyes. His feet remained planted in the muck of self-loathing, utterly restraining him. He was stuck in layers of despair; it was impossible to move forward.

And so, stuck he remained.

■ ■ ■

Kyla

It took Valen's tears a half hour or so to dry up, Kyla providing comfort all the while. When the demorinkin seemed fairly more composed, Kyla recommended he go relax to recuperate. He did not argue that plan, his demeanor exhausted as Kyla brought him towards the private quarters.

She opened the doors and gestured for him to walk past. His steps were slow as he found Rorrik's room and opened the door, shutting it behind him as he headed inside. Kyla lingered in the double doors, pity for the demorinkin swelling within her. '*Poor cub...*'

He was just a young man, of course he was going to be curious about dating. It was unfortunate and tragic that his very normal interest had led to his capture. She hoped he could eventually forgive himself, but knew that day was likely far off. '*It's a process… He'll need love and encouragement until then.*'

She closed the doors and walked through the kitchen and into the living room, finding Rorrik there lying on a couch, his face buried in the cushions. He tensed up at her footsteps.

"Rorrik… I don't know what to do with you," Kyla began sternly, her son flinching as she spoke. "I had specifically told you *not* to tell him anything. That information was unneeded for him right now!"

Kyla had asked all her children to keep quiet with what had happened on the watch so that they might avoid any unnecessary drama for the demorinkin. She hadn't anticipated that would be an issue, but, apparently, she had been wrong to assume so.

"He knew something was up, though!" Rorrik lifted his head as he protested, his eyes guilty. "I wanted to let him know it wasn't anything too bad, or else he'd worry even more!"

"Still, Rorrik, you disobeyed! Again!" Kyla snapped, her patience gone. "You should have let *me* be the one to discuss it with him. If you really want to help I need you to actually *listen* to me!"

Rorrik dodged her gaze in shame as she was firm with him.

"Head upstairs and help Walter for the rest of the day! I do not want to hear any complaints, go!"

Rorrik groaned and rolled off the couch to get to his feet, his tail dragging behind him as he moved out of the room. Kyla followed him all the way to the stairs, her eyes never leaving him until he reached the top.

She shook her head and headed back into the meeting room, shutting the door behind her. She approached the table and reached into a compartment found within a lamp that hung above. The felidaren retrieved the recorder that was housed there and sat back down in the chair she had conducted the questions in, a sigh leaving her.

She began to run through the recording, transcribing the conversation onto paper in the process. Her mind dwelt on the information that had been revealed in her questioning. She couldn't fend off disappointment that Valen had not had more answers to offer, but that was nobody's fault. They would have to accept and work with what they were given.

The recording reached the end of the questioning and she turned it off before Valen's episode could begin, her empathy marking her troubled and unwilling to hear it again.

A headache pounded in her skull and the felidaren staved off tiredness as she gathered both the new and old transcripts into the file on the table. Today had been a worse day for her health; the baby was not only acting up, but she felt exhausted and strained from her other condition.

Her earlier argument with Niem had certainly not helped; the fight had riled her symptoms even further. Niem had been furious, taking the news of the family being followed as justification that the demorinkin should not be there. He argued that not only was the boy's presence endangering the family, but *now* he was disrupting their children's training, as well.

Kyla had matched his fury, her typical pleasantness and patience gone as she once again met the face of her mate's snarling disapproval. She was too exhausted to defend herself and so she jumped to attacking Niem's behavior instead. He had just returned from a week-long trip and *this* was how he greeted her?! He was acting despicably!

They had both fired unkind words at one another before Kyla had screamed that he could find a different bed that night. "You're not welcome in mine!"

He had called her selfish and turned to leave, Kyla rebutting that *he* was the selfish one. Niem had frozen but kept his mouth shut, the fight finishing on that note.

Kyla sighed away the memory of their dispute. Relations with her mate felt like they were nothing but stiff and tense as of late. It seemed more often than not that they were at odds with one another, having little make up time and almost no positive interaction. '*He never really did recover from me choosing to keep Aylan…*' Kyla glanced down at her pregnant belly, moving a hand to rest on it. '*Why can't he just understand?*'

She shook her head to chase off her musings. She could not focus on her relational troubles at the moment; she had a job to do.

She grabbed the folder and scooted out of her chair, her head pulsing and her vision blurring as she stood up. Dizziness struck and she was suddenly stumbling to the floor, grabbing at the chair to slow her fall.

She remained on the floor as exhaustion seized her, a faint ringing in her ears and stars in her vision as she tried to compose herself. Breathing hard, she could find no strength to pull herself up as the episode worsened, sweat clinging to her brow.

Getting those transcripts over to Avalene would have to wait, she decided.

Chapter 26

Rorrik

Rorrik scrubbed at the bar, his ears flat and his mood sour.

"What did you do to earn yourself cleaning duty?" Walter asked him, the human male leaning against the back counter, watching the felidaren do his job for him.

'*So much for 'helping' Walter…*'

Walter was the barkeep for The Den and a long-time friend of the family. He was a good sport with a decent sense of humor but knew when to stand up and end nonsense if it got too rowdy, a useful trait as a bartender.

The human was a bit on the heavier side, both in weight and in muscle. A crown of wavy red hair covered his head and a thick, braided beard adorned his chin. His creamy, white skin was dotted with several freckles, not only on his face but also on his meaty arms, which were normally exposed in the tank top and apron he typically wore. His face was angular and wide in shape and he was aged somewhere in his thirties. Rorrik had always thought he looked a bit older than what he truly was.

"I don't want to talk about it…" the felidaren responded to his question in a mutter.

Walter grunted at that, seemingly amused. "Fair enough. Once you're done with the bar, go on and scrub all the tables. After that there's some dishes waiting for you in the sink. Hop to it!"

Rorrik groaned with a hiss, miserable. He normally wasn't so opposed to cleaning, but when it was a punishment the chore was always peskier. That, and there were lots and lots of tables and even more dishes. '*This is going to take forever!*'

His eyes longingly gazed out the windows next to the grand fireplace in the lobby. He *should* be outside training today but instead he was scraping his paw pads raw with scrubbing. All of it had the power to leave him feeling undignified, but it was his own fault that he was there in the first place.

After all, he had proven he was unable to watch his own back after yesterday, earning him home confinement until his older brothers figured everything out. His apparent lack of skill had only grown more and more upsetting as the repercussions panned out. His confidence felt slighted over the whole ordeal; he should have been able to notice the man. It made him feel like he was still just a kit after all.

Tears of frustration warned and he bit his lip in effort to contain them. He definitely didn't want to cry about it, that would only make him feel even *more* like a child.

He scrubbed on and on; from the bar to the tables to the dishes, the day plodding by. More chores awaited him beyond that, such as sweeping the floor, scrubbing the fish tank, and taking inventory of the supply room. The sun had long disappeared from the sky when Walter finally dismissed him.

"For a good day's work I think you've earned yourself a nice meal," the barkeep told him, presenting a bowl of the inn's renowned soup. It was a thick and creamy chicken broth loaded with potato dumplings, cheese, and various vegetables.

Rorrik cleared the bowl in a hurry, his belly eager for food after all his hard work.

Walter gave Rorrik a pat on the back when he was ready to go. "Make sure you behave yourself, Rorrik. Have a good one."

Rorrik was too tired to sass and so he merely nodded. "You too, Walter."

Exhausted and demoralized, Rorrik headed down into the hideout, yawning. Having not received very good sleep the night before, he was looking forward to snuggling into his bed and falling asleep.

His brothers were gathered in the living room when he arrived downstairs, throwing him one last hurdle to leap before he could do so.

"There's the naughty kitten," Jate laughed from a couch. "What did you do to get stuck working the inn?"

Rorrik growled at his brother, having no patience to humor him.

"Uh oh, someone is grumpy!" Quinn snickered from next to Jate.

"Don't make any sudden movements or else he'll attack!" Jate teased.

"Nooo!" Talis giggled from the floor. "He's gonna get us!"

Rorrik ignored them, not in the mood to play along.

"You missed dinner, Rorrik," Gavin mentioned from an armchair.

"Walter gave me a bowl of soup, it's fine," Rorrik mumbled.

"Awww, lucky! We got stuck eating Gavin's cooking!" Calvin piped up from the floor next to Talis. There was something between them, Rorrik noticing that it was the broken practice lock from earlier.

"Mom isn't feeling well," Gavin explained. "So I had to make dinner."

Rorrik frowned at that, worry adding to the negativity weighing down his spirit. "Is she okay?"

"She's fine, she just needs to rest. Looks like you could use some rest yourself."

"Yeah, you look beat!" Jate said.

Rorrik's shoulders bumped in a shrug. "Yeah…"

"Well, good night, then," Quinn smiled. "Sleep well!"

"Goodnight!" the rest of his brothers echoed.

He tiredly nodded at them all. "Goodnight…"

The felidaren headed to the private quarters without delay and opened the door to his room. He was walking over to collapse into his bed when he suddenly noticed with a jump that Valen was already lying there. The demorinkin was fast asleep, undisturbed by Rorrik's entry.

He immediately remembered their arrangement upon seeing him there. *'Duh, I'm sleeping on the loft bed.'* He truly didn't mind; he had simply forgotten.

He quietly climbed up into the bed and snuggled into the comforter, noting it already smelt like Valen. He sighed deeply and closed his eyes, slumber finding him far quicker than the previous night.

■   ■   ■

Kyla

"We couldn't find any record of the boy's family," Avalene spoke from over her corresponder. "Not in Riverview or any city in the Akarthi area. It's as though they never existed."

"Well, that's not too surprising," Kyla replied. "He did mention his mother worked at the town hall. If they were hunted, she probably made sure their existence wasn't on the books."

"A fair guess," Avalene sighed. "Well, I'll call you if anything else comes up."

Kyla yawned. "Remember to get some rest, Avalene."

The call went dead without her friend agreeing.

■   ■   ■

It was later that night, amidst the baby's kicking and the pounding of her head, that she heard the door open. She looked over her shoulder and saw Niem standing in the doorway.

She quit staring and furrowed her brow into her pillow. "I told you to find a different place to sleep," she tried to say firmly, although it came out weaker than she intended.

She felt the bed dip with his weight and then his arms wrap around her from behind. He pulled her close and she could not stop herself from melting into him, lulled by his intimacy.

"Why are you letting this boy disrupt our life so much, Kyla? Why are you letting it disrupt *us*?" her mate softly asked, his voice calm.

Anger flared and she scooted away, his advance ruined. "I've already explained myself, Niem."

"I just don't understand, Kyla. None of this is worth the risk or sacrifice." Niem had no anger in his tone.

"I won't abandon him, Niem! He needs us. Why are YOU letting it get in the way of us?" Kyla redirected the question.

"Because you acted without my console or opinion. Because you continue to push for more when I have already been more than patient," Niem let out a sigh, his breath hitting her hair. "I feel like you don't respect me as your mate."

Kyla frowned at that and turned over to face him. "I'm... I'm sorry... I just knew you'd say no and I... I *had* to help him, Niem. Please understand."

Niem's eyes were staring into hers, their typical intensity softened. "What is it with you and this boy, Kyla? You have never done this with any of the other children you've saved..."

"None of the other children I've saved were ever almost beheaded right in front of us," Kyla elaborated, matching her mate's calm.

"Porte could have kept him safe, Kyla. She's kept the prisoners out of prying eyes; the boy would have been *fine*," Niem pointed out, stressing his words but still delivering them mildly.

"I won't apologize for being extra cautious, Niem," Kyla said, endeavoring to keep herself pleasant. "You know we have the resources and experience to help this child. Why can't you just think of it as another job?"

"Because there are far more risks to this than a normal job, Kyla," Niem answered, still maintaining his cool.

"Perhaps, but we're getting handsome pay! We've taken risks in the past if it was worth the reward, why is it so different now?"

Niem stared at her for a long moment then sighed. "I don't want to fight about this any longer. I take it you expect to house him here indefinitely?"

Kyla didn't nod at first, but then, firmly, she did.

Niem closed his eyes. "Fine."

Kyla wasn't sure how to respond. Knowing her husband and the businessman he was, she was sure there would be a catch.

Even so, she decided to cuddle into him and give a purr, relieved. "Thank you..."

It was silent for a few minutes until Niem broke the quiet. "The boy knows some magic, then."

"He does, yes. What tipped you off?"

"He broke a practice lock earlier with a spell."

"Did he?" Kyla was surprised to hear that. "What was he doing with a practice lock?"

"Talis pushed it on him, asked him to unlock it with magic."

"...And he listened?"

"Tried to, yes."

That was intriguing; did Valen house curiosities in the type of work they did? She could not help but wonder, however… "Why are you bringing this up?"

Niem cleared his throat. "If he's staying here I expect him to eventually pull his weight."

Kyla yanked herself out of their embrace. "We can't ask that of him!"

"We help him and he helps us. It's basic business, Kyla."

"We're already being compensated for helping him. He owes us nothing."

"*You* owe me after all you've pulled."

"He is not a commodity to exchange!"

"We can give him the illusion of choice if his free will concerns you," he pressed coolly.

"Niem!"

"Why are you arguing me on this, Kyla? I am suggesting what should be expected, if anything."

"He shouldn't even be leaving the hideout until his attackers are dealt with!"

"Then he starts after they are dealt with," Niem suggested, unfazed. The usual intensity in his yellow eyes returned. "Do not bother arguing. You got your way, I will now get mine."

Kyla frowned, unable to deny that her mate was likely correct. "How do you even know it's worth the trouble? He's not even trained."

He grunted at that. "We're taking enough risks, might as well stack another on."

Kyla's frown grew. "What do you plan to do with him?"

"Gavin mentioned he has shape-shifting capabilities. That along with the access of magic has many uses."

Kyla sighed as guilt and worry bombarded her. "Let's just see where this all goes."

"We know where it's going: we help the boy, and he returns the favor. If you have such a problem with it then you can return responsibility to Porte."

Kyla turned away from him and she rolled over, unhappy. "Fine, Niem. But know that I don't support it."

She felt Niem's arms once again wrap around her. "We're even, then."

Kyla wanted to squirm out of his spooning but sighed instead. '*He's right*…' "I suppose we are, yes."

She felt his tongue began to lick at her neck gently. "I've missed you…" he breathed out.

Kyla couldn't help but melt into her mate's advance, unable to turn away his affection. "Is that so?"

A purr began to rumble out of him, his licking continuing as he nodded.

Kyla felt a smirk born from mischief threaten. "Prove it, then," the tortoiseshell challenged, subtly arching herself against him.

Niem did just that, the two of them finally coming into agreement.

. . .

Avalene

'*They're late...*' Avalene once again checked the clock on her desk, anxious. The warden's men should have arrived a few minutes ago, and yet they were nowhere to be seen or heard from. '*He better have sent someone competent. This is nothing to scoff at!*'

Avalene was impatient to get the prisoners out of the warehouse and into the jail. Ever since the interrogations, the behavior of their captives had turned... unsettling. At least, in light of their fire and animation in the questioning. Each one of them had grown incredibly quiet and still; they sat in their cells with their eyes closed, motionless as could be, chests barely lifting with each breath. They had not touched the food or drink that was offered, and they did not respond when spoken to. It was as though they were in a trance or meditating, and Avalene did not like it one bit.

It was two nights since the interrogations had taken place. The warden had promised to send an able team to confiscate and transport the prisoners as soon as he could, which was tonight at two in the morning. It was currently 2:15 and their tardiness was utterly unappreciated.

She was ready to call Jarome to demand answers when suddenly Felicity walked into the room.

"They're here," her associate told her.

'*Finally.*' Avalene stood up at once to go meet them, Felicity following.

A uniformed team of six had arrived via three black vans. One of them stepped up when Avalene arrived, a female terran, Avalene pinning her to be the head of the squad. "Miss Porte, I presume?"

"You're late," Avalene rebuked.

"Our apologies, ma'am. We were told to take extra precautions on the way here."

"You should have left early to accommodate for that. How can I trust you're an able team if you arrive late?"

"Well, ma'am, if you doubt our skill you don't have to trust us with anything. We can leave," the terran said with a hint of irritation.

"Don't be ludicrous. Now, come. Let's get this done and over with."

Avalene led them into the warehouse and where they kept the prisoners, her nerves on edge. They arrived in front of the old, emptied storage rooms that served as their cells.

Avalene nodded to the heavyset door and Felicity went forward to unlock the several locks keeping the rooms secure. Two of the warden's officers stepped up as she did so, ready to head inside.

Felicity moved aside as the last lock clicked open, and the officers hurried into the room, finding the prisoner just as Avalene's people had left her, eerily still and quiet. Her handcuffs still held her, yet unrest still plagued Avalene. The prisoner did not protest in the slightest as they restrained her and began to guide her out, her mangled hair hiding her face.

The same process repeated for the other two prisoners, their behavior mirroring each other. They began to drag them out of the warehouse and towards one of the vans the warden's men had arrived in. They were loaded into the back of the vehicle, one of the officers remaining with the prisoners as the doors were closed and locked.

Avalene watched as the rest of the officers piled into the other two vans. She approached the female terran as she was stepping into the leading vehicle of the line.

"I'll be following along to confirm the task is done," the vigilante told the officer.

The dwarf furrowed her brow. "Miss Porte, we are more than capable of handling this without your babysitting."

"I'd rather not gamble and find out otherwise," Avalene retorted. "Forgive me for being cautious but it is critical that these prisoners are transported somewhere secure. I'll be following along, that's that."

The terran appeared annoyed but did not protest. She slammed the door shut in Avalene's face and started the engine, the other vehicles following suit.

Avalene went to sit in her own car, Felicity joining her in the passenger seat.

"Do you really not trust them?"

"It's the prisoners I don't trust..." Avalene muttered to the brevin, turning the ignition.

"What do you mean?"

Avalene was not sure how to explain it; she simply could not fight off a sense of worry. Perhaps it was the unsettling behavior of the prisoners or the fact that the guards had been late or the idea that if anything were to fail horrible repercussions could follow. "I just need to see them arrive at the prison. Then I can know they're in able hands."

Felicity gave a firm nod of understanding.

The convoy began to drive off, Avalene moving out along with them.

"Go ahead and tune in on their chatter," Avalene told Felicity, gesturing to the car radio.

The brevin nodded and did just that.

"Gods, what a bitch! Who does she think she is?" a male voice spoke over the radio.

"Phet above, I know! It was only fifteen minutes! What's her deal, anyway? The warden doesn't send us out to pick up prisoners from just anybody," a different male voice said.

"Didn't she used to work for the government or something?" another voice gossiped, this one female. "But then she got fired?"

"Wait, I thought she quit?" yet another added, also female.

"Enough, all of you. Drop it." Avalene recognized the speaker as the female terran. "Let's just focus on finishing the job."

The radio went quiet after that.

As time passed, the road drew closer to the main city as the lake came into view. They began driving across Dell Bridge, a few minutes' drive across.

The radio chatter returned. "Uhhh, Officer Emveil? The prisoners are talking in some sort of... *weird* language to each other. Should I shut them up?" a new voice said.

"What do you think, Padvek?! Put an end to it!"

"Right. Uh, hey! No talking!" Silence. "Hey! I said no—"

Suddenly, there was a deafening boom, and the middle vehicle's back doors flew open and off their hinges, a loud scream over the radio sounding in the same moment. The doors, as well as a flailing body, crashed into the third van in a splatter of blood and glass, the driver swerving in a failed attempt to dodge.

Avalene and the rest of the convoy slammed on their brakes, squealing to a stop.

"Padvek?! What on Azyria happened back there?! Report!"

A view of the middle van's exposed trunk was allowed thanks to the third vehicle having swerved out of the way. Avalene noticed someone jump out of the van, mangled, long hair telling that it was the female prisoner. Her handcuffs were glowing red as if they were burning hot and the prisoner snapped them apart with a determined yank, the bands falling away in a fiery display.

Avalene's stomach lurched with terror. 'No! No!' She hurriedly moved to take off her seat belt, the mechanism fussing after slamming on the brakes as she had.

She was unbuckled and ready to open the door when another thunderous boom split her ears. The third van's tail end was suddenly crashing into their vehicle, forcing them back several feet, the windshield shattering and the airbags deploying.

Disorientation gripped Avalene as her ears rang and her head throbbed. She forced her eyes to blink open and saw wreckage in front of them, a blazing fire up ahead as car alarms screamed.

'The prisoner!' Alive with adrenaline, Avalene pushed past the airbag and out of the vehicle, her ears still muffled with ringing. The vigilante ran out onto the road, stumbling. She frantically looked all around, catching no sight nor sign of the prisoner. She hustled to the edge of the bridge and stared off the side, stars in her vision as she desperately searched for any hint of them, spotting nothing but dark, flowing water. '*Shit! No, no!*'

Her vision redirected on the wreckage, shock slamming her. The middle van was now a fiery mess of metal and billowing smoke. The front van had been blown forward a few yards and rolled onto its side, while the third had been pushed back into Avalene's car, its front window smashed and bloodied with gore. "What in all the realms happened?!"

"I don't know, Porte!" Felicity answered from next to her, a fresh cut splitting open her forehead.

Avalene could not recall when her associate had arrived at her side, but the human didn't linger on it. "Call the police!"

Felicity instantly did as she was told. Avalene hurriedly dialed for the warden on her own corresponder.

"Patience isn't your virtue, is it? They'll be there soon, Avalene," the warden answered with snark.

"Jarome! There was an explosion on Dell Bridge — your convey is totaled and a prisoner escaped!"

"What?!" the candidaren barked. "Wait, slow down! What happened?!"

"We were driving over Dell Bridge when the van carrying the prisoners blew out its back! A prisoner got out and an explosion followed right after! The van is in flames and the other two are wrecked!"

"H-How is that possible, Avalene?! Who on earth were you having us transport — I thought you said they were just members of some organization harassing you?!"

"Extremists! I said *extremists*! I have to go!" She hung up the corresponder, her eyes once again scanning the water for any clue of the prisoner — *ex*-prisoner. Still she saw nothing.

"The police are on their way," Felicity said.

Avalene stiffly nodded, her eyes never leaving the lake, adrenaline blaring within her. Her hands shaking, she once again lifted her corresponder. She had a few more calls to make.

Chapter 27

ᑅalen

Valen shot into sitting up, his heart beating fast as he startled awake. The memory of his dream vanished instantly, but not the terror. He breathed hard in an attempt to compose himself, yet his fear was loath to leave him.

He looked around the room, panic striking him as he did not recognize where he was. He then noticed something up high near the ceiling, his heart catching in terror. He gaped at it, dread overwhelming him.

He was still eying it when recognition dawned on him. He was staring up at Rorrik in the loft bed, and he was in the felidaren's room. As though on cue, the tabby made sleepy sounds and shifted his position, his face now visible to the demorinkin.

Valen felt silly for once again being fooled by his surroundings upon awakening. He exhaled shakily, shooing off the remnants of his consternation.

As it departed him, he noticed he *really* had to use the bathroom. Valen felt thankful that his awful dream had not caused him to soil himself, the thought of any further humiliation was not a kind scenario to imagine.

He moved off the bed and hobbled out of the room and into the hallway, the dimmed lights there telling that it was still nighttime. Valen had pieced together that the lights dimmed when it was time for bed, being they were bright for the remainder of the day. He appreciated all the light he got as he made his way down the hall and stopped in front of the first bathroom door.

He gave a quick knock, silence answering. He hurried in and shut the door, sparing no time in making his way to the toilet.

Valen had been priorly uncomfortable using the bathroom in the family quarters but necessity bought out his awkwardness. He was relieved to relieve himself.

He took his time, knowing that the rest of the family should be asleep, thus he could relax. When he was finished, he flushed and went to wash his hands, allowing himself a look in the mirror.

It seemed the cut on his head was finally healing up. His black hair was shaggy and uncombed, considering he had not attended to it in weeks. His skin was drab and sunken, courtesy of the stress that hounded him constantly and stole any comfortable sleep. He looked as pathetic as he felt, and he found himself hating his reflection. He turned to leave, bothered.

When he arrived back in the hallway he spotted Mrs. Catty outside Rorrik's door.

"Where is he?!"

"I-I don't know!" Valen heard Rorrik cry from within.

'Are they talking about me?' Why was Mrs. Catty so panicked? "Uh, I just went to the restroom," Valen spoke up sheepishly.

The felidaren jumped at his voice and whipped to face him, relief splashing over her features. "Oh, thank Nocturna…"

Valen became uneasy. "What's wrong?"

"I had just come to check on you, and you weren't there. It startled me." The mother turned to look back into Rorrik's room, appearing thoughtful. "Has Rorrik shown you the emergency exit out of his room?"

Valen frowned as he shook his head; he had never been told of any emergency exits.

Mrs. Catty put a hand on his back and led him into the bedroom. "It's probably better for you to know, just in case."

They arrived in front of the wall between the two beds, Mrs. Catty barely squeezing by the chair. She pointed to a panel in the wall. "Push on this panel here, and then slide to the right." She then demonstrated, the wall giving way and sliding open, Valen gasping as it did so.

"Follow me, kit," Mrs. Catty urged before pushing through the opening, a feat for her pregnant form.

Valen hesitantly obeyed, still unnerved by her behavior. They stepped out into a very narrow hallway that was modestly lit, a ladder resting in the middle of the space.

Mrs. Catty pointed to the ladder. "If you ever needed to escape, listen carefully: You'll climb up that ladder and find yourself in a very cramped room. Turn to the right and push in the panel on the wall directly in front of you, just like in Rorrik's room. You'll find yourself in a closet. When you leave the closet, you'll be in a hallway. Head straight then turn left at the corner. At the end of the hallway is a set of doors that lead outside." Mrs. Catty looked to consider something. "Why don't we practice? Head upstairs and follow the instructions I gave you until you reach the closet. Don't leave the closet, just come back down."

Valen's mind had trouble grasping what she was saying. "So I head up and then I…"

"Will find yourself in a cramped room. Turn to the right and push in the panel there. You'll see a closet beyond. Don't walk into the closet, just come back down."

Valen nodded in apprehension. He walked up to the ladder and stared up, spotting another dim lightbulb on the ceiling of the room that laid above. He ascended the ladder and found himself in a very tight space, just as Mrs. Catty had mentioned. It was hardly three by three feet.

"Now turn right," Mrs. Catty instructed from below.

He did so, a flat panel in the wall laying directly in front of him. He pushed on it like Mrs. Catty had demonstrated, but the wall did not budge.

"It won't move!" Valen moaned, straining.

"You have to push it really hard. It can be tricky."

Valen pushed harder, and the wall finally gave way with a click.

"Now slide," Mrs. Catty directed.

He did so with a grunt, a dark closet coming into view, barely illuminated from the spare light of the room he stood in.

"If you were escaping right now, you'd head through that closet door, go straight, turn left at the corner, and head outside through the doors found at the end of the hallway. So, tell me, Valen, what would you do?"

"I'd, uh... I'd leave the closet, go straight, turn left, head outside," Valen repeated, a potential escape striking as an unnerving prospect to map out.

"Very good! It's important you memorize that. While it is highly unlikely you will ever need to escape, it's never a bad plan to be prepared. Go ahead and close that panel and head back down."

Valen pressed back on the panel before sliding it closed. With that, he maneuvered his way back down the ladder, Mrs. Catty waiting at the bottom.

The tortoiseshell led him back in front of the passage leading to Rorrik's room. She stopped before heading inside and pointed to a button on the wall next to the opening.

"If you're escaping, you can hit this button to make the door close behind you. They are found next to all of the secret doors." She pressed the switch and the panel snapped back into place, just as explained. "It can be all the difference if you are being chased."

Valen nodded, trying not to tremble.

Mrs. Catty knocked at the panel. "Can you open back up, Rorrik?"

Valen heard some shuffling and then the panel click as the wall slid open.

"After you, cub," Mrs. Catty said.

Valen walked through the opening, Mrs. Catty following close behind. Rorrik was standing on the queen bed to make room for them to walk in.

Valen walked past the bed so he would not be in Mrs. Catty's way, and the mother shifted the panel back into place. "We will go over the other escapes routes in the morning. For now, why don't we all get some more sleep?"

'*Other escape routes?*' Valen could sense that something was amiss, but wasn't sure if he wanted to know what. "O-okay," he forced out, nervous.

The felidaren sighed. "Sorry to disturb you. I had a nightmare of my own." She walked up and wrapped her arms around the demorinkin, squeezing him tight. "Goodnight, Valen. Sleep soundly."

With that, she left, the door of Rorrik's room gently closing behind her.

Valen went to sit on the queen bed, perplexed and anxious.

"Sooo, that was pretty cool, huh?" Rorrik then asked.

"What?" Valen replied, not following.

"The escape route!" The tabby plopped down next to him, the bed bouncing.

"Y-yeah…" 'Cool' wasn't exactly the word that popped into his mind. The fact that the family had escape routes in the first place made Valen feel restless.

"…What's wrong?"

"I just…" Valen gave a quivering sigh. "I don't know how I'm going to sleep after that…"

"After what?"

"Your mom seemed pretty freaked out…" Valen recalled when he had initially seen her in the hallway, how panicked she had seemed.

"You heard her, she had a nightmare! She was just scared to see you gone." Rorrik then added, "Nightmares are scary, you should know…"

Valen flushed with humility. "You're right. Okay…"

Rorrik leapt from the queen bed and clung onto a support of the loft bed before scurrying up into it. He peeked over the edge, giving a frown. "…You going to be okay?"

Valen forced a sloppy nod. "I… I think so."

In truth, Valen wasn't quite sure what to think.

• • •Following breakfast the next morning, a mage was called to alter the private quarter's doors so that Valen would have access.

"Go ahead and grip the handles with both hands. Keep still until I tell you it's fine to move," the wizardess, a middle-aged gnome with peppered, red hair and vibrant, orange skin, instructed him. She had the look of a professional, her fancy fiber armor and draping silk sleeves marking her as dignified. She carried a sizable bag with her, likely full of magical supplies and things of the sort.

Valen gripped the handles of the doors with both hands and held, just as he was told.

The gnome spoke an incantation, and the doors began to glow. A symbol that resembled a feline's head appeared above the handles, its eyes glowing with an intense yellow. The cat's maw opened, and runes were suddenly visible in the general vicinity of the door, the air their canvas.

Valen gasped in surprise at the display and proceeded to gawk, fascinated. It was not the first time he had seen a mage access the runes packed within an enchantment anchor, considering the several times he had watched his father enchant items, but the sight was no less mystifying.

He studied the strings of rucana floating in front of him, scanning for any familiar runes. The spell decorating the air was the most complicated formula he had ever witnessed, but he did notice that part of the formula was similar to the spell he knew that holds a door in place.

"How does it work?" the demorinkin couldn't help but ask, intrigued.

The gnome grunted. "That's a secret."

"The runes are right there, though, aren't they?" He gestured to the formula with his head.

The mage's expression went crooked and she briefly glanced at him before setting her attention back on the runes. "You're saying you can see them?"

Valen blinked and tilted his head. "Am I not supposed to?"

"Unless you have the correct spell cast, no," the gnome answered with a narrowing of her eyes.

Valen had no memory of casting anything; he must have accidentally manifested the spell.

"Well, I— Sometimes I accidentally cast spells," Valen admitted hurriedly. "I didn't—"

The gnome waved him off and gave a single chuckle of amusement. "I get it, you must be a sorcerer."

Valen nodded, thankful she understood.

The gnome went back to focusing on the formula. Runes began to shift and change within the body of it, her hand making small gestures in front of her simultaneously. "So, you're claiming you understand this?"

Valen bumped his shoulders in a shrug and his face warmed. "I know a thing or two, but..." He went back to studying the formula, a plethora of unknown symbols and complicated syntax everywhere he looked. "This is a bit beyond my level..."

"It's good you know anything at all," the gnome commented. "Too many sorcerers don't bother understanding magic, especially at your age."

Valen grinned weakly and his blush deepened, his pride tickled. "I think it's important to understand." His father's advice echoed in his mind.

"It is important, indeed. So, how much magic do you know, then?" the gnome inquired as she went on with the spell, the formula continuing to alter in real time. Valen found her concentration impressive.

"A couple dozen different spells. Mostly illusions and alterations. I actually know a spell similar to this one," his head gestured to the runes, "just a lot less... complicated."

The wizardess chuckled before smirking at him. "Well, I'd keep learning and honing your magic. Panther pays well for a good spell."

Valen tilted his head, not understanding what she meant. 'Panther?' He glanced at the symbol mounted above the handles, the cat's yellow eyes glaring into his. The image kept him captivated, something about the sight familiar to him.

The runes then disappeared from the air and the glow left the door, the feline's head along with it. Valen blinked, slow to react. How long had he been staring at the symbol?

"Alright, go ahead and try the doors," the mage told him.

Valen did so, finding the passage complacent.

"Well! Looks like my work is complete, then," the gnome said with a clap. "Good luck to you, youngster."

With that, she picked up her bag and walked into the kitchen. Valen followed along, having been told to return to Mrs. Catty when the job was completed.

"I'm done here, Spot. The boy has unrestricted access," the gnome reported.

"Oh, good! We'll include the pay in your check for the week," Mrs. Catty answered from the table. "Thank you, Pepperglow. You're free to leave."

"Anytime. I'll be off." The gnome walked back into the hallway, leaving them alone.

"Good to finally have that sorted out, huh?" the felidaren asked with a warm smile.

Valen nodded in reply and offered a mild grin.

"Well, if that's all done." The mother scooted out of the chair and stood up. "I can show you the other escape exits."

Valen's grin vanished, his worries from the night before hurrying back into the forefront of his mind. His fascination with the rucana had been a nice escape, but it was only a distraction. "Okay…"

Mrs. Catty noted his apprehension. "Come on, it will be good to get you acquainted with them. It won't take long."

■ ■ ■

Valen's mind was overwhelmed with a mess of information as Mrs. Catty showed him each emergency exit after another. There were so many of them, some having their own special directions on how to not only activate the passage but where to go upon opening it. There was one in the pantry of the kitchen, several leading out of the bedrooms (both family and guest), another in between the two family bathrooms, and yet another found within the entryway.

The one in the walk-in pantry was hidden up in the ceiling, requiring some climbing to get to. Mrs. Catty had instructed to hoist himself up on the shelving that scaled the wall until he could reach the ceiling. There, he was to push and slide on a panel in the ceiling, like how the other door in Rorrik's room was activated. With the panel slid out of the way, a fold-up ladder could be pulled out. Mrs. Catty told him that the ladder led into a narrow hall that he would head straight down and then turn left. Waiting at the end was another secret door that worked like just like the rest of them, opening via push and slide. Mrs. Catty stressed that it was very important he closed that last passage, being it led into part of the building that lay above the hideout.

The next several that were found in the bedrooms all emptied into the same place Rorrik's door had led to. Mrs. Catty did not bring him to each one, rather pointed out that each bedroom on the left side of the private quarters all had the same type of passage that was in Rorrik's room. She then showed him that the three guest bedrooms that lay at the end of the guest wings also had an alike door, marked by a slighter darker panel in the wall. She also drew attention to an additional passage in the main hallway of the hideout that led into the same escape route, this door marked by a sconce on the opposing wall.

Following that, she showed him where the passage that lay in between the two bathrooms of the private quarters was. To activate it, Mrs. Catty pulled at a sconce in between the restroom doors and a pop in the wall responded. She instructed that he would then push on the wall and it would flip, acting as a rotational door. From there was a ladder that would deliver him into a cramped room. On the wall to the front upon arriving was a push and slide door that led outside, and to the back was an alike door that led into a closet.

Finally, the last passage was shown in the entryway, this door activated by turning a light fixture that hung above the buffet at the end of the hall. The door slid open on its own after Mrs. Catty turned it, a room lying beyond. She actually brought him into this passage, and a space revealed that was full of lockers and boasted a wall loaded with several supplies. Valen could not stop himself from gaping at the collection, spotting all sorts of gear; from weapons, to armor, to rope, to grappling hooks, and more.

Mrs. Catty pointed to a ladder that sat at the far end of the room. "That leads you into a narrow space. There is a discolored panel along the front wall that works just like the others to open it. This door also directly leads into the building above so make certain you close it behind you."

Valen already could not recall which other door he needed to make sure was closed; he had already forgotten much of what she had told him. He felt utterly overwhelmed.

"That's all the passages, then," Mrs. Catty concluded, the words filling Valen with relief.

His relief was shaken as the felidaren approached the wall lined with gear, her green eyes seemingly searching for something. Her gaze landed on a set of fiber bracers that boasted decorative rucanic etchings, and she removed them from their perch. She studied the set briefly before holding them out to Valen. "Here, you should take these."

Surprise twisted Valen's face. "W-what? Why?" He gingerly accepted the bracers with a frown and looked down to inspect them. Judging by the decorative runes, he supposed the set was enchanted. He turned the bracers over and found the symbol for 'magic armor' inscribed on their fastening belts, further backing that assumption.

"Just in case of the worst, you should have a way to defend yourself," Mrs. Catty spoke matter-of-factly.

Valen's mind spun at what she was suggesting. What was with the abrupt shift in her behavior; why was there suddenly so much concern over 'the worst' happening? His feelings of turmoil translated to his expression, and Mrs. Catty noticed his consternation.

"I'm sorry, Valen, but these are necessary precautions..."

"Why is it so 'necessary' all of a sudden?!" Valen didn't think the question through as it fell out of his mouth, alarm in his tone.

Mrs. Catty looked back the way they came in. "Let's talk about that in the kitchen."

"B-but, I don't even know how to use these!" Valen fretted, remembering all the failed attempts at activating his father's bracers.

Mrs. Catty waved off that comment and went to leave the room. "We can discuss that later. Come on, let's go sit down."

Valen's frown grew at her dismissal and he followed her out of the passage, his steps wobbly. She readjusted the light fixture she had turned to open the door, and the panel returned to its prior spot in the wall.

"All of the doors I showed you will eventually slide back into place on their own, but it's still a good idea to close them behind you."

Valen gave a weak nod, tired and raw from all the information.

She led him into the kitchen and they sat down at the table, Valen placing the bracers down on its surface, his attention fixated on them. He thought about the shock and fear he had felt upon receiving his father's set and how acquiring this new pair made him feel no different. He stared at the decorative marks upon them, the rune for 'fortify' the centerpiece of their design.

It was silent for a minute or so, the air growing tense.

"...Valen," Mrs. Catty then began, her tone serious. "Do you want to be informed on what's going on?"

The question hit Valen hard with indecision. One part of him desired more information, but the other was too overwhelmed with fear to want to know. He remembered Mrs. Catty's panic from the night before; did he really want to find out what had upset her so?

He squeezed his eyes shut. "I... I don't know..." How could he be prepared for anything if he didn't know what was going on? Or, was there anything he even *could* do to prepare? If not, surely he was better off not knowing? But, if he knew something was going on, wouldn't not knowing only make his worry worse? Then again, if it was something really bad, would knowing be more distressing than not?

Tears welled as his mind went back and forth. "I don't know!" he repeated.

"I will respect your wishes, whatever they are," Mrs. Catty told him softly. She cleared her throat. "I, myself, think it's a better idea for you to be updated. Even though it may be distressing, knowing how we plan to combat them may be comforting, in turn."

Valen bit at his lip, her point gaining traction in the debate within him. He *knew* the Fangs of Hellbane were out there and that they were trying to find him, what he *didn't* know was what the family planned to do about it.

It frightened him to learn of any negative news, but he had to trust that he was in able hands.

A trembling sigh left him. "O-Okay. I... I want to know."

"You're positive?" Mrs. Catty pressed.

Valen swallowed hard as he nodded his head.

"Alright." Mrs. Catty returned his nod. She was quiet for a few moments, her hands steepled. "Well... Last night, one of the prisoners that had attacked you escaped from our control. The other two evidently sacrificed themselves so she could get away, and we were unable to track down where she went."

Valen's stomach dropped with dread at the news.

Mrs. Catty went on. "This means that we have no choice but to accept that the Fangs of Hellbane now know your identity."

Valen's brow crimped with confusion. "Wait, what? Know my identity? I thought they already did?"

Mrs. Catty frowned, appearing guilty. "When we said your name to get them to talk, they revealed they had not known you were a Vaaskiir. That knowledge had a... definite impact on them. We have to assume they will be working harder than ever to find you."

Valen paled at that information, and his guts gave another flip.

Mrs. Catty saw his panic and talked fast. "We plan to use that to our advantage, however."

"How?" Valen croaked out, nausea parading him.

"You know that our family is being closely watched and followed. The Fangs will be more desperate to track us down, which means they'll be easier to manipulate — less cautious."

Valen let her speak, his body proceeding its fit.

"We plan to let them follow us and get them to think our hideout is somewhere different. From there we can put together a trap. We also are going to follow whoever is snooping and see where they go and who they report to. We've got our work cut out for us."

Valen tried to listen to the logic of the plan, but fear still suffocated him, disallowing him any solace. His gaze dropped to stare at his lap as he was unable to stave off regret from asking to be informed. Deep down he knew it was for the better, but that reasoning did not translate well in his distressed mind.

"...I know you are very frightened, Valen. Please, try to trust that we are doing everything in our power to put an end to this. We *will* protect you."

'*Just trust us,*' he recalled Rorrik's words. The demorinkin set his eyes back on her, and the two shared a long look, Valen's apprehension versus the family's confidence.

Valen found his anxiety losing the fight, overwhelmed by the intensity in her eyes.

"I... I'll try. Thank you..."

223

Mrs. Catty's features bent into a warm grin. "It's our pleasure."

With that, she stood up. "I hate to leave you alone, but I have a meeting to get to. I'm sure Talis and Calvin are around somewhere, perhaps they can keep you company?"

Valen could recall which brothers she spoke of, to his surprise. Talis was the youngest sibling, and Calvin was secondly so. "Alright." He saw no issue with them hanging around.

"If you need some privacy, we have disallowed them from going into Rorrik's room for now. Don't be afraid to be firm with them, either, they can take it." The mother shook her head with a single chuckle. Her eyes then fell on the bracers, and the amusement in her expression faded. "I'll have to arrange for someone to teach you how to use those. I'll see if they can come by tomorrow."

Valen felt an inkling of excitement over the prospect, but it was quickly snuffed out by the context of the situation.

The mother offered him a grin of support. "It'll work out fine, don't worry." She glanced towards the clock in the room and clicked her tongue. "Well, I need to be on my way. May Nocturna keep a watchful eye on you."

Chapter 28

Valen

Valen was tentatively poking around the rec room in the private quarters when he heard the pitter patter of little kitten feet. He set his attention on the archway right as Talis and Calvin slid into view, their tails frizzed.

"You really want to play?!" Talis questioned excitedly.

Valen answered with a mix of a shrug and a nod.

"Yay! I love playing with you; it's funny!"

"He cheats with magic, though," Calvin contributed, grimacing.

"I think his magic is fun! I don't mind!"

"So, you like my spells, huh?" The corners of Valen's mouth twitched in a slight grin.

"Yeah, yeah! You should do more!" Talis hopped over the chair Valen was standing in front of and landed on the furniture with a soft thud, his agility impressive. The kitten leaned towards the demorinkin, his green eyes large with wonder.

"Like what?" Valen's grin grew at entertaining the young felidaren. The two brothers were a welcome distraction. The demorinkin had always been fond of children; they were interesting to interact with.

"Ummm!" Talis' eyes went about the room as he thought. "Uhhh!"

"You should turn Talis green!" Calvin snickered.

Valen smirked at that. "If you say so..." He performed the spell via a hand gesture, much of its power drawn from within him.

Talis' gray fur responded as it blended into a facade of bright green. Calvin began to guffaw wildly and Talis gasped.

"I've got to see this!" the youngest brother squealed, leaping off the chair and scurrying off, seemingly to find a mirror.

Calvin was on Talis' heels, laughing all the while. Valen also followed along, mostly so he could maintain concentration on the spell. Talis led them into a bathroom and he gave a joyful giggle when he saw his reflection.

"You actually turned me green!" Talis hooted, amused.

"Well, not *actually*," Valen clarified from the doorway, grinning.

Talis quit his staring to look over at Valen, puzzled. "What do you mean?"

"It's an illusion. It's not actually real, it's a trick."

Talis hopped up and down excitedly. "Whoa! What other illusions can you do?!"

Valen concentrated on another spell.

"Talis! Calvin! Where are you?" Mrs. Catty's voice called out, a product of his trickery.

The boys jumped.

"Mom?! But she's in the meeting!" Calvin said, startled.

Valen smiled knowingly. "She is, isn't she?"

They both caught on, Talis looking thrilled and Calvin crossing his arms.

"Hey! That's not fair!" Calvin pouted.

Valen chuckled at that.

"It's dumb how *we* can't be in the meeting... Everyone else gets to be there..." Calvin grumbled.

"Yeah! We're part of the family, too!"

Valen gave a sideways look at that. '*So the rest of the family is in the meeting?*' He wasn't sure how to respond to the young brothers; he figured they were left out because of their age.

"Hey, how come *you're* not at the meeting?" Talis inquired Valen, his head giving a dramatic tilt.

Valen blinked. "Why would I be?"

"It's about you, isn't it?" Calvin added.

'*It is?*' Valen frowned, uncomfortable from the question. "I, uh..." He tried to think of a reason to excuse his absence but could not find one. He had just agreed to be in the loop, yet he was sitting out of a meeting that apparently dealt with his predicament? He began to feel self-conscious. Then, he began to feel a tad offended. Mrs. Catty hadn't even invited him!

"I'm not really sure why I'm not there..." Valen mumbled, having trouble hiding his offense.

Calvin appeared to take note of his mood as he squinted at him. He then perked up. "Oh, oh! We should go spy!"

"Yeah!" Talis jumped excitedly, his tail poofing with excitement. "Let's be spies!"

"Wait, what?! No!" Valen shot down, shocked at their suggestion. "I can't leave the hideout, anyways!"

Talis giggled at that. "We don't have to leave, silly!"

"Yeah, it's right here in the hideout. Wow, you don't know anything, do you?" Calvin scoffed.

Valen flushed. "Still! We aren't spying on anybody!"

"Why not? It's a meeting about you and they're leaving you out! Aren't you curious?"

Valen's frown grew, Calvin's point having too much merit for comfort. "They must have their reasons for leaving me out..."

"Wasn't Mom *just* asking you if you want to know stuff?"

'*He heard that?*' Valen's frown intensified as the plan became more and more tempting. '*I shouldn't...*' His discontentment over the situation festered and he felt a nudging of mischief within him.

Calvin didn't wait for an answer. "Let's go!"

The brothers pushed past Valen in the doorway and hurried down the hall, their tails flapping behind them.

Valen set after them, trying to match their haste but falling short. '*Am I really doing this?*'

They ran until they reached the entryway, in which they began a creep. Valen was amazed at how their footfalls suddenly became so silent; he could not hear them if he tried!

He attempted his own sneaking, the floorboards antagonizing his efforts.

Talis gave a mute giggle at his endeavor; Calvin rolled his eyes.

They snuck into the room with the staircase and then up to the door where Valen had been questioned a couple of times. '*Duh, the meeting room!*'

They huddled up against the wall, adrenaline pumping through Valen as he began to hear voices from within. The brothers began to press their heads to the wall and Valen hesitated in following suit. '*You shouldn't be doing this!*'

He pressed an ear up to the wall, regardless.

"...which is why I believe it's best we lure them into a trap. We might not have the luxury to take a milder course of action," he heard Mrs. Catty say. "Time isn't our friend here, boys."

"I see your reasoning, Mom," a brother's voice said, his mellow tone suggesting the oldest. Valen's mind fell short on his name. "It just seems risky."

"I think we have the clearance to be risky," the mother replied. "The timing could not be more perfect for a more direct approach. The Fangs are going to be desperate if their behavior in the interrogations is anything to be counted on."

"I think Mom has the right idea," another brother contributed, Valen unsure of whom. "If they're already following us we might as well take advantage of it. I think a head-on approach is acceptable."

"Perhaps we should gather as much information as we can from our stalker first?" a different brother said. "See if they can give us any other promising leads? They have to report to someone, eventually, yes?"

"Well, we plan to follow them, trap or not. We could wait around and see if we get any leads, yes, but in doing so we might surpass our opportunity to easily manipulate them. We have to rile them by giving them a scent," Mrs. Catty rebutted.

"Besides, if we're going to find a stalker again we'll have to purposely be spotted," a brother remarked. "We might as well kill two birds with one stone and start planting a seed while we're being followed."

"I'm sure Miss Porte won't like a more reckless plan," the oldest brother pointed out.

"Porte will agree to it. She's not opposed to risk if it's appropriate. I think we have the right idea here."

Valen suddenly heard Talis gasp and Calvin quietly groan. He looked to the brothers and noticed they were staring at something. He followed their eyes...

...and spotted their father looking directly at them, standing at the foot of the steps. His arrival had been completely undetected by the demorinkin.

Valen's guts flipped with dread and regret slapped him hard. He sloppily pushed himself away from the wall, propelled by guilt.

Their father glared, his yellow eyes narrowed and disapproving, silent. The demorinkin was about to stumble out an apology when the black-furred felidaren jabbed a finger towards the exit, his stiff demeanor keeping.

'W...*what?*' Valen was utterly bewildered. They had just been caught *spying* and that was all the disapproval they got?

Talis grabbed Valen's arm and dragged him off, the demorinkin complying. They went back into the entryway and then the living room, the brothers bursting into laughter upon arriving.

"Whoopsie! Guess we got caught," the youngest trilled.

Valen's confusion didn't relent. "That's it? We're not in trouble?"

"You really don't know anything," Calvin guffawed.

"It's training!" Talis giggled.

'*For what, exactly?*'

■　■　■

Rorrik

Rorrik sat in the meeting room silently as his family discussed what to do about the latest development, his head slightly dipped and his eyes on the table. He had been surprised to be invited to the meeting by his mother, considering his prior slip-up. He could not ignore a sensation of inferiority, his bleeding confidence suggesting he should not be there.

His mother had started the meeting off by announcing that one of the Fangs of Hellbane prisoners had escaped the night before. '*So Valen was right when he thought something had happened...*' She had told them that it could be twisted into good news if they played their cards right and proceeded to describe a plan to set a trap for the demorin hunters.

Each of his older brothers had something to say about the plan. Jate was supportive, Gavin was cautious, and Quinn was analytical. Rorrik was unsure of what he himself thought of the plan; his distraught self-esteem had him feeling too naive to generate a solid opinion.

They all seemed to be coming into agreement on the plan when his mother turned her attention on him. "What do you think, Rorrik?"

Rorrik quit his slouching and cleared his throat. "Uhhh, I..." He still was unsure. They all seemed to have come into agreement, so: "I think it's a good plan!"

"...You look uncertain," Gavin observed.

Rorrik shrugged and had difficulty fending off a frown. "I'm... just not sure what to think..."

"Well, why do you think it's a good plan?" his mother inquired.

"Um, we get to take advantage of being followed, like Jate said," Rorrik offered.

"And what *don't* you like about it?" Quinn asked.

"Well, like Gavin said it seems risky... But like Mom pointed out we have the clearance to—"

"I thought we were asking what *you* think," Jate laughed. "Not us!"

Rorrik's cheeks grew hot with embarrassment. "I don't know what *I* think!" His ears drooped and his eyes fell on the table. "I don't know anything..."

"Sure you do, little brother!" Jate affirmed, slapping him on the back.

His mother frowned at him. "That's not like you. Is this about the watch?"

Rorrik slid lower into his chair as she hit the nail on the head.

"Oh, come on, Rorrik, it's fine! You're still learning," Jate encouraged. "That guy was hard to spot! Even I barely noticed him."

Rorrik's shoulders inched in a shrug and he kept quiet, unconvinced.

"Jate told me you were the one to think of how to escape the shop, Rorrik," his parent said. "You showed skill in how to handle being followed and were able to get away. You showed competence that day."

"Yeah, but I didn't notice him in the first place!" Rorrik snapped. "You all couldn't trust me to leave the Den because I proved I can't watch my back — just like Calvin and Talis! I'm still just a kit!" Tears of frustration burned, to his humiliation.

"We're just being cautious, Rorrik. Even *we've* barely left," Gavin contributed.

"Indeed, it was nothing against you, little brother," Quinn added. "Understand that risky situations call for circumspection. We're just being careful."

"Your brothers are right, Rorrik," his mother said. "I know your confidence has been shaken, but mistakes happen so we can learn from them."

"Yeah, we've all made loots of mistakes," Jate chuckled.

"And still do," Quinn nodded.

"Some of us more than others." Gavin smirked. "But, joking aside, mistakes are all a part of the process. You should be proud that you were able to rectify yours so seamlessly."

"Yeah! That was a great plan you had to get us out of there," Jate complimented. "Really, Rorrik, cheer up!"

Rorrik processed his family's advice, their words of encouragement chipping at the weight crushing his self-esteem. He felt too bashful to say anything, humbled by their praise.

"Perhaps it would help to get back on the horse?" his mother suggested.

All the brothers turned their attention on her.

"What do you mean?" Rorrik wondered.

"Well... We need someone to lead on the spy in our plan," the tortoiseshell smirked. "Would you like to act as bait?"

Rorrik sat much straighter. "Really?!"

"That's an important job," Gavin commented. "But I think you can do it."

"Yeah! After all, the name of the game is pretending to *not* spot anybody," Jate guffawed.

Rorrik blushed at his brother's quip but did not let it hamper his spirits. "I want to do it!"

"You'll have a lot weighing on your shoulders," his mother warned. "Are you comfortable with that responsibility?"

Rorrik felt a tug from his dying inferiority but could wrestle it down. "I can do it!"

"Well, let's discuss how we plan to exactly go about this. The goal is to get them to think our hideout is someplace else. You'll need to get them to follow you and not tip them off that you are aware of their presence. You'll have to act convincingly, or they might detect that something is up."

"I know!"

"So where *is* our hideout, anyways?" Quinn wondered.

"That's still being determined," their parent replied. "I have an idea but I need to run it past your father as well as our people. Avalene, too."

"And what's this idea?" Jate pushed.

"There's the unused safe house on Token Boulevard. There's still some functional tunnels out of there, and it won't be the end of the world if something backfires horribly."

"What would an example of backfiring be?" Jate pondered.

"The place being blown to bits or collapsed. I'm thinking that won't be an issue, though."

"What makes you so sure?" Gavin said.

"Well, they've shown they know how to blow up a vehicle and yet when they attacked Valen they merely stopped the car. I think they're wanting a more personal touch to whatever plan they initiate. From what I can see, they'd hate to collapse the building on him rather than cast the final blow themselves."

230

"So we're actually planning on having them think Valen is there, then?" Gavin asked for clarification.

"That's the plan."

"We should probably throw the spy a few bones, then," Jate proposed. "Maybe have Rorrik talk to one of us while the stalker is in earshot, have a vague conversation about Valen."

"You mean like what Rorrik and you did before?" Gavin teased with a smirk.

Jate and Rorrik exchanged a look.

"A *little* less vague than that, but you've got the right idea!" Jate laughed.

"I agree. We'll make sure to give him some juicy conversation to eavesdrop on," their mother concurred. "Let alone a lot of movement in and out of the 'hideout' for them to witness. We have to make this convincing."

"So how are the particulars going to work? Are we going to be spying on the person as they're spying on Rorrik?" Quinn brought up.

"I think it's best you all follow, yes," the tortoiseshell agreed. "Keep an eye out from several vantages. It's important you remain undetected."

"How about when it comes time to follow the spy?" Jate brought up.

"I can follow him on foot. I have the most experience tailing," Gavin proposed.

"And I can keep an eye from the higher ground," Jate offered.

"Me, too!" Rorrik also volunteered.

"I've actually been working on a bug," Quinn piped up. "I can get it ready by tomorrow! It's in the shape of a gold piece, so long as you can plant it in his pocket we should be, well, golden!" He guffawed at his joke, Jate and Rorrik having a laugh, too.

"You're *sure* it will be ready?" their mother challenged, serious. "We don't have room for any... unexpected repercussions, Quinn."

"All of my calculations tell of success!" Quinn assured. "I took apart one of Bluebird's old mics and made only a few necessary adjustments."

"...Such as?"

"Well, it had to fit inside a coin!" Quinn said. "The mic was in a case that was a taaad too thick before, so I had to give it a new housing. That called for rerouting some of the wires, but it's been working swimmingly in my tests!" The brother then scratched at his chin, his look turning sideways. "The only snag is it gets a little... hot."

"Hot?" Rorrik echoed.

"Indeed. If it runs for more than, say... twenty minutes or so, it starts to heat up rather noticeably."

"I fear that's a damning trait," their mother worried. "If it's going to be in his pocket, he's going to notice it heating up."

"Hmmm. There might be a way around it," Quinn mused.

Everyone waited.

"It seems exercising the mic is what gets it bothered. If I can rig it to only transmit on cue and have it rest the remainder of the time, perhaps it can work out."

"And how do you plan to do that?" Gavin wondered.

"I have my ways," Quinn snickered. "To put it simply, it would require a little more tweaking under the hood."

"And you can get that finished and ready to go by tomorrow?" Their mother sounded incredulous. "Without the threat of any unexpected outcomes?"

"I believe I'll manage, yeah! Keep in mind, though, it means we will not get constant chatter. We'd have to be choosey of when we snoop." Quinn began to giggle. "We also have to hope he won't spend it on his lunch."

"How long does the charge hold for?" Jate asked.

"That's... a complicated answer. When it would heat up in my tests it tended to burn out pretty quickly, but if we're only pushing it every so often, well, who knows!"

"*We* better know," Jate laughed. "Not everybody gets a kick out of the unexpected, Quinn."

Quinn chortled in response. "I'll run some more tests, would that be satisfactory?"

"It would." Their mother nodded. "We'll need to know exactly what to expect out of it. We don't have room for the unexpected."

"So, when exactly are we going to start all of this?" Rorrik wondered.

"There's still preparations to make and I have a few more people to talk to," their parent replied. "Hopefully no later than the day after tomorrow."

"Are we just lying low until then?" Gavin asked.

"It's probably best to, yes. We'll discuss this in more depth after I get the green light from your father and Avalene." She stood up. "Quinn, make *certain* that bug is field-ready. The rest of you, stay here while we're still preparing." She gave them all a firm nod. "I'm so proud of you boys. You're all shaping up to be able professionals."

Rorrik couldn't help but smile at that, his prior loss of confidence a departed memory.

"Aw, thanks, Mom," Jate chuckled.

"Your little criminals have all grown up," Gavin jested.

Their mother laughed at that. "You've got some growing up to do yet, all of you!" She headed for the door, turning to face them one last time before leaving. "May the lady of luck smile on each and every one of you."

Chapter 29

Valen

Valen had retreated to Rorrik's room following the earlier excitement, remorseful after his decision to spy. Why had he allowed being left out of the meeting to bother him so badly? It sounded like it was to merely discuss schematics of the plan Mrs. Catty had already shared with him, nothing the demorinkin had to be there for.

He was embarrassed and ashamed over his immaturity. Being an elder to the young brothers, he should be an example for Calvin and Talis, not encouraging them to indulge in such behavior.

Then again, apparently, their father condoned it all in the name of 'training', as Talis kept putting it. Valen could not help but be unnerved by it all. He supposed the act of spying was a desirable skill for a vigilante, sure, but where was the line drawn? What other acts were excused in the name of 'training'?

The brothers had been disappointed to hear that Valen 'wanted to lie down', but they had shockingly respected his escape to Rorrik's room, regardless. Valen had been resting on Rorrik's bed when he felt an itch to busy his mind, distressing thoughts earning more leeway in his boredom.

He summoned the courage and left the room, finding the place empty, the two young ones nowhere to be spotted. He made his way to the guest bedroom he had been staying in before, everything still there as he had left it, save for the bed being stripped of its comforter and sheet.

He went to the nightstand and pulled out the packets he had placed in its drawer. As he stood up, his eyes found the dresser, his father's vest still neatly folded on top, the pair of the clothes Rorrik bought him resting underneath it.

Valen frowned heavily at the clothing as he felt a surge of emotion, a concoction of both the good and bad feelings the garment inflicted. He was happy to have the vest back, of course, but the betrayal of his father's enchantment still stung woefully. It hurt to look at the vest and be reminded of all the self-doubt and confusion it now imposed on him; he wondered how he could ever wear it again.

He could not just let it become unused, however! Guilt settled in, ashamed at the fuss his pride was generating. It was his late father's gift and the only possession he still owned from his old life, and yet he was going to just refuse to wear it in the name of ego?

He picked it up, the vivid scarlet color showing as if it were new, the tailor's work an impressive feat. No obvious cuts or blemishes showed on the garment's body, as if they were magically undone. *'I suppose they could have been...'*

He folded the article and slung it across his arm with a sigh. He then grabbed the rest of the clothing from the dresser, including the spare clothes Rorrik was lending him, and walked out of the room, closing the door behind him.

He returned to Rorrik's room without any interruption or issue and set the vest and new clothes on top of the felidaren's dresser, deciding he was still not ready to wear them. He placed the other clothing Rorrik was lending next to the pile, feeling too invasive to place them in the drawers.

The demorinkin approached the desk underneath the loft bed and sat in the chair there. He delved into one of the packets he had retrieved, his mind ready for the distraction.

He was about a half hour into the lesson and solving a math problem when the door opened. He looked over and saw Rorrik standing in the threshold.

"Hey!" the tabby greeted before bouncing up. His emerald eyes fell on the packet. "Anything interesting?"

"Uh, just algebra and integers," Valen replied through a mild grin.

"So, Quinn's idea of fun, then."

"Quinn is..." Valen trailed off, raking his memory for which brother that was.

"The crazy one," Rorrik reminded with a chortle. "The one who likes to tinker and build things."

Valen remembered Quinn and his zany introduction a few days prior, and then their more typical meeting at dinner. "Ohhh, right. Sorry, you have a lot of brothers."

Rorrik guffawed at that. "And my parents still aren't done!"

Valen was reminded of Mrs. Catty's pregnancy. "I'm only assuming you're going to get another brother soon?"

"Yep!" Rorrik nodded. "That'll make seven of us!"

Valen smiled, albeit a tad overwhelmed. "You'd think your parents are building an army."

"Ha! Something like that," Rorrik giggled.

Valen tilted his head, wondering how much of the felidaren's comment was a joke.

"So, I heard you're in the loop now!" Rorrik changed the subject.

Worry slithered into Valen's demeanor. *'Word travels quick in this family...'* "I agreed to be, yeah."

"Well, our plan is great!" Rorrik gushed. "We're going to spring a trap, and I get to be the bait!"

Valen's features fell into a frown. "Bait? What do you mean?"

"It's my job to trick the stalker into thinking our hideout is somewhere different! The spy is going to follow me while I pretend not to see him. It's going to be so cool!" The tabby flopped onto the bed with a happy sigh. "It'll be my third *real* mission!"

Valen did not share his excitement. "Will you be okay?"

"Of course! This is the kind of thing I've been training for!"

'*There's mention of training again...*' "Um... Rorrik..." Valen started, awkwardness setting in.

"Hm? What's wrong?"

"Ah... What does your family... *do* exactly?" Valen worded uncomfortably.

Rorrik blinked at him before smiling wide, a fang poking out. "Lots of things!"

"Okay, but like what?"

Rorrik sat up with a chuckle. "Rescuing you, for one!"

"So are you like... vigilantes or something, then?"

Rorrik blinked before bobbing his head in a nod. "Sure!"

"Sure?" Valen repeated. "Sure *meaning...*?"

Rorrik laughed. "Sure!"

Valen returned his vision to the packet, unsure of how to feel over Rorrik's response. He could not shake the feeling that the felidaren was dodging something. '*Why am I worrying about it? They're helping me, aren't they?*'

He again switched the topic. "Anyway, my mom is still getting ready for the plan and we have to lie low for the rest of the day and probably tomorrow, too. What do you want to do?"

Valen looked back to the felidaren. "I'm not sure. What is there to do?"

"Well, I guess there *is* school." Rorrik pointed to his packet. "But, much more thrillingly, there's also... ping pong!" The felidaren gracefully rolled off the bed and past Valen's chair with ease. "Let's go play! Come on, I'll show you how!"

Valen scooted out of the chair to follow, his concerns over the family falling into the back of his mind.

■ ■ ■

Kyla

She found Niem upstairs at the bar, eating his lunch in solitude. She sat down next to him and smiled pleasantly at her mate.

"The meeting was a success," she reported.

Niem swallowed his bite of food. "You had some spies."

It did not surprise her that Calvin and Talis had snooped. "That's no shocker," she chuckled.

"I think it might be," Niem disagreed. "There was three of them."

Kyla's eyes went wide as she was shocked, indeed. "You mean...?"

Niem nodded.

Kyla processed the news, finding it hard to believe. "Well, that's certainly interesting..." Why had Valen spied on the meeting? Had the boys suggested it and he been too complacent to protest?

Niem nodded again, slower this time. "It *is* interesting..."

Kyla studied her mate with narrowed eyes. "I imagine you're happy with this development."

Niem gave a single chuckle, a rare gesture out of her mate. "You're worried about having the boy work for us and yet he's already showing interest."

"Just because he was eavesdropping doesn't mean anything." Kyla shook her head. "He was probably talked into it by the boys, anyhow."

"He still went along with it, did he not? He clearly wasn't trying to stop them." Niem veered on smug.

Kyla attempted to picture Valen spying and no mental image answered; he simply struck as too polite and sweet.

She wondered how much of the meeting they had listened in on. Kyla tried to remember everything covered in the talk and could not recall anything too sensitive.

The felidaren pushed aside her musings so that she could get back on task. "Well, how much spying did *you* do?"

"None. I assumed you'd fill me in."

"You assumed right." It was the reason she had come to talk to him, after all. "I think we have a good plan figured out, we just have to... work out a few factors and smooth down the details."

Niem nodded and gulped down the remainder of his drink before sliding off the barstool, Kyla following suit. He tapped a fork against his plate and Walter came by to sweep up the dish instantly.

He and Kyla began to walk towards the back, both giving a brief glance at the lobby to double check for any prying eyes. Normally it was not a concern to be more open and relaxed in the inn, being they had their people looking out to warn of any overly curious guests, but times were cautious.

The pair entered the employees-only section of the establishment and walked up to the storage room doors, Niem pulling out his key. He unlocked the door and they silently entered the room, Kyla relocking the door from the inside with a deadbolt lock. Niem headed over to turn the steel bands on the appropriate barrel and pushed in the back of the container, a satisfying click in the wall responding. They pushed through the now loose rotational panel in the wall, and the secret passage shifted closed behind them, returning to its facade of inconspicuousness. A faint whisper of gears resetting and pressure building hit Kyla's trained feline ears, telling her that the passage was recuperating.

They walked to and down the steps, Kyla finally deeming it appropriate to begin her briefing, the soundproofed walls bestowing her confidence. "Well, we decided that if we're going to be followed we might as well offer them a red herring."

"I knew it," Niem grumbled as they reached the floor. "That's just your style."

"Style aside, it's appropriate!" They walked into the meeting room. "We have an opportunity to manipulate them, so, why wouldn't we?"

"So what's this red herring you're planning?"

"We aim to get them to think our hideout is somewhere different. I was thinking possibly Token's old safe house."

Niem gave a hiss and then an unimpressed sigh. "That'll take a lot of preparation if it's going to be convincing. We'll also need eyes on the building constantly. That kind of manpower isn't cheap, Kyla."

"I'm sure Avalene will contribute some of her people to the job. This is her case, anyways, remember?"

Niem scoffed. "Then why are we still so involved?"

"Because the paycheck is pretty, Niem. We've been over this." Kyla hit him with her tail. "So, what do you think, is that something we can manage?"

Niem hissed yet again. "Why something so complicated? Can't we just tail the spy?"

"We plan to, of course."

"So why is a trap needed?"

"The trap is ideal because we get to play on the demorin hunter's desperation. We might not get a better opportunity."

Niem was quiet for a lengthy second. He then shook his head. "Alright, fine. If you think this is the better course of action, Kyla."

The tortoiseshell was surprised her mate was not fighting her on the plan. She could not help but grin at him. "You're in an awfully good mood, aren't you?"

Niem glanced over at her with a scoff. "Don't push it."

■　■　■

Avalene agreed to meet her that evening. When Kyla walked into Avalene's office, the human had her eyes on a booklet in front of her, her facial features strained with concentration.

The human adjusted her reading glasses and nodded at the felidaren's arrival. "Hello, Kyla. I take it you have news."

"Not so much news as a plan," Kyla clarified. "Before I run it by you, though, how have things been?"

"Hectic." Avalene tiredly shook her head and sighed. "The warden has been furious, the police are prying too deep, and my recon team has yet to deliver any solid leads on anything of value."

"What about the accident? Have we been able to piece together what exactly happened there?"

"The prisoners definitely used magic, that we're sure of. My rucanic expert thinks that the prisoners were able to cast the spells due to their apparent mediating," Avalene said. "By concentrating deeply and conserving all their energy for days, they were able to focus all of their strength into their rucanic reserves. He mentioned that the strain of casting the spells probably did the other two in, which would explain why there was no effort to escape on their part. He estimates some sort of force spell blew off the doors, and another spell caused the car engine to burst. As for the one who got away, it seems she used a heat-related spell to weaken the metal to break it apart. Since her spell was considerably less taxing, she still had the energy to escape."

"And they were able to do all of that without any kind of somatic gestures?" Kyla asked, disturbed but also impressed.

Avalene nodded gravely. "Whether that was possible by the gift of desperation or great rucanic skill — or both — it is concerning." The vigilante clicked her tongue. "Anyways, how are things on your end?"

"Well, I think we've worked out a pretty good plan, if you're wanting to hear it."

"I'm all ears, Kyla, please," Avalene urged, gesturing to one of the arm chairs in front of her desk.

Kyla took a seat. "As you know, we've had a spy poking around," she began. "We were thinking of giving them something to run off of and—"

"You want to spring a trap."

Kyla nodded firmly.

Avalene gave a sharp exhale. "Is that a risk we really should be taking, Kyla? You just heard of what they did on that bridge. You want to invite that same type of danger onto your doorstep?"

"Our fake doorstep, yes," Kyla quipped. "Besides, I doubt it'll come down to explosions. They could have blown up the vehicle Valen was originally being transported in, but they didn't. I think they want to strike the kill themselves."

"A fair point, but still, Kyla..." Avalene crossed her arms, unconvinced. "We have safer options to work with here. See who the spy is reporting to, for instance."

"We plan to," Kyla assured. "Think about it, though, Avalene. When the rest of them learn of Valen's identity they're going to be desperate, if we can expect the same intensity they showed in the interrogations! The trap allows us to play on their heightened emotions, which we may not get another chance at. I'm afraid that if we give them too long their emotions will cool, and they'll get more cautious."

Avalene kept her arms crossed. "If they're fanatical, Kyla, their emotions will likely never die down."

Kyla felt a wavering of confidence in her logic. "Perhaps, but you can't deny there will be a more desperate push immediately! Especially if we rile them with a scent early!"

Avalene held Kyla's eyes. "I think you just want to hit them back," she suggested coolly.

Kyla did not look away and she swallowed hard. It was a fair observation. "Is that such a bad thing?"

"No, but it *is* a risky thing. We don't even know the full extent of who we're dealing with, Kyla. We should research our enemy before picking a fight with them."

"The fight has *already* been picked, Avalene," Kyla stressed, irritation sprouting. "They're coming for Valen whether we're ready or not. We might as well put ourselves in a position we have better control in."

Avalene considered that. "Alright, say we go through with your plan. You lead on the spy, and they are tricked to believe your hideout is… where exactly?"

"The old safe house on Token."

"Right. So, they run and tell this to their client, and they will surely be ordered to scope out the place. What do you expect them to find?"

"The details are still being sorted through," Kyla reminded. "But essentially that Valen is being kept there, and there is some sort of hole in our security."

"And when they report that to their client, how do you expect to know what the Fangs will do about it?"

"We'll know the rough idea of their plan because of the hole," Kyla said. "You don't find a weakness in security and then ignore it."

"So, your trap is sprung. What is it exactly?"

"Again, details are being worked out, but we'll probably incapacitate them through some sort of means. Whether it's chemically, magically, or by preemptive strike. From there we capture them."

"A small team will likely be sent, just like the van attack," Avalene said. "So what do we plan to do about the rest of their numbers, however much there even are?"

"Well, we don't necessarily know only three will be sent. The Fangs didn't know Valen was a Vaaskiir for that attack, remember. But, even if it is just a small team, we're hoping our snooping will reveal more and more about these demorin hunters. Your recon team is also on the case. Something *has* to come up eventually. We might only have a small amount of them captured, sure, but it's a few less than we'll have to deal with in the future."

Avalene continued to fire questions. "And how do you plan to restrain them? Considering our previous prisoners are no longer prisoners, I suggest a sound plan."

"Well, we know they used some sort of magic to escape. We'll have to invest in rucanic draining cuffs or set up an anti-magic field. We won't give them access to their spells."

"Their resolve is solid, Kyla," Avalene warned. "They mediated for days and were thus able to generate extremely powerful spells that should have not been possible in their state. Even with sapping cuffs or an anti-magic field, it could prove problematic."

"Jarome has housed plenty of rogue mages in his prison," Kyla pointed out. "We'll hand them over to him, then. I wager he'll send a better convoy after last time."

Avalene sighed, long and drawn out. "If he even agrees to send another..."

"These people are endangering the city, of course he'll agree to it."

Avalene closed her eyes and massaged her brow, her glasses bumping upwards. "So, after your trap has been sprung, the Fangs will be much harder to fool. Are you sure this is how you want to spend your surprise attack?"

"I believe it's a worthy time to. It's better to do this before they get to know us, after all. They don't know how competent we are right now, so they're more likely to underestimate us."

"A reasonable observation."

"Sooo," Kyla ventured, "are you on board, then?"

Avalene was quiet, her lips jutted with consideration. "You were right when you said they're coming whether we're ready or not. I think you have the right idea to swing the situation in our favor. A little control is always appreciated."

Kyla smiled at her old friend. "I'm glad we're on the same page."

"So, how are you planning to keep tabs on the spy?"

"Gavin will be tailing him, and the rest of my eldest will be helping out. Quinn is also finishing up a bug we hope to use."

Avalene nodded, satisfied with that response. "Well, do keep me updated with the details..." The vigilante sighed and stood up from her desk, stretching. "I'm sore for a walk. I've sat in this cursed chair since last night."

"Haven't slept yet?" Kyla raised her eyebrows.

"With what time?" Avalene shook her head. "This is the ugliest case I've ever worked on. I never thought my job would brush shoulders with people like these."

"Well, if these people are ready and willing to hurt a child than it's right in the job description, isn't it? It's a little different then what we're used to, but that doesn't mean we can't handle it."

"I hope you're right about that, Kyla..." Avalene muttered, wrinkles of worry weighing down her brow. "Truly, I do..."

Chapter 30

Rorrik

It turned out Valen really enjoyed ping pong.

Rorrik had brought him into the rec room and run down the basics of the game to the demorinkin, Valen learning quickly. At first he was fairly clumsy with the paddle and his dexterity left much to be desired, but then he began to improve with practice. As he got the hang of the game, he became more confident; he was even able to barely retaliate to a few of Rorrik's trickier serves.

Most impressive was that the demorinkin actually seemed to be having fun; Rorrik had never heard Valen laugh so much. It was encouraging to see him finally loosen up and relax a little.

It was getting to be later that afternoon when Jate, Calvin, and Talis noticed their sport and joined in. They were all eager to show Valen their "special moves", the demorinkin a good sport to their tomfoolery. Valen never won a game but did not seem discouraged by the fact.

Late in the evening Rorrik's mother returned home, once again with takeout. This time it was pizza, much to the pleasure of all the siblings.

There were three choices in pizza: plain cheese, pepperoni with bacon, and supreme. The siblings grabbed their slices enthusiastically, Rorrik grabbing two pieces of the pepperoni and another of the supreme.

He looked over to see what Valen was doing and spotted him talking with his mother.

"No, it's alright. I think I... I think I'll try a piece," he heard Valen tell her.

"If you're sure you're alright with that, great!" his mother replied. "Mind the grease, though. Your stomach is still adjusting."

Valen was going to try a piece of pizza?! The demorinkin hadn't eaten anything other than bread and eggs since his rescue! *'Oh, and that cupcake...'*

Rorrik couldn't help but smile as the demorinkin grabbed a plate and gingerly placed a plain cheese piece on it. He came and sat down next to Rorrik at the table, offering the felidaren a bashful glance and a shrug.

Rorrik continued beaming at him and playfully bumped the demorinkin with his shoulder. He was glad Valen was feeling good enough to try a different meal.

Valen slowly lifted the pizza to his mouth and took a small, tentative bite, his eyes closing blissfully as he chewed. He swallowed and exhaled a light sigh. "That's... that's *delicious.*"

"Isn't it? Pantino's has the best pizza in this part of the city!" Rorrik gushed.

Valen replied with a weak grin but then realized the whole table was gawking at him, chasing away his smile as a blush formed on his cheeks.

"He's eating the pizza!" Talis yelled out in surprise, mid-bite of his own plain cheese slice.

Jate smiled as he gave Valen a nod and returned to his own pizza. He had grabbed all supreme pieces, four on his plate total; well, three and a half now.

Calvin, who had grabbed two pepperoni, rolled his eyes. "Took him long enough."

"Talis, Calvin, that's enough," their mother scolded. "Be respectful."

"It's alright," Valen dismissed with an awkward chuckle. He studied his slice and brought it up to take another bite, and then another.

Rorrik noticed he was so busy staring that he had not even touched his own plate yet. He got to it, starting with a pepperoni piece.

"Where's Gavin and Quinn?" their mother asked, sitting down with a plate herself. She had grabbed two supreme pieces.

"Quinn is at the shop and Gavin was upstairs last I saw him," Jate answered. "He was talking to Dad."

Their parent nodded slowly. "Well, I'll have someone run a plate to Quinn later. As for your other brother, he—"

"Will grab himself a plate, yes," Gavin's voice suddenly interrupted.

Rorrik turned to see the eldest walking into the kitchen.

"Couldn't ignore the scent of pizza any longer, eh?" Jate joked.

Gavin offered a brief smirk. "Sorry I'm late."

"Don't worry about it," their mother said.

Gavin fetched a plate of two supreme pieces and a pepperoni and sat down at the table with the rest of them.

Dinner went by in relative silence, a quiet meal by comparison for the family. Valen had eaten his entire slice, his gaze remaining on his empty plate after doing so. When Rorrik had asked if he was going to get more, the demorinkin had shaken his head.

Following dinner, Valen headed for Rorrik's room, the tabby following along. Valen headed for the bed and sat down, his eyes falling on the packet he had left unfinished earlier that day.

Rorrik plopped down on the bed next to him. The tabby lay back, his belly happy and full from the pizza. "So, did you have fun today?"

Valen met his eyes and gave a weak grin. "I did, yeah..."

Rorrik smiled at him. "That's great!"

Valen broke eye contact and looked to the floor, the grin melting away. He began to look thoughtful.

"Well, what do you want to do tonight?" Rorrik asked him.

Valen's shoulders bumped in a shrug, his demeanor quickly worsening as a frown drug down the corners of his lips.

"...Is something wrong?"

Valen sighed. "I just..." he started, his brow wrinkling. "I don't know how to feel sometimes..."

Rorrik sat back up. "What do you mean?"

"I can't shake this..." Valen searched for the word. "...*guilt*. Every time I even *slightly* feel okay I just... It comes right back and..." His voice thickened with emotion.

Rorrik frowned at him and his ears pressed back. "I'm sorry..."

Valen shook his head and his eyes clenched shut. "No, *I'm* sorry..."

Rorrik wasn't sure what to say to help him. Therefore, instead of using his words he used his touch, giving the demorinkin a light headbutt on his shoulder. He kept his head there, still searching his mind for something to say. "It's okay to feel better, Valen..."

Valen flinched at that and then the demorinkin was dipping his head. Rorrik stared up at him, his own frown growing.

"I just... I always get reminded of —" Valen shakily started to say before the door flung open. In ran Calvin and Talis, Rorrik pulling away from Valen at the intrusion.

The two of them pounced on Rorrik and slammed him into the mattress, Valen hopping up and off the bed to avoid being dragged into it.

"Surprise attack!" his youngest brother squealed.

"We totally got you!" Calvin laughed boastfully.

Rorrik attempted to wrestle them off him. "Knock it off!"

Talis only giggled, and Calvin gave a snicker.

"Seriously!" Rorrik growled, his ears flat with irritation. "You guys aren't even allowed in here!" He finally managed to kick them off him.

"Awww! But we want to play more!" Talis whined.

"We were allowed in here before!" Calvin complained.

"Rorrik, it's okay..." Valen assured in a quiet voice.

Rorrik turned to look at the demorinkin, spotting him hastily wiping at his eyes. The tabby's heart twisted, and he cursed his little brothers' terrible timing.

"He says it's okay so it's okay!" Calvin pushed, stubborn.

"Yeah!" Talis ungracefully nodded his head in agreement.

"You don't get it!" Rorrik told them both, stern. "He's just being nice!"

"Whaaat! No, he liked playing with us earlier! He even played spies with us!"

"*Talis!*" Calvin snapped, hitting him on the arm.

Rorrik's eyebrows raised. "Spies?" He glanced at Valen and noticed the demorinkin was standing straighter, his eyes worried and his face growing increasingly red.

"You *spied*?" the tabby questioned him, surprised.

"I—They—" Valen sputtered guiltily, alarm in his voice.

Rorrik could not hold back laughter. "No way! On what?!"

"The meeting, duh," Calvin answered with a scoff. "Not like there's anything else to do. I hate being stuck here!"

"Dad caught us, though," Talis added. "So we didn't get to spy much…"

Rorrik turned back to Valen, the demorinkin still looking positively uncomfortable.

"I'm sorry!" Valen desperately apologized. "I don't know what came over me!"

"Sorry? It's fine!" Rorrik excused with a chuckle, waving his hand. The tabby was way more amused than offended.

"No, it's not fine! I wasn't invited for a reason; I shouldn't have eavesdropped!"

"You weren't invited because we were just figuring out the specifics of the plan. It's not like it was secretive or anything. Don't sweat it!"

"I still invaded your privacy," Valen pressed. "It was wrong!"

Rorrik blinked as his look went sideways. "I mean… I guess. But it's not a big deal."

"Yes, it is!"

Rorrik had no idea how to respond. He wasn't sure why Valen was being so insistent that *he* was in the wrong; Rorrik had said it was fine!

"What, does privacy mean *nothing* in this family?"

The brothers looked in between each other.

"Uhhh," Rorrik trailed off.

Valen face palmed with a shake of his head. "You know what? Never mind…"

Rorrik felt awkward at Valen's behavior; he was not used to someone making spying such a big deal.

Talis seemed unfazed as he began to roll around on the bed. "This bed is sooo big! We could ALL sleep on it!"

"How come you get a bigger bed, anyways?" Calvin muttered sourly.

Rorrik's impatience with his siblings returned. "Because I'm older! Seriously, if you guys don't leave I'm going to go get Mom!" the tabby warned.

"Oh, come on, Rorrik!" Calvin protested with a groan.

"We don't have to play; we can just cuddle!" Talis tried, snuggling into the blankets with a sputter of a purr.

"No!" Rorrik began pushing them off the bed. "Just go!"

His siblings finally listened and they headed for the door, Talis bummed and Calvin annoyed.

"Jerk!" Calvin spat before slamming the door.

Rorrik felt a pinch of remorse at kicking his brothers out, but what choice did he have? It wasn't the time for their antics!

Valen sat back down on the bed with a sigh, his face still hidden by his palm. "You didn't have to make them leave," he said quietly.

Rorrik shrugged and looked down at the comforter. "I figured you... weren't really in the mood, though." He remembered the demorinkin's behavior before his brothers had intruded.

Valen gave a very slow nod and he finally dropped his hand from his face. He met Rorrik's eyes.

"Well, thanks..." Valen's lips twitched with an attempt of a grin but the expression was stunted by his melancholy.

Rorrik could not hold his eyes as he nodded in reply. His focus drifted up towards the loft bed and his expression fell. Perhaps that night still wasn't a suitable time to do sleepover things... He had kicked his brothers out in the name of minding Valen's feelings, and yet he himself was asking Valen of things that he wasn't up for. He had to think of what Valen needed, not what he himself wanted. *'He had just seemed so much better today...'*

"You're probably tired, huh?" Rorrik asked him.

Valen nodded and dropped his gaze onto the floor.

"Okay, I can let you go to bed, then." He hopped from the mattress and scurried over to flip the light switch, the room falling into partial darkness, the nightlight in the corner glowing dimly.

Rorrik was ready to head out the door when he heard Valen sigh.

"...I'm sorry, Rorrik," the demorinkin mumbled, his eyes still on the floor.

Rorrik shook his head at the demorinkin. "Don't apologize, it's okay!" he encouraged, successful in keeping his disappointment out of his tone.

Valen glanced over at him and held his eyes for a moment. The demorinkin then sighed yet again and looked away, his attention falling onto the bed. He began to tuck himself in, the tabby watching all the while.

Rorrik went to head out the door. "Goodnight, Valen..."

"Goodnight..." the demorinkin mumbled in reply.

Rorrik closed the door, unable to stave off a frown any longer. He sighed and went off to busy himself; the felidaren was much too awake to even try going to sleep. Normally bedtime was a few hours after dinner, not directly following it, after all.

He found Jate and Gavin sitting in the rec room, their eyes on the television up on the wall. Rorrik sat down next to them, his bummed demeanor holding.

"What's with the frown, Rorrik?" Jate wondered.

"Valen is bothered again..." Rorrik sighed.

"Is that a surprise?" Gavin asked.

Rorrik thought about that. "No, not really..." His shoulders raised in a drawn-out shrug. "I just... he had fun today, so I thought..."

"This kind of thing is complicated, Rorrik," Gavin explained. "He's still recovering from what happened, and he is in mourning. It's a process. One moment he might be happy and the next he might be sad."

"Gavin is right, kit," Jate agreed. "Just be patient with him."

"He said he doesn't know how to feel... He was about to say something else when Calvin and Talis ran in," Rorrik said.

The older brothers looked to each other and winced.

"Ooh, sorry about that... We should have kept them busy," Jate apologized.

"I was able to get them out, it's okay." His eyes found the TV to see what they were watching. It looked like some sort of detective show, Gavin's favorite.

"Did he just go to bed, then?" Jate asked.

"Yeah..."

"Well, rest will help," Gavin supposed.

Rorrik wanted to believe his brothers. 'It's a process...' he internally repeated their wisdom. 'I just have to be patient.'

．．．

Rorrik had trouble getting and staying asleep throughout the night, anticipation over the job rendering him restless. His mind kept dwelling on the excitement to come and how great it would be to put their plan into motion. Nervousness also occasionally surfaced, considering he had never done a job so big before. He could not help but worry if he was ready, but his enthusiasm was quick to convince him.

He was lying there staring up at the ceiling when he heard Valen shifting from down below. The tabby blinked and peered off the edge of the loft bed, spotting Valen rocking his head back and forth, a wince on his face.

"N-no..." the demorinkin murmured, his expression tightening. A whimper began to leave him, and his body flinched before quickly turning over. He continued to moan and whine, his body scrunching up.

'He's having a bad dream.' The felidaren hurried down from the loft bed and gently shook at Valen's shoulders.

"Hey, Valen, wake up," the tabby tried.

Valen didn't respond as he continued to move his head back and forth, his face still in a grimace.

Rorrik pressed his ears back and shook a little harder. "You gotta wake up, Valen, come on..."

It took a little more stimulation but the demorinkin eventually snapped open his eyes, his look turning surprised. He sat up in a hurry and breathed hard, disoriented.

"You okay?"

Valen jumped at Rorrik's worried voice and set his attention on the tabby, his mouth falling open. He stared for a few moments before looking away, easing himself back into lying down. Tears began to pool, and he moved a hand up to cover his face, his shoulders jumping with a sob.

246

He started to cry, and so Rorrik crawled onto the bed and sat next to him, putting a hand on his arm. "It's okay," the tabby attempted to soothe.

Valen's tears didn't relent, the bed shaking with his sobs.

Rorrik frowned as he failed to help. The tabby considered how to proceed, thinking back to how he would comfort his brothers after a nightmare. *'We'd always cuddle...'*

He hesitantly decided to lay down next to the demorinkin and nuzzled into his shoulder. He started a purr, hoping it would help like it did during Valen's prior panic episode.

Valen's sobs eventually began to ebb and he sniffled, his hand still hiding his face. Rorrik continued his purring, his cheek brushed up against the demorinkin.

A few minutes passed, Valen's crying growing fainter and fainter. Finally, the demorinkin sighed and his hand moved from his face and onto his forehead, his hair pushing up.

Rorrik peered up at him, his expression anxious and his purring ceasing.

Valen opened his eyes and glanced down at the tabby, the two of them making eye contact. Valen adjusted so that he was facing Rorrik and wrapped his arms around the felidaren, squeezing tight.

Rorrik could not stave off surprise but did not fight his embrace. He returned the hug, his purr returning. He buried his head into Valen's neck, taking in his scent and warmth.

"Thank you..." Valen said, his voice thick with emotion.

Rorrik nuzzled into his friend. "It's going to be okay..."

The two remained cuddled for several minutes, Rorrik growing sleepy from the warmth of their huddle. If he didn't move soon he figured he would fall asleep and so, he began to gently pull away.

Valen let it happen; he dodged Rorrik's gaze as the felidaren sat up.

Rorrik was turning to go when Valen shakily said, "Please don't leave..."

The felidaren's ears perked and he looked back to the demorinkin. Valen was cradling his chest, his head dipped and his shoulders scrunched.

Rorrik's heart gave a flutter and he immediately lay back down, starting a purr yet again. He was more than happy to stay.

Valen did not move as Rorrik returned to his spot next to him, his arms still wrapped around his torso. The demorinkin then rolled onto his back and his eyes opened to stare at the ceiling, his yellow irises twinkling in the dim lighting of the room.

Rorrik snuggled into his side and Valen raised an arm to drape it across the felidaren. The tabby placed his head on his chest and the sound of Valen's heartbeat hit his ears.

Valen let go of a trembling sigh. "I miss him so much..." he started, his chest giving a shudder as another storm of tears threatened. "I don't even know what to do... It doesn't feel real..." He squeezed his eyes shut and his free hand covered his face, a sob falling out of him. "I wake up and he's not there and it hurts so bad every time… I miss him… *I miss him…*"

'*He's talking about his brother…*' Rorrik snuggled even closer to Valen, his empathy swelling. The tabby nuzzled into him, hoping to ward off even just a fraction of Valen's agony.

Valen coughed out another sob. "I promised him and now he's gone. It's all my fault…" His body shuddered as he bawled. "I miss him… I miss him…"

Rorrik had no words to offer the demorinkin and so he continued to snuggle and purr, feeling helpless against the barrage of Valen's grief.

Time stretched on as Valen wept and Rorrik attempted to provide solace. Eventually, the demorinkin's crying began to wane. He had been quiet for a few minutes when Rorrik noticed that his breathing had become softer and slower. The felidaren peeked up at him and noticed his eyes were closed, hinting that he had fallen back asleep.

Rorrik placed his head back down on Valen's chest and closed his own eyes, searching for slumber, himself. It answered quickly and the two remained cuddled together, sound asleep.

Chapter 31

Valen

Valen felt Karreo next to him as he began to come to. He sleepily rolled over and nestled into his little brother, a sigh departing his chest. He had missed his younger sibling terribly; it had been so long since the demorinkin had turned over and found him there.

He was enjoying his companionship when a rumbling began to hit his ears and vibrate against his chest. He focused on it and realized it was a purr.

Valen was pulled out of the remainder of his slumber and opened his eyes, finding it was not Karreo at all, but Rorrik. The felidaren was sleeping with his back to Valen, the demorinkin cuddled into him from behind.

Realization slammed him and his heart splintered. He scooted away and sat up, bringing a hand up to his forehead as sadness and shock resonated through him. He squeezed his eyes shut, exhausted and broken from the reminder that his baby brother was gone.

Rorrik turned over so he was facing Valen and gave a sleepy exhale, his purr jumbling in the process; he still seemed to be sleeping.

Valen stared down at the tabby, recalling the events from the night before. Valen remembered waking up from an emotional nightmare about Karreo and the felidaren being there to comfort him. Rorrik had laid down with him, and Valen had been too desperate for companionship to let the felidaren leave. His face flushed at the memory, embarrassed he had been so needy. *'He didn't seem to mind, though…'* For whatever reason, that added to his blush.

The felidaren seemed comfortable enough being physical with him. He remembered Talis mentioning cuddling instead of playing the night before, too. Valen had once heard that felidaren were a touchy-feely lot with those they liked and accepted; it would seem that was true for this family.

The demorinkin tried to shoo away his feelings of embarrassment but they were loath to leave him. Rorrik then started to stir next to him and apprehension joined his humility. How would Rorrik react in light of the night before? Valen was nervous to find out.

The felidaren stretched with a massive yawn and his claws unsheathed to scratch briefly at the sheets, Valen impressed at how much his body bended. Rorrik rolled onto his back as his emerald eyes cracked open, his vision quickly finding Valen. He yawned again, his fangs showing off in the display.

"Morning," the felidaren greeted, casual enough.

Valen felt awkward, regardless. "Morning," he forced the reply.

Rorrik sat up and had another hearty stretch. He then regarded Valen with a tiny frown. "How are you feeling?"

Valen didn't hold his eyes. He fought a sigh and shrugged, letting that be his answer.

Rorrik gently leaned into him. "Well, I'm here if you need me…"

Valen flushed as his feelings of embarrassment worsened.

To his relief, Rorrik didn't linger in the gesture and scooted off the bed, his tail twitching behind him. He approached the dresser and tilted his head, his eyes catching the clothing sitting on top of it.

"Hey, when did your vest get in here?"

Valen shrunk. "I, uh… When I got the school packets I brought all my stuff in here…"

"Oh! Okay." He glanced back at him. "I'm going to take a shower. You can take one, too, if you want. The towels are in the cabinet next to the toilet."

Valen's insides churned at the idea of a shower, but he knew he needed one. He gave a hesitant nod.

"Since there's two bathrooms we can take our showers at the same time," Rorrik said. "Come on, let's go get clean!"

■ ■ ■

At the tabby's own request, Rorrik went into the bathroom with him to show how the shower worked. It was a single knob that turned from left to right, hot on one end and cold on the other, just like the guest showers. To activate the shower one pulled a tab on the faucet upwards.

"If you want, you can take a bath instead," Rorrik suggested, pointing to the tub. "You're not in any kind of rush, sooo…"

Valen was tempted by that plan, but the luxury of it discouraged him. Still, it was better than reliving his trauma through a shower… He began to seriously consider it.

"The shower head pops off if you want to wash your hair in the tub easier," Rorrik mentioned. He showed how to remove the nozzle then returned it to the bearing. "I think that's it! Like I said, towels are in the cabinet there." He pointed to the container next to the toilet.

Valen nodded and offered a weak grin. "Thanks."

The felidaren smiled and left the room, leaving him alone. The demorinkin walked up to lock the door and gave a nervous exhale. He had never stripped down in the family quarters before, and he was more than reluctant to do so.

250

Valen summoned all his courage and bared himself slowly and warily, cursing how exposed he felt. He eyed the door, afraid someone would come barging in or knock frantically. He hated how bothered he felt in nothing but his skin, the shadow of his trauma an influencing one.

He grabbed a towel from the cabinet and hung it on a bar hanging next to the tub. He leaned down to start the tap, his free hand reaching out to test the temperature as it poured, the flow of water through the faucet considerably less triggering than the downpour of a shower head. Even still, the water felt too cold for too long, psyching him out. Eventually, it reached an ideal temperature, and he decided he was not brave enough for a shower. He put the stopper in, and the tub began to fill with a bath.

He didn't wait for it to fill all the way before lowering himself in, the feel of the water as it began to pool around him an experience he had long been denied. He had last taken a bath in the comfort of his family home two lives ago, the night he had packed for his 'trip'. The memory stung to recall and so he took in what was around him, trying to focus on the present rather than his biting past. It was easier said than done.

The tub continued to fill up, the water soothing to his still tender muscles. He splashed some up onto his bare torso, the liquid soaking him with warmth.

'*Just relax...*' He closed his eyes and eased himself into lying down, his eyes closing. The water soaked his hair, and he dunked his head back so the entirety of it got wet. He had always liked soaking his hair in a bath; he enjoyed the way it floated and sprawled about when submersed.

Soon the water reached a good amount and he pushed in the knob with his foot, the flow of water ceasing. He melted into the heat of the bath and appreciated its therapeutic embrace. Guilt was quick to tail his pleasure but he was too desperate for peace to linger on the negativity festering within him. He just wanted to relax for a little while, even if he knew he did not deserve it.

He forced himself to think about something else and found his mind dwelling on the night before. He could not lie that it had been comforting to have someone close in the midst of his nightmares and grief. Although it had been jarring to wake up thinking the tabby was his little brother, he could not deny that it had been nice to have someone nearby, regardless.

His body grew hot with embarrassment as he thought about Rorrik's purring. For whatever reason, it had a lulling effect on the demorinkin; he was bashful at how much it helped in the brunt of his episodes. Something about it calmed him, whether it was the feel of faint rumbling, the sound of the noise, or both. He could not deny it provided a great amount of respite.

He felt too ashamed at even entertaining the idea of asking Rorrik to sleep in the bed with him. It made him feel like a desperate child, scared and bothered from nightmares and longing shamelessly for solace. '*Child or not... it's true...*'

The reminder of the family's mission entered his mind without warning, and Valen felt a familiar kick of dread, guilt quick to join it. He was terrified of the Fangs of Hellbane and appreciated the family's help, but their sacrifice troubled him. He knew it was their job and that it was their choice to help him, but the idea they were risking their wellbeing for him was worrisome. Valen felt guilty over accepting their assistance; he did not feel worthy of help and was ashamed at the idea of getting it.

He was attempting to clear his mind when he realized that he had to scrub himself clean at some point. With a sigh, his eyes scanned for soap, finding a bottle of body wash on a rack hanging from the showerhead. He would have to stand up to reach it.

He hoisted himself up and stood, reaching out to grab the bottle. He noticed shampoo next to the soap on the rack and froze with temptation. His hair was dry and brittle from using body soap as long as he had; it would surely thank him to get the hydration it needed. His guiltiness protested, demanding that he should not indulge himself. He grabbed both bottles anyway.

He placed them on the side of the tub and eyed the shower head with worry. It would most definitely be easier to wash his hair with the nozzle, as Rorrik had stated, but it was still a shower. Perhaps it would feel different if he held it close enough to his scalp?

He grabbed the nozzle off its bearing and returned to the water, the warmth of the bath welcoming him back. He eyed the showerhead in his hands and let it hang until he was ready to use it.

He got to scrubbing his body with the soap, making it as brief as he did in his previous showers. As had become usual, the sensation of touching his privates bothered him, his body unable to shake the phantom of the terrible hands that had been there before, yanking and fingering and assessing. It was enough to make his skin crawl, and he wished it all would go away. It was not happening to him now, so why did it still impact him so?

He finally finished and didn't delay with pouring some shampoo into his palm. He lathered it into his hair, his claws massaging the product deep into his scalp. He could practically feel his hair drink up the hydration it had been denied for so long. It lifted his spirits a tad, despite the ever-present suggestion that he stay miserable.

He eyed the shower head and sucked in a deep breath. He turned the water on and held his hand in the faucet stream, waiting for it to reach an ideal temperature. When it did, he flipped the tab on the faucet, the noise of water whirling through the pipes, up into the shower, and then down the nozzle sounding. Water came rushing from the shower head, hitting the tile of the wall but not him.

He felt the water with his hand and it proved warm. He trusted in logic and brought the shower head to his soapy scalp, the stream soaking him instantly. He gasped but did not pull away, the temperature proving warm despite the persuasion of his trauma.

When he was all rinsed off, he turned off the tap and stood up from the water, realizing how dirty it had become with a glance downwards.

He unplugged the stopper, grabbed the towel, and patted himself dry. Next came dressing into the clothes he had brought into the bathroom with him, more of Rorrik's spare sweatpants and t-shirt.

He checked his reflection in the mirror, his hair wet and sprawled every which way from using the towel to help dry it. His expression went crooked as he attempted to run his fingers through his locks, a mess of knots thwarting the effort. He despised that his hair had become so mangled; what good was shampoo if he wasn't even taking care of it?

When was the last time he had even combed it? It had been before he left the clock tower prior to that last date with Siena, he realized, the knowledge tearing at him. He had used to fuss over his appearance so much, and now it had fallen into ruin, just like the rest of him.

He sighed and looked away from the mirror, the sink coming into view. He noticed a woven basket that housed a comb sitting on the counter. Valen frowned as more temptation taunted him. He weighed brushing his hair, his misery versus his desire to feel better.

Another victory was earned for his spirits as he reached out for the comb and caressed his fingers along its bristles. A brush had been one of the first things he had earned back on the streets of Akarth, Valen having understood what being groomed did for his morale.

He worked the comb through his hair, the knots catching constantly. He was persistent but gentle as he worked through them, careful not to snap his locks. It took him a solid twenty minutes, but his hair eventually succumbed to his priming. He ran a hand through it yet again, and no knots protested this time around.

A smile broke involuntarily. He adjusted his hair part and studied his reflection, a glimpse of the old him staring back.

The smile vanished as his guilt finally caught up with him. It was extra insistent after ignoring it for so long, relentless as it bullied him into feeling despicable for taking care of himself.

He frowned and the glimpse of his old self flickered away, replaced instead by his tormented present reflection.

He sighed and turned to leave, wondering how he could ever move on.

. . .

Kyla

The tortoiseshell had awoken earlier that morning than she normally did, a restless night rendering her eager to get out of bed. She had walked down the hallway to poke her head into Rorrik's room so she could check on Valen, something that had become habit over the last few days.

She had seen that Rorrik and the demorinkin sleeping soundly on the same mattress. She wondered what had spurred her son into relocating to the queen bed and figured Valen must have had another nightmare; she was relieved he had Rorrik there to help him.

She had gone out to relax on the roof of the inn, watching as the sunrise bathed the city in light. She found solace in the wake of dawn, the new day arriving with the promise of a clean slate. She had a lot to piece together in the time to come; the mission needed much preparation, indeed.

Amongst that preparation was arranging Pepperglow to come and train Valen in the rucanic. She called the mage on her corresponder upon returning to the basement.

It didn't take more than two rings for the wizardess to answer. "'Morning, Spot. It's a little early for chitchat, so I take it you have a job for me?"

"That's right," the tortoiseshell confirmed. "I was wondering if you could come train our rescue in activating enchantments. You'll be compensated."

"The kid needs help learning how to trigger runes, eh?" Pepperglow replied with an amused grunt. "Sure, I can do that. When?"

"I was hoping you could come by today, if you're available. I know it's short notice…"

"Today works fine. Is that all?"

"Actually," the queen started, "we're still unsure of what he's entirely capable of magically, which can prove very dangerous in case the hideout is attacked. I was—"

"Dangerous? You really think he could pose a danger? I thought he was just some rookie kid?"

"He knows a very powerful constrict spell," Kyla corrected, the memory of said spell replaying in her mind's eye. "He cast it to save his life when he was being attacked before. We should make sure he's not going to do anything worse, for everyone's safety."

"I wasn't aware he was that powerful. I suppose it's not a surprise – he's obviously got demorin blood flowing through him. What are you thinking, then? A stress test to see what he can do?"

"He's in too fragile of a state to do a stress test." The felidaren had considered that option herself but decided against it. While the results of the test would reveal the most powerful spells Valen knew, the price of discovering that information would be forcing Valen into believing something terrible was happening to him. Stress tests were notoriously brutal on their recipients; it was the last thing Valen needed after so much pain and trauma. "Instead, I was wondering if you could start training him in how to use a spell slinger."

"Spell slinger, huh? Ah, you're thinking that if he has a weapon it won't come down to him being forced into something drastic?"

"You got it. I have one available in the equipment room that he can use."

"Great. Anything else?"

"Nope, that's it. Thank you, Pepperglow. That will be all."

She went on to complete her next tasks: getting a shower and preparing breakfast for her family. She was delving into the latter when Jate walked into the kitchen.

"'Morning," her son greeted with a kiss on the cheek. "Busy day ahead, huh?"

"That's the plan," Kyla replied. "We have a lot to piece together if we're going to make this work."

Her son nodded. "Well, let me know if you need my help!"

"On mission prep or breakfast?" his mother quipped with a grin.

Jate laughed. "Both!"

"Well, for starters you can beat some eggs."

"Consider it done."

Gavin eventually arrived in the kitchen and also kissed her good morning.

"Quinn isn't in his room, so we can assume he's still at the shop," he announced.

Kyla nodded. "I checked in with our watch. He's still there."

Gavin shook his head and Jate laughed.

"Hopefully his brain doesn't overheat while trying to get that bug not to!" Jate chortled.

Gavin smirked at that. "You know him, he has a tendency to get tapped into projects."

"Especially ones with deadlines," the mother reminded. "Gavin, go ahead and get some fruit together for a salad. Jate, butter some bread, will you?"

Her sons obeyed without protest.

Calvin and Talis then came running down the hall, chasing one another.

"TALIS!" Calvin bellowed, hot on Talis' trail. "GIVE IT BACK!"

"Boys!" Kyla shouted at their backs. "What is going on?!"

"Talis took my bouncy ball!"

"I didn't! This one is mine!"

"No, it isn't!" Calvin screeched. "Mine is the green one! Yours is the blue one! You LOST yours!"

"Na-uh! You're lying! YOU lost yours!"

"Boys, it's too early for this!" Kyla scolded. She looked to Gavin. "Handle that, please?"

He nodded and went to do as she asked.

"You can always share and play together with the bouncy ball," she heard her eldest tell him.

"Not in the living room, take it to the hall!" Kyla stressed.

"I don't want to play with him! He took my bouncy ball!" Calvin whined.

"I didn't!"

"It doesn't matter whose it is, if you can't agree to play together then no one will get to play with it," Gavin warned.

"What! No! Mooom!" Calvin yowled.

"Listen to your brother!" Kyla told him.

"Come ooon!" The ten-year-old protested. "This is so dumb! It's mine!"

"No, it's mine!" Talis fought.

"It's about to be *mine*," Gavin said. "Hand it here."

"Nooo!" Kyla heard hurried footsteps start up again and turned around to see Talis run off, Calvin on his heels as well as Gavin this time.

'*Gods above...*' She wondered if her youngest children were going stir crazy from being cooped up. '*Hopefully we can get everything all sorted out soon enough...*'

Rorrik then walked into the kitchen, his fur damp and his eyebrows raised. "Whoa, what did I miss?"

"Bouncy ball drama," Jate answered with a snicker.

Kyla noted Rorrik was alone. "Where's Valen?"

"He's taking a bath."

"That's great news." The mother smiled; self-care was always a big step in the wake of trauma. "We can put a plate aside for him."

Kyla was laying everything out on the island counter when Gavin and the two youngest walked back into the kitchen, Talis crying and Calvin looking grumpy. Gavin had the bouncy ball in his hands and placed it in his pocket.

"Breakfast is ready, boys. Quit those crocodile tears and come eat," the mother ordered.

The family all sat down to eat, sans Valen. The meal in total was toast, scrambled eggs, fruit salad, and ham.

"So, we have a lot to get figured out today in preparation for our mission," Kyla told her boys. "Following breakfast, I'm going to a meeting with some of our people to discuss how we're going to shape up the old safe house. Gavin, Jate, Rorrik, I want you three coming with on that."

Rorrik perked up, and Gavin and Jate nodded.

"Calvin, Talis, I expect you to work on school today."

Talis started crying again. "I hate school! *I* want to do something exciting! It's no fair!"

"Yeah! We've been stuck here for days! It's so boring!" Calvin moaned in indignation.

"I'm sorry, boys, that's just the way it has to be right now!" Kyla sighed. "You'll be able to leave again after we get more of this straightened out."

Calvin and Talis appeared less than satisfied with that answer. They both proceeded their pouting, Kyla feeling a kick of pity for them. They were too young and full of energy to be locked up like they had been.

"How long is that even going to take?" Calvin questioned in aggravation.

"That's still uncertain, cub. Understand that sometimes in our line of work we have to stay hidden. If you want to be successful, you have to know when to lie low."

"Mom's right," Gavin nodded. "You want to be successful, don't you?"

Calvin crossed his arms and jutted his eyes away from his brother, ignoring him.

Kyla went on, "Anyway, I've arranged it so Valen will be training in magic with Pepperglow today. Rorrik, could you let him know before we leave?"

Rorrik looked somewhat surprised before nodding. "Uh, yeah, I'll let him know!"

"What?! So Valen gets to train and we have to do school?!" Calvin proceeded to whine.

"I want to train, too!" Talis added to the chorus of complaints.

Kyla shook her head at her children. "You will be doing school work today, that's final."

"Ugh!" Calvin stomped. "I—"

"*Enough,*" Kyla interrupted, her tone darkening. "No more complaints. Do what you're told."

Calvin and Talis shut their mouths, but their expressions still broadcasted the sour thoughts on their tongues.

The family finished their breakfast in silence following that, the youngest brothers pouting and the oldest siblings mindful.

"Well, I leave for that meeting in half an hour," Kyla announced. "I expect the three of you to be ready by then. I'll be waiting upstairs. Jate, Calvin, it's your turn to do dishes."

Calvin groaned loudly and Jate chuckled.

"Come on, kit, it won't take long."

"I'm not a kit!" Calvin wailed in protest.

The mother shook her head and dropped her plate off in the sink. With that, she headed upstairs.

■   ■   ■

Rorrik

Rorrik was sitting at the desk in his room waiting for the demorinkin to finish his bath, the felidaren's mind busy with thoughts of the job ahead. It wasn't long before he heard footsteps approaching, and a freshly groomed Valen stepped through the doorway.

Rorrik noticed immediately that something was different about him. The tabby could not help but stare, realizing that for the first time Valen's black hair was neatly combed and parted. He found himself admiring how the demorinkin's locks now fell, all the knots that had been mangling and twisting it before nowhere to be seen. There was also a sheen that had not been there previously, rendering Valen considerably healthier looking.

The two of them locked eyes, Rorrik's surprise showing in his expression.

Valen's features bent with confusion and he gave an uncertain grin. "...what?"

Rorrik gave his friend a toothy smile. "You combed your hair!"

Valen's look turned sheepish and he broke eye contact with the tabby. A tiny shrug lifted his shoulders.

"It looks great!" The fur on his cheeks warmed.

Valen received Rorrik's compliment with a frown, and another shrug hardly nudged his shoulders.

Rorrik's smile dissipated. "...are you alright?"

Valen sighed and sluggishly made his way to the bed, sitting down on the edge. "It's like I said yesterday... I don't know how to feel sometimes..."

Rorrik turned around in his chair so he was facing the backrest. He waited for Valen to go on, his green eyes worried.

Valen was slow to continue. "It's like... even when I want to feel better... the guilt eventually catches up, and I end up feeling worse." He put a hand up to his forehead, his dark hair scrunching beneath his touch. "I just... want to feel okay, but how am I going to ever again? I..." The demorinkin shook his head and his hand moved to cover his eyes, hiding his face.

Rorrik desperately searched himself for words of comfort. He recalled his conversation with his brothers from the night before. "It's... a process. You just have to give it time," he warily told his friend. "You're still healing..."

A shuddery exhale left Valen. "I don't know how I'm ever going to heal..."

Rorrik frowned heavily, wishing he knew the answer to that. He proceeded his search for something meaningful to say. "I'm here to help... however I can." The warmth on his cheeks intensified. "We'll figure it out. Don't worry!"

Valen peeked at him from beneath his hand before unveiling his face, and the two of them held each other's gaze.

"...Thanks, Rorrik," Valen breathed through a weak grin, his voice thick. Rorrik spotted a faint blush coloring the demorinkin's cheeks.

Rorrik's own blush went hotter at the sight. "Ah, no problem!" he replied, his voice nearly cracking. Sudden embarrassment swept over him, and the two broke eye contact. The felidaren gripped at the chair, his claws retracting and catching in the wood. He wondered why he was blushing and wrestling sheepishness; it wasn't like him to be shy. Well, sometimes talking to pretty girls made him shy, but…Valen wasn't a pretty girl!

Both were quiet in the following moments, rendering Rorrik even more awkward. He remembered why he was there. "Oh! My mom said to tell you that you're having magic training today."

Valen snapped his attention back on Rorrik with a look of surprise. "What, really?"

Rorrik bobbed his head in a nod. "That should be fun, huh?"

Valen weakly grinned and it struck Rorrik as uncertain. The demorinkin looked away and rubbed at the back of his neck. "Maybe…"

Rorrik tilted his head. "I thought you liked magic?"

"I do…" Valen agreed. "It's just… what I have to learn is a bit nerve wracking, considering…" the demorinkin trailed off, but Rorrik waited, his head still tilted.

Valen grimaced as he was forced to continue and shrugged. "It's to protect myself in case of… the worst…"

Clarity splashed upon Rorrik, soaking him with understanding. "Oh!" His ears pressed back as he once again found himself searching for something to say. He offered his friend a supporting smile. "Well, at least what you're learning is fun, right? Sure, it's for your protection, but it's really unlikely you'll have to use what you learn! At least… for *that*."

Valen looked thoughtful before letting out a sigh. "We'll see…"

Chapter 32

Rorrik

Rorrik's mother stood in front of the mass of workers that had been summoned for the task ahead, the scent of stale air thick in the room. There were twenty gathered total, including Rorrik and his older brothers. They had mustered in the den of the Token safe house, the furniture of the room showing its abandonment via a layer of dust.

"We've got a lot to accomplish if we want to whip this place into shape," the tortoiseshell started. "But, if we work efficiently we'll be done in no time."

"What's the plan?" a worker Rorrik did not recognize questioned, leading the felidaren to assume it was one of Miss Porte's people.

Miss Porte had sent a team of five to help prepare the safe house. Rorrik had noticed earlier with a kick of annoyance that Tommik, the brevin from the mission when he found Valen's vest, was among that team. He had avoided the brevin thus far and was ready to be moody if their paths crossed.

"First off, this place has enough dust to be a crypt, not an active safe house," his mother said. "Which means making it look lived-in is paramount. We need to not only dust but also dirty the place enough to make it look convincing."

"That seems a bit counterproductive," Jate snickered from next to Rorrik.

"It may seem that way, but if the place is too clean then it raises suspicion of its own. We're aiming to make it seem occupied."

There were several nods from the crowd.

"We also need to get some equipment moved in here. Weapons, food, surveillance—"

"There's a system still set up," Dalf mentioned from his chair in the corner. "It'll need some new wires if you want it to actually work, however."

Dalf, an old, wrinkly, bearded human male, was the caretaker and owner of the safe house. Though, it would seem he was lacking in the 'caretaker' department, considering the dust and abandonment of the place. Rorrik had not dealt with the human much, but Dalf did manage to look the same age every time the felidaren saw him, no older and no younger. Gavin said it was because he was a wizard and had frozen his physical aging, which had always puzzled Rorrik. If the man was magical, surely he could make himself look younger?

"We want it to work, yes. It will be important to have visuals on our visitors," his mother said. "We also need to organize some watches and generate some movement in and out of here; give our spy a show."

More nods answered her.

"Remember, though, we're trying to make the place look tempting to attack. We need to devise some kind of hole in our security. Any ideas?"

"Perhaps the guard shift is slow and lax?" a worker spoke up.

"That *can* work, but we need something more tempting, something that will give them a bigger time window," the tortoiseshell replied.

"*Window,* eh? Perhaps we were a tad foolish setting up our outside surveillance?" Dalf contributed. "Thus, the east wall is not very well guarded?"

Rorrik's mother excitedly nodded her head and pointed towards the wizard. "That's good! It gives them an opportunity to infiltrate without worry. It should be easy enough to spot for our snoop, too."

"What about the trap itself?" Rorrik recognized the voice as Tommik's, and his ears went flat.

"Well, I was thinking that we could fool them into seeing the demorinkin and lead them into a specific room where we have the means to incapacitate them," she explained. "Any ideas?"

"Pacifying them with magic is too risky, judging by their prior escape," Gavin pointed out. "They might be able to counter any spell."

"I was thinking the same. We can also assume they will be well-armed, so a preemptive strike and engaging them is riskier than it has to be. I think chemicals are our best bet."

"That is wisest. Have a particular one in mind?" Dalf wondered.

"That I do. Glowmist. It'll act quickly and cause minimal damage."

Rorrik had heard of the substance in his training. Glowmist was a heavy smoke composed of a rapid-acting hallucinogen — crushed and magically fermented Goldena seeds, if he remembered correctly. Recipients of the mist experienced vivid disorientation in all the senses (most famously the eyes, which are bombarded with visions of overwhelming color and brightness, hence the name). This overload of information causes a daze that can persist for minutes to an hour.

"Won't Glowmist only cause them to fall into a trance?" Tommik criticized.

"We merely need them to be hindered, not completely out cold," she said. "I can think of no others that would instantly work and not cause damage."

"Who cares if we damage them, though?" Tommik grumbled. "Loonies deserve it, I say."

"Whether they deserve it or not is irrelevant. We need their brains and bodies intact for questioning." Her eyes scanned her crew. "Any other questions or concerns?"

"How exactly do we plan to trick them into spotting the demorinkin?" one of his parents' workers asked. Rorrik could not recall her name but recognized her face, a common phenomenon when it came to much of their family's workforce. This particular employee was a lithely built gaian with marbled, smooth skin of black and white. She towered amongst of the rest of them (especially Tommik); Rorrik estimated her height to be easily eight feet.

"I'm thinking an illusion. That minimizes risk on our part," the tortoiseshell suggested.

"And what if they aren't fooled?" another voice asked, this one belonging to a male seakin with black scales that boasted an iridescence of green and blue. Rorrik blanked out on his name, as well.

"The whole point of infiltrating the safe house is to find the demorinkin. I think our guests will be easier to fool than not," his mother argued. "Remember, we're dealing with fanatics here."

"True as that may be, we should still be prepared for the worst," Dalf advised.

"We'll have the upper hand in a preemptive strike if it comes down to it," the tortoiseshell pointed out. "But I doubt it will."

"Even if you doubt it, it is good to have a plan for the worst," Dalf said. He then giggled. "However, the trouble with plans is we cannot plan for everything, no? It is good that our work celebrates those who can think on their feet."

"Indeed," she smiled. "But, if everything goes smoothly we shouldn't have to do much of that." She looked over the crowd. "Anything else?"

Silence was her reply.

The queen addressed them with a nod of determination. "Then let's get to work!"

. . .

Valen

"Concentrate," Pepperglow instructed yet again, her voice slow and even, patient. "Search for the flow of runa within you. Focus on it."

Valen attempted to do as his teacher told, but progress was evading him as it had been for the past half an hour. They were both sitting in the living room of the hideout, cross-legged on the floor, their eyes closed to better hone concentration.

Upon arriving for the lesson earlier, Pepperglow had briefly introduced herself before asking him if he knew the process behind activating enchantments, to which he had answered, "You awaken the runes by applying pure rucanic energy."

"Correct," she had smirked. "How much do you know about drawing pure rucanic energy out of your own reserves?"

"I know the steps of the process, but… I've never been able to succeed at it." He had been humble to admit it, although it was no secret, considering her presence there to teach him.

"And what's the process?" Pepperglow had prompted.

"Find your inner current of runa, direct the flow out of yourself, and then concentrate it onto your target."

"You know your stuff; good," the mage had nodded approvingly. "Well, let's start with meditating. Like you said, channeling your runa is about locating the rucanic current within yourself and then manipulating it. Can't do smack until you find it, which takes a lot of concentration, especially at your level. Don't you worry, though, it gets faster and easier with practice."

It was certainly not getting any faster nor easier at the time. He was finding it difficult to focus at all, the influence of his anxiety souring the effort. The reminder of why he was being taught the lesson was wont to seep into his mind, breeding more hesitation than concentration.

Thus, success continued to dodge him. The most headway he accomplished was feeling an occasional brushing of his current, but it was brief and fleeting, taunting him more than encouraging him.

He was starting to become frustrated; it had never been this difficult to locate the flow of runa within himself before!

"You are too wound up," Pepperglow noted. "Frustration will only rob your focus further. Breathe. Inhale." The mage took in a long gulp of air and held it deep within her abdomen. She then released it. "Exhale."

Valen mirrored her breathing, as he had several times prior, to no avail. The agitation within him grew as nothing seemed to be getting any better, only worse.

"…you seem more than just frustrated," Pepperglow observed. "Very anxious."

Valen's brow scrunched and his shoulders tensed.

"Is it true? Are you anxious?"

Valen's frustration accumulated further. "Why wouldn't I be?" he grumbled, his eyes opening and jutting away to stare at the wall.

Pepperglow grunted at that. "What's making you anxious?"

"The fact that I'm learning this so the people hunting me down won't kill me!" Valen spat, the fire of his agitation overheating his nerves.

"Ah, so you're afraid, then?" the gnome assumed, contrastingly calm.

Valen squeezed his eyes shut, the vision of his attacker's golden, glaring eyes flashing through his consciousness. A shudder snaked down his spine, and his throat grew tight. He could only nod; he was very afraid, indeed.

"Well, there is a good reason you're afraid," Pepperglow scoffed. "You should be."

Valen flinched and turned to look at her, his face contorting with hurt and confusion. Why would she *tell him* to be afraid?!

She saw his face and chuckled. "Look, youngster, fear is something we all feel. It's there for a reason; without fear we don't understand what's at stake."

"But I don't want to know!" Valen snapped, exasperated. "Why would I?!"

Pepperglow's brow rose. "Shush, of course you want to understand. Let me tell you why."

Valen waited, despairingly incredulous.

"It's not going to do you any good to ignore the situation and convince yourself everything is alright — it's not. Admitting there is an issue is the first step to solving it. The admittance of that issue is fear."

"B-but I can't even focus!" Valen cried. "How is fear supposed to help me?!"

"Well, youngster, fear is a two-way street; you can either let it control and cripple you, or you can channel it into resolve to help yourself," the gnome explained. "Ever hear the concept of 'fight or flight'?"

Valen weakly nodded, remembering the phrase from one of his biology lessons. Fight or flight was the physiological response to fear.

"That's what it all boils down to. By using fear as a propeller, we can find the strength to conquer our endeavors."

He began to understand Pepperglow's point, to which a feeling of despair responded. He hung his head as fear swirled within him, clenching him tight within its influence, in control. "But... I... I can't do that..."

"Nonsense. From what I understand you've been through a lot and yet you're still here. You've found the ability to conquer your fear before; how?"

Valen searched himself for when he felt his bravest and being Karreo's older sibling and caretaker was the answer. "I could for my brother... I *had* to..." His vision began to blur with tears born from remembrance and pain. "Without him... I... I can't be strong..."

The mage appeared thoughtful. "I've heard that you're alive because you were able to save yourself with a spell. You claim you can't be strong, and yet you've already shown you can be! You have fight in you, you've already proven it."

Valen's face scrunched with a perplexed frown. He still did not understand why he had saved himself, considering all the despair and negativity that unceasingly hounded him. The idea of succumbing to death seemed far more appealing than cutting himself on the broken glass of his old life; what was left but scattered debris and pain? "I still don't understand why I didn't just..." He hesitated. "...let them kill me..."

He could feel Pepperglow's eyes on him. She was quiet for a few charged moments, then, "Are you suggesting that you want to die?"

Valen's throat strained further and his shoulders lifted in a meager shrug.

"...youngster, if you wanted to die you would have let them kill you," Pepperglow said. "You obviously don't."

"That's what I don't understand!" Valen wailed. "Everything is wrong and broken! It's never going to get better and yet I... I..." He put his face in his hands, the moisture of his tears smearing on his palms.

"...I think part of you refuses to accept that," the mage offered gently. "That part of you is still holding onto hope."

"*Hope*?" That was the very *opposite* of what he was feeling. He lifted his gaze back on to her, his face heavy with defeat.

The gnome nodded. "I think it's that very hope that gave you the will to cast the spell."

"But that makes no sense! I don't have any hope!"

"Perhaps not on the surface. But it would seem deep down you're not ready to give up."

Valen's lip shuddered as he processed her words. He closed his eyes and thought back to the attack, attempting to decipher what had sparked the rally for his survival. He pictured his assailant's golden glare, the shining of her sword as she raised it high, the terror that had struck him before her blade could, and the desperate shouting within him that had demanded he fight back. Was that because of hope; could Pepperglow be right?

"Some of you still believes that not all is lost, and that there is still something worth fighting for," Pepperglow said as he reflected. "Ultimately, hope is what gives meaning to our efforts. If we don't have expectations for what it means to overcome, we don't have a reason to fight. Hope gives us a destination, a reason."

Despite his initial skepticism, he was finding himself convinced that she had a point. Why else would he have preserved his own life? Valen cracked open his eyes to stare at his teacher, wanting to believe her.

"Let hope give you the assurance to press on now. I think you can do it." The gnome then smirked. "You've already shown you can, after all."

Valen looked down to his lap, considering. Even if hope had spurred him back then, did he still have hope now? All the developments that had occurred since his rescue answered that wonder. Despite the murk of his despair, a twinkle of hope *did* appear to be shining dimly up ahead, promising a dawn after the night.

He experienced a flicker of determination before his fear snuffed it out, eager to show it was still in control. "But I... I'm still afraid..." Valen muttered weakly.

"Admitting it is the first step, like we discussed. Now, you must channel it into resolve," the mage replied. She then scrunched her face as though she were mulling over a thought. "You know, it's not too unlike activating an enchantment. You have your problem, the enchanted item. You require resolve to conquer that problem, the pure rucanic energy. You must acknowledge your fear, the flow of runa within you. You then channel that fear, just as you redirect your runa. Your fear is manifested into resolve, and your runa is expelled as pure rucanic energy. You apply that resolve to conquer your issue, just like you direct that pure rucanic energy onto the runes to activate the enchantment. Do you understand?"

Valen listened intently, her analogy striking him with clarity. He nodded.

"Right, so, let's try it. Close your eyes," Pepperglow instructed.

Valen did so.

"Find your fear."

Valen did not have to search; it was everywhere within his mind.

"Now, find your runa."

Valen took in a long breath and attempted to apply Pepperglow's metaphor. He concentrated on his emotions and how charged they were in response to his fear. He let go of the breath and focused on his feelings, embracing them rather than shunning them. A link connecting his mental state and rucanic reserves revealed, establishing a bridge. He followed the path and at last was greeted with a definite current of his runa.

He gasped lightly. "I can feel it."

"Good! Now, you must direct it, just as you must channel your fear," Pepperglow advised. "Focus on its flow. Do not fight the current, redirect it. This is the same with your fear. Do not deny it, own it."

Valen bit down on his lip and focused on the flow of his runa. It was running faster than he had ever experienced, its pace in conjunction with adrenaline born from anxiety. '*I am afraid.*' He delved into both the current of his runa and his fear, matching their flow. He let it all wash over him, heightening his self-awareness. He did not deny his fear nor try to dampen its effect on his runa; instead, he redirected it just as Pepperglow told him.

'*I can fight…*' He influenced the flow of his runa towards his palms and his fear towards strength. He thought of the hope that assured him before and allowed it to validate him in that moment. '*I want to fight!*'

Both his runa and his emotions surged along their newfound course until finally Valen felt raw magic pour into his fingertips and a similar power awaken within his spirit.

Without delay, he laid his hands on top of the bracers and let the power buzzing within him climax. A surge of pure rucanic energy was expelled onto the bracer and his fear erupted into resolve.

The bracers gave a magical chime and flashed with magic – he had activated them!

Valen stared down at the armor set, stunned from the rush of power. What he had just accomplished dawned on him with an overwhelming surge of excitement. "I did it!" A smile erupted on his face. "I did it!" he repeated.

"You sure did!" Pepperglow gushed with a laugh. "They won't do you any good on the floor, though. Put them on, youngster!"

Valen did so, his hands shaking. He fastened the armor onto his forearms and gazed at them in awe, the surprise from his victory still fresh. *'I did it!'*

"Any idea how much magic you pumped into them?" Pepperglow asked him.

His mind was slow to digest her question. "I, uh, um, no," he admitted in a stutter, the words sloppy from his shock. "But... my current was really fast..."

Pepperglow chortled, apparently amused. "Hopefully you didn't drain yourself too much. That's not the only magic item you're going to work with today."

Valen's brow wrinkled with confusion and he sized the gnome with a curious look.

She grinned at him. "Spot wants me to train you in a spell slinger. I plan to get some practice done today, if your reserves aren't tapped dry."

Valen's eyes doubled in size. "A spell slinger?!"

"You heard right," Pepperglow nodded. "What do you say to that, then?"

"I—ah—yes!" Valen stammered out. He had not dreamt of wielding a blaster anytime soon, let alone at all, considering spell slingers were the weapons of accomplished magic wielders. *'Just like a real mage!'*

Apprehension tailed the thrill, warning of the seriousness and dangers of using such a weapon, but the euphoria of activating the bracers and general excitement of using a spell slinger overwhelmed his worry.

"You seem excited, good!" Pepperglow said. "You should be. Learning how to use a spell slinger is a momentous step of your magical journey. Come, follow me." She stood up off the floor and began to head towards the stairs. Valen followed, his heart still galloping.

He could feel a faint humming coming from the bracers, sending a tickle into his forearms that spread into his shoulders and down his spine. If he concentrated he could sense a magical barrier surrounding him, molding to fit around his body. If the spell was the Mage Armor he had learned about prior, then the barrier would act like a force field, protecting him from harm. The extent of that protection depended on the amount of runa pumped into the runes and the formula of the spell itself. He assumed the bracers were enchanted with an intermediate spell, not too demanding in runa, something that would bestow him general protection. If necessary (such as bracing for an explosion), he could augment the spell by pumping in more runa, but the quality of the runes could only be improved so far.

They went into the entryway of the hideout and passed the stairs, entering the meeting room. The room was dark and unoccupied and they kept walking until they arrived in front of the back wall. Valen became confused; where was she taking him?

The gnome answered his wonder by nonchalantly pushing in a plank on the wall. A solid click replied, followed by the sound of shifting. Part of the wall then retracted, and a dim hallway revealed ahead.

Valen jumped back, startled. *'Another secret passage?!'* Why had Mrs. Catty not shown him this one?

Pepperglow snickered. "Relax, youngster. Nothing but mannequins and targets ahead." She stepped into the secret passage and Valen followed, perplexed as to why it had still been a secret to him.

"This leads to a training room, then?" he guessed.

"That's correct."

'I guess there was no reason to show me that... it's not an exit.'

The hallway was a short walk, a closed door lying at the end of it. Pepperglow pushed it open without pause, and they walked into the room ahead, Valen impressed by what he saw.

It was a well-lit area at least the size of a medium sports court. A mannequin stood at one end of the room, several ring markings adorning its body. Valen guessed that they were targets, being the location of the markings highlighted the head, chest, and other crucial areas for attack.

On the back wall were three tracks of metal running along the floor, spanning from one end of the room to the other. Valen wondered what those were for.

"Well, let's dive into this while you still have a connection to your flow," Pepperglow interrupted his examination. The gnome dug into her bag and pulled out a spell slinger, his breath catching at the sight of it.

It was a typical-sized blaster, around two hand lengths in size, and it was shaped rather mundanely, the handle plain and the barrel uninspired in design. If he were truthful, he expected something... flashier. He had pictured heroes from stories and their intricate spell slingers, their barrels molded into shapes of dragons, griffons, fire, or trees, their handles an extension of such designs. This spell slinger resembled no such artistry.

He must have done a poor job masking his disappointment. "You look heartbroken, youngster!" Pepperglow snorted. "Look, this one is nothing special, but it's just for training. Spot has a much nicer one for you if you can manage it."

Valen's cheeks warmed with humility. *'Oh, that makes sense.'* "Spot?" he then repeated. Pepperglow had used that name before, too.

She grunted and flashed a smirk. "Kyla, as you know her."

"Oh!" Valen recalled Mrs. Catty's speckled fur and found the nickname apt.

"Anyhow, let's get this rolling. Here, youngster." She offered the weapon out to him and Valen's nerves finally wrestled back influence. He was still learning how to channel his runa and keep his sorcery powers under control; if he took that weapon he could accidentally fire it!

Pepperglow took note of his apprehension. "Don't worry, youngster, watch." She aimed it towards him and his guts gave a violent churn.

"W-wait—" he tried, but the blaster flashed into life, the runes in the barrel glowing as it fired. Valen squeezed his eyes shut and screamed, expecting pain, but instead heard something splash.

He forced open his eyes and examined himself, spotting a blue, gooey, paint-like substance coating the forcefield wrapping around him. He gawked at the strange liquid, shock still rattling his system.

"You didn't think I'd actually hurt you, did you?" the gnome giggled. "It's just a training slinger. It shoots magical paint, nothing harmful."

"Whoa!" Valen continued to study the substance, relieved it was nothing dangerous. A thought then hit him as he rubbed a finger into it, it's sticky texture clinging to him. "Isn't it a bit messy to clean up?"

"It certainly would be, but that's where being magical is handy! It disappears on its own after a few minutes," Pepperglow explained. She held the blaster back out for him.

"That's really convenient!" Assured that it was safe for him to handle, he gingerly received the weapon, a grin breaking free. While the blaster was plainly designed and nothing dangerous, Valen could hardly wrap his mind around the fact that he was holding an actual spell slinger. Adrenaline coursed through him, his emotions clumsy from the rush.

He turned the blaster in his hands as he eagerly studied it. He peered into the barrel and spotted decorative runes there, recognizing the symbols as part of the conjuration school of magic, but that being the extent of his knowledge. He assumed the anchor for the actual runes was found inside the handle, and a couple of screws there encouraged that suspicion.

"Ready to get started?"

Valen pulled his attention from the spell slinger and onto his teacher. "Yes, ma'am."

"Well, youngster, first things first. That weapon may not be dangerous, but it's best to start teaching you to have safe form now. When holding any blaster, make sure it's pointed away from yourself and your comrades. Keep it at a slight downward angle until you're ready to fire."

Valen adjusted his hold on the blaster, tipping the barrel downwards.

"Very good!" Pepperglow nodded, and began walking towards the back wall. "The fact you were able to conduct your flow at all has me confident you have a solid grasp on it. I take it you've had prior training?"

"I had a pair of bracers that I practiced with," Valen answered. "I had gotten close to expelling my runa before, but had never succeeded up until now."

"Let's keep that up, then." The gnome stomped her foot into the ground, and there was a click and then some clanking.

Valen jumped as something burst upwards from one of the tracks running along the back of the room. It was a humanoid-shaped target, several rings decorating its shape. It stood in place from where it popped up from, waiting.

"Try to hit the targets," Pepperglow directed. "You should still have connection to your flow. Just do it like you did before."

"Uh... alright!" Valen stared at the target, his chest tightening as he pictured a scenario where it was not a practice-thing but a real enemy. It made him feel scared, but he ushered in that sensation rather than burying it.

'I am afraid...' He aimed the blaster towards the silhouette, his eyes narrowing with focus and intensity. 'But I can fight!' He called upon his flow of runa and it instantly replied, his connection from before still fresh. He guided the current, his grasp on the blaster tightening as he felt runa rush into his fingertips.

He expelled the rucanic energy into the handle, and the weapon buzzed with power before firing, causing a mild kickback. In the blink of an eye paint was... soaking the wall behind the target, entirely missing its intended trajectory.

Valen frowned as the drama of the moment was hampered by his missed shot.

"Well, at least you fired it!" Pepperglow encouraged through a snicker. "Go on and try again!"

Valen lifted the blaster for a second time, the corners of his mouth heavy.

"It might help to loosen your grip, youngster. You're too tense — clenching it like that messes with your aim. Relax!"

Valen removed the tension from his grip.

"That's a bit *too* loose. You don't want the kickback to knock it out of your hands! Also, see how the barrel is drooping? Just a bit tighter, youngster," the gnome further instructed.

Valen nodded and again modified his grip, not too tight and not too loose.

"Right, good. Go on and shoot!"

Valen shook off his discouragement and took in a breath. He called upon his runa yet again and applied it, the spell slinger vibrating into life. The weapon fired its sticky ammo, and a burst of blue paint hit his mark, soaking the torso of the target.

Valen about dropped the spell slinger as disbelief slammed him. "I hit it!"

"There you go, youngster!" Pepperglow cheered.

The target retreated back into the metal track, and another sprung up a few feet off.

"Don't stop now, keep at it!"

Without delay, Valen aimed the spell slinger at his new target and shot.

Chapter 33

Valen

Valen sat at the kitchen table, beads of sweat lining his brow and his breathing labored, the draining of his rucanic reserves leaving him physically strained.

His lesson with the spell slinger had lasted about an hour. He had hit a fair number of the targets before the depletion of his magical reserves became too strenuous. Pepperglow had congratulated him before leading him into the kitchen, mentioning that she had something that would help boost his energy.

The mage was presently filling a kettle with water at the sink. Upon finishing she cast a spell, and the pot began to whistle briefly before quieting. She then poured the water into a mug that housed a tea bag she had retrieved from her bag.

"This will help recharge your reserves faster," she said as she worked. "It's millina root. It contains an agent that promotes runa recovery. Very appreciated after exerting oneself magically, as you have."

He had heard of millina before; tasted it, even, unfortunately. His father had liked to make tea with it, but Valen had been less than fond of its bitter taste.

"I've had it before…" Valen told her in a mumble, his tongue shriveling at the memory.

Pepperglow's shoulders bounced with a chortle. "You have, huh? Bet you're eager, then."

"Something like that," Valen weakly chuckled. He had to admit that despite the root's unpleasant flavor, he *was* curious to try it again. The demorinkin wondered how much he would notice the root's healing properties, and if it would help remedy his physical exhaustion as well.

"It's definitely an acquired taste," the gnome continued to giggle. She reached into a cabinet and took out a bowl of sugar cubes and then a spoon from a drawer. "Sugar helps, though."

Valen had never tried it sweetened; his father had always had his cup straight. His curiosity was further piqued.

Pepperglow placed the kettle down on the stove and grabbed the supplies from the counter. She delivered them in front of Valen, and the tea's stench hit his nose, dampening his eagerness to try it.

"Let it sit for a minute or so and then drink up. I'll be right back," the gnome told him. With that, she walked out of the kitchen and left him alone.

He was willing to wait, the acrid odor of the drink discouraging any urgency. He grimaced down at the cup as the minute passed, bracing himself to sample it, his sense of taste and smell balking. Despite the protest, he dropped a cube of sugar into the mug and stirred, watching as the square of sweetness dissolved.

He called upon his earlier courage, took in a deep breath, and lifted the mug to his lips to have a sip.

Steaming hot bitterness splashed upon his tongue, striking him with disgust. He gagged and tightened his face with repugnance, the aftermath of the sip wreaking havoc on his taste buds. The sweetness from the sugar was nowhere to be tasted, overshadowed by the root's stark bitterness.

And so, he dropped in another cube. And then another. And then one more beyond that. Four cubes of sugar *should* be enough to tame the cup of wretchedness, at least he hoped so.

He stirred the mug, its sour steam wafting up into his face. He decided to wait for it to cool off before trying another dreaded mouthful. It had not only been grossly bitter but uncomfortably hot. *'Just like Dad's cup used to be...'*

As Valen waited for the drink to cool he was thoughtful over his father. He remembered walking into his old home's kitchen, yawning and groggy from sleep, spotting his dad sipping at his usual cup of millina root tea while reading a book. The demorinkin's heart panged at the memory, his grief swelling. He had once thought he was as healed as he could be over his parents' death, and yet the wound was reopened and bleeding again, a consequence of his trauma.

Valen gazed down at the mug sadly, wishing his father could be there to explain why he drank it, as he always did when asked why he tolerated the beverage. "It's good for me," his parent had always said. "It assists my runa production and keeps me on my toes. Well, on my good foot, at least." His father normally wasn't one for wisecracks, but he had always been fond of that particular joke.

Valen sighed, and it disrupted the steam coming from the cup. Seeing that, he began to gently blow at the mug, helping it cool faster.

He then lifted the cup for a second time, mirroring an image of his father doing the same in his mind's eye. The demorinkin sipped at it and a much sweeter, yet still alarmingly bitter, taste filled his mouth. He grimaced but decided he could tolerate it. He took another sip, and then a gulp; he just wanted to get it over with.

It took a few sizable mouthfuls but he finally downed the entire drink, a bizarre aftertaste of bittersweetness staining his tongue.

"Good, good, you finished it!" Pepperglow's voice signaled her return. "That wasn't so bad, huh?"

He shrugged, still recovering from both the taste of the drink and the ache of his memories.

"You'll get used to it, youngster. After you start feeling the kick from that cup you'll understand why the taste is worth acquiring," the mage chuckled. She then sat down across from him at the table. "The way you handled that training slinger shows you can wield the real deal in an emergency. Of course, I want you to continue practicing with the training slinger, but just in case…" The gnome placed down a blaster and holster onto the table. "You should take this."

Valen's heart skipped a beat, his eyes doubling in size. This spell slinger was a *much* better representation of the hero's weapons he had imagined. The barrel was shaped in the likeness of a roaring feline, its snarling mouth open to fire spells. Its broad, thick tail wrapped down the length of the handle, which boasted intricate engravings of runes and letters from a language he did not recognize. He spotted the rune for 'force' amongst the markings, acting as a main centerpiece of the design. The weapon's color was a deep ebony with an occasional splash of yellow found in the runes and the eyes of the cat.

"It's got a safety built in," Pepperglow pointed out. She gestured to a switch above the handle. "When it's on, the runes won't activate. You'll be keeping it that way unless you *really* need to fire it. As I said, this is *just* for emergencies."

Valen gawked at the weapon, his mind still processing the fact that it was being offered to him.

"If you ever *do* need to shoot, don't be worried about finding your current on time. Even inexperienced wizards can focus on their flow when it really counts, and you're a sorcerer. Your powers are much more innate," the gnome gave a smirk, "which corresponds nicely with instinct."

He managed to pull his eyes from the spell slinger and gaped at Pepperglow, his expression a chimera of excitement and apprehension.

The gnome's smirk grew. "Go on and take it, youngster! Don't be scared of it, it's impossible to fire with that safety on."

With a trembling hand, he did so, his eyes saucers. The weapon had a noticeable weight to it as he took it, proving much heavier than the training slinger felt. He wondered how much of that was his own mind's trickery.

"Well, what do you think? A bit fancier, eh?"

"I-it's amazing!" Valen complimented, still in awe.

"The spell it fires is force-based, so each shot is a concentrated kinetic blast. If you can manage to augment the spell, it can also deliver a force push upon impact," the gnome informed. "So be careful indoors — wouldn't want to be rearranging furniture."

Noting the feline's commanding pose, Valen found it fitting that the weapon quite literally pushed the target around.

The demorinkin placed the spell slinger back down gently and eyed its holster. The sheath matched the black of the blaster and was embroidered with runes and letters akin to that on the handle. It was horizontal in stature and attached to a belt.

"That holster goes on your hip and sits at the small of your back. Go ahead and make sure it fits."

His hands still shaking, he grabbed the belt and wrapped it around himself, the sheath pushing on his back. He tightened the belt to its limit but still it sagged, his sweatpants and their lack of belt loops providing no support.

Pepperglow snickered upon looking him over. "Might help to not wear sweatpants, but that should do."

Valen wasn't sure he agreed; it felt loose enough to slip.

"Go ahead and complete the look. Holster the slinger, youngster," Pepperglow prompted.

The demorinkin reached out for the weapon and picked it up, his nerves still rendering his touch unsteady. He twisted his body and awkwardly maneuvered the weapon into the holster, the sheath realizing the weapon's weight and drooping further. The pressure of the blaster on his back was uncomfortable and heavy, but his excitement was stubborn to dampen.

His teacher placed the training slinger, which was tucked into a simple, beltless sheath, onto the table as well as a tin container. "Well, I want you to keep practicing with this training slinger on your own time. Do you remember how to get into that training room?"

Valen nodded, the instructions fresh in his mind after her showing it to him upon the end of his lesson.

"And how to activate the targets?"

He again nodded; she had taught him that, too.

"Good! I'm leaving you a box of millina root tea bags." She gestured to the tin container. "Make sure you have a cup each time you strain yourself magically, but don't exceed three cups a day. Understand?"

"Yes, ma'am." Valen once more bobbed his head in a nod.

"Good, good!" The gnome stood up from her chair and slung her bag over her shoulder. "Well, that'll be all today. I'll be back tomorrow. Until then, youngster!"

■ ■ ■

Rorrik

Rorrik stepped down the stairs to the hideout, his tail in a tick and his brow furrowed. The felidaren pulsed with annoyance, an earlier spat with Tommik lapping his memory. The day had gone fine up until he was leaving the safe house that evening. He had been excused earlier than his older brothers on the account that he had a more taxing job to do the following day.

Apparently, though, the brevin just couldn't let Rorrik slip away without pestering him.

"What is she thinking having *you* be the bait for this?" Tommik had whined to his tail. "That investigation of the base was one thing, but this? This is something for a professional. You're still just a brat!"

Unlike last time, Rorrik did not have Shannine around to quell the brevin's griping. "I'm more than ready for this," the felidaren had growled without turning around. "You don't know anything."

"Pff! I know a lot more than you, kitten!" Tommik had shot back. "Honestly, the nepotism here is ridiculous; this is all just because you're Panther's kid!"

Rorrik's ears had gone flat at that comment. "It's *because* I know what I'm doing; I've been training all my life!" he spat in a hiss.

"Your very *short* life, yes," Tommik had proceeded to pester. "I don't think you're ready for this, kitten."

"Well, it's a good thing your opinion matters, huh?" Rorrik had remarked in a mocking tone.

"When you get knocked down a peg it better not cost the rest of us," Tommik had warned in a snarl. With that, the brevin had stormed off, his head of messy curls shaking.

The whole exchange had darkened Rorrik's mood. The ghost of his doubt was back to haunt him, threatening to reopen the wound on his confidence. He endeavored to not linger in the negativity and instead aligned himself with the assurance his family had instilled in him. He had to trust in his training and abilities. '*I know I can do this.*'

He had reached the foot of the stairs when something exploded on his chest with a splash. The felidaren was immediately torn from his thoughts and jumped back in alarm, his tail frizzing. His ears flat with disorientation, he examined the hit, finding a sticky, blue goo soaking his torso.

Laughter erupted, and he turned his attention on the source, spotting… Valen? The demorinkin was standing in the threshold of the entryway, hunched over with laughter.

"I got you!" the demorinkin guffawed. "Oh, man, I got you! I've waited here forever but that was so, so worth it!" He laughed and laughed.

Rorrik's mind was slow to process the oddity of what he was seeing. Despite it, the felidaren let out a laugh of his own and again studied the goo clinging to his chest. "What did you do?!"

"I shot you!" Valen answered through a jumble of giggles.

"I see that, but with what?" Rorrik poked a claw at the mystery substance.

"With this!" The demorinkin stood straighter and hefted something that resembled a blaster in his hands.

Rorrik gasped and hopped up for a closer look. "Is that a spell slinger?!" Was that why Valen was receiving magical training, to learn how to wield a blaster?!

"Well, *this* is just a training slinger," Valen clarified through a smile. "But look!" He turned around and showed his back to Rorrik, revealing a holster resting on his hips; poking out of the sheath was another blaster. "*This* is the real deal!"

"Whoa! No way!" Rorrik studied the holster, feeling as though he had seen its design before. "Where did you get it?!"

"Your mom wanted me to have it!" Valen answered. The demorinkin reached back with his free hand to unsheathe the weapon, and the body of the spell slinger came into view.

Rorrik recognized it immediately; it was the spare blaster from the equipment room. It had been a long while since it had been loaned out, and Valen was the first person to wield it that Rorrik had personally met.

"That's so cool!" the tabby gushed excitedly. He knew Valen was magically inclined, but hadn't been aware the demorinkin was powerful enough to wield a spell slinger!

"Isn't it?!" Valen matched his tone. The demorinkin returned the weapon back to its holster. "It's just for emergencies, though. I'm still training." Valen nodded towards the training slinger. "Have to improve my aim and such."

That made Rorrik smirk, and he gestured towards his gooey chest. "Well, I hope you know that was a cheap shot."

Valen chuckled almost smugly. "I still hit you!"

"Sure, okay," Rorrik agreed in a drawn-out shrug. "But, can you do it again?" In an instant, he was twirling past Valen nimbly and scurrying away before the demorinkin could blink.

The tabby had reached the living room when Valen finally reacted with a hoot. "Hey, get back here!"

Rorrik had no such plans. He proceeded to flee, and a blue streak shot past him and burst onto one of the couches.

The tabby laughed in a goading fashion. "Missed me!" He spun around to have a quick look at Valen, finding him standing in the archway, aiming the blaster with a look of determination.

Another glob of blue answered his taunting, and Rorrik dodged it through a side jump, albeit narrowly.

He would have to keep moving if he wanted to remain more gray than blue. He hopped the half wall to the kitchen and ducked behind it before more sticky ammo could strike him.

Hurried footsteps told him that Valen was changing position. Rorrik waited for the footfalls to near the kitchen, and then stood to deftly leap back over the half wall and into the living room. As he did so, he spotted a bullet of blue in his peripherals.

Rorrik fell onto the couch next to the half wall and rolled, keeping momentum. His feet found the floor, and he spun around to get another visual on his attacker.

Valen was already poised to shoot again; Rorrik had to duck to prevent another blast of blue from coating his chest.

Rorrik hollered out with amusement. "Close!"

Valen scoffed and shot yet again, Rorrik barely dodging. The felidaren took off towards the entry hallway, Valen hot on his tail.

The tabby turned the corner into the main hallway and ran down it, weaving to and fro to throw off Valen's aim. His efforts proved worthwhile as the demorinkin shot another glob at him, missing. He burst towards the kitchen in a sprint, trying to put some distance between them.

The tabby made it to his destination and ducked behind the island for cover, his heart thumping with thrill. He peered from the corner of his hiding place and saw Valen arrive, the demorinkin's blaster outstretched and ready to shoot. When his friend did not immediately see Rorrik, however, the intensity was sapped from his pose and he glanced around, puzzled.

The felidaren had to stifle a giggle. Valen's gaze started to scrutinize the room, and so Rorrik quit his peeking. Instead, he perked his ears to track the demorinkin's movements. It was more than easy to hear his friend; his footfalls were loud, the floorboards snitching on his every step. '*Valen really needs to learn how to sneak; I didn't even know the floorboards could be that noisy!*'

The demorinkin neared the island, and so the felidaren silently slunk to the other side of it, keeping low. Valen continued his patrol around the kitchen, Rorrik remaining undetected as he once again slipped out of view.

Valen's steps suggested he was heading towards the living room. Rorrik smirked and decided to sneak back towards the hallway, feeling smug that he had fooled his friend.

He tip-toed towards his escape, his vision focused on Valen standing in the entrance of the living room, the demorinkin's back to him. Rorrik felt cocky enough to let out a loud laugh.

"Over here, Valen!" he shouted.

"I know," Valen's voice came from in *front* of him, instead.

Startled, Rorrik whipped his attention to his front, just in time to witness a lopping blast of blue hit him square in the chest. The force of impact had him ungracefully falling back on his tail.

Valen once more bellowed out with laughter. "I got you again!"

Rorrik sat there in stupefaction, his green eyes round with surprise. "But, you—" the felidaren stammered, turning to get a visual on the Valen he had seen in the living room, only to spot nothing.

"You were hiding," Valen said through his guffaws. "So I cast an illusion to have a look around. You revealed you were in the kitchen, so I decided to lure you over here for a clear shot." The demorinkin continued to bounce with chuckle after chuckle.

Rorrik flushed with humility. It had been an illusion?! "But I even heard you!"

"I don't walk that loud, do I?" Valen snorted. "But thanks for thinking so!"

The footfalls *had* been awfully loud, even for Valen. But... "What does that have to do with anything?"

"Louder noises are easier to replicate. I'm still getting the hang of illusions that can move and make sounds," the demorinkin elaborated. "Glad to know they're convincing enough to fool someone!"

Rorrik's fur was still warm from being tricked. "Well, you would have never hit me without your magic," the felidaren taunted with a smirk.

"It's a good thing I have it, then," Valen said through a smirk of his own, looking awfully pleased with himself.

Rorrik shook his head with a chuckle. "Maybe for you!"

Valen replied with more laughter, and Rorrik couldn't help but laugh, too. The demorinkin's laugh was a wonderful sound to hear, even if it was at the expense of his own ego.

As their giggling waned, Rorrik directed his attention to his blue-coated chest with a sideways grin. "Man, this stuff looks fun to clean up..."

"Actually, it's magical paint! It fades away on its own after a few minutes!" Valen revealed.

"Really?" Rorrik coated the end of a finger into the viscous substance, his ears perking and his head tilting. "That's convenient!" He sniffed at the paint, its odor reminding him of rubber.

"I thought so, too!" The demorinkin held out a hand to help him up.

Rorrik was about to take it but noticed Valen was trembling. "Whoa, are you okay?" the tabby wondered with a frown, the memory of Valen passing out after tag fresh in his mind.

Valen offered a weak smile. "Don't worry, I'm just a little worn out. It's alright, though, I have something that will help."

Rorrik finally took his hand and was pulled to his feet. Valen walked up to the kitchen island, Rorrik following after him.

"My teacher left me some millina root tea bags," the demorinkin said while opening a tin box. "When I use my runa, like earlier, I get tired out. This root helps promote runa recovery." He fetched a mug and spoon from the cupboard and placed a tea bag into the cup. "I was still recovering from my lesson earlier, so I was already pretty tired." He smugly smiled at Rorrik. "It was worth it, though."

Rorrik leaned on the counter and jokingly rolled his eyes. "Yeah, yeah."

Valen turned to grab a kettle that was already on the stove, and Rorrik heard water sloshing in it. The demorinkin closed his eyes, and seconds later the pot began to whistle and blow steam from its spout.

Rorrik was impressed. "Wow, you can make it just boil like that?"

"Yeah, it's not too hard of a spell," Valen answered with a wince, looking tired, contrary to his statement. "I've known it for a while." He poured the hot water into the mug, and a sour odor attacked Rorrik's nose.

The tabby's ears shot back with disgust. "It doesn't smell very good!"

Valen laughed at that. "It doesn't taste any better than it smells, trust me." The demorinkin fetched some sugar and dropped several cubes into the liquid. He began to stir the tea, casting out its stench further into the air.

"It must help a lot if you're willing to drink that," Rorrik muttered, his face wrinkled to better ward off the smell.

Valen chuckled. "It certainly helped me earlier. It made me feel a lot better, and I was really tired."

The two fell into silence, Valen's eyes on the mug and Rorrik's on Valen. The demorinkin's demeanor was different than Rorrik had ever experienced before. Even with his exhaustion wearing him down, he seemed… happier, more confident.

Valen appeared to sense his staring and glanced at him. "Hm?"

Rorrik smiled at his friend. "Today went well, then?"

Valen's gaze dropped back down to the mug and he grinned. "Yeah, yeah it did." The demorinkin went back to stirring the tea. "It was pretty tough at first, but… it got better."

"That's great!" Rorrik told him excitedly. "I'm glad!"

Valen once again looked up at him and smiled warmly. "Me, too."

■　■　■

Due to his mother and older brothers staying out late on their job, dinner was made and brought down by Walter. The meal had been a beef stew with bread, and Valen had accepted and eaten a bowl, quite eagerly, even. Following that, the two of them had been tired enough for bed.

Rorrik was lying up in the loft bed, his mind swelled with thoughts concerning the next day. Worry and excitement took turns punctuating his musing, and the flip flopping was driving him mad. One moment he could hardly wait to prove himself and take on another *real* job, but then the next Tommik's snarling voice was echoing through his memory and eroding his confidence.

He turned over towards the wall in a huff, hissing out a sigh.

"…is something wrong?" Valen's voice came from the queen bed below.

Rorrik jumped at the question; he had thought the demorinkin was already sleeping.

"No, it's — I'm fine," Rorrik's bluff was so poor it made him wince.

"…what's bothering you?" Valen pushed gently.

Rorrik considered how to answer. "It's just hard to get to sleep… You know, with tomorrow…"

"…you're nervous, then?"

Rorrik sighed. "…a little."

Valen was quiet for a few moments. "Well, like you told me, this is what you've been training for, right?"

Rorrik moved so he could look down at the demorinkin. Valen was lying on his side, his yellow eyes looking up at him intently.

The felidaren nodded in reply. "All my life."

Valen broke eye contact and rolled onto his back. He appeared to be considering something, then, "You don't have to do this, Rorrik…"

Valen's words summoned determination, and suddenly Rorrik didn't feel quite as nervous.

"Maybe," the felidaren admitted. "But I want to."

Chapter 34

Rorrik

Rorrik scanned the busy square in front of him with an inconspicuous glance, his senses alert despite his nonchalant demeanor. He was lounging by the fountain in the heart of Farpoint plaza, hoping his presence there would catch the eye of their prior snoop. If Rorrik had come to the location before, logic would encourage the spy to return there to look for him. At least, that was the hope. Thus far, his presence had attracted no attention, but the tabby was ready to be patient.

"You're not drawing attention to yourself by just sitting there," Jate's voice buzzed in his ear via a tiny earpiece. "Maybe you should get off your tail and go browse some shops or something."

"Good plan," Gavin's voice, too, came from the radio. "The spy could be hanging back, watching you out of view. If you start moving around, we have a better chance to spot him."

Rorrik made sure not to make any reply to their advice. As far as anybody was concerned, he was alone and not being chatted to by his older siblings, who were watching from different vantages around the location.

He went on to explore the offerings of the market, feigning intrigue over the many stalls and shops as he went. He noticed several merchants regard him with an accusing eye, wary he was there to swipe their goods, but that was the extent of his admirers. As the day stretched on and the crowd began to thin, he was still a stalker short.

The sky was freshly indigo with dusk when Gavin's voice sounded over the radio. "The market is closing soon; we'll just have to try again tomorrow."

"Guess our spy was poking somewhere else today. If he's worth his whiskers, though, he has eyes here that noticed you. He'll definitely be around tomorrow!" Jate's encouragement came right after.

Rorrik was thankful necessity kept him from having to reply to his siblings; he was bummed and short on words. He had been hoping to prove himself that day, but establishing his worth would have to wait.

The brothers went their separate ways, as was common when reporting back to their hideout. Rorrik headed for the bus stop on Waypoint, his tail feeling heavy as it kept trying to drag with disappointment.

He moved with a decent flow of people as they left the plaza. The felidaren spotted a few shoppers grab at their bags and reposition them in front of themselves when they noticed him, an attempt to ward off pickpocketing. Rorrik ignored their assumptions and kept on his way, too tired to find it amusing.

Eventually, he was one of many boarding the bus. He found an empty seat and turned his attention to the window, his ears slouched and his whiskers drooped. No one sat by him as the bus filled up and drove off.

His stop arrived after an uneventful ride, and he headed for his next connection. As he walked, he spared a glance at the people that had shared his stop, an important habit when making his way home. Most patrons went their separate ways, but a handful arrived at the next bus stop with him.

He boarded that bus and then the next on his elaborate route, his journey purposefully complicated to help detect any followers. While departing the last bus, he once again gave a quick glance around and noticed a common denominator amongst all the faces he'd spotted at every stop.

It was a middle-aged human male wearing a gray shirt and tinted glasses, which was a mundane enough get-up, but the man's presence there likely suggested he was following the tabby. After all, one didn't normally take consecutive bus routes that tend to overlap and backtrack.

Upon realizing he was not alone, his heart jumpstarted and the fur along his spine bristled. '*Act natural!*' He bluffed away the effects of his adrenaline and kept walking as though nothing was amiss, and when he turned the corner the man followed.

'*I have to let Gavin and Jate know!*' Nonchalantly, Rorrik pulled out his corresponder and hastily typed a writ message to his siblings. 'Missed my stop at Cedar Street.' They would know the meaning behind his message; the phrasing was a predetermined indicator he was being followed.

He continued to fiddle with his communicator, pretending to be distracted, when in truth he was still conscious of his surroundings. The spy began to slow down to put some space between them and restore obscurity, but Rorrik was none fooled.

'*He might suspect that I know he's following me. I have to make it look like I shook him so he believes the safe house isn't just a trap.*'

The tabby was close to Pine Front, a part of town that housed several night-life locations, thus crowds to get lost in. Conveniently, it was also relatively close to the safe house; only about five blocks or so separated them.

He stuffed his corresponder back into his pocket and headed for his new destination, his heart thumping with every step.

"We got your message, Rorrik. Carry on with the plan. We'll get a visual on you soon," Gavin's voice calmly vibrated in Rorrik's earpiece. "Until then, keep your senses sharp."

"Good for you for spotting him on your own!" Jate added. "You're doing great!"

His brother's comment filled him with a surge of pride that had a grin twitching briefly on his lips. The remaining doubt Tommik's words had instilled in him was at last dismissed. *'I can do this!'*

Rorrik didn't have to walk far before finding the commotion of night life. As he drew closer to his destination, the sidewalks grew denser, the noise louder. The bustle of Pine Front was not easily missed, even from a couple of blocks away.

He arrived at the main street, his whiskers twitching with stimulation as he weaved through the mass of patrons. A stench of alcohol and sweat hung in the air like a haze, assaulting his keen sense of smell. Constant shouting and laughter boomed in his head, even with his ears flat. The bustle was not easily missed, indeed.

As he made his way, he witnessed several peddlers loudly calling out slogans and advertisements for their wares. Many shop owners attempted to stop people with a hurried pitch and a forceful show of their product, to which most ignored, but the merchants were tenacious. Rorrik noticed a stall owner actively block a man's path, slap a hat on him, and then demand money for it. The tactic had succeeded by what Rorrik assumed to be the grace of liquor; the man had forked up the cash and went on his way with a stumble.

Rorrik finally glanced behind him to check his back, but if the stalker was following he could not tell; the swell of people was thick and his height didn't bestow an impressive view. *'What if I lost him?'*

Rorrik broke free of the rush to stop at a stall that displayed tribal mats and tapestries. The hanging merchandise created a short maze of patterns and color; it was a perfect opportunity for Rorrik to get tabs on his follower.

He stepped up with mock interest in the wares, positioning himself so that he was partially obscured to the road, but not completely. He needed to give a convincing show to the spy, but he couldn't be too effective, either; he wasn't *actually* trying to shake him.

The sounds of bickering alerted Rorrik that the shopkeep was occupied in a conversation with a customer. The owner, a felidaren queen with spotted, gray fur, was having a heated discussion with a human woman.

"You're trying to rip me off with these obnoxious prices!" the human accused. "I bet these aren't even official tribal pieces — you're probably just some scheming, alley cat fake!"

"You want authenticity but don't want to pay for it," the felidaren hissed with a thick north-felidaren accent. "So be it! Take your pennies and go buy from Monti's Mats or some other mangy rip-off. You get what you pay for there — I'll bet my pelt *those* are fake!"

Their argument pressed on, but Rorrik's attention was diverted as he noticed a familiar figure in his peripherals. The spy was approaching the stall but stopped at the farthest end of the maze of tapestries, his attention seemingly on the art.

Rorrik continued to browse briefly before setting off again, and with a sweeping glance, he could spot the spy follow.

"Hanging out in Pine Front, eh? Aren't you a little young for that?" Jate was suddenly quipping. "I'm almost to your location. Don't have too much fun until I get there!"

"I'm already here," Gavin mentioned right after.

Jate laughed. "Didn't know we were racing, Gavin."

Gavin chuckled before going on, "We still have to get that bug on him. Rorrik, stall for a little bit. I'm setting something up near the tail of the street."

Rorrik stopped at another stand with a preoccupied owner to kill time like his brother ordered. The merchant, a floraling male, was wrapping up a sale with a client in a much more agreeable exchange than the other he had just witnessed. This stall was selling intricate, painted wooden plates and other dishes, all depicting traditional floraling artistry, complete with a hefty price tag; even more pricey than the felidaren's mats, he realized. Regardless, the customer had not complained.

The spy arrived at the next stand over, and although he did not appear to be watching the felidaren, Rorrik knew he still was.

Another minute or so of feigned browsing passed by.

"Alright, go ahead and start leading him towards Top Notch Hats, near the end of the street," Gavin instructed. "I have the merchant paid off to give him a pretty… spirited pitch. I'll get the bug on him while he's occupied. Go ahead and rush off during the pitch, he'll be especially distracted if he's trying to watch where you're going."

"That'll make it look like you think you shook him, too," Jate added. "I'll make sure he doesn't *actually* lose you, don't worry. I'm here now and have a good vantage."

Rorrik moved to lead the spy towards their trap, his tail twitching with excitement. After some walking, he saw Top Notch Hats and went up to the stall, his chest tightening with adrenaline.

The felidaren hadn't even begun to browse the merchandise when he heard the rowdy, buttery voice of what seemed to be Gavin's paid-off peddler.

"Good sir! Ah, what stylish glasses you have! Handsome, wonderful! But you can do better, sir! Look, look at all the glasses I have here! And all the hats that would complete your motif!"

With a fleeting peek, Rorrik spotted the spy being accosted as the shop keep blocked his path and attempted to shove merchandise on his person. Without wasting another valuable second, the tabby hastily walked away from the stall and back into the crowd, quicker than he knew he should if he were trying to be inconspicuous about it, but that wasn't quite the goal.

"It's on him," Gavin reported.

"And he's on you still, Rorrik! Keep it up!" Jate told him.

Rorrik reached the end of Pine Front's main street and turned the corner, his pace still brisk as he left behind the bustle and commotion. He could now head for the safe house, having 'shaken' the spy, who in truth was still on his tail, as Jate assured him. His older sibling proceeded to keep an eye out from higher ground, feeding Rorrik frequent updates on the status of his follower. Finally, Rorrik arrived at the safe house, and the stalker was there to witness it.

Jate was waiting on the porch, annoyed, a look on his face that reminded Rorrik of their father.

"You're late, kitten," his brother scolded.

"I was being followed," Rorrik excused too loudly. "But, don't worry! I was able to shake him at Pine Front!"

"You're *sure*?" Jate hissed, sounding doubtful.

"I did! He got held up by a peddler and I got away!"

Jate appeared convinced. "Fine, then."

Rorrik pretended to look around before cautiously wondering, "So... is he doing any better today?"

Jate hissed and slapped him on the arm. "Not out here!"

With that, the two brothers slipped inside the house. After the door clicked closed and they moved into the next room, they both burst into laughter, their facades disappearing immediately.

"Nice Dad impression!" Rorrik playfully nudged his older brother.

"You think so? I thought the scowl really completed it," Jate replied in a snicker.

"He just wrote something down, and now he's on the move," Gavin's voice buzzed in both of their ears, ceasing their giggling. "Come on, let's see where he goes."

■ ■ ■

Rorrik sat up on a roof adjacent to a nice restaurant, the sound of the lake splashing behind him. Jate was on his own perch from across the street, scoring the brothers two different vantages.

While tailing their admirer, the brothers had found themselves in Lakeview Circle, a nicer section of town that ran along the coast of Lake Conigan. Lakeview was well regarded for its beauty, as thorough landscaping accentuated the streets and embellished most buildings. There were many gardens and parks found within the area, made all the more lovely by the presence of the lake. Lakeview was especially popular with tourists, so a steady flow of people still pulsed up and down the street despite the hour.

Rorrik watched from his aerial view as Gavin headed into the restaurant their stalker had just entered moments ago. His sibling looked nothing like what Rorrik was used to; by the trickery of makeup and a pinch of magic,

Gavin was able to become an entirely different person. No tail or whiskers or evidence of fur made up his appearance; instead, he had the form of a dark-skinned floraling.

Following the spy had not been difficult, but there had been a snag when the man hopped on a one-stop bus to Lakeview. While Gavin had boarded the bus without issue, it was too risky for Jate and Rorrik to follow suit, considering their undisguised appearances. Thus, the two had scrambled to find a taxi instead. Fortunately, they had been able to keep up fine; beat the bus to the stop, even.

From there, the snoop had led them to the restaurant they were currently looking on. It was a nice-looking establishment but nothing especially fancy, considering that none of the patrons were dressed formally. It did boast a very elaborate garden that wrapped around the sides of the building, however, beautifying an otherwise drab alley. To the back of the building was a patio area that extended out onto the lake.

"Can you grab us something to go?" Jate joked to their brother over the radio. "I'm getting pretty hungry."

Of course, Gavin did not reply; he was in the same circumstance Rorrik had been in earlier. Their sibling was supposed to be alone, not exchanging snark over the radio.

The brothers kept watch as the minutes began to pass, scrutinizing the people who entered and left the restaurant closely. Rorrik then felt a buzzing coming from his corresponder in his pocket.

He took out the device and glanced down at its display, seeing a writ message from Gavin: 'They went into a private room on the west wall. Can you use a window to get a visual?'

"You're the closer between us, Rorrik. Can you manage that?" Jate asked over the radio.

Rorrik didn't have to think about it. He could not keep excitement from his tone as he replied, "Yeah, I've got it!"

"Alright, keep to the shadows!"

Rorrik creeped down from his perch and lowered himself into the garden between the two buildings, his feline eyes struggling none with the gloom of the night. It was by far the nicest alley he had ever been in; bushes and flowers replaced the typical crates and trash. The change wasn't just pretty to look at, either; the flora would help his job of maintaining obscurity much easier.

He tip-toed through the mulch, steering clear of the garden lights that were dotted around the premise. He peered into one of the several windows along the wall, spotting many tables and people. 'Definitely not a private room.'

Window after window revealed nothing but more common seating until finally he glimpsed into the last window and saw what he was looking for.

A sheer curtain obstructed his view, but he could still make out the form of two people sitting at a large table, one of whom matched the likeness of the spy. The other had a head of flowing, blonde hair that contrasted dark, but radiant, bronze skin.

"I have a visual," Rorrik whispered to his brothers.

" —ou in the mood for? I was thinking perhaps poultry, something light, but savory," a rich, unfamiliar voice said over the radio.

"I'll have whatever you're having," another voice replied, flat in tone.

'*Gavin must be running the bug!*' Gavin had the remote to toggle the transmission. The bug was set to broadcast to their frequency, so they could all listen in.

"Chicken it is, then! Would you care for any wine? I've been craving Akarthi spirits, as of late," the first man said. Through the sheerness of the curtain, Rorrik could gather that it was the blonde talking.

"If you want to fork out the Pines for that kind of thing." The figure that resembled the spy shrugged his shoulders, revealing to be the other speaker.

"Of course! Why should we not indulge? It is a happy occasion, is it not?" the contact insisted.

"That's his contact, the other voice is the spy," Rorrik informed quietly.

The stalker crossed his arms and grunted. "If you insist."

"I do!" the blonde assured. His attention found something on the table. "What appetizer do you think would complement the chicken?"

"I'm not any good at that palate business." The spy sounded short on patience. "Just order something."

"You're not 'very good' at the manners business, either. Won't you just be a good sport and let me treat you? You are a very dear friend, and I plan to treat you as such."

"I get it. You're buttering me up," the spy muttered. "But I'm telling you, it doesn't matter if it's the stuffed mushrooms or the shrimp scampi, *just order something.*"

The blonde eyed the spy for several, tense moments before saying, "Very well." He then gave a clap.

Another figure hustled into the room, clad in black and white, feminine in form. Rorrik figured that she must be the server.

"Sirs?" she questioned.

"My good friend and I are ready to order," the contact said.

"Of course. What can I get for you?"

"We will be having—"

The feed cut off and the thick wall reduced the voices to a faint murmur.

"What? You don't think their meal plan is important enough to snoop on, Gavin?" Jate chuckled. "I get it, though. We don't want to run that bug needlessly."

It was true; according to what Quinn had said, the bug grew hotter the more it was exercised. They had to be careful of when they ran it, lest the spy notice his pocket overheating.

"Didn't know we were eavesdropping on a date instead of a meeting," Jate proceeded to quip. "Seems our spy isn't one for pampering, huh?"

Rorrik attempted to concentrate his hearing on the meeting instead of his brother's fooling, but even with his honed senses, he could barely make anything out. He would have to use his eyes to judge when it was an ideal opportunity to run the bug again.

The server hurried off after the blonde finished his order and the table fell into a stiff silence. The spy's gaze began to wander about the room, spurring Rorrik into ducking as his attention moved towards the window. While the felidaren was not positioned right up on the glass, he did not want to risk detection, regardless.

The tabby waited a good minute before peering through the glass warily. The server had returned and was placing an ice bucket down on the table, a bottle of wine resting in its chilly embrace. She was quick to leave the two of them alone again.

The silence continued, so Rorrik took the opportunity to thoroughly study the contact. The man's bronze skin appeared to faintly glow in the lighting of the room, while his blonde hair was lustrous and thick. What was most impressive was his eyes; even through the vague imagery of the curtains, they shown with a glinting amber that was far from mundane. Rorrik was reminded of how Avalene's prior prisoners had been described; it became clear that he was very likely staring at one of the Fangs of Hellbane.

His hackles raised and his stomach twisted with disgust and anger. A growl threatened in his throat but he did not betray his secrecy.

"I think it's one of the Fangs," he hissed into the radio.

"Really? What makes you say that?" Jate wondered.

"His eyes..." Rorrik replied. "They're just like the prisoners'. And he has blonde hair."

"Huh..." Jate didn't have a quip for that. "...what are they doing now?"

"They're just sitting there not talking."

"Well, let us know if something interesting starts to happen."

It wasn't until another few minutes passed that something finally did. The contact reached for the wine and began to speak.

"They're saying something!" Rorrik alerted his siblings.

"—ave you kept up with the antics of our new sport team?" the blonde started, his tone rinsed of the prior tension. He filled up a wine glass and gently nudged it over to the stalker. "I heard they have been producing impressive numbers."

The spy shrugged and took up the glass to have a sip. "Yeah, the Cougars, they've been doing alright — better than everyone expected. Lost some money on that one..."

The blonde raised a brow as he poured a glass for himself. "A betting man, are we?"

The snoop shrugged yet again. "Not often, but that seemed like easy money. They didn't exactly draft a bunch of superstars."

"Indeed, it is rather surprising, but equally heroic! I hear they are projected to rise high in the standings, perhaps even make the playoffs!"

"I wouldn't say that, but, who knows, they've surprised everyone so far," the spy said.

"They're talking about sports? Do we have the right table?" Jate remarked in a snicker, mirroring Rorrik's own thinking.

"So, which team do you tend to root for?" the blonde questioned, dragging on the small talk.

"I normally go for the—" The feed once again cut off, a smart choice on Gavin's part.

It was not the last of the small talk. Every time the conversation picked up, it was over shallow subjects, from sports to stocks to weather. The brothers had yet to overhear what they were listening for, and each time they exercised the bug, the risk of it burning too hot grew. It was starting to wear on Rorrik's nerves, and he was not alone in his annoyance.

For the spy's patience was deteriorating, as well. His replies became more and more curt as the meal dragged on, course after course. The table was waiting on dessert, the bug currently off, when Rorrik noticed the stalker slam a hand down on the table.

"Run it!" the felidaren spurred his brother abruptly.

"—ridiculous! We both know why I'm here, why haven't we gotten to business?" the spy demanded.

The contact was hardly fazed. "I thought we would enjoy dinner before delving into more serious matters. But! If you are *so* eager to dive into your report, you can start by explaining why it took you *triple* the amount of time to get results." The contact's golden stare was sharp.

The stalker looked humbled before scrunching his face with exasperation. "That isn't my fault! It wasn't easy finding information; they have their furry asses covered! It was only because of some brat slipping up that I even got anywhere!"

"Are you admitting incompetence?" the blonde inquired with mock pleasantness.

The spy's face flushed. "N-no! And if you're even thinking about dropping me for the job then good luck finding another contact! Everyone else is paid off or too lousy to bother with!"

The supposed Fangs member stared at him for a long second before giving a wry sort of grin. "Fair enough. Tell me what you've found then."

"Not until I know I have the rest of the job!" the snoop resisted.

"There is nothing to fear over that." The contact reached into his jacket and retrieved a plump coin purse. "But if your worries are persistent, I have payment for the rest of the job here." He slid the money across the table.

The spy sat straighter at the sight of it. He grabbed the money and began to quickly count the coins before nodding to himself. "Alright, fine..."

"Well?" the blonde pushed.

"I found your cats." The snoop pocketed the money. "I was able to track down their hideout by following some inexperienced kitten. Why they're trusting a brat like that is a mystery, but anyways. He led me to a house, and it seems they've got your guy there."

"What gave birth to that assumption?" The Fangs member had a glint in his eye that had the power to disturb Rorrik.

"He asked a buddy how '*he*' was doing, and his friend was quick to shut him up and get him inside."

The blonde steepled his hands and nodded. "And the address of this location?"

The spy slid across a small piece of paper.

The demorin hunter swept up the paper and gave it a glance before stuffing it in his jacket. "What you have found is very promising. However, we both know your work is not yet done. As was agreed, you are to continue spying. We must find out more before proceeding."

The stalker gave a firm nod. "I've got my work cut out for me. I'll have more news for you soon."

"Isn't that an exciting prospect?" The Fangs member smiled as he took a sip from his glass of Akarthi wine. "I'm glad we were able to enjoy dinner after all."

With that, the feed cut out, just as their desserts arrived. As the two ate their black mousse cake in agreeable silence, Rorrik looked on, his head and guts swirling with revulsion. He was disturbed and angry; scared and disgusted.

"Uh, well, looks like they fell for it!" Jate's chipper voice chimed over the radio, contrasting Rorrik's dysphoria. "So, that's great news!"

Rorrik didn't reply at first. "...Yeah," he finally said in a growl. "We'll get them." He wanted nothing more.

It came time to pay the check, and the Fangs member covered it. The spy then said something and reached into his pocket. As he did so, his face wrinkled in confusion and he pulled out a lone coin.

Rorrik's adrenaline skyrocketed. '*It's the bug!*' Was it too hot from running it as long as they had? Would the spy suspect foul play upon finding a rogue coin in his pocket? Would their spies now know they were being spied on, in turn?!

All Rorrik's worries were answered as the spy gave a shake of his head and placed the coin down along with a few others.

'*Did he... just tip with it?*'

Rorrik could hardly believe it. The two men shook hands and scooted out of their chairs to leave, the bug remaining on the table, being conveniently left behind.

"G-Gavin, he tipped with the bug!" Rorrik told in a hurry, his mind still snagged with disbelief.

"He did not! Did he notice it was hot?" Jate said.

"I—I couldn't tell! He didn't seem to think twice about it!"

"Quinn must have really outdone himself on this one," Jate marveled. "He deserved that day-long nap!"

The men having left, Rorrik was about to sneak away when he noticed Gavin slip into the open door of the private room. His brother approached the table, palmed the bug, and left the room in a single, seamless action. Only seconds later, the server returned to the table and collected what was left of the tip, unaware that it was ten cedars short. It was enough to make Rorrik smirk as he began to sneak off. *'We're so cool!'*

The tabby tip-toed to the edge of the garden and slipped out of the bushes while pretending to zip up his pants. If anyone were to question him being hidden in the foliage, they could use their imagination.

"I've got a visual on them leaving the restaurant. Blondie is getting into a black vehicle, a Panther, it looks like," Jate shared. "I'm writing down the plates now. Are we going to try to follow?"

"We don't have the means to follow a car right now," Gavin replied. "I think we've got enough to go on. Good work, both of you. Let's call it a day."

Chapter 35

Avalene

The plates of the vehicle matched a company car for a chauffeuring business called Leonel's Lifts. Avalene had heard of the service before and knew it to be a dignified company whose clients were equally proud. However, there *were* whispers of them dealing with shady affairs in western Sengard, which, judging by their most recent customer, was not a baseless accusation.

Avalene had pushed for her certified detective, armed with a warrant, to look into the company's records, but Kyla had not supported the plan.

"If someone comes knocking to look at records it will tip off the Fangs," her old friend had argued. "We need to preserve obscurity."

Avalene had been loath to agree but could not deny that the queen had a point. "Breaking into the premises has its own risks," she had still tried.

Kyla had chuckled at that. "That's why I plan to have Bluebird do it — she'll be in and out of there, Leonel's and the Fangs none the wiser."

"If you believe this is the appropriate way to proceed," Avalene had surrendered with a sigh. "Just please, be clean about it."

Avalene now sat in her office the next day, the oldest of Kyla's children there to debrief her on how the job had gone.

"Blue and I were able to infiltrate the premises and search their records," Gavin informed politely.

Avalene was impressed at how much Kyla's son had grown; the tabby had certainly become a capable young man. "I take it you remained undetected and left no traces?"

Gavin adopted a subtle smirk. "We were able to bypass security using a magic scrambler and a few tricks. As far as the cameras saw and the motion detectors felt, it was a quiet, unremarkable night."

"Very good. So, what did you find?"

"Well, the car we saw pick up the Fangs member is supposedly out of commission. According to the paperwork, it's in the garage receiving repairs — has been for a week now. On top of that, there is no record of *any* of their vehicles picking up a client from that restaurant, but we know better."

Avalene slowly nodded as she digested the news. "Whoever got into that car didn't want it on the books."

Gavin confirmed with a nod. "We're going to post an eye to watch the activity of that car, see where it goes and who it picks up. With any luck, Blondie is a regular customer."

Avalene dipped her head. "We can only wait and see."

■ ■ ■

Rorrik

The next two days went according to plan. The spy had been back to snoop both days, and the family had made sure to put on a convincing show. They had orchestrated plenty of activity in and out of the safe house and had even sent Dalf out to 'repair' the outside surveillance, an effort to show the spy the hole in their security.

The snoop must have found something, for at the end of the second day their eye on Leonel's Lifts told them that the car picked up the blonde man from a park in west Sengard and delivered him to the same restaurant in Lakeview. They could assume another meeting had happened, which meant an attack could be impending. Luckily, the Token safe house was ready for them.

When the eye had attempted to follow Blondie after dinner, they had lost him when he entered a lounge called the Roosting Dove. When he was followed inside, evidence of him was nowhere to be spotted. Therefore, there was now surveillance on that business as well.

Rorrik had returned both nights to an excited Valen who was eager to gush about his magic lessons before using the felidaren for target practice. Rorrik was thrilled to oblige, even though he always lost to Valen's tricks. Playing with the demorinkin was a lot of fun, made even better by seeing his friend so happy.

Exhaustion from their busy schedules always had the two of them eager for bed, and the two nights had passed without the demorinkin having any apparent nightmares. It would seem Valen was finally feeling better.

On the third morning, Rorrik was kneeling down to pick up his hamper for laundry day when he noticed a sleeve poking out from under the bed. Upon closer examination, he identified it as belonging to the shirt he had picked up while shaking the spy at Farpoint Plaza; he must have missed the laundry basket when he took it off before.

The felidaren gave an amused scoff and picked up the shirt. The article wasn't exactly his style, but he could see Valen wearing it.

"Hey, Valen, do you like this?" Rorrik asked, holding out the shirt.

Valen was sitting over at the desk working on a packet. "Hm?" The demorinkin's eyes moved to briefly study the shirt and he nodded. "Yeah, I like it. Why?"

"I don't really want it. You can have it!" Rorrik offered. He tossed the article over, and Valen caught it.

"Thank you!" The demorinkin turned the article in his hands, further exploring it. His face then crimped with confusion. "Wait, this has a price tag. Why did you buy this if you didn't want it?"

"Uhh—" Rorrik blinked at the demorinkin, taken off guard by the observation. Did the felidaren have any reason to not be upfront? The family's work was obvious to the demorinkin already, was it not?

A smirk twitched on Rorrik's lips and his shoulders lifted in exaggerated shrug. "Well, I didn't exactly, you know...*buy* it."

Valen narrowed his eyes at him. "...what do you mean?"

"Back when Jate and I were being followed, we used a shop to shake the spy. We had to create a diversion so we could sneak out back, so we pretended to try on clothes. Since we could use a makeover to help disguise ourselves, we—"

"You *stole* this?!" Valen interrupted, his yellow eyes saucers.

Rorrik's ears shot back at the demorinkin's alarm, and his smirk became an uncomfortable grin. "Well, *stole* is a strong word—"

"No, it is not a strong word!" Valen fought. "That's what you did!"

"Okay, sure, but we had to! It was necessary!" Rorrik hurriedly defended.

"Necessary?!" Valen echoed, incredulous.

Rorrik's words tumbled out in a rush. "We had to make ourselves look different to help shake the spy! It's — it's just what you have to do sometimes in our line of work!"

"And what *is* your line of work, huh?!" Valen demanded, his shock morphing into anger. "Don't dodge the question!"

Rorrik gave a nervous smile before tilting his head. "You... really haven't figured it out?"

They held each other's gaze for several tense moments before Valen looked away, squeezing his eyes shut.

"You're... you're criminals..." the demorinkin uttered quietly, his tone defeated.

Rorrik's ears returned to the side of his head. "Um... is that..." He hesitated. "...a problem?"

Valen remained sitting there with his eyes scrunched, silent.

Worry slammed into Rorrik when the demorinkin did not reply. "It's not like we just steal stuff! We help people, too! We saved you, didn't we?" He frowned at his friend, desperate for his favor. "It's not like we're bad people..."

Valen kept quiet for another long moment before cracking open his eyes. The demorinkin was about to say something when Jate's voice spoke up instead.

"Hey, Rorrik, we gotta get moving!" his older brother urged from the doorway before noticing the tension smothering the room. "...Uh, is everything alright?"

Rorrik's frown doubled; he wasn't that sure.

"You heard him, Rorrik..." Valen said in a small voice without looking over. "You better go..."

"Um, if you guys need a moment —" Jate offered.

"Just *go!*" Valen snapped with an abrupt burst of anger, jabbing a claw at the door.

Rorrik's tail frizzed, and he hustled out of the room, almost dropping the laundry basket as he fled. Jate was quick to make way for him, and they shut the door without skipping a beat.

"Whoa! What happened?" his older sibling frantically questioned in felidaren as they hurried down the hall.

Rorrik couldn't help but feel small as he admitted, "He... he found out..."

■ ■ ■

Valen

Valen gazed down at the shirt bundled in his lap, its price tag glaring back at him. The demorinkin was not sure why he felt so surprised and betrayed; he had known, he had just not wanted to admit it.

But now there was no denying it. Rorrik had confirmed it himself: the family, his saviors and current caretakers, were a band of criminals.

His throat felt swollen with stress as he tried to force a swallow down. It was all terribly ironic. He had not been wanting to associate himself with illegal practices and crime, and yet there he sat in the heart of a rogue hideout, a guest of thieves.

He felt incredibly foolish for not forcing himself to realize it sooner. It had simply been easier to stuff his suspicions into the back of his mind to worry about later, but now everything was crashing back, overwhelming him.

Part of him still endeavored to deny it. Valen longed to view the family as the good people he believed them to be, but the reality of the situation was contradictory. How could they be good if they were criminals?

Samitri Dayas popped into his brain to challenge that assumption. Valen recalled the librarian and how he had helped Valen with magic training despite the illegality of it. That made Mr. Dayas a criminal, and yet Valen had not seen him as a bad person. If anything, he had looked up to the floraling and agreed that the government didn't need its nose in everything.

With a blush, Valen realized he himself had not exactly regarded the law with much care. He remembered the fake permit he had purchased to pursue magic training and his original intention at the market before discovering his riddle game. He had been planning to steal, the very thing he was so appalled about. Even his continued pursuit in magic was far from law abiding.

Which meant Valen *himself* was a criminal, and yet he did not see himself as a bad person.

'But it's *different!*' his conscious debated. '*I've been driven by necessity!*' He was going to steal to feed himself and his brother. He was learning magic because…

…well, there wasn't much necessity to that, was there?

He puffed out a frustrated sigh and tossed the shirt across the room. His head found his hands, and he squeezed at the hair caught in his palms.

'*It's not like I'm hurting anyone, though! Neither was Mr. Dayas! What Rorrik did was harmful to that shop!*

'*…But it wasn't needless. He was driven by necessity too. It's not like he stole just to steal.*' His mind hung on that thought, unsure of what to feel about it.

'*They did rescue me, too… That's not bad, is it?*'

But what if they actually *did* do bad things? Did they ever steal just to steal? Did they ever smuggle harmful, illegal substances? Did they ever hurt people? Worse yet, did they ever… *kill* people?

A chill snaked down Valen's spine, causing him to shudder. What the family exactly did was still a question, and once again his imagination was the only answer he had.

'*They can't be* that *bad…*' Optimistic logic stepped in to curb his discomfiture. '*Why would they work for that Porte lady, then? She helps rescue kids. That's a good thing to do!*'

The demorinkin felt helpless as an internal battle of tug-of-war began to wage. One moment he was excusing the family, and then the next he was accusing them. It was confusing and stressful, and he just wanted to cut the rope, force it to end.

He would soon have that ability. His magic lessons started within the hour, and those were always the perfect distraction. Nothing quite tore his mind from his troubles like the rucanic.

He stood up with a groan and went to wait for Pepperglow in the living room.

On his way out, he caught a glimpse of the shirt on the floor, its price tag seeing him off.

Valen sat hunched over on a couch in the living room, upset enough for tears. He had only minutes ago walked into the room to find Mrs. Catty there waiting for him.

"There you are! How are you?" she had greeted, pleasant.

He hadn't been able to hold her eyes; all he saw there was a reminder of his internal conflict.

"I-I'm doing fine," he had fibbed rather obviously.

"...what's the matter, cub?" she had tried, but he quickly dismissed her question with a shake of his head.

"I don't want to talk about it." *'I just want to do my magic.'*

"...alright. Just know that you can always talk to me."

In that moment, he hated how she reminded him of his mother. He didn't want to think of Mrs. Catty as a motherly figure, it only exemplified his confusion.

"Well, I hate to break this to you, but your lessons will have to be put on hold for now," the tortoiseshell had gone on to reveal. "Pepperglow is needed at the Token safe house in case we get a bite on the trap."

The news had him feeling akin to shattering glass; it exploded across his fragile emotions and mercilessly smashed his spirit into tiny, scattered pieces.

His shock and disappointment had been palpable on his face, and it spurred Mrs. Catty to frown.

"I'm sorry," she had said. "Even more sorry because I have to leave. We need to be ready in case something happens. I'll be back later."

Following that, she had left to let him to sift through the debris of his demolished morale.

But he wasn't to sulk by his lonesome for long. A weight plopped next to him on the couch, and he glanced over to find Talis.

"What're you doing?" the tiny kitten inquired with round, curious eyes.

"Uh—" Valen was remarkably far from willing to entertain the child; he was desperate to be alone. He stiffly stood up to leave. "I'm going to go lie down." The two youngest normally respected when he retreated to Rorrik's room.

"What, whyyy?!" Talis mewled with disappointment. "I really wanted to play!"

"I-I'm sorry. I just—" Why did he even need an excuse? "I'm sorry." He moved to leave the room, awkward and upset.

"But I'm sooo bored!" Talis kept on. "Ugh! I just want to go outside again!"

Valen stopped in his tracks as Talis' words pierced him; the kitten sounded *exactly* like Karreo. Struck with grief, his insides twisted and his hands went to grasp at the sides of his head.

"...Ummm, Valen? Are you okay?" Talis worried, Valen hearing Karreo's voice intertwining with his.

Valen tried to swallow but found himself unable. He stared forward, his expression taut with pain. "Why... why can't you go outside?" The words spilt out without him willing them to.

"I have to lie low!" On the corner of his eye, Valen could see Talis' shoulders scrunch up as though the felidaren were hiding. "It's safer that way!"

'...He can't leave because of me!' He began to shake his head wildly as his emotions overcame him.

"What's wrong?!" Talis whined with confusion.

Valen looked back at the young tabby and saw Karreo's face instead.

"I..." the demorinkin choked out. He squeezed his eyes shut but still saw the image of his deceased brother. Guilt constricted him, forcing out his next words. "I... I'm sorry you can't go outside..."

"It's okay! Mom says it's not forever!"

'For Karreo it was.' The grief within him multiplied, and he fled the room in a disoriented speed walk.

"Valen, come back! I just want to play!" Talis whimpered, but Valen did not stop nor reply.

He retreated to Rorrik's bedroom and slammed the door before collapsing onto the queen bed. The dam finally broke, and tears poured out in a flood, relentless.

The guilt was becoming too heavy to carry. 'This is all my fault!'

■ ■ ■

Rorrik

The spy had returned to snoop for a third day, which meant pulling more theatrics in the form of movement in and out of the building. The sun was close to setting when Rorrik was told it was his turn to put on a show.

He left the safe house and started heading down the street, appearing cautious in his actions.

He was reaching the end of the block when Gavin's voice vibrated in Rorrik's earpiece. "You've got a tail, Rorrik. The spy is following you."

The spy was tagging along? That was new behavior; for the past two days, he had stayed put when casing the safe house.

"Ooh, pressure is on to look like you're doing something more important than a milk run," Jate joked over the radio. "I'll follow along."

Rorrik wasn't sure what to pretend to do. He brainstormed ideas as he went, wondering what could be a good ruse.

As he weighed how to proceed, he turned onto Conifer Street, a quieter road that ran through a neighborhood. As he headed down the way, ideas were stubborn to come to him, perhaps in part because of his mood. It was difficult not to linger on the prior conflict with Valen; Rorrik felt terrible that the demorinkin had reacted so negatively to the family business. It bothered the tabby that he did not seem to have Valen's favor anymore; he just wanted the demorinkin to like him, but had that been ruined?

Rorrik's ears twitched as sounds of commotion and grunting started up ahead. He spotted two human men struggling with a wooden buffet as they attempted to shuffle it towards a sizable moving van.

Rorrik watched the endeavor; the furniture looked awfully heavy, perhaps too heavy for only two movers?

One of the men took notice of him. "Hey, kid! Can you give us a hand with moving this stuff? Our friends bailed on us. We'll pay you!"

Rorrik perked up at the idea of compensation. "Uh, sure," he agreed with a shrug. The felidaren had helped his brothers move things all the time; he knew the power of working together made moving furniture many times easier.

"Thanks, man! You're a lifesaver!" the other human said.

"Aw, isn't that kind of you?" Jate's voice cooed over the radio. "Rorrik the humanitarian!"

"Hey, how strong are you, kid?" the first man then questioned.

Rorrik's shoulders lightly bounced and he smirked. "Pretty strong."

"Great! Can you grab this end, then? My arms are killing me!"

"Uh, yeah, sure!"

The human passed over his hold of the buffet and its heaviness automatically stressed Rorrik's arms. Luckily, the man moved so he was holding the midsection of the buffet, significantly removing much of the strain.

"Alright, let's get this hunk of junk on that truck!" the second man pushed.

They moved the mass of wood towards and up the ramp, Rorrik leading. With a glance back, he saw that the van already housed a mattress, which was resting up against the back wall.

He stopped to ask, "So, where are we putting this?"

"Just towards the back," the first man said.

Rorrik nodded and once again began to move, but the two men pushed off too quickly, knocking him off balance.

"Hey, ah, wait, I'm slipping!"

But they did not slow down. Instead, they sped up, spurring him into losing his footing all together. He shouted out as he fell back into the mattress.

"...Rorrik? You okay in there?" Jate asked through a nervous chuckle.

The next instant the buffet was ramming into his stomach, incapacitating him. The felidaren desperately tried to react, but the air had been knocked out of his chest.

The truck then went dark as Rorrik heard the slam of the trailer closing.

"Rorrik! Rorrik! It's a trap!" Jate was suddenly shouting over the radio in a panic. "Rorrik!"

The vehicle roared into life, and Rorrik could feel the pressure of it taking off. The tabby was too stunned to move as the men shoved the buffet aside and kneeled in front of him. In movements too quick for him to counter, they forced his hands behind his back and zip tied him.

"Rorrik!" Jate's voice once again called. "Shit! *Shi*—"

His brother's alarm cut off as one of the men yanked the earpiece out. A gag then wrapped around his mouth, and a hood was pulled over his head, snuffing out the view of the trailer around him.

"We've got him," the first man's voice said. "Be ready for the switch."

Panic usurped surprise as Rorrik finally recovered from the impact of the buffet. He started to struggle, but a swift punch to the gut had him reliving the impact of the furniture for a second round. He moaned against the gag as pain and shock wracked him.

A couple of terrifying minutes passed, Rorrik too scared to move in fear of another punch. His mind kept trying to wrap around the situation but it could not—would not—process it. *'This isn't happening!'*

Suddenly, by the sound of it, the trailer was yanked open, and Rorrik was being strong-armed into standing up. The two men began to drag him, and then he was being pushed down into an uncomfortably tight spot. Another slam sounded, this one right in his ears.

With that, Rorrik once again felt the pressure of movement, spurring him to believe that he had been stuffed into a trunk.

'This isn't happening!' Disbelief and fear gripped Rorrik so tightly that he could hardly breathe. *'This isn't happening!'*

■ ■ ■

Valen

Valen was exhausted from grief when a frantic knocking came at the door. He was pushing himself up to answer, but the door burst open before he could, revealing Mrs. Catty.

"Up, up, *now*," she ordered strictly. She hastily made her way to the back wall and pushed at the secret board, triggering the escape exit.

Valen stumbled off the bed, his cheeks still wet with moisture. "What's going on?!"

"Move. *Now.*" Mrs. Catty grabbed his shoulders and pushed him through the narrow passage.

They arrived in the narrow hallway beyond, and the felidaren went to scramble up the ladder. "After me, hurry!" the felidaren spurred in a bark.

Confusion and fear muddled his mind and movements as Mrs. Catty guided him through the secret passage she had explained a few nights prior.

They stepped from a closet and into a hallway. She grabbed his shoulders and began to rush them forward until they reached a set of doors that appeared to lead outside.

As they hurried through the doorway, daylight soaked Valen for the first time in weeks, blinding him. He winced against the sun as Mrs. Catty shoved him towards a car that was parked on the side of the road. A worried looking Quinn was standing by the vehicle and opened the door when they neared.

Mrs. Catty forced Valen in the car and slammed the door shut. She then entered the vehicle from the driver's door, Quinn from the passenger's. Valen noticed that Talis and Calvin were sitting next to him in the back, the kittens looking soberer than he had ever witnessed them before.

Without wasting another second, Mrs. Catty sped off, watching the road with a determined stare.

Valen could not find his voice as he sat there in consternation. "Wh... wh..." he attempted, but the words clung to his throat. "Wh... wh—what— what is going on?!" he finally spat it out, his voice cracking with alarm.

Mrs. Catty met his worried gaze in the rearview mirror. "We're relocating you all to Denbrook."

"W-why?!" Valen cried.

"We've been compromised." Mrs. Catty broke eye contact, and Valen noticed that her eyes were glossy with threatening tears. "...Rorrik was kidnapped."

Chapter 36

Valen

"Rorrik was kidnapped."

Valen was enslaved with torturous consternation as the words ricocheted in his ears. He desperately endeavored to deny what he had just heard; he could not bring himself to accept it.

But Mrs. Catty went on, forcing him out of his denial. "We have to assume the Fangs know all our secrets," she spoke from the front seat, her voice strained, but absolute. Her eyes remained glossy but never overflowed with tears as she stared straight ahead. "Which is why we have to relocate."

"Is Rorrik going to be okay?!" Talis whimpered. "Mom?!"

"Baby, cub, we're going to find him," Mrs. Catty told her son. "We have people on it. We're going to find him," she repeated, perhaps partially for herself.

"This is all because of Valen!" Calvin tearfully accused.

The guilt already crushing Valen intensified as the kitten's remark struck him like a whip. The young felidaren was right; if it weren't for Valen, Rorrik would be safe, not...

"It is *not* Valen's fault!" Mrs. Catty snapped. "Don't you say that!"

"But it is!" Calvin screamed. "All this is happening because of him!"

"Calvin!" Quinn barked as he turned in his seat to face his younger sibling. "We can't point fingers! We have to stick together!"

Calvin thrashed and kicked at the floor. "I don't want to! I hate him!"

"That is enough!" Mrs. Catty yelled, her voice booming in the small vehicle. "We need to remain calm!"

Guilt constricted Valen tighter and tighter still; he was dangerously close to suffocating. Mrs. Catty's earlier words began to echo in his mind. *'We have to assume the Fangs know all our secrets.'* With a chilling realization Valen finally understood what she meant: Rorrik was going to be tortured. *'No! No! Rorrik, no! Gods, this is all my fault!'* Valen could not bear all the terrible things that were happening because of him. *'This should have never happened! It's all my fault!'*

A ringing coming from Mrs. Catty's person then disrupted the turmoil.

"Quinn!" the mother said hurriedly. "My corresponder!"

The tabby retrieved the device from her pocket and looked down at its display. "It's Miss Porte!"

"Put her on," Mrs. Catty ordered briskly, Quinn doing so. "Hello?!"

"Kyla, we received a ransom on my public line from the Fangs," Avalene reported without delay.

Mrs. Catty's shimmering eyes widened. "What?!"

"We'll discuss it at more length in person," Miss Porte went on. "Bring your kids and meet me at the safe house in Cliffton." The call went dead before Mrs. Catty could respond.

The car was quiet for a lengthy, stunned second.

Mrs. Catty turned the car around. "Quinn, call your aunt. We're not heading to Denbrook after all."

■ ■ ■

Avalene

Within the hour, the family had all mustered in the cramped walls of the Cliffton safe house, an ideal location due to its unused status in the whole Fangs ordeal. Valen and the two youngest had been ordered to remain in one of the bedrooms while Avalene, Kyla, Niem, and the three oldest gathered in the dining room to discuss how to handle the development.

Avalene scanned the room with a grave stare, the air heavy from the gravity of their predicament. "This is the message they left." She activated the recorder and a feminine voice began to speak.

"We have captured your child and have every means to subject him to the consequences that he is deserving of. That is, unless we can come into agreement. We both possess something the other desires. We have your child, and you have our target. Perhaps we can arrange an exchange?

"If you hand over the demorin, we will hand over the boy. We will withhold harm from befalling the child until then. However, if you fail to respond by tomorrow morning or reject our offer, he will befall the fate a hell sympathizer is befitting of.

"You have been presented a golden opportunity. If Vaaskiir is handed over without struggle, you will have your precious child back *and* we will no longer have our quarrel, a rare convenience for the grievances you have committed against our cause.

"Our offer is well worth considering. Is the blood of your child a price you are willing to pay to protect this hellborn? The choice is clear: hand him over and bring this all to an end."

The room digested the recording in pensive silence.

306

Kyla was the first to speak. "Well, maybe we can work this to our advantage," the queen suggested cautiously. "We can always pretend to play along and then get the jump on them."

"You think they're not expecting that?" Niem huffed from his spot in a corner. The ebony felidaren was outstandingly broody; Avalene could tell he was worried for his son.

"Of course they are! But we're smarter than them!" Kyla pushed.

"Are we? I believe we sit on the hoodwinked side of the equation," Avalene reminded, her brow tight with stress.

"I-it's my fault. I should have— I really should have noticed something was weird about it!" Jate spoke up in a tone Avalene had never heard him use, a far cry from the quips he normally cracked. The tabby's demeanor was jittery and sunken. "I—I—"

Gavin put a hand on his brother's arm. "Jate, you couldn't have known. We have to accept what happened and move forward."

"Your brother is right. We can all sit here and... and blame ourselves but that's not going to help anyone," Kyla said with a shake of her head. "We have to deal with the choices we've made."

She appeared to be speaking more to herself than to Jate.

Avalene redirected the conversation. "Well, let's say we try to trick them. How would we approach the switch off?"

Kyla mulled on it for a second. "Well, we could—"

"Just stop it!" Valen's voice suddenly interjected. He charged into the room, distraught. "It's not worth it! Just give me up!"

The meeting had to take a moment to react to his intrusion and then another for his outburst.

"What in all the realms are you saying?" Kyla said with disbelief.

"I'm sick and tired of people getting hurt because of me!" Valen cried through a tear-soaked grimace. "Just stop it! Please!"

"Absolutely not!" Kyla rejected. "Valen! Be reasonable!"

"I *am* being reasonable! I don't want you to do this anymore! Give me up!"

Kyla shook her head. "I'm not arguing with you on this!"

But Valen kept on. "Your *own* son has been kidnapped! It's all my—"

"This is no one's fault but my own!" Kyla cut him off in a shout. "I will deal with the decisions I have made, Valen Vaaskiir!"

"Why are you doing this?!" Valen matched her tone. "I don't understand!"

"It was my choice to help you, and I plan on seeing that through!" Kyla answered, firm.

"It's not worth it!" Valen slammed a fist down on the table. "Just give me up!"

Kyla hissed and gestured to her mate. "I can't handle this right now! Niem, get him out of here!"

Niem went to approach Valen, but the demorinkin left the room by his own power. He hurried off, the room falling into an uncomfortable silence.

The mother let go of a long sigh. "We need to think of something. We don't have much time."

■ ■ ■

Valen

Valen fled from the meeting and into one of the empty bedrooms, stumbling as he went. The voice from the recording was a sinister echo in his thoughts, fueling all his self-hatred and remorse. He wished he had never heard it, but morbid curiosity had driven him to eavesdrop.

He slammed his back against the wall and slid down its length until he crashed on the floor. Guilt and anger rocked him, frenzied by the severity of his despondency.

'*I can't do this anymore!*' He was too crippled by fear and despair, too exhausted by pain and grief. The hope he had thought he had was gone, snuffed out by the cold reality he could no longer deny. His existence brought nothing but pain; he hated himself and all the damage he had done. The grief of losing his family and failing his baby brother was simply too powerful to overcome. He not only was hurting others by existing, he was hurting himself, too.

Nausea boiled in his stomach, scalding his chest and throat. He just wanted it all to go away, to fix what he had broken.

And yet Mrs. Catty would not let him. Even though giving himself up would save Rorrik's life, she still refused. He choked out a sob and punched at the floor, beside himself with frustration.

'*If she won't do it, I will!*' He was far too frightened to deliver himself to the Fangs and meet whatever end they had planned for him, but there was another way.

He reached towards the holster on his hip, his hand trembling. He gripped the weapon sitting at the small of his back and pulled it from its resting place, the blaster feeling heavier than ever before.

He stared down at the spell slinger, the nausea in his guts bubbling up his throat. His eyes were glued to the safety as adrenaline coursed like acid through his system.

'*If I'm dead, they'll have no choice.*' The demorinkin didn't take his eyes from the weapon. '*They'll have to give me up. Rorrik will be safe. Everything will be fixed.*

'I... I won't have to do this anymore. I can finally see my family again. Everything will be fixed. Everything will be fixed!'

He clenched the weapon until his knuckles flushed pink. He squeezed his eyes closed and coughed out a sob, the taste of bile souring his mouth. He began to rock as all the feelings rampaging within him began a crescendo, spurring him on.

'Everything will be fixed... Everything will be fixed...' He raised the blaster so it was in front of his face and opened his eyes to stare down the barrel, the runes staring back.

He clicked off the safety, causing a burst of fear that was immediately mauled by determination. 'Everything will be fixed...'

He put the blaster to his head and another sob forced itself out of him, complete with more bile. He bit his lower lip, tasting blood, and once again pinched his eyes closed. 'Everything will be fixed!'

He called upon his runa and it was quick to respond, a gift of his adrenaline. He attempted to channel his current as he had several times over the last few days, but the flow was sloppy and erratic, foiling his efforts.

'Everything will be fixed!' He again tried to surge his flow towards his fingertips but it proceeded to evade him. 'Everything will be fixed!' He tried and tried, only to be met with the same result.

With a flare of shame, he recognized the familiar block of fear was preventing him. 'Why can't I just be strong enough?!'

Valen then heard the sound of footsteps, and he popped open his eyes to see Niem standing directly in front of him, the felidaren's intense yellow glare on the demorinkin.

Valen gaped at the felidaren, too startled to move.

They held each other's eyes for several seconds. Then, the black-furred felidaren shook his head at the demorinkin.

"That won't fix anything," Niem told him, gruff. The felidaren maintained his commanding stare for another long second and then walked away, adding, "You know that."

Shock rattled Valen as the power of his determination was obliterated, and he dropped the blaster. As it clattered to the ground, he buried his face into his knees and wailed out in agony and shame.

Chapter 37

Rorrik

Rorrik hit the floor with a harsh, graceless thump, having been shoved by his captors. He coughed out an inhale of dust the floor had greeted him with and waited for more rough handling, but it did not come.

Instead, he heard footsteps make their way away from him, and then a door slammed shut. Rorrik kept his ears perked, braced for any sounds or movement elsewhere in the room, but he detected nothing. It would seem he had been left alone.

He could still hardly process what had happened; his best (and most fearful) guess was that he had been kidnapped by the Fangs. The felidaren had spent a good hour in the cramped space that he supposed was a trunk before he was being forcefully removed and pushed along. They carried him into a building before shoving him into the room he was in now.

Although the hood still robbed him of his vision, he could figure that he was in a very old place; the stench of dust and wood rot was all around him. Contrastingly, he could also trace ghosts of incense on the air, sighs of herb and flowers.

However, the felidaren had no time to smell the flowers if he wanted any chance at freedom. If the Fangs *were* his captors, his escape meant *everything*, including, very likely, his own life.

He moved so he was sitting up and began weaseling his restrained arms down his back. He slipped them past his bottom and then around his legs, bringing his arms to his front instead of his back.

He slipped his hands past the hood and pushed the gag upwards, allowing his mouth access to the binds. His tongue felt for the lock in the zip tie, and he bit down on the plastic as hard as he could. It took a couple of chomps, but a pop finally responded, signaling surrender. The zip tie fell to the floor, and he removed the hood and gag from his head.

A dark room revealed itself, his feline eyes adjusting to the gloom. There was no furniture or windows, and when he studied the only door he noted that there was no opening mechanism. A line of dim light leaked in from underneath the door, and Rorrik heard someone cough on the other side. *'Shit! Not that way!'*

The tabby got to his feet, his blood pulsing loud in his ears. He had to act quick and think even faster. He consulted his lifetime of training, determined to discover a way out.

He studied the walls and noticed a decrepit air duct near the ceiling. *'That might work!'* He scurried up to it, his footsteps mute. He nimbly jumped and grabbed at the bars, the metal whining in protest. The felidaren shifted his weight, and the vent was yanked free, sprinkling a rain of rust on him.

Rorrik's feet found the ground silently and he inspected the opening, only to be disappointed. Even with his remarkably flexible, lithe form, the space was hardly big enough to allow him passage. Discouraging him further was the presence of rust; it lined the duct like moss, endangering the integrity of the vent. Even if he could fit, would it even hold him? Dispirited, he put the cover down on the floor; he would have to find another way.

Panic began to poison his concentration, and he started a worried pace. If the door had no mechanism to compromise (not to mention a guard on the other side) and there were no windows to escape or a vent to crawl out of, what options did he have?

He paced back and forth, his tail cutting through the dusty air as it thrashed. He moved about the room, desperately scanning the walls and ceiling. *'There has to be a way! There has to be a—'*

Squeak.

He froze, his ears perking and his vision honing in on the plank he was standing on. Even with his sneaking, the board had sounded when he stepped on it.

His foot applied pressure, and the plank wobbled against his weight with another squeak. *'It's loose! I can hide in here!'* Rorrik kneeled to pry the floor open, moving fast. The board came free after some convincing, and a narrow, cobweb-ridden space about a foot by five feet lay beneath; a tight squeeze, but a possible one!

Rorrik immediately began nestling himself down into the cranny, paying any potential creepy tenants no mind. Footsteps and voices then started outside the door, causing Rorrik's panic to flare.

The tabby hurried into lying on his side and slid the plank back over the space. As the board attempted to fall into place, however, he noticed his tail was caught outside, preventing it.

He attempted to pull his tail inside, but the opening was too tight. Rorrik's alarm erupted tenfold as the sound of a door knob twisting hit his ears.

He lifted the board just enough to allow his tail entry and closed it in the same second the door opened. Rorrik had to consciously keep himself from crying out in fear; he squeezed his eyes closed, and his ears dug into the side of his head.

Whoever entered the room was quick to notice he was missing. In a language he did not recognize, they began to yell, their tone confused and angry. Rorrik heard them stomp across the room, their every step rattling him. They drew near his hiding spot, Rorrik bracing himself for the worst, but they kept walking.

The felidaren let go of a tense breath, relieved, but then a metallic clang bounded across the floor, landing nearly on top of his hiding spot. Rorrik's fur bristled with apprehension and he was back to holding his breath. *'What was that?!'*

Nothing came of it as the steps left the room in an agitated gait. Rorrik did not hear the door close after them.

More chatter started outside the room, growing louder and more alarmed in tone. Rorrik could feel faint vibrations of people hurrying about elsewhere in the building; several sets of feet were on the move.

A booming voice then shouted, and Rorrik felt someone clomp up to the room. Another voice frantically responded, submissive and afraid. The first voice roared something, and the second voice stuttered out a worried reply. They went back and forth a couple more rounds, and then there was the scraping sound of a weapon unsheathing.

The second voice cried out and there were multiple, fleshy, splashing noises and a solid thump hitting the floor close by. The unmistakable tang of blood struck Rorrik's sense of smell, elucidating what had just happened; someone, probably the guard that had been assigned to the room, had just been cut down.

Rorrik was still processing that when something wet hit his face, hot on his fur. With horror and disgust, he realized it was blood. It continued to leak into the plank, soaking him.

The board shook as the owner of the voice stormed off, leaving the body to drain blood and guts into the floor. The stench of the wound seeped into the air, curdling Rorrik's already bothered stomach. Nausea joined the sensations bombarding him, threatening sickness. Rorrik desperately fought against his repulsion; he had to stay put, even if it meant marinating in gore.

Rorrik wrestled with a fermenting sensation of restlessness as time passed by, drip by drip. The odor of the wound only worsened as Rorrik was forced to linger in his hiding place, blood sinking deep into his fur. Vomit inched up the felidaren's throat but he was able to keep it there by the influence of terror. If he spewed, he would make noise, potentially leading to detection.

He could still feel and hear commotion happening across the building. Several voices screamed and footfalls scampered in the distance; the place had fallen into a frenzy, and it was all because of him. That fact both satisfied and terrified him.

The clamor persisted for a solid hour before finally simmering down. Achy from hiding and crusty with dried blood, Rorrik summoned all his courage and tentatively lifted the board to peek out into the darkness.

Inches away was the vent he had removed from the air duct. *'That must have been the metallic bang from before!'* That would mean someone had forcefully moved it across the room. *'Do they think I escaped through the duct?'* Rorrik hadn't exactly intended to create that ruse, but was thankful he had.

Only a few feet off was the stinking corpse of the guard, still lying where they had been cut down. Rorrik stared at the body, horror twisting his face and souring his guts. He had never seen a dead person before. It simply overwhelmed him; he wanted to move on and leave the death behind, but his training told him to check the body.

He stiffly pulled himself out of the nook, his muscles protesting, groggy and tight from his hiding. He crawled towards the corpse, his fur standing on end with anxiety as he moved out into the open. It seemed that at any moment someone would come walking by and notice him, and his endeavor would be undone. He would be interrogated and tortured and killed, failing everyone. He pushed those thoughts back; he couldn't lose his head now.

Remaining on all fours, he arrived in front of the body, making sure to avoid the pool of blood. The felidaren got an eyeful of the several gashes that had been the death of the guard; all the wounds were deep cuts, save for a single puncture hole gaping in their chest. Rorrik didn't dare stare for long as the gore unsettled him.

He studied the face of the guard, pinning them to be male. Even in death, their skin glimmered in the faint lighting from the hallway, similar to the contact at the restaurant. Their lifeless, copper eyes stared off into nothing, unblinking. Rorrik found that even more unsettling than the wounds and tore his attention away, troubled.

He shut his eyes as the nausea in his guts worsened, fueled by the disturbing imagery and smell of decay. He reminded himself of his training, desperate for motivation. *'I have to do this...'*

He mustered his strength into resolve and swallowed hard, forcing down vomit. *'...for Valen!'*

His eyes snapped open and found the body's belt, spotting a weapon there, an elaborate longsword sporting a familiar fanged hilt. It was the same weapon the prisoners had used, confirming his suspicions towards his captors. He was in Fangs of Hellbane territory, indeed.

Although he had figured, it was still sobering to be confirmed. He wrestled his apprehension into submission and proceeded to search the body.

There was an earpiece in the guard's ear that Rorrik assumed to be a radio. The felidaren considered grabbing it, but remembered the language they spoke was unknown to him. He left it behind; it would do him no good and possibly alert the Fangs to his presence. *'It might have a tracking device in it. Can't be giving away my position!'*

Nothing else particularly noteworthy about the body revealed as he searched. They wore a typical looking tunic that was embroidered with a shining trim of gold, paired with mundane pants. Their pockets had nothing of worth or significance, and so Rorrik decided he could finally move on.

...out into the hall. As though on cue, the lights barely illuminating the space beyond flickered, humming with a faint buzz. The open door beckoned him, and he didn't delay another moment. He set off in a creep, silent as could be.

He paused in the threshold and peered into the dim hallway, his ears erect to detect any sounds. No one seemed to be wandering about that he could hear or see, and so he tiptoed out into the hall, his tail bristling with adrenaline.

At the end of the hall to the left was a window, presenting Rorrik with a choice: he could escape now or try to find out more information. His instincts and fear begged him to flee for safety, but his training disagreed. If he were indeed in Fangs territory, he had found himself in an invaluable opportunity. He could assume he was in a type of headquarters, and where there was HQ there was intelligence. He had to at least *try* to find information before running for it. '*I have to do this. For Valen!*'

He turned right, leaving the window, and its safety, behind.

The hall turned a corner and he stopped to poke his head around the bend. Nothing but dull hallway awaited him, camera-less and abandoned.

He noticed an ajar door and approached it warily, arriving without issue. He peeked into the room and his stomach dropped at what he saw.

It appeared to be his would-be torture room. A belted chair sat ominously in a corner, joined by a table displaying an assortment of instruments, from knives to hammers to hooks. A shudder ran down Rorrik's spine as he was once again reminded of the intensity of his situation.

He proceeded to study the space and noticed another table with supplies. Instead of torture equipment, however, it appeared to be covered with gadgets.

The tabby crept into the room to have a closer look. Upon inspection, Rorrik pinned the first device as a recorder and the second as a translator, useful assets for interrogation.

Conveniently useful for intelligence gathering, as well. Any past conducted interrogations were potentially captured on the recorder, while the translator removed the language barrier he had hit. He pocketed the recorder and hooked the translator around his ear.

The tabby turned his attention on the assortment of torture instruments and armed himself with a knife. If things were to get hairy, he wouldn't be defenseless.

He took one last check about the room for anything else notable, discovering nothing. With that, he snuck back out into the hall upon making certain the coast was clear.

He gazed at the path ahead of him, weighing how to proceed. About halfway down the hall there was another bend, and when Rorrik peeked down it, he noticed two more doors and an archway. He decided to head that way.

With a quick glance, Rorrik saw that the archway led into a living room area. The place was empty, although it looked fairly lived in, judging by the clutter.

Nothing particularly interesting stuck out, and so Rorrik directed his focus towards one of the two doors. It was barely hanging open, and when Rorrik checked inside, he saw the makings of a bathroom. Moonlight leaked in from a window. *'Another exit!'*

He still was not ready to leave, however. He pulled his gaze away from freedom and set it towards the other door. It was closed, and when Rorrik put his ear up to listen for any sign of inhabitants, silence was his answer.

A quick test of the handle revealed the door was unlocked, so he mustered his courage and headed inside.

The room appeared to be an office space, as it had a few desks, bookshelf storage, and a large map up on the wall. *'This looks promising!'*

He slunk up to the bookshelf to assess it, finding a collection of binders labelled in a mystery language. It was unfortunate his translator was merely a vocal one; he still had a language barrier to contend with, after all. *'I might not be able to read it, but I can bring it back to someone who can.'*

He scrutinized the binders, calling upon his training to decipher which one was worth grabbing. He had to be choosey, considering he had no bag to stuff binder after binder in. He would have to carry whatever he took with his hands.

The whole shelf was dusty, but there was a binder that appeared cleaner than the others, suggesting that it was accessed more often. Its position on the shelf further supported that observation; it wasn't neatly pushed back like all the others. It was likely grabbed enough to not bother obsessing over tidiness.

He carefully pulled the binder free from the shelf and cracked it open to spare a quick look inside, finding tables that were reminiscent of a contact page. If that were true, it was definitely the binder to grab.

He set his attention onto the massive map, instantly recognizing it as Sengard. Multiple pins and strings decorated the face, and Rorrik got right to memorizing them, another task his training had prepared him for. Much of his conditioning had taught him to quickly retain things, a valuable gift in their line of work.

He spent a minute absorbing the map before moving on to hunt through the desk drawers; supplies and empty forms were all he found.

He glanced down at the binder in his hands, thought about the map in his memory, and decided that he had found enough information to excuse an escape. He headed out of the room, eager to get his tail out of there.

He arrived back in the hall, finding it empty, as it had been his entire investigation. He could not help but find that odd; where was any kind of patrol?

As though to answer his question, Rorrik began to hear faint voices and movement coming in his direction.

The felidaren's adrenaline spiked, and he searched for a place to hide. A counter stood a few feet away, offering refuge. He ducked into the furniture, pressing into a pile of towels inside, and waited with bated breath as the voices grew closer and closer.

"I am aware Arch Cloudhook is trying to send a message to us, but I wish they would remove Philan's body already. It is not helping anybody just rotting there, fouling the air like that," a female voice complained, still far off.

It seemed his translator was working.

"Never seen the Arch that angry before. I reckon Phil will be bones by the time they move him," another female voice replied. "Best we get used to the stench."

"I am still pressed to believe that felidaren got through the vents!" the first voice said, drawing closer. "Poor Philan, that wasn't his fault. Who could have anticipated that to happen?"

"Those cats are remarkably pesky," the second voice noted. "The Arch was really counting on that ransom."

'Ransom?'

"It is an unfortunate development," the first voice replied from directly in front of the buffet. "I wonder what we are going to try now?"

"Not like we'll know until later. We're stuck doing patrol while everyone else is at that meeting," the second voice grunted.

'Meeting?'

"If I'm honest, though," the voice went on. "I'd rather be where it's quiet rather than contend with that mess downstairs. Even *with* the stench up here." The voices grew farther away. "Gods, things have really fallen apart since Arch Levaris ascended..."

"Watch your tongue! The Arch will slice it off if he hears you saying things like that!"

"*Pfft*. He's too occupied spitting fire downstairs to hear."

"Marrith!"

"What? It's true, is it not?"

"That doesn't warrant..."

Rorrik could no longer make out their words, signaling their departure.

The tabby cautiously left his hiding spot, mindful over the exchange he had just eavesdropped on. If there was a meeting going on, that would explain the emptiness. He looked to where the guards had come from, noticing another bend at the end of the hall. A staircase lay beyond, heading downwards. Judging by the guard's remarks, the meeting was happening there.

His nerves alit, he started down the steps. Escaping would have to wait; catching that meeting was invaluable.

As he descended, a muffled, shouting voice reached his ears. By the time he cleared the last step he could make out what it was saying.

"This is inexcusable! A disgrace! The lot of you deserve hellfire for this slipup!" a male voice spat.

The commotion was coming from behind a door that lay straight ahead. The space Rorrik found himself in was small and without any cover, grinding his nerves further. He pressed up against the wall, feeling utterly exposed.

"Arch Cloudhook, I believe you've badgered them quite enough," a female voice said, firm. "Time is not our ally. We *must* discuss our next move!"

"Do not order me around, Vallika!" the male voice, Arch Cloudhook, apparently, roared. "I am Arch! Not *you*!"

"Then behave like one!" the woman, Vallika, rebutted. "While you throw your tantrum we are wasting valuable time! That felidaren could be reaching his base any moment, and yet you —"

"We will know when he reaches it! Our eye is posted on the building!"

"But we need to be ready for when he does!" Vallika pressed. "Enough with this, already!"

"Vallika is right, Arch. We need to focus on our next plan of action," a mild-mannered male voice contributed, Rorrik recognizing it as the contact from the restaurant. "We must be ready for a potential counterattack."

"Bah! Why have we been so incompetent to face these meddling felidarens?!" Arch Cloudhook huffed. "Can anyone explain that to me?!"

Rorrik remembered the recorder in his pocket with a start. He pulled it out and began to record.

"At least we know where their base is, Arch, sir," a new voice said.

"But how do we know it's not just a trap?" another voice spoke up.

"I say just firebomb the cursed place!" yet another voice yelled out.

"But what if Vaaskiir truly is there? You know the commandment: our fangs must be the one to slay him!"

'Fangs?' He was reminded of their sword hilts. 'Do they mean their swords?'

"Blindly firebombing is a gamble we cannot take," the mild-mannered male said. "I suggest we send an accomplished group of five to search the place. If Vaaskiir is nowhere to be found, then we have no reason to relent."

"I approve," Vallika affirmed. "Arch?"

"Levaris would be disgusted with us all," Arch Cloudhook groaned. "We should have slayed that demorin that first night. The fact we don't even know where the beast is is very telling!"

"Arch?!" Vallika growled.

"Very well!" Arch Cloudhook snapped. "But, if he is found, you are *not* to kill him — that honor will be reserved to me!"

"It will be done, Arch," a chorus of voices answered.

"It best be — we cannot afford any more errors! The fact we lost that ransom is simply —"

"We technically have not lost it *yet*," the mild-mannered male informed. "We have until our ex-prisoner reaches his base for the felidarens to potentially accept our demands. We should hold onto the ransom until we see him return. We still might have leverage, after all."

Rorrik's stomach churned as he processed the conversation. Were the Fangs charging Valen as the price of his release? *'They would never agree to that!'* At least he hoped.

"It is nothing we should rely on," Vallika said. "We cannot stay here — we must leave as soon as possible. Our first priority should be cleaning the building of all sensitive material. Then, I say we rig up the place with wire trap explosives. If they return searching for us, then they will pay the price."

"I was thinking very similar," the mild-mannered male agreed, punctuated with a single chuckle. "Does this idea appeal to you, Arch?"

"Get it done!" Cloudhook snarled. "Or so help me, Xerstelle!"

Rorrik figured the meeting was soon coming to an end, and so he hustled towards the stairs, clicking the recorder off. The pressure was on to get out of the building before the place fell into chaos again, let alone back to his family to alert them of his escape!

He reached the top of the steps and stopped briefly to listen for any movement ahead. Instead, he heard it coming from behind him, forcing him forward.

The felidaren cleared the corner and spotted that the bathroom door was still hanging open. He scuttled up and slipped inside, clicking the door closed quietly. He noticed a lock on the knob and exercised it. *'Nothing unusual about a locked bathroom door!'*

He stopped to breathe for a moment, burdened by the effects of his adrenaline. His fur was damp from beads of sweat, and he couldn't stop trembling. He lashed his tail and exhaled through clenched fangs. *'Remember your training! Keep it together!'*

He approached the window, which sat above the toilet and was narrow in stature, and had a look outside. The black of night awaited him, offering shadows of cover, Nocturna's gift to rogues. *'May shadows guide me,'* he prayed.

He stepped up on the toilet, placed the binder down, and unlocked the window. He attempted to open it, but to his dismay it turned out to be jammed.

His ears shot back and he hefted the window again and then once more. *'Come on! Open!'*

The sound of the doorknob jiggling made him freeze immediately, his tail doubling with fluff. A knock followed.

Rorrik's body blared with alarm as he desperately thought of what to do. Should he jam the door? Break the glass and run for it? Or maybe —

...the tabby loudly cleared his throat.

"Oh, sorry, sorry!" someone frantically apologized. "Did the lights go out in there again? The wiring in this ancient place is so faulty. Um, anyway, take your time..." Rorrik heard soft footfalls step away from the door.

Rorrik stood there on the toilet, his tail still frazzled, a mixture of surprise and relief. *'That was... convenient.'* He had picked a good room to make his escape from, apparently.

He went back to trying the window. It was stubborn, but he proved more tenacious as he finally pried it open with a yank, almost falling over. He cut out the screen with his knife and poked his head outside for a better view of what awaited him.

He was on ground level and a cluster of bushes lay below. The window appeared to be on the side of the house, and a street lay beyond, blurred by fog.

He dropped the binder into the bushes, the foliage shaking softly as it fell past. He followed right after, slipping through the window with ease by the blessing of his lithe form. He lowered himself into the bushes, doing his best not to rattle the landscaping. He found the ground, picked up the binder, and crept along the side of the house, letting the bushes be his cover.

He reached the end of the wall and looked around to further situate himself. He was in a residential area of the city, an unfamiliar one, at that. His eyes searched for a street sign and he spotted one across the road: Petal Dance Terrace.

He recognized the name on the map he had priorly memorized. The street was in the northern section of Sengard, and if he kept down it, he would soon find himself in more familiar territory.

He didn't have time to waste. Shadows guiding him, he kept low and took off into the night.

. . .

Kyla

Dawn was soon approaching, and they still did not have a solid plan.

Kyla paced the room, too strained with stress to hide her worry. The mother wracked her brain for the umpteenth time, desperate for a solution.

"...a word with my mate, please," Niem stiffly asked.

Avalene nodded and left the room, leaving them alone. Their oldest children had earlier left to comfort their siblings and get some rest in case something happened.

Niem stepped in front of Kyla to block her pacing, and she buried her face into his shoulders, fighting a sob.

"You were right, Niem. Gods, you were right. He's gone and it's all my fault. This is all my fault!" She shook as guilt bombarded her, goading tears.

Niem's arms wrapped around her, firm but warm. "We always knew something like this could happen, Kyla. It is the risk we always take with our line of work."

"But this whole thing was my idea!" Kyla croaked.

"This could have happened on any other assignment, Kyla," her mate spoke softly, contrasting his usual tone. "A job is a job, as you said before. Rorrik knew that. He understood the risk."

Kyla shook her head, her remorse still rampant. "Did he, Niem?" She thought of her child, barely thirteen years old, shy of manhood. "We subjected him to this! We forced this line of work on our children!"

"…Kyla."

She thought of Valen and Niem's plans for him. "We gave them no choice!"

"Kyla! Get ahold of yourself," Niem said, biting back a hiss. "You're speaking nonsense!"

"We… we forced this on them…" Kyla sobbed.

"Kyla." Niem grabbed her shoulders looked her in the eye. "You can't just regret everything at the first sign of trouble. This is our life and the choices we've made. You have to live with that."

The mother cried as despair drowned her. "We failed him, Niem…"

Niem didn't move or reply at first. Then, his arms once again wrapped around her, pulling her close. Her mate buried his face into her hair and he held her. "He… he just wasn't ready…"

Avalene then burst back into the room, interrupting their grief. "We found him!"

The two parents broke their embrace in shock.

"What?!" Niem demanded.

"Rather, he found us!" Avalene clarified. "He was able to escape and find help. He's on his way here now."

Kyla had no words. She looked to her mate and melted back into his arms, overcome with relief.

Rorrik was ready after all.

Chapter 38

Kyla

The sky was a soft purple when the car finally pulled up to the Cliffton safe house, right at dawn. Kyla was waiting in the foyer as she watched from a window, her tail ticking with anticipation.

Rorrik stepped out of the vehicle, and Kyla's stomach dropped; her son was covered from head to toe in blood. Her mind instantly took off with terrible explanations, fretting over what her child must have been through.

Rorrik hustled up to the porch, and Kyla opened the door for him, shutting it right upon his entry.

"Rorrik!" the mother cupped her son's cheeks in her hands, her eyes worried. "Rorrik, are you hurt?!"

"I'm fine, Mom!" Rorrik replied, fast. "I—"

"What did they do to you?!" Her eyes fell on his bloodied body, scanning for any gashes or mutilations or—

"Nothing, nothing! The blood isn't mine!" he hurriedly assured. He hefted something in his arms, a binder. "I need to—"

"*Rorrik!*" Jate then cried out, followed by a chorus of the rest of her sons. All five of them rushed up to their brother and swept him up in a group hug.

Kyla stepped aside and watched her children, her eyes shining with tears. Niem's arm draped across her shoulder, and she leaned into her mate, awash with relief.

"Rorrik! I-I'm so sorry!" Jate frantically apologized.

"Did you get the bad guys?!" Talis questioned, his eyes huge.

"We thought you were gonna die!" Calvin gargled with a sob.

"Wait, you're covered in blood!" Quinn realized, startled.

At that, Rorrik's siblings broke the embrace, and they all gasped.

"Rorrik! Are you alright?" Gavin worried.

"It's okay! I'm okay!" Rorrik dispelled any alarm. "I—I need to get to a map!"

"A map?" Talis repeated with a tilt of his head. "Why?"

"There's one in the office," Avalene then contributed from the hallway. She turned around and set off down the hall. "Come with me."

Rorrik hustled after the vigilante, the rest of the family following along.

They arrived in the office, and Rorrik scurried up to a large map on the wall. He began to mark the surface using pins and string that were in a compartment underneath the map, his tail swishing as he worked.

After a few minutes, he gave a long exhale and scanned his handiwork. "Okay! Good to get that out!"

"And what is that, exactly?" Gavin stepped up to study the map along with Kyla.

The queen noted a few familiar locations, the Token safe house being one of them. Others were Farpoint Plaza, the restaurant from Lakeview Circle, and Leonel's Lifts.

"It's a bunch of locations and roads the Fangs had marked down." Rorrik pointed to a large red pin in northern Sengard. "That's where I escaped from. They are planning to ditch it and rig it with explosives, though."

"Oh! Uhh, well!" Jate hesitantly chuckled. "I think you have a bit of explaining to do..."

"Tell us, Rorrik, tell us!" Talis jumped up and down with excitement.

"Why don't you get clean first?" Kyla suggested, antsy to see her son blood-free. "After you finish up, we can sit and talk in the dining room."

．．．

"After I was taken they brought me to a really old house," Rorrik began his story, fresh from the shower, his fur still damp. He wore an extra pair of clothes that had been in storage and smelt of moth balls, but it was an improvement from blood. "They locked me in a room by myself, so I was able to get my binds and stuff off. The room had no windows or furniture, and there was no doorknob on the door. The vent was too small to squeeze through, sooo I hid in the floor!"

"The floor?" Jate echoed, his brow raising.

"Yeah! A plank was loose so I was able to pull it up and hide under it," Rorrik elaborated through a smile. He seemed eager enough to share what had happened. "I barely got my tail inside before someone barged into the room! They realized I was gone and the place went crazy! They assumed I escaped through the vent!"

"Whoooa!" Talis cooed.

"So, how did you get all bloody?" Calvin cut in, grudgingly wiping at his cheek to smear out past tears.

"Uh, well..." Rorrik's excitement dampened, and he looked down with a shrug. "When I was hiding, um... The guard of the room was... killed. They didn't move his body... so..." Her son again shrugged.

"What? What happened?!" Talis pressed, his green eyes saucers.

Kyla frowned as Rorrik hesitated.

"His blood… seeped into the floor…" Rorrik's ears pressed back, and he shuddered. "So I got… you know… covered."

"Grooooooss!" Talis and Calvin shrieked.

Kyla's frown grew, and she rubbed at her son's back. She had been hoping he had managed to come out of the situation unscathed, but his behavior suggested otherwise.

"Oh, geez, Rorrik…" Jate appeared guilty. "That's…"

"What happened next?" Gavin guided the conversation forward.

"Uh, well…" Rorrik shook his head and forced a grin. "I waited until things died down, and then I left my hiding place. I… searched the body and found the same sword the prisoners used. Seeing that, I knew for sure it was the Fangs who took me.

"I needed to try and find information before leaving, so I explored. There was, um… an interrogation room and I found these there…" He placed a recorder and translator earpiece down on the table. "I also found an office that had that map and a bookshelf full of binders. I grabbed this one because it looked to be used the most." He set the binder he had been carrying down next to the other items.

"After that I was going to escape, but then I began to hear guards and had to hide. I heard them talking about a meeting downstairs, so I went to eavesdrop on that.

"I actually recorded it," Rorrik gestured to the recorder. "It was in a different language, but I could understand because I was wearing the translator. The leader was ticked that I had escaped. They decided they are going to attack the Token safe house with a group of five soon. If Valen isn't there, they said they're going to firebomb it."

Rorrik's demeanor then turned terrified. "Wait! Where is Valen? You didn't agree to the ransom, did you?!"

"What? No! Of course not!" Kyla immediately dismissed. "I'm sure he's just resting right now."

"Oh, okay…" Rorrik appeared relieved, and he let go of a sigh. "Um, anyway, then they decided they're going to clear the building of any sensitive material and rig it up to explode with trip wires. The meeting was ending so I went to escape. I left through a window in the bathroom." Rorrik then giggled. "Someone even knocked, but I just pretended to be using it! They bought it, and I was able to get away!"

The rest of her children joined Rorrik's giggling.

"A smart room to make your escape from!" Quinn remarked with a little clap.

"Wonder how long it took them to notice you were dumping them instead of taking a dump," Jate snickered.

"Alright, alright," Kyla said through a tiny smirk of her own. "Go on, Rorrik."

"After that I was able to recognize the street I was on, Petal Dance Terrace, because of the map. I followed the road until I hit North Street and found Mr. Viggo's shop."

Viggo, a gray-furred felidaren, was an old friend of Niem's. The two had done business for years, even before Kyla's involvement with her mate. Viggo served as a contact for the black market and acted as the family's middleman in several dealings with it.

"He called you guys and, well, you know the rest."

Avalene had sent a car out to pick up Rorrik and bring him to the Cliffton safe house.

"The Fangs are holding out on the ransom until I get back to base, which they think is the Token safe house. So until they spot me return there, I think they won't be taking any action."

"Very good. You've done well, Rorrik," Avalene said. "What you've found will help the investigation along tremendously."

"We're very proud of you," Kyla also congratulated. "It was very brave to search for information before escaping."

"You proved yourself," Niem then said, causing Rorrik to jump and look towards his father, surprise in his eyes. Niem offered him a firm nod. "Good work."

Rorrik's shock was stubborn to fade, but then his expression burst into a smile, bright with pride.

"Well, cub," Kyla started, her grin warm. "If they didn't get any information out of you, then let's head home."

■ ■ ■

Valen

The memory of what Valen had nearly done was a constant in his thoughts, overwhelming him with remorse and mortification. The blaster had since been returned to its holster, pressing uncomfortably on his back, its weight a crushing reminder. It scared the demorinkin to realize the weapon had been by his head only hours before, poised to shoot and end his life. He had been longing to fix everything, but nothing would have been fixed if he had succeeded. On the contrary, everything would have been ruined. It would not have gotten Rorrik back, and he would be dead.

He begged himself not to linger on it, but the realization ricocheted across his consciousness, slamming him with adrenaline and nausea each time it skipped and bounced.

326

Following his attempt, Valen had suffered through painstakingly long hours of shame and despair, tortured and alone. He had relocated to the bathroom to spew several times, and there he had remained, sleepless, until Mrs. Catty found him and told that Rorrik had escaped and was alright. Valen had been unable to believe it, but Rorrik had returned, regardless, living proof.

Self-contempt had held Valen back as the family had their reunion. The demorinkin had watched from afar, too guilt-ridden and shaken up to face them, especially Rorrik.

He had eavesdropped on Rorrik's explanation, his guts twisting as he digested what the felidaren had been through. The demorinkin hated how his new friend's life and wellbeing had been put into such severe jeopardy. *'It's all because of me...'*

He wanted to be relieved Rorrik was alright, but his anxiety discouraged the feeling. Instead, all he could experience was worry. The situation had turned out fine, but what if it hadn't? What about what was still to come? Terrible possibilities tortured Valen, feeding the guilt that ever constricted him.

"Wait! Where is Valen?!" Rorrik had eventually wondered with alarm.

Valen had been spooked into retreating at the question. As he fled, he could still hear Rorrik go on. "You didn't agree to the ransom, did you?!"

Valen once again felt the sharp sting of shame, its venom flooding his mind and body. *'They didn't, but I... I tried to.'*

He had fled to the bathroom and locked himself inside, and there he stayed. He sat on the toilet, struggling as his memories were once again poisoned with flashbacks of the prior night.

A few minutes passed, and then a spirited knock came at the door. "Valen, hey, are you in there?" It was Rorrik.

Valen was utterly unwilling to see him just yet. He kept quiet, unsure of how to respond.

"Valen?" Rorrik tried the door, finding it locked. "...are you alright?"

Valen attempted to reply but his throat was too tight. "I... I'll..." The words finally squeezed free, strained. "I'll be right out..."

"Okay, hurry up, we're going to head back to the Den!"

The demorinkin's head found his hands, and he sighed through a wince. He flushed the toilet to mask what his true purpose had been and washed his hands. His nerves white-hot, he unlocked the door and pushed it open.

Rorrik was standing a few feet off, leaning against the wall. The felidaren turned to look and beamed at Valen, the sight stirring a jumble of emotions in the demorinkin.

Valen stepped up to embrace his friend in a tight hug. "I-I'm so happy you're okay..." Valen sighed, tears pooling as relief finally washed over him. The demorinkin squeezed him tighter, and Rorrik returned the embrace with a nuzzle and a chuckle.

"Looks like the Fangs are going to have to try a little harder, huh?" the felidaren said, joyfully smug.

Valen didn't reply. He hoped the Fangs would never have another chance, but the truth was sobering.

Rorrik broke the hug and regarded Valen with excitement. "Wait until I tell you what happened! You're not going to believe it!"

"I'm not sure I want to believe it..." Valen mumbled, unable to hold the felidaren's eyes. "It should have never happened..."

"It's fine, Valen!" Rorrik instantly excused.

"No, it's not!" Valen's tone rose with frustration.

"Valen, *hey*." Rorrik grabbed his shoulders and instigated eye contact. "I'm *okay*. I got away! It's fine!"

Valen stared for a long moment before shaking his head. "No," he repeated, his relief evaporating under the scorching heat of his worry. "It's not."

"Boys! Are you ready to go?" Mrs. Catty's voice then called from down the hall.

Valen looked away and headed towards Mrs. Catty without another word. Rorrik followed him with a frown, matching the demorinkin's silence.

■ ■ ■

The car ride back to the Den had been terrible. Valen, entirely exposed and threatened from being outside, had been too overwhelmed to even peek out the window. His vision had remained locked on his feet as the vehicle drove along, the noises around him slurring as panic set in. He kept expecting the car to have its tires blown out or someone to smash through the windshield, but it never happened. After a time Valen had lost track of, Mrs. Catty was opening the door and helping him out.

She had brought him up to a wall on the side of a building and pushed in a few bricks. She had then shouldered the wall and it gave way, revealing a passage. She ushered him inside and guided him through one of the several escape routes, this time down into the hideout rather than out of it.

Upon arriving, Miss Porte apparently had more questions for Rorrik.

"We have to conduct a proper debrief," she had told the tabby. "We need to know more specifics about what you saw. It won't take long."

The two had went into the meeting room and Valen, unwilling for company or socialization, took refuge in Rorrik's bedroom.

The demorinkin had lain down on the bed, substantially exhausted thanks to no rest the night before, yet sleep still evaded him. His mind was much too rattled to settle down.

He must have fallen asleep, regardless, for he was suddenly waking up with a start to Rorrik opening the door.

"Sorry! Didn't mean to scare you," Rorrik apologized with a yawn. The felidaren was visibly exhausted.

Valen blinked, his eyes fuzzy and his mind foggy with sleep.

"Are you hungry? My mom put aside a plate for you."

Valen immediately shook his head. Despite the hollow emptiness in his belly, his melancholy robbed him of any appetite.

"Well, a plate is in the fridge if you change your mind," Rorrik informed him through another yawn. He climbed into the loft bed and collapsed onto the mattress. "There is," another yawn, "going to be... a... meeting tomorrow morning..." He snuggled into the blanket and sighed. "Goodnight..."

'*Goodnight*?' Had Valen slept the day away?

A few moments passed, and Rorrik's breathing told he had already fallen asleep.

Valen settled back down, now wide awake, the negativity that had been burdening him regrouping. Like a lighthouse guiding him back to turmoil, his suicide attempt flashed through his mind.

Denial flared at calling it a suicide attempt, but that's what it had been. He had tried to take his own life, as troubled as that made him feel.

'*I just wanted Rorrik to be safe... for everything to be fixed!*' For the umpteenth time, he was reminded that it would have fixed nothing and ruined everything. Valen winced against remorse as it harassed him yet again.

'*I... I don't want to die...*' He had certainly felt differently hours before. Despair had carved his outlook into a tunnel vision of pain and suffering.

He had not been able to go on, the pain was unbearable, and yet he still had not been able to shoot the blaster. He had labelled that a symbol of weakness at the time, but Niem's words repeated in his mind to challenge that.

"That won't fix anything. You know that."

Was Niem right? Had Valen known, deep down, that his actions would fix nothing?

Time crept by as Valen's mind hung on that wonder. '*Even if exactly what I expected to happen happened... if they used my dead body to get Rorrik back... they would have felt like they failed me. They're doing this all for me...*' He remembered Mrs. Catty and her steadfastness in keeping him safe as he argued with her. '*Me killing myself would have made it all for nothing.*'

Niem was right, he *had* known that. He had not wanted to admit it and act regardless of it, but he *had* known. His fear of death was not from weakness, rather born from the rational part of him that knew it was not the answer. He had feared the consequences of his actions, a brave thing to do in the thick of his despair.

He suddenly felt a pressure next to him on the bed and something nestle up against his back. He flipped over with a start and found Rorrik there.

"Uh," the tabby seemed embarrassed as he dodged Valen's gaze. "I... I can't sleep..."

Valen gaped at the felidaren, still recovering from the intrusion. His mind stumbled for a reply, but Rorrik kept talking.

"I just... I keep..." The felidaren sighed, his ears pressing back. "I keep falling asleep, but then... I keep dreaming I'm back in the floor..." Rorrik shuddered and his shoulders scrunched. "The blood i-is dripping on me... but I can't move... It starts to drown me, and th-then I wake up..."

Valen finally sobered, and his expression fell into a heavy frown. "Rorrik..."

"E-either that or someone opens it up and they grab me," Rorrik shakily added. "I don't... I don't know why it keeps happening... I... I know it sounds silly... it's not like I'm there anymore, but..."

Valen's heart burst with empathy, and he shook his head. "No, no, I get it..." The demorinkin recalled the terrible revisits of his trauma that plagued him in both in sleep and in waking. "I know exactly how that is..."

Rorrik sniffled and buried his face into Valen's chest. "It just... keeps happening..."

The demorinkin blushed at Rorrik's closeness, but his arms wrapped around and pulled the felidaren close, regardless. "Well, I'm here," he softly assured, his hands gently brushing Rorrik's shoulders. "You can relax..."

Rorrik responded with a faint, jumbled purr, and he snuggled closer to the demorinkin. It wasn't long before the purr was fizzling out and Rorrik's breathing turned soft, telling Valen that he was back asleep.

Equipped with fresh guilt, Valen carefully rolled so he was on his back, Rorrik remaining curled up against him. Once again, the family protecting him had come at a cost, this time being Rorrik's mental wellbeing.

His guilt morphed into frustration as it festered. Rorrik, the family, Miss Porte — they were all sacrificing so much, and what was Valen even doing to help? This was *his* problem, and yet responsibility had fallen on everyone else! He had done nothing but cower as others stepped in and fought his battles. The demorinkin couldn't just sit back and watch any longer — he refused to! '*I can't just hide forever!*'

Valen set his gaze on Rorrik, remembering the blood that had drenched the felidaren's fur, the same blood that now soaked the tabby in his nightmares. '*I have to... for Rorrik!*'

A wind of determination breathed onto the ashes of his resolve, and a flame flickered back into life, burning hot. '*I... I can fight...*' He recalled the despair of his suicide attempt and shoved it away, rejecting it. He grasped for the hope that had motivated him before and held onto it tight. '*I want to fight!*'

Chapter 39

Rorrik

Rorrik awoke to warm sheets but no Valen. The tabby sat up with a stretch and squinted about the room, wondering where the demorinkin had gone. The bed still harbored his heat, suggesting he had not been away for too long.

Rorrik sleepily lay back down, his limbs still heavy and aching from exhaustion. Even with the naps he had taken on the car ride home from Cliffton and after the debrief with Avalene, he had still gotten scarce sleep for over a day. He had not been to bed for a solid thirty-six hours before finally crashing the night before, a fact his sore muscles and grogginess had been keen on reminding him.

Yet, despite his fatigue, nightmares had hounded him, further preventing solid sleep. The memory of blood and gore unceasingly dripped into his subconscious, disturbing him far more than he expected it would. His mother had been worried about him before he had headed to bed despite his reassurance that he was fine. His nightmares testified against that claim.

Luckily, Valen's comfort had been enough to calm and lull him into a lasting slumber. If the felidaren had any more nightmares while in Valen's arms, he did not remember them.

The debrief with Avalene had lasted about an hour. He had explained in further detail the rooms he had explored and the building's security measures. He had also made note of the conversation he had overheard between the guards and how it highlighted apparent unhappiness and unease in the organization, which was further hinted at in the Fangs' meeting. Avalene had recorded the debrief and mentioned that she already had people investigating the intelligence he had gathered.

He was falling back asleep when the door opened and Valen walked in, damp and wearing a fresh pair of Rorrik's clothes. Rorrik noticed in groggy admiration that the demorinkin's black hair was combed handsomely again.

Valen noticed him staring and offered a sheepish grin. "Hey…" The demorinkin walked up to the desk and picked up his spell slinger holster to wrap it around himself. "Sorry, I had to get a shower."

Valen taking showers was always a good sign! Rorrik shook his head to dismiss the demorinkin's apology and yawned. "Don't worry about it!" He snuggled into the bed, its warmth and comfort having him in no rush to leave it. "Man, I'm still really tired…"

"Well, it's pretty early still…" Valen mentioned. "When I looked at the clock about half an hour ago it said it was five."

The meeting was at seven, which meant Rorrik still had time to sleep. He cozied into the sheets, a faint purr bubbling in his chest.

"Well, I'm going to go eat," Valen said. "You can get more sleep."

Rorrik was way ahead of him.

■ ■ ■

Valen

Valen was nibbling at a piece of toasted bread when Mrs. Catty walked into the kitchen, her entrance striking him with apprehension. Surely, Niem had told her about what Valen had almost done, and she was there to talk to him about it. Humility and dread tightened his throat, seizing his latest bite of bread.

"Good morning! You're up awfully early," the mother greeted, her tone casual.

Valen forced down his food with a wince, bracing for the worst. "'M-morning…"

Mrs. Catty filled a kettle before placing it on the stove to heat up. "Did Rorrik tell you about the meeting that's happening in a couple hours?"

The demorinkin answered via a hesitant nod.

"Good, good," the tortoiseshell said. She fetched a mug from the cupboard and placed a tea bag within it. "Did you get good rest yesterday? I know the night before had been… tough…"

Valen tensed at the question as alarm blared within him. He clamped his eyes shut and sunk in his chair with shame, at a loss of what to say.

The felidaren sighed. "At least everything turned out." She took the seat next to him and he could spot her watching him with his peripherals. A tense silence passed, then, "Valen…"

'Here it comes…' The demorinkin's body felt overheated.

"I'm… sorry my emotions got the better of me in the meeting," the mother told him, her ears folded back. "…Can you forgive me?"

Valen was thrown off balance as the conversation veered in a different direction. He turned to face her, his own ears dipped. "O-of course…" His gaze trailed to the table. "I'm… I'm sorry, too…" 'For… everything.'

She draped an arm around his shoulder and pulled him close. "Apology accepted, cub. It was a… stressful time."

332

He lingered in her embrace, still expecting the worst, but then the mother stood up. She walked over to the stove just as the kettle started to whistle.

"Would you like some tea, kit?"

"No, thank you..."

She prepared her tea and returned to the table, where she proceeded to drink in silence. Valen waited and waited for her to say something, but she never did.

...Did she not know? Had Niem not mentioned anything? He must not have, for the mother never did bring up his attempt.

The nervous knot in Valen's stomach slowly came undone. Whatever Niem's reasons for not telling, Valen was relieved he didn't.

■ ■ ■

Kyla

Kyla sized the room with a determined stare. Niem, their four oldest sons, and Valen sat at the meeting room table, while Pepperglow and Avalene listened over a corresponder. Seeing that they were all prepared, she began.

"Thanks to the intelligence Rorrik has gathered, we know an infiltration is coming on the Token safe house. We have not heard back from the Fangs concerning the ransom, which means they still might be holding out on it. If that's true, we can assume they won't be acting until after Rorrik returns to the Token safe house. We know the Fangs are sending a group of five and can anticipate they will move under the cover of night, but we must be ready for them at any time.

"Our plan is simple. We have the old office downstairs rigged to leak out the glowmist from the vents remotely. As for getting them there, the Fangs will likely utilize the hole in our security by breaking into the window on the east wall, which puts them close to the stairs. Pepperglow will cast an illusion of Valen standing there and lead them down the steps, down the hall, and into the room. Then, Jarome's—"

Valen shot to his feet. "I-I want to do it! I want to cast the illusion!"

The room turned to look at the demorinkin, startled.

"I-I have to do something!" Valen kept on, speaking fast, determined. "I'm tired of everybody else fighting my battles for me while I just —*just*— sit back and feel helpless!" He slammed a fist down on the table. "I can't anymore — please! I'm *so sick* of feeling helpless!"

His outburst was met with surprised silence.

Kyla was the first to break it. "Absolutely not!"

Valen seemed ready to argue, but suddenly Niem cleared his throat. "I think he should do it."

Kyla whipped to glare at him. "*Niem!*"

"If he wants to help himself, then who are we to stop him?" Niem debated, steady but firm. Her mate looked to Valen and offered a firm nod. "He deserves the chance."

Valen appeared taken aback by Niem's approval as he held the felidaren's gaze with round, confused eyes.

"I for one know he's a capable mage," Pepperglow then contributed over the speaker. "If he knows the spell, then why not?"

"He does know the spell! His illusions are really good!" Rorrik added enthusiastically. "He's fooled me, he can fool them!"

"No, no!" Kyla shot them all down. "It's too risky! If the Fangs get a hold of him, they'll—"

"They're only there to capture him!" Rorrik reminded. "It's not like his life is in immediate danger!"

That was true. "Yes, but—"

"Rorrik has a point, Spot," Pepperglow said over the speaker. "The Fangs are not there to kill him. It's an opportune time for him to help."

"I can do this, Mrs. Catty!" Valen's voice came from behind her, despite the demorinkin sitting across the table. When the tortoiseshell glanced back, she spotted Valen standing there, a convincing illusionary copy. "*Please!*"

She turned and faced the real Valen, her brow heavy with worry. "Valen..."

"I can't just hide forever!" the genuine demorinkin pleaded. "I need to do this!"

The mother held Valen's gaze, her worried green on his determined yellow. The demorinkin kept firm, looking far different than the helpless boy they had rescued only a couple of weeks before. He had a fire about him, one that would likely continue burning even if she were to refuse him. Niem's words replayed in her mind. '*Who are we to stop him?*'

She let go of a breath, her gaze still locked with his. "You're *sure* you want to do this?"

"I am," Valen replied, certain.

"I can do this," the illusion added from behind her.

Kyla slowly nodded, her worry still weighing her brow. She dropped her attention on the table and sighed. "Avalene? What do you think?"

"It's his choice," the vigilante replied over the speaker. "If he's capable, then I will not argue it."

Kyla closed her eyes in a nod. "Alright." She took a moment to accept it and opened her eyes to regard Valen. "It's settled, then."

■ ■ ■

Valen

Valen was brought into the Token safe house using a set of tunnels that led in and out of the premises. Upon arriving, Pepperglow walked him through the exact steps of the plan. "I won't ask you to practice the actual illusion," the gnome said. "You need to conserve every last bit of your runa."

To make the feat less demanding on his reserves, it was agreed that Valen himself would stand at the top of the steps rather than an illusionary copy. Once spotted, he would flee down the steps and take refuge in a wardrobe at the foot of the stairs. From there, he would cast his illusionary double, earn the Fang's pursuit, and then follow along from behind to ensure he maintained proper focus on the spell.

The room containing the glowmist trap lay at the end of a long, winding hall that composed of two turns. "Sorry for the lengthy sprint," Pepperglow apologized. "It works best in the old office because of its compact size — the other rooms down here are too big and would thin out the gas, which would substantially slow down the effect."

From a quick peek into the other rooms, Valen had to agree. The basement composed of a large utility room, a large recreational room, a large bunk room, and a large community bathroom. It was worth the lengthy sprint, indeed.

Once the Fangs were incapacitated by the glowmist, a group of the warden's men would rush into the room and restrain them with sapping cuffs. The group would be standing by in the utility room next door to the office, ready to spring into action when needed.

Valen was given a radio and translator earpiece. "You'll need to be able to understand what the Fangs are saying," Pepperglow said. "The radio is so we can update you and keep in touch." Lastly, he was handed a remote with a single button. "This will trigger the gas. Once the Fangs get into the room, shut the door on them and press that switch."

Once it was certain Valen knew the steps, Rorrik was given the signal to orchestrate his return to the safe house.

"Now all we can do is wait," his mentor said. The two of them sat on the top step of the stairwell. "It can happen any time now, so be ready."

Valen had thought he was ready, but as her words hit him, he experienced a surge of doubt. Fear took the opportunity to sneak attack him, and he was abruptly toppled over with worry. *'What am I doing?! I can't do this!'*

Pepperglow took note of his mood shift. "What's the trouble, youngster?"

Valen couldn't wrestle down a frown. He shrugged, too ashamed to voice his inner turmoil.

"Guessing the fear is setting in?" Pepperglow tried.

Valen's frown grew as she hit the nail on the head.

"Well, youngster, it's just like we've talked about," the gnome said. "Channel that fear into resolve, just like before. You sounded mighty determined in that meeting; just remember what made you stand up and let that be your battle cry." The mage had a chuckle. "Like you yourself said, you can do this, youngster."

Valen's determination found fuel in Pepperglow's words and he was able to guide his confidence back to its feet, albeit with wobbly knees. He owned his fear rather than rejecting it. *'I am afraid... but I can fight!'* He remembered the night before and his rally for action. *'I want to fight!'*

Time passed by, painstakingly slow. Pepperglow remained with him, offering support through her company.

His worry and doubt kept surfacing, but his determination burned all the hotter. Even so, Valen struggled with nervous apprehension as the hours stretched on, terrified for the Fangs to finally strike, but exhausted from waiting for it.

The clock was nearly midnight when Jate's voice spoke over the radio. "We've got company! There's a group of five approaching the east wall!"

"Everybody in position!" Mrs. Catty's voice came right after.

Valen's heart leapt into his throat, and he sloppily got to his feet, his legs weak. Pepperglow ruffled his hair and chuckled.

"You can do this, youngster," she encouraged before heading down the steps to hide in the utility room with the warden's men, as was earlier agreed.

Valen's doubt gave a final push, but he couldn't listen to it now. The Fangs were coming, ready or not.

"They're cutting through the window with a flame cutter," another brother informed. "They're reaching in and unlocking it now. Window is open, and they're coming through. Be ready!"

Valen could hear movement in the room across from him, causing his panic to blare. Despite it, he remained put, his blood pulsing impossibly loud in his ears.

The door slowly opened with a foreboding croak, and from the darkness of the room shined multiple pairs of golden eyes. They immediately honed in on the demorinkin, and out stepped the first Fangs member, their brass skin glowing in the haze of dust and dim light.

Valen didn't have to feign any kind of terror or shock. He gaped at them, his parents' murderers, realizing just how fragile the situation truly was.

The demorinkin rocketed down the steps, adrenaline alive in his blood, but something hit his back, like a burst of air. He screamed, but it did not come out. He realized in mystification that his steps made no sound as he cleared the stairs. *'They must have hit me with a silence spell!'* Valen had never felt so relieved that most of his spells came to him through innate power; he required no spoken incantations to trigger them.

He dove into the wardrobe and shut it without skipping a beat. Peering through the lattice, he manifested the illusion just in time for the Fangs to reach the foot of the steps. There were three of them total.

"There he is! Restrain him!" one of the Fangs growled in a harsh whisper.

Valen had the illusion flee, making careful note to make its movements mute.

"We found him and are in pursuit, Markai. Keep our exit open!" another hissed into a radio.

They set off after the copy, and Valen didn't delay in leaving his hiding spot. He followed along hot on their trail, his steps conveniently silenced.

They cleared the first corner and then the second. The Fangs were nearly ready to follow the copy into the room when one of them spared a look behind them, immediately spotting the real Valen.

"Hey!" the member shouted. "It's a trick! He's behind us!"

Valen's stomach plummeted with panic. *'Shit! Shit! Shit!'* He turned tail and fled back around the corner, the Fangs now chasing him instead of the copy. The illusion was off; he had to use himself as bait instead.

He had to think fast if the plan was still going to work. If he was to lead them into the room, it meant getting past them. Valen came upon a buffet next to the community bathroom and an idea flashed into his mind.

He whipped his spell slinger out and aimed it behind the buffet before summoning his runa to shoot, his flow responding instantly. With a massive burst of magic, the blaster fired and its force slammed into the furniture with a loud bang. The buffet was propelled towards the corner that lay beyond, twisting as it flew. It slammed into the Fangs as they arrived around the bend, forcing them up against the wall. Valen found it aptly ironic as he remembered Rorrik's kidnapping. *'Who's hit by a buffet now?!'*

Summoning every last bit of his courage, he ran straight by them as they struggled with the furniture, the hairs on his neck standing as he passed.

"Hey! Hey! He's getting away!"

Valen didn't look back as he charged into the open threshold of the office. He hid behind the door and waited, stinging sweat dripping down into his eyes. Footsteps clamored closer and closer, and the Fangs finally burst into the office. Valen shoved the door closed and punched the button on the remote.

A thick stream of glowmist began to pour from the vent just as one of the Fangs pinned Valen against the wall, her hand on his throat. Valen beheld a clear view of the member as her amber eyes drilled into him, draped by her rusty blonde hair. The sight brought him back to the moment he was pulled from the car and terror overcame him.

"We've got him!" the Fangs member grinned. She was reaching for something on her belt when Valen's vision went hazy and full of milk. Stars and bursts of color followed the white, and the image of the woman holding him twirled and morphed.

The hand on his neck left, or so it felt; his sensations were growing more and more muddled.

"WHAAA—tssss goooooooooo....oo...OO...oiiinnnggg.... Onnn!" a voice demanded, slurring unnaturally.

Valen's consciousness started to slip as color and brightness flashed all about him, the exertion from his spells and stress weighing him down as he sank towards the floor. He surrendered to the overstimulation and closed his eyes.

He was then being shaken awake, blips of color still dotting his vision, even against the blackness of his closed eyes. He cracked them open and saw Mrs. Catty staring at him instead of the Fangs member, her face mildly distorted.

"Wee got theeem!" the tortoiseshell beamed with a slight slur.

Valen was slow to process her words as he struggled to calibrate himself with reality, his senses still raw from the glowmist. When it finally hit him, he pushed himself up off the floor, his limbs feeling gummy. He stumbled, but the felidaren caught him.

"They're in Jarome's custody now!" Mrs. Catty went on. She lifted him to his feet and embraced him in a tight hug. "You did it, Valen! You did it!"

Chapter 40

Avalene

"Our new prisoners aren't talking," Avalene began, seated at her desk the next morning, the binder Rorrik brought back spread open in front of her.

"That's to be expected," Kyla commented from over a corresponder.

"However, we have been reviewing the intelligence your son brought back," Avalene went on. "It's pieced together a few questions we've had."

"Oh yeah? Like what?"

"First off, the language they're using is Celestine, the tongue of celestelles from the realm of Stellaar. Judging by the Fangs' remarkable appearances, it is probable that they are celestelles or at the very least have celestine roots. My expert thinks the latter; she says our prisoners don't appear pureblood."

"So, they're celestborn, huh?" Kyla sounded thoughtful. "That makes sense. Celestelles and demorins aren't the biggest fans of each other."

"While true, they are especially motivated in their hatred," Avalene noted. "They had mentioned being the 'light of Korinthis' and 'piercing sword of Nathalia' before. We can assume that statement largely contributes to their mindset."

"Now if only we knew what that meant," Kyla said through a strained chuckle.

"We might have a lead, actually." Avalene set her attention on the binder and adjusted her reading glasses. "The binder Rorrik stole is a contact book, and on the first page there is a scholar. I imagine, being a knowledge dealer for the Fangs, they could answer that question."

"We should definitely pay them a visit then."

"There was also a weapons dealer and a detective listed on the front page. We plan to send teams to bring them back for questioning."

"Sounds great, but how do you expect to get them to comply?"

"We've got enough reason to warrant their arrest," Avalene answered simply.

The felidaren chuckled. "That should help."

"Anyhow…" Avalene's gaze found the recording transcripts on her desk and she scanned over them. "We reviewed the recorder and found an interrogation on one of Sniver's servants."

"Sniver?" Kyla repeated, her tone curious. "The scholar who had purchased Valen?"

"Correct. From the sound of it, the interrogation happened before the Fangs murdered him. They were demanding security information and sensitive knowledge concerning Sniver's… collection. They got quite a bit out of the servant before announcing they meant to kill Sniver. According to them, lusting after a demorin was enough to deserve retribution."

"Guess that answers why they killed him," Kyla muttered.

"Indeed…" Avalene sighed as a headache began to pound in her skull. "Did you send a team to defuse the Petal Dance premises yet?"

"We did. They already have the bombs neutralized and are doing a thorough search of the building. It's looking like the Fangs left a tidy house, though."

"Well, we are not without leads," Avalene reminded, closing the binder. "I think we have enough to go on from here."

■ ■ ■

The teams had been sent out at the same time to prevent any alarm or warning from spreading amongst the contacts, let alone the Fangs. Hugo took his team to get the weapons dealer while Mindi brought a team to find the detective. Avalene herself led the last team to bring back the scholar.

The ex-government worker drove the car along in silence, en route for the scholar's library. The rest of her team, Felicity and Shannine, sat in the back seat, matching the quiet.

"We are getting close," Avalene informed. "Be ready, both of you."

The ringing of her corresponder then sounded, and the vigilante tapped her earpiece to answer. "Hello?"

"Porte! We just got to the detective's house and he—he's dead!" Mindi's voice hurriedly answered.

Avalene was taken aback. "What?!"

"We broke in after no one came to the door, and we found him dead," the vulpen explained. "It was staged to look like suicide, but we found too much sign of struggle. Someone definitely framed it."

Avalene wrestled with shock and frustration as she digested the development. "Continue searching the premises — find out what you can!"

"Already on it, Porte." With that, the call went dead.

Avalene took a few moments to curb her surprise and anger. "…the detective was killed," she informed gravely.

"Killed?!" Felicity echoed in alarm.

Shannine cursed in elvish. "Likely silenced by the Fangs..." the floraling hissed.

Avalene was about to reply, but her corresponder went off again. She answered with another tap to her earpiece. "Report!"

"Porte, the dealer is dead," Hugo's voice spoke stiffly. "Looked to be attacked. Obvious struggle. Made quite the mess..."

"No!" the vigilante snapped, her frustration peaking. "Search the premises, find out what you can!"

"We'll alert you if we find anything," the terran answered, ending the call.

"Damn it! The dealer, too!" The human slammed her foot down on the accelerator, and the car sped closer to the library. "We have to hurry!"

■ ■ ■

The team ran up to the door of the library and briskly knocked. Instead of an answer, they heard commotion coming from within the building, shouting and slamming.

Avalene's alarm blared, and she tried the door, finding it jammed. "Shannine!"

The floraling was already on it. She pounded a small crowbar into the crack of the door using a hammer and tugged hard, the sound of splintering wood protesting. With a few more yanks, the door finally gave, and the three of them rushed inside.

A flash of blue light blinded them upon entry, and Avalene shielded her eyes. A loud bang followed the light and then more screaming.

Avalene forced open her eyes and saw up ahead, amongst a few downed shelves and scattered books, a conflict between two people. A robed individual, likely the scholar, was clenching their side and aiming a braided stick at another person. Avalene recognized the other figure's fanged sword hilt immediately. 'It's a member of the Fangs!' With a churn of apprehension, the human noticed that the weapon's length was bloodied.

"Cover the exits!" Avalene hissed to her team, and the two of them set off with a nod.

The vigilante pulled out her blaster and aimed it towards the Fangs member. "Stop right there!"

The Fangs member flinched at the sound of her voice and swung to glare at her, spotting her poised weapon with narrowed eyes.

Another blue flash of light overcame the room, and an incantation was belted out. A screeching beam of magic was fired from the braided stick and connected with the Fangs member, knocking them back several feet into a pillar.

The robed individual spat something out in celestine before falling to their knees. Avalene gasped and was about to run over but the scholar shook their head and pointed towards the Fangs member.

"Don't be daft! Get the sorry bitch!" they demanded in an elderly, female voice.

Avalene nodded and turned her attention on the Fangs member. They were weakly pushing to their feet, their golden blonde hair hanging in tangles across their face. They still gripped their sword with knuckles of flushed white, showing their strain.

Avalene once again aimed her blaster at the extremist. "Drop your weapon! You're injured and outnumbered!"

"You will not shoot me," the Fangs member growled in a female voice. "I am much too valuable to you alive."

Avalene kept the firearm on her. "Drop. Your. Weapon."

Instead, the Fangs member cried out an incantation, and a thick fog poured into the area. Avalene winced into the dense cloud, unable to see anything. Dread enveloped her. *'No!'*

Suddenly another shouted incantation, courtesy of the scholar, whisked away the fog, revealing the Fang running for a window. Shannine swiftly moved to block the exit and tossed a bolo at the celestborn's feet, tripping her up. The Fangs member crashed to the floor with a pained grunt, and Shannine went to kick away her sword and pin her arms to her back. The extremist did not fight as sapping cuffs were clamped to her wrists, and the elf yanked her into standing. Felicity hustled up, a corresponder to the brevin's ear as she frantically spoke, likely to Jarome's men.

Avalene looked towards the scholar and approached to help her to her feet. As the vigilante did so, she noticed the intensity of the wound on the elder's side.

"Come on," Avalene said, guiding the scholar towards the exit. "We need to get you medical attention."

The scholar scoffed but did not resist.

■ ■ ■

"The wound is stabilized," Felicity reported from over a corresponder, hours later. "Even though she lost some blood, the doctor says her injuries aren't fatal. She'll recover."

"Good," Avalene sighed with relief. "Remain there and keep me updated."

"Will do, Porte."

With that, Avalene ended the call. She massaged the tension knotting her brow and let go of another sigh. She was sat in a break room of the jail, waiting for permission to interrogate their newest prisoner. The vigilante

342

had already made all her calls and arrangements, which meant there was naught to do but wait.

And so, wait she did. It was a solid four hours until one of Jarome's men finally walked into the room.

"Miss Porte," he greeted with a dip of his head. He sat down at the table right as Avalene stood up from it. "I know you're eager to get down there and demand some answers, but there's a couple of things to go over that I'm certain you'll find relevant."

Avalene smothered down her impatience and returned to her seat. "Alright, then. Let's hear it."

"We were going through their gear when we noticed something curious," the guard said. "The uniform is different than our other prisoners."

Avalene's face crimped with intrigue and consideration. "Do you have a comparison?"

The guard reached into a bag and pulled out a shirt. "This belongs to one of our other prisoners," he said, gesturing to a familiar white tunic lined with a strip of gold. He then presented another fabric. "And this belongs to our newest prisoner."

Avalene immediately spotted the difference. The color was not only changed, a blue rather than white, but the golden trim housed an elaborate design within its stitches. A symbol also decorated the chest, a pair of wings crossed by a sword, a suggestion of shining light behind it.

"Their armor is also far more decorated as well as their sword. We find it interesting that all of our prior prisoners had the same equipment, but this one is different. What do you think?"

Avalene remembered her prior prisoners and their identical uniforms and weapons. "It's definitely relevant." She mulled on what it could mean. "I'm thinking their status differs from our other prisoners; uniform color is often a clear sign of rank."

The guard nodded. "We were thinking the same."

"This was a sensitive mission for the Fangs, clearly," Avalene went on. "And they were sent alone. Thus, we can assume they're a higher rank than the others."

The guard nodded again. "The uniforms are not the only noteworthy oddity," he then added.

Avalene tilted her head. "What else?"

"Their behavior is different," the guard elaborated. "The other prisoners have a very… dedicated vibe and reserved mannerisms, but this one… they're different. They didn't fight us, calmly answered our questions…" He shook his head and shrugged. "They're actually cooperating."

Avalene scrunched her brow and rubbed her chin, unsure of what to make of it. Her first instinct was suspicion. "That is… interesting…"

The guard stood up. "Well, if you're ready, we can head down and have you check her out yourself."

Avalene rose to her feet and nodded. "Let's."

■ ■ ■

Upon clearing the copious security measures and flight after flight of stairs, they finally arrived in front of a windowed room. The prisoner awaited inside, bound to her chair and flanked by two guards.

Avalene mustered a deep breath and nodded to her guide. He nodded in return and opened the door, both stepping inside.

There was already evidence that the prisoner was different. Instead of hanging her head, she watched Avalene evenly, even offering a nod. Her golden blonde hair was pulled back into a bun, thus out of her face, showing off a striking beauty through her sharp cheekbones and full eyelashes. The celestborn's gold stare did not leave Avalene, rendering her uncomfortable, but her professionalism was not betrayed.

The vigilante sat down and returned the look. She held it for a lengthy few moments. "You're different," the human finally said.

The celestborn's lips twitched. "By what logic have you come to that conclusion?"

"Your gear differs from the others," Avalene answered. "And your behavior is compliant."

"I have it on good reason to be compliant," the Fangs member said through a subtle smirk. "However, before we delve into that, let us have a proper introduction..."

Avalene narrowed her eyes, but the celestborn carried on.

"I am Vallika Fatecry," the Fangs member introduced. "One of three leaders of the Fangs of Hellbane."

Chapter 41

Kyla

"The prisoner is cooperating," Avalene told from over a corresponder, sounding tired.

Kyla couldn't believe it. "Seriously?"

"As strange as it sounds, yes." The human paused before going on uneasily, "And that's... that's not all."

Kyla narrowed her eyes. "What do you mean?"

Avalene sighed before replying. "I think you should come by and talk to her yourself."

"Good idea," Kyla agreed. "I'm on my way."

"Don't delay." The call ended.

Avalene's behavior had both unsettled and intrigued the felidaren. Despite the hour being late, she pushed out of bed and began getting ready to leave.

"Where are you off to?" Niem questioned from their bed as she pulled on a fresh shirt.

"The prisoner is cooperating. Avalene wants me to come by and speak with them."

Niem's brow knotted. "Why? Is something wrong?"

"I'm... not sure," Kyla admitted, remembering Avalene's behavior. "But if they're cooperating, that's a good thing." '...*Right?*'

■ ■ ■

"I... don't understand." The felidaren squinted at the prisoner with scrutiny and confusion. "You want to *help* us?"

"That is what I said," the apparent leader replied, holding her head high despite the madness she had just suggested.

"And why in all the realms would you want to do that?" Kyla sharply inquired, endeavoring to keep her cool.

"Simple. Our goals align," Vallika evenly responded.

Kyla balked at that, and her cool was lost. "How could they *possibly* align?!" she demanded in frustration, holding back a growl.

"We both wish the Fangs of Hellbane were no more." She went on calmly before Kyla could reply. "I cannot look on the organization I once had unfaltering pride in without being overcome with revulsion and shame." Her calmness began to dissipate, evaporated by the boiling of anger. "It has grown weak and lame by the guidance of the scourge it tentatively calls its arch; it spits on the legacy it has built up and perverts the very name of the Fangs of Hellbane. It is unfit to exist any longer and has reached a point beyond redemption. Salvation will only come through eradication." By the end of it the prisoner was seething, but then her features hardened into a cool stare, much like lava becoming rock. "You wish to eradicate the Fangs of Hellbane; this is why our goals align."

Kyla shook her head, snagged on how bizarre it all sounded; she was unwilling to wrap her mind around what the leader was suggesting. "You honestly expect us to believe any of that?"

"It is the truth. I cannot further tolerate what the Fangs of Hellbane have become. It *must* be destroyed — to honor all our fore-archs and the very cause we serve."

Kyla glared at the demorin hunter, her hackles raised. "That's a *tad* extreme, don't you think?"

"I do not," the celestborn answered, resolute. "It is the only way."

Kyla was far from convinced. "*Why?*"

"I have already explained myself."

"Well, explain it again," Kyla pressed.

Vallika's amber gaze squinted at the felidaren, perturbed. "The organization has fallen into ruin. Our arch is unfit and despicable. Our members are incompetent and without dedication or passion. Our numbers are pitiful, and our prestige is a husk of what it once was. The Fangs of Hellbane dishonors all it once existed to be."

Kyla remembered the recording Rorrik captured of the Fangs' meeting and the guards he had overheard, all of it testifying to what Vallika was saying.

But Kyla was still not ready to buy it.

"How would you even help us?!" the tortoiseshell hissed.

"I have a plan," Vallika revealed.

Kyla scoffed. "And how exactly do you expect us to trust you?!"

"There is no obligation," the leader shrugged. "I am merely reaching my hand out. I implore you to take it, being time is running short, and our goals align."

Kyla was silent for a few moments, her expression squeezing into a narrow glare. "Why should we even accept your help?"

"Because I am your best chance to end this. You will find that my plan presents a golden opportunity that would be sorely missed if you refuse. You will never again get a chance to end the Fangs altogether. Despite the betrayal of our pride, it is within everyone's best interest."

Kyla processed that with an uneasy heart and stomach, unsure of what to feel. Her gut still didn't trust the situation.

"You can't expect us to agree either way until you disclose your plan," Avalene said from behind Kyla.

Vallika's lips twitched. "Yes, of course." She sized them both for a moment before starting. "Very soon there is a meeting happening amongst all of the Fangs of Hellbane on how to handle Vaaskiir. With all our numbers gathered at once, it is a pivotal time to make an attack. By this I do not just mean with weapons, but also with words. Many of our members have low morale; all they need is a push to throw them off balance. If I were to attend this meeting, I can force that push. If a leader speaks up on how low the organization has fallen *and* turns against our arch, discord is sure to follow. If there is discord, then they will be far easier to overwhelm."

Kyla scoffed yet again. "Sounds a lot like a trap."

The celestborn shrugged. "That is your call to make. You can either keep me here and miss the opportunity, or go along with my plan and finish this."

"And why are you necessary? Couldn't you just give us the location of the meeting?" Kyla proposed.

"And rob me of the chance to rectify this damned mess?" Vallika shook her head. "No. I will be going. This is part of the agreement. I have the power to make the sweep much more successful. Although many feel doubt, they still endeavor to bury it. If I can give them assurance, they will be significantly hindered."

"And if we refuse to let you go?" Kyla growled.

"Then you miss out on a solid lead and an opportunity you will never again have. Only the leaders know the place of our conference, and I will not reveal it until there is an agreement."

"And what makes you think we won't force you to tell us where the meeting is?" Avalene challenged.

Vallika gave a bitter laugh. "Is that a threat of torture? How contradictory to the treatment of your earlier prisoners!" The celestborn smirked, her golden eyes glinting. "Besides, I'm afraid I won't give you that chance."

"What are you getting at?" Kyla snarled.

"If you refuse my plan, then I will be forced to act drastically," the demorin hunter warned.

"Meaning?"

"I have been trained to will myself into death with a spell if I was ever to be captured, to prevent spilling sensitive information. If you are going to refuse my terms, all of the information I have will be lost to my grave."

"A spell?!" Kyla repeated incredulously. "Check your wrists, you're wearing sapping cuffs!"

Vallika's smirk held. "You doubt the true power of determination. It is not an incredibly demanding spell; I could muster enough runa even with these hunks of metal draining my reserves." The celestborn sneered. "It's simply a hole in the ship."

Kyla recalled their past prisoners and their escape from the convoy. "You're bluffing," the tortoiseshell still accused, her stomach twisting.

"Perhaps, but do you really want to gamble and find out otherwise? Accept my terms and put an end to this damned lost cause. I am helping you more than inconveniencing you."

In that moment, Kyla recognized Vallika's voice as the one from the ransom.

"So, your terms are you want to be present at the meeting?" Avalene asked for clarification.

Vallika nodded. "That is correct."

"You would not be let out of our sights," Avalene pointed out.

The celestborn did not seem put off by that. "Of course."

Kyla was bombarded by indecision and suspicion. "We'll have to discuss this at more length."

"Do what you need," Vallika said. "However, time is of the essence. I wouldn't delay, lest you miss an important meeting."

■ ■ ■

"I don't like it," Kyla spoke in the privacy of another room, her ears pressed back.

"Neither do I," Avalene agreed with a sigh. "We need more information before agreeing or disagreeing to anything."

"The scholar?" Kyla guessed.

"That, and our other prisoners," Avalene responded. "It will be telling to see how they react to one of their leaders scheming to turn on them."

Kyla gave a firm nod. "They can also help shed some light on if what Vallika is saying is true."

"My thoughts exactly. Let's get some rest, and then get to it in the morning."

Chapter 42

Kyla

The scholar was still being treated at the central Sengardian hospital for her wounds. Accompanied by Avalene, Kyla headed there early the next morning, ready to find some answers.

The scholar was awake when the two of them entered the hospital room, her ribs neatly wrapped with fresh bandages that smelt of medicine. She was an aged celestborn with white hair and vivid, silvery eyes, the first celestelle Kyla had seen without the trademark gold. Despite her age, she still boasted a dignified beauty, not youthful but rather rich and refined. The elder huffed when her platinum gaze found them.

"I was wondering when you were going to show up." The scholar eyed Kyla with a squint. "Who's the cat?"

"The cat is named Kyla," the tortoiseshell answered with a twitch of a smirk. "And what may we call you?"

"Oditha," the scholar replied curtly. "Oditha Windsong." Her attention fell on Avalene. "So, you're Porte, eh?"

"That is correct." Avalene dipped her head in a nod. "It's fortunate you are alright, Oditha Windsong. If my team had arrived any later I'm unsure we could have said the same."

Oditha scoffed through a horse cough. "Bah. I had a bit more fight left in me yet; I wasn't about to let that bitch off easily. But you have my thanks for intervening." The elder's expression then crimped with scrutiny. "I have to wonder why you were there in the first place, though."

"We were there to question you over your affiliation with the Fangs of Hellbane," Avalene revealed evenly. "And those questions still remain."

"Ah..." Oditha had a chuckle and sputtered out another cough. "You must be those thorns they griped on about." Her laughter didn't cease. "You've caused the Fangs of Hellbane quite the headache, from what I've heard."

"That's good news," Kyla quipped with a touch of bitterness.

"Considering I bleed because of their fangs, I agree," Oditha grunted with equal bitterness. "Although terms had been rocky for the past few months, I never imagined they'd be out for my blood."

"Rocky?" Avalene echoed. "What do you mean?"

Oditha appeared thoughtful for a moment before shaking her head with a pronounced grimace. "Not like there's any reason to hide the dirty laundry after that stunt they pulled. Simply put, ever since Arch Levaris ascended, the Fangs have been... out of sorts. Our work relations suffered duly."

'*Out of sorts?*' That would testify to Vallika's testimony.

"And what were those work relations?" Avalene pressed.

"My private library and all my scholarly connections have been at their disposal for years," the elder explained. "We did not interact much, but when we did it was respectful and agreeable. However, in the last few months, that changed. They turned rude and entitled and often disregarded me. Most likely due to all the new blood — Cloudhook doesn't have the same pull on the new recruits as Levaris did."

"You keep mentioning this Levaris character," Kyla cut in. "Who is this?"

"Levaris served as the old arch, the leader," the scholar informed. "Upon his ascending, he appointed Cloudhook to take his place."

Avalene narrowed her eyes. "Ascending?"

"His passing," Oditha elaborated. "The death of his mortal self, and the beginning of his celesteon, if he was so found fit."

Avalene and Kyla shared a look of confusion.

"What do you mean by that?" Kyla wondered.

"While it is rare for those who do not have pure celestine lineage, it is possible for all celestborn to ascend into a second life as an immortal celesteon. Our actions in our mortal time decide this fate. If we impact the realms in a way that is deemed substantial and suitable to the Forerunners, we are decided worthy enough to ascend."

Kyla crossed her arms as discomfort began to fester in her gut. "So, Levaris was worthy enough?"

Oditha shrugged. "Many believe he was, including himself."

"And what do you think?" Kyla questioned, her tone sharpened.

"It is so rare for non-purebloods to ascend. Despite the Fangs of Hellbane's efforts to purge evil in our realm, I am doubtful it gained enough attention from the Forerunners," Oditha admitted.

Kyla's ears curled back at that. "Purge evil? You mean mindlessly slaughter demorinkind!"

Oditha regarded Kyla with curiosity. She then smirked. "To the Fangs of Hellbane that is one and the same."

"And what about to you?!" Kyla demanded, her temper flaring.

Oditha shrugged again. "Demorins and their kin have a hard time escaping their dark lineage and roots. More likely than not do they fall on the wrong path."

Kyla was ready to snarl out a reply, but Avalene sized her with a commanding look, stopping her. Kyla flushed with passion as her emotions blared within her, but she held her tongue, respecting Avalene's wishes.

"What or who are the Forerunners?" Avalene redirected the conversation.

"Heaven above! Do I have to explain everything?" Oditha grumbled with exasperation. "The Forerunners are a congress of celesteons and quasi deities that determine who is befitting of celesteon. They were appointed by Stellaar's king and god himself, Xerstelle."

Avalene nodded slowly and went quiet, appearing thoughtful. She then faced the elder with a firm stare. "So, why do you think the Fangs wanted you dead?"

The scholar's wrinkled face darkened. "Probably on the account that I'm a loose end and not important enough to protect. Whatever you've been doing to the Fangs has them desperate; they sent Vallika herself to deal with me."

"And what were they afraid of you telling us?"

The celestborn sighed, and her lips twisted with consideration. "Names, probably. History. Much of which I've already shared."

"You mentioned Vallika," Kyla stepped in. "Who is she within the Fangs?"

"Vallika Fatecry is one of the three leaders," Oditha replied. "The other two are Nathian Thestis and Davarin Cloudhook, the arch."

With that, the scholar confirmed Vallika's name and rank. Despite it, Kyla still felt uneasy.

"You mentioned history; can you enlighten us on who Korinthis and Nathalia are, then?" Avalene brought up.

"Ah," the elder smiled. "I have several books that can explain that far better than I can. Get me a sheet of paper and something to write with, will you?"

Avalene retrieved such from her bag and handed it over.

Oditha quickly sprawled something down on the page and then handed it back to Avalene. "Head back to my library and give this to the girl who will answer the door. She is my apprentice and granddaughter."

Avalene and Kyla both spared a look at the note. It read:

'Nadelyn, these women are the ones who are helping me and have been given permission to look at my library. Direct them to the collection concerning Korinthis and Nathalia, please.'

Under the note was a symbol that faintly glowed with a magical aura, likely a signature to prove authenticity.

Avalene folded the sheet and stuffed it in her pocket. "We'll do that."

Kyla narrowed her eyes at the scholar. "So, if you support what the Fangs are doing, then why are you helping us?"

Oditha's aged face folded into a smirk. "The Fangs and I have no more partnership after yesterday's development. If they were so quick to be rid of me, then I will return the favor."

■   ■   ■

"Hm, the door is new," Avalene commented as they stepped up to the entrance of the library.

"Well, you *did* break it down," Kyla snickered. "So, that's not surprising, is it?"

"Hmph. No, it's not," Avalene said through one of her rare smirks.

They knocked, and a pretty teenager with vivid silver eyes that matched Oditha's answered the door, looking wary. Her hair was a pale blonde that barely reached her shoulders.

"The scholar is out," she said in a polite voice. "I'm sorry, but the library is closed."

"We are here at your grandmother's request," Avalene informed her, handing over the note. "This is from her."

The girl tilted her head and received the message, curious. She read it before looking back on them, her eyes large. "You're the ones who helped my grandmother?!"

Avalene's head bobbed in a single nod. "Yes. She is still healing at Central, as I'm sure you've been kept aware."

The girl hurriedly nodded. "Thank you for your help!" She stepped aside and beckoned inside the open door. "I can show you to the collection."

The two of them stepped inside without delay. Inside still showed evidence of the struggle that had happened the day prior, as a couple of the shelves were still knocked over and books were strewn about.

"What is your name, young lady?" Avalene questioned as they went.

"Nadelyn. And yourselves?"

"I am Avalene Porte and this is my colleague."

"Call me Kyla," the felidaren finished.

"It's a pleasure." Nadelyn bowed her head.

They arrived in front of an intact shelf, and Nadelyn gestured to it. "Here it is. I will be nearby if you have any questions."

Avalene nodded. "Thank you, Nadelyn."

With that, the girl walked off and began gathering some of the books that littered the floor.

"Well!" The felidaren started to scan the shelf. "Let's see here…"

There were several thick books boasting titles in elaborate fonts, but the one that caught Kyla's eye was called *The Light that Pierces*, its gold-trimmed bookend glinting with a sheen that caught in the sunbeams pouring in from a window. When Kyla pulled it from the shelf, a kick of dust followed; it had to have been a long time since it was last retrieved.

The cover was lined with the same gold sheen and displayed a depiction of two celestelles, one male and one female, both poised for battle holding longswords that glinted when the book was tilted. Behind them was a bright light burst, and that, too, shimmered in the light.

Kyla remembered the prisoner's words: *'The shining light of Korinthis and the piercing sword of Nathalia…'* She offered Avalene a wry grin and showed off the cover. "Wonder if we have the right collection?"

Avalene shook her head to dismiss the felidaren's kidding and continued glancing through the shelf herself.

Kyla cracked open the book, and the smell of aged paper and dust puffed into the air. She scanned the text on the first page, which was large, embellished and decorated with intricate patterns.

I, Korinthis Sunstrike, have so forth dedicated my mortal life to the servitude of all that is good and holy. I am not alone in my purpose; Nathalia Johana raises up her sword alongside mine, committing to the same cause. We have pledged ourselves to the never yielding mission of eradicating evil and all that wish to jeopardize harmony. We have left our home realm of Stellaar behind and come to the aid of the realm Azyria, a place of discord and corruption. We hunt all that is evil and will not rest so long as our breath still lifts our chests. We are warriors of valor and stewards of peace. Xerstelle above, bless our efforts and look upon us with pride, we will go forth and glorify your name.

Kyla read the passage, her face tight and her fur bristling. While it read noble enough, these were the same individuals that the Fangs of Hellbane modeled their organization after. If the Fangs were of any indication, 'all that is evil' was a broad and stubborn statement that ensnared all demorin kind, regardless of their actions.

"Looks like they were self-proclaimed hunters of evil who came to Azyria from Stellaar," Kyla shared.

She continued to flip through the book, pictures of slain monsters and demorins speeding by. It all began to blend together until something demanded her attention, a picture of a golden-haired individual with a broken halo above their head. She found the page and studied the picture, seeing that the wrongdoer Korinthis and Nathalia had bested appeared to be *celestine*. With stunned intrigue, the felidaren read the passage preluding it.

It is within my time of serving righteousness that an impactive and largely misunderstood sentiment of life has been instilled in me. Evil can, in fact, come from anywhere, anyone, and anything. Even that which is understood as good and is trusted as good can bring forth darkness. From the brilliant rays of a loud, boastful light can there be a shadow of corruption cast. It is paramount that we, as servers of righteousness, remain vigilant and wise in discernment. All is not that it appears to be.

Kyla turned the page, seeing a horned individual, a *demorin*, standing between Korinthis and Nathalia without conflict. She read on.

As such, we must also remember that while evil can come from anywhere, so can good. We, too, must practice discernment with what we perceive as flawed and evil. I once was blind from perceptions born of prejudice and internalized hatred, but throughout my travels those perceptions have been eroded away, clearing my outlook.

One's lineage does not seal their fate and determine their alignment. Every life is unique and different, and there is no generalization that adequately describes an entire people. I have learned this with humility, and I have learned this well.

Kyla was overcome with confusion. The book, supposedly penned by the very Korinthis the Fangs of Hellbane dedicated their cause of slaying demorinkind to, completely and utterly contradicted their mindset.

Kyla read it again and then again, the passage making less sense the more she read it.

"...Kyla? What is it?" Avalene asked, apprehensive.

Kyla handed the book over. "This doesn't make sense..."

Avalene read the passage and the same puzzlement found the vigilante's expression.

"Maybe we really do have the wrong collection..." Kyla hesitantly jested, only half joking.

Avalene jutted her lip and shook her head. "Let's continue looking through the books and see what else we find."

■ ■ ■

The books all agreed on one thing: Korinthis and Nathalia were able to ascend as celesteons because of their heroic deeds. However, Korinthis' lesson was not touched on in any of the other books they glanced through. Contrastingly, some of the books even preached the opposite, that demorins were to never be trusted and were inferior of their celestine cousins.

"I don't understand..." Kyla mumbled, her focus on a book in her lap, a depiction of an impaled demorin showing on the current page. "How did they all get it so wrong? Korinthis himself said it!"

"It is not a lesson many celestelles take kindly to, I'm sure," Avalene reasoned. "It is easier to pick and choose what topics one agrees with and ignore the uncomfortable ones. I believe that is what happened here. Many do not appreciate coming to terms with a belief that challenges their established ideas."

Kyla's ears flattened with disdain and she scoffed. "So, they cherry picked, basically?"

"It appears so. That, and over time, common understanding of Korinthis and Nathalia's deeds grew more and more perverse and radicalized. Cue extremists like the Fangs."

Kyla hissed out a sigh. "It's terrible that the Fangs are claiming to be doing this in Korinthis and Nathalia's stead but are actually just insulting what they stood for..."

"It is ironic. But a common fate for many causes, unfortunately." The vigilante began to return the books they had flipped through to their spot on the shelf. "We should really get back to the jail to speak with the other prisoners. I can assign someone to keep looking into this and log what they find."

Kyla nodded and closed the book in her lap, the picture of the slain demorin disappearing back into its pages.

■ ■ ■

Avalene

Avalene stared at the prisoner in front of her, braced to go through the same routine the others had already put her through: silence and grimacing.

The celestborn sat there with her rusty blonde hair hanging in her eyes, masking most of her expression.

"We have captured and imprisoned one of your leaders," Avalene began. "Vallika Fatecry."

The prisoner's shoulders jerked but that was her only reply.

"She has cooperated so far..." Avalene spoke slowly and clearly. "And has even requested partnership with us." She let the words hang.

The prisoner slightly lifted her head, and Avalene caught a glimpse of her amber irises, which were thin with consideration.

"...Vallika plans to turn on the Fangs of Hellbane," Avalene told her evenly, the words still sounding strange even to her own ears.

At first, the prisoner did nothing. Then, her shoulders began to bounce. A snicker slipped free and grew into full-fledged laughter.

Avalene endeavored to retain composure, but her eyebrows still raised.

"*Wow!*" the prisoner guffawed. "It really has all gone to shit!" She continued her giggling and began to shake her head.

Avalene watched the celestborn, her face tight.

"That doesn't surprise me," the prisoner chuckled on. "Not at all... not at all..."

"And why is that?" the vigilante firmly asked.

"Because the Fangs of Hellbane are crumbling into ruin!" the prisoner cried. "Vaaskiir must be pleased! Ever since he killed Levaris it's all spiraled downward!"

"...Vaaskiir?" They couldn't be talking about Valen...?

"The father of that brat you're protecting!" the prisoner elaborated. "Our Fangs got him but, Xerstelle above, was he ready for us! We played right into his hands!"

Avalene cocked her head. Valen's father had been the one to kill Levaris? "How?"

"They had a trap laid for us — him and his wretched mate. He drew us into some ruins and took down Levaris before collapsing the place on us all. Now more than half of our numbers are dead, and Cloudhook is in charge, soiling everything!"

"When was this?"

"Shy of a year ago." The celestborn shook her head, her blonde hair flying to and fro. "Vallika must be fed up with it all! Don't blame her. I can't even remember the reason I'm doing this anymore! Without Levaris it just... it's all..." Their demeanor turned somber. "Nothing makes sense anymore."

"...Why?" Avalene pried.

"Levaris had a way of... making it all seem worth it," the prisoner sighed. "He had that charisma about him. It all was so easy to understand back then... But now, with him gone, it all grows harder to justify..."

The low morale Vallika had spoken of was exposed. "Are you alone in that struggle?"

The prisoner snorted. "No! Everyone tries to hide it, but we're all just lying to ourselves!"

Avalene slowly nodded as more and more of Vallika's words were verified. "Well, you don't have to lie to yourself anymore, do you?"

The prisoner snickered and hung her head, her shoulders trembling, Avalene spotting a tear splash on the table past the curtain of her hair.

■ ■ ■

Kyla

"You're certain about this, Kyla?" Niem's voice came from over the corresponder, hesitant.

"All of what she said was verified through the scholar and one of the prisoners. It's the best lead we have right now," Kyla replied, stifling down her own hesitation.

Her mate sighed. "Well, I trust your judgment."

Kyla weakly grinned. "Good to know."

"Stay safe, Kyla."

"I will." With that, she ended the call.

The felidaren leaned back into the wall and closed her eyes, nerves torturing her insides. She still did not like the plan, but they had been given enough reason to accept it. She did her best to make peace with it, but peace did not come.

"Ready?" Avalene asked after a minute or so of her wallowing.

Kyla pushed herself off the wall and jerked her head in a nod. Avalene returned the gesture, and the two of them headed into the room beyond where Vallika sat waiting. The celestborn's golden gaze held them as they both walked up and joined her at the table.

"Alright," Kyla said. "We agree."

Chapter 43

Valen

Valen had spent the entirety of the day training with Pepperglow, as was the case the day before. He had just finished his post-lesson millina root tea when Mrs. Catty came walking into the kitchen.

"Hey there," she greeted, taking a seat across from him. "How was your lesson?"

Valen offered a mild smile. "It went well. I'm getting better at augmenting the bracers!"

Mrs. Catty returned his smile. "That's great! I'm glad you're improving."

She then sobered, and Valen felt a stirring of apprehension.

"Valen, we've been talking with the prisoners," the mother gently began. "We learned something today that you should know…"

Valen's apprehension intensified. "…what is it?"

"It's about your parents."

A heavy stone thunked in Valen's gut, stealing his breath away.

"Your father was the one who killed the Fangs of Hellbane's prior leader," Mrs. Catty told him. "About a year ago."

Valen gaped at Mrs. Catty as his mind grappled with shock.

"He and your mother apparently led the Fangs into some ruins and, upon killing Levaris, collapsed the place on them all, taking out more than half of them." Her hand moved across the table to hold his. "Because of this, the Fangs have been left in a compromised state. Their morale is low without their old leader, and their numbers are dwindling. Your parents impacted the situation in a way that is invaluable to us. Because of them, the Fangs will be possible to overwhelm and defeat." She squeezed his hand. "We cannot thank them enough…"

Valen dropped his gaze to the table, surprise still rattling him. He tried to process the news, but shock hampered the effort.

Mrs. Catty's hand again squeezed his. "They went down with a fight."

It all finally hit the demorinkin, and he shut his eyes as a plethora of emotions bombarded him; grief over his parents' death, anger from the Fangs hunting them, pride in his parents for fighting back, and relief at finally having closure. His emotions sloppily shuffled and exchanged

359

dominance, rendering him unsure of what to feel or say. The stone is his gut remained, heavy and constricting.

He cracked his eyes open to stare at Mrs. Catty, his expression a product of his inner conflict.

The felidaren frowned before walking over to wrap her arms around him. Valen did not return the hug as his inner discord surged on.

"I know it still hurts…" she whispered to him with a squeeze. "But, now you have closure."

His heart panged, and he leaned into the mother's embrace, recalling the warmth of his own mother's arms. His heart finally decided it was feeling grief, and he winced against a dry sob, his chest tight and his throat swollen.

Mrs. Catty held him as he mourned, both of them silent. A few minutes passed, and she broke the embrace with a sigh, taking the seat next to him.

"There is something else that I have to bring to your attention," the felidaren mentioned, almost warily.

Valen's stomach twisted with anxiety at the prospect.

Mrs. Catty stared at him for a long moment. "One of the prisoners we captured, the one that attacked the scholar, is one of the leaders of the Fangs."

The demorinkin's eyes went wide.

"…She proposed an idea to us that we had trouble accepting but found suitable support as we investigated…" Mrs. Catty went on. "She is going to help us stop the Fangs of Hellbane."

Valen was stupefied. "What?!"

"It sounds bizarre, I know, but we believe she's being sincere," Mrs. Catty kept her voice even. "Her argument is that the Fangs have become despicable since the death of their old leader, and that only stopping the organization will bring rectification."

Anger usurped grief. "No!" the demorinkin yelled with a thrash of his tail. "I don't want her help!"

Mrs. Catty regarded his outburst with a tight frown. "I understand how you feel, I really do—"

"No, you don't!" Valen scooted out of his chair with force. "They killed my parents! They ruined *everything*!" He turned to leave in a huff, but Mrs. Catty grabbed his arm to stop him.

"Valen, wait—"

The demorinkin yanked himself free. "Why are you even trusting her?!"

"Because what she is saying has been confirmed to be true," Mrs. Catty argued. "And she is giving us an opportunity to end this."

"What do you mean?!" Valen demanded.

"She has revealed the time and location of a meeting the entire organization is attending. She is going to crash it and speak against their leader. We will be able to overwhelm them in the discourse."

Valen's anger boiled on. "We don't need her help!"

Mrs. Catty let go of a sigh. "Sometimes, Valen, we need to put aside our pride to do what needs to be done. I don't like it, either, but this is the best plan we have."

Valen bristled further at that. "No, it's not!" He once again turned to leave, and this time Mrs. Catty let him go.

．．．

Valen had holed himself up in his old guest bedroom for about an hour before Rorrik found him.

"What are you doing in here?" the felidaren wondered from the threshold.

Valen was laying on the bed with his face to the wall. "What do you want?" he muttered without turning around, his mood still dark with anger.

"Uh..." Rorrik sounded uncomfortable. "There's a meeting starting soon. My mom said you should be there..."

Valen's shoulders stiffened. "Why? It's not like my opinion matters..."

"...What's with you?" Rorrik asked with a hint of annoyance.

"Maybe the fact that we're collaborating with my parents' murderer?!" Valen spat. "That might do it!"

Rorrik was silent for a lengthy moment. "She's going to help us *stop* the Fangs, Valen..."

"But she *is* a Fang!" Valen argued. "I don't want her help!"

"But because of her we're going to be able to stop them! You want to stop them, don't you?!"

Valen didn't want to hear it. "Just leave me alone!"

"You have to come to the meeting, Valen!" Rorrik pushed.

Valen made no move nor reply.

"...You're not going to help us stop them, then?" Rorrik accused, incredulous.

The demorinkin hissed out a sigh and sat up grudgingly. He scooted off the bed and marched towards the door, avoiding Rorrik's gaze. He slipped past the felidaren and headed for the meeting room, his tail thrashing with every step.

．．．

"Our scouts have confirmed the place is clear and matches the map Vallika drew up," Mrs. Catty began the meeting, which was composed of the oldest four felidaren siblings, their mother, and Valen.

The demorinkin was sulking in a corner with his arms crossed, his attitude no secret.

"The location is a shrine dedicated to Korinthis and Nathalia that is carved into a cliffside, a perfect location for an ambush. The meeting begins tomorrow night at midnight. According to Vallika and the prisoner, we are up against roughly fifty members. We have organized about sixty on our side between our people, Avalene's, and the warden's. The schematics of our plan will be further decided when we get there. The shrine is about a two-hour drive and requires a bit of off-roading to get to. We'll all be leaving here very shortly to prepare."

The mother paused and regarded her sons with a sigh. "Well, do you boys think you're ready for this?"

Each of her children answered with a confident nod.

"Of course!" Rorrik assured.

"It's what we've been trained for," Gavin said.

The tortoiseshell nodded before turning to look at Valen. "And what about you, Valen?"

Valen tensed up and nodded, unable to keep her gaze.

"You're positive?" Mrs. Catty pressed. "Remember, you don't have to do this."

Valen stared at his feet, his brow knotted as he muttered, "Yes, I do…"

"…You don't," the mother pointed out delicately. "But, if you want to, we won't stop you."

The demorinkin nodded firmly. "I do."

Mrs. Catty returned the nod. "Then get ready, all of you! We leave in an hour."

∎ ∎ ∎

Valen sat in the living room, his stomach in knots as anger and nervousness fought for control of his mood. He was already prepared to leave, as Mrs. Catty had given him a backpack of supplies and his armor and weapon were already equipped. Amongst the equipment was a translator earpiece so that they would understand the Fangs.

The brothers had scurried off to don their own equipment, leaving Valen alone to wait for them.

Another few minutes passed of Valen staring at his feet before Rorrik was suddenly in front of him, startling the demorinkin.

"Check me out!" the felidaren exclaimed.

Valen lifted his head to do so and was taken off guard at what he saw. Rorrik was wearing snug-fitting pieces of maroon fiber armor that did well to accentuate his lithe form and render him professional looking. Valen admired him from head to toe, finding himself appreciating the shape of the felidaren's torso and the angle of his hips. Rorrik turned around, and Valen was met with a sightly view of the tabby's rear, riling a blush out of the demorinkin. His lower abdomen tingled and he tore his gaze from the felidaren, suppressing his stimulation with a surge of discomfort and panic.

"Isn't it cool?!" Rorrik spun back around. "I got this set for my birthday! It's—" The tabby's sentence cut off. "Oh... you're still mad..."

Valen's cheeks flushed hotter. "No, you— it looks great!" His heart hiccupped, and he swallowed hard.

"You're not even looking..." Rorrik pointed out.

Valen forced his attention back on Rorrik, awkward. "I did, honest! I'm sorry, I'm just..." His vision trailed back to his feet. "...overwhelmed."

Rorrik sat down next to him on the couch. "I get it..." He leaned into the demorinkin, goading Valen's overstimulation further. "Remember that we're in this together, at least."

Valen forced a nod, his heart thumping as he endeavored to recover.

"If you're both ready, we should head upstairs," Gavin then said from the entry archway.

Rorrik hopped to his feet, dragging Valen along with him. "Come on!"

■ ■ ■

Valen stepped out of the car, the smell of pine and earth greeting him. He gazed around the wooded area they had arrived at, his demorin eyes struggling little with the gloom of night. A chorus of bugs and other woodland creatures filled the air, a sound he had not heard for many months.

Rorrik joined his side. "I don't see a shrine?"

"It's a small hike to get to it," Gavin informed.

Jate snickered. "Luckily for us city slickers, there's a trail!" The felidaren walked up to the edge of the foliage and pointed to a stone step that was being overrun by plants and leaf litter. Several other steps waited beyond, beckoning.

Mrs. Catty pulled a folded, camouflage tarp from the trunk that was coated with fake moss and leaves. "Boys, help me hide the car, will you?"

The brothers draped the tarp over the car while Valen hung back, unsure of how to help.

"Valen, why don't you look for some branches with a lot of leaf cover?" Mrs. Catty suggested.

Relieved to make himself useful, Valen did so, finding more than a few fitting pieces of fallen foliage on the crowded forest floor. He delivered them to Mrs. Catty, and she placed them over the vehicle strategically. Before long, the car blended in effectively with the forested landscape.

"Alright, let's move on," Mrs. Catty ordered, approaching the steps. She started up them, her footsteps quiet despite the cluster of dead leaves underfoot. The brothers followed, matching her stealth. Valen frowned as his first step yielded a crunch and his next sounded with a rustle. '*How do they do that?!*'

Rorrik giggled from in front of him. "Playing in the leaves, Valen?"

Valen flushed with humility. "I'm sorry!"

"Try putting your weight on the balls of your feet," Rorrik offered advice.

Valen tried. While it did help some, there was still plenty to be desired.

"It takes lots of practice," Rorrik assured. "Don't worry!"

They eventually arrived at the end of the steps and a clearing revealed itself, framed by the wall of a cliff side. Stepping stones laid out the path ahead, obstructed by prairie grass and weeds. They walked along, the cliff face growing taller as they drew closer. The stepping stones led them across a bend and what lay beyond took Valen's breath away.

Several pillars of white stone towered ahead, supporting a tall structure of the same pale stone that spanned between an opening in the cliff side. The building boasted brilliant craftsmanship, its walls embellished with several patterns and intricacies. Archways lined the walls like windows, offering a peek at what lay beyond: two giant statues that towered at least two stories high.

At the foot of the pillars was a tunnel, and Avalene was waiting at the opening. "Good to see you made it."

"It's quite the place!" Mrs. Catty said, gaping up at the structure.

Avalene nodded before turning around to head inside. "Come, let's not waste time."

Valen had a look down the tunnel and spotted a courtyard ahead, a modest fountain at the heart of it. The group followed Avalene inside, and they stepped into a yard of healthy green grass, free of weeds and evenly trimmed. Marble masonry made the way to a platform which was accessed by a set of rounded steps. An altar adorned the middle of the stage, and standing behind it was the statues Valen had witnessed prior, towering over the courtyard with their swords crossed, a vivid ball of light shining where their blades met.

Bordering the courtyard were two extensions of the building that had greeted them, wings carved out of the rock that composed of the cliff side. Archways spanned across the length of them, murals of figures that matched the likeness of the statues decorating the walls beyond. The wings were three stories total while the front structure was four, nearly matching the height of the cliff.

"What do you think, Spot?" a familiar voice wondered. Valen turned to see Pepperglow approaching.

"I think we've got our work cut out for us," the felidaren answered with a look around. "There's plenty of places for our people to hide and only one exit for the Fangs."

"Fatecry mentioned there's an escape route but we're already blocking that off," Avalene said. "We have our work cut out for us, indeed."

Mrs. Catty nodded, her eyes on the building above. "I'm thinking my people can hide on the second and third stories. From there they can shoot tranquilizer darts to incapacitate the Fangs. Avalene, your people can close in and round them up. Once we have everyone cuffed, we can send them off with the warden's people."

"I was thinking the same," Avalene concurred.

Mrs. Catty looked to Valen. "You and Rorrik will be on the fourth story with Pepperglow. I don't want you any closer than you have to be during the attack."

That was fair. They both accepted with a nod, and Rorrik nudged Valen playfully, smiling wide.

"You can help by casting illusions to create diversions and draw people in for clearer shots," the mother said. "Can you do that?"

Valen nodded, trying to appear confident.

Mrs. Catty returned the nod. "Alright! Let's look around and pin down exact positions."

■ ■ ■

It was decided that eight people would man the second floor with another eight manning the third. Avalene's people, thirty strong, would be waiting in the surrounding woods until they were signaled over the radio to move forward and block the exit.

Valen was sitting up on the second floor gazing down at the courtyard below, his demeanor pensive. Uneasiness enveloped him as he spotted more and more workers arrive, their presence suggesting that the situation was finally coming to a head, a fact he was scared to realize.

"It's getting late, youngster. Perhaps you should get some sleep," Pepperglow interrupted his brooding. "There's a camp set up nearby."

His brow wrinkled. "I doubt I could sleep right now…"

"It's worth a shot. You need your rest to replenish your runa reserves." The mage placed a gentle hand on his shoulder. "Come on, I'll walk you there."

Valen scooted back and pushed to his feet, his movements sluggish. He spared the courtyard one last look and noticed there were more people arriving. Adrenaline and shock pierced him when he noticed that the group was escorting a member of the Fangs. Both her arms and legs were bound with shackles, and her skin shone with radiance in the blue light of the moon. He was still gaping in shock when she lifted her head and peered towards him, their eyes meeting. Time slowed as they regarded one another, her golden gaze entrancing him.

Another long second passed before Valen's anger came roaring back, hardening his expression into an intense glare.

"What is it?" Pepperglow inquired, following Valen's gaze. "Ah... Vallika. One of the leaders, as I'm sure you've been told."

'That's her?!' The prisoner, Vallika, was spurred forward. Her attention left him, but Valen's did not leave her. The demorinkin's anger peaked and a wave of resolve overcame him. He shot towards the steps, but Pepperglow grabbed his arm, stopping him.

"Whoa, youngster! Where are you off to?"

He fought the mage's grip but it was too firm. "Let me go!"

Pepperglow shook her head. "Can't do that until I know what you're up to."

"I have to talk to her!" Valen insisted with a struggle. "I have to!"

"Vallika?"

Valen jerked his head in a nod.

Pepperglow's lips puckered with consideration. "Let me run it by Spot—"

"Run what by Spot?" Mrs. Catty's voice then came from the stairs. The felidaren finished the steps, her eyes squinted.

"I have to talk to Vallika!" Valen exclaimed, resolute.

Mrs. Catty stared at him for a few tense moments before sighing. "...Alright. I understand."

■　■　■

Vallika was flanked by two guards and chained to one of the pillars in the courtyard when Valen approached, Mrs. Catty at his back. The celestborn lifted her head at his arrival and her lips spread into a smirk.

"Ah, young Vaaskiir..." Her amber eyes shimmered. "What a pleasure."

Valen's resolve did not abandon him. "Why are the Fangs of Hellbane hunting my family?!" he demanded.

Vallika's brow raised. "Has your own heritage been lost?"

Valen replied with a heated glare.

"Ah, I see..." Vallika shook her head. "Perhaps that is not surprising, considering the shame your name carries."

"What do you mean?!" Valen growled.

"Your ancestor claimed to be worthy amongst celestelles," Vallika told him.

Valen already knew that. "What does that even mean?!"

"That he rejected his brethren and surrounded himself with celestine company and influence."

Valen's expression rippled with confusion. "How is that a bad thing?!"

"He is a demorin and cannot escape his heritage. In trying he insulted celestellekind and dirtied the accomplishments of Approphas and Kaliina."

"Approphas and Kaliina?" Valen echoed.

"Valiant celestelles who fought and succeeded to seal away an ancient artifact from the hands of evil," Vallika explained. "Vaaskiir, in his foolishness, endeavored to assist them, but by doing so insulted their cause."

"Just because he's a demorin?!" Valen accused, incredulous.

Vallika nodded.

"So, you're hunting us only because my ancestor tried to be *good*?"

"The Fangs hunt your bloodline because of Vaaskiir's foolishness, indeed." Her smirk then stretched. "Of course, the damage your father did has them more eager than ever to spill *your* blood."

Valen's chest clenched.

"What your father did has Cloudhook sick with vengeance. However, it is in vain. The damage he cast on the Fangs of Hellbane was grave and has left it bleeding and crippled." Vallika chuckled. "How fitting that his son will help cast the final blow?"

Valen forced down a swallow. "I *will* finish it."

Vallika's smirk kept. "That is the plan."

■　■　■

Valen lay on his back in the uncomfortable embrace of a bedroll, his heart swarming with emotion. Sleep evaded him as he was mindful over his parents and how their actions had impacted the situation. It was because of them that the Fangs were compromised, as both Mrs. Catty and Vallika had pointed out.

As the demorinkin's mind hung on that thought, the pride in his parents finally shined through the muck of grief and the fire of anger. They had refused to go quietly and done all they could to get rid of the Fangs of Hellbane; Valen was amazed at his parent's bravery and tenacity. '*Dad, Mom... Thank you.*'

The relief of closure found him in the afterglow of his pride, bittersweet but appreciated. It stoked the flames of his resolve, the fire burning hotter than ever, the demorinkin wanting nothing more than to finish what his parents had started.

Chapter 44

Valen

"It's not that hard!" Rorrik said, scuttling up the tree with ease, bits of bark chipping off in his wake. "Just use your claws!"

Valen stared up at him from the ground, unconvinced. "I don't know, Rorrik…"

The felidaren paused on a branch that hung about ten feet up, his tail dangling. "Come on! At least try!"

The demorinkin's expression tightened with determination as he stepped up to the tree. His claws clenched into the bark, and he attempted to hoist himself upwards, his arms protesting. His feet lifted to provide further support, but the slippery sole of his shoes merely slid off the trunk, and he dropped back to the ground with a grunt.

"It's easier without shoes," Rorrik commented in a snicker.

"Of course you would say that," Valen replied through a sideways grin. "You're always barefoot."

Rorrik laughed. "For a reason! I don't know why people even bother with shoes."

"Probably because not everybody has protective pads," Valen pointed out.

Rorrik playfully rolled his eyes. "Try it! It's easier to climb, trust me!"

Valen shrugged and slipped off his socks and shoes, the feel of pine needles on his feet surprisingly soft. He once again attempted to scale up the trunk and was shocked when Rorrik proved to be correct. His feet could bend to fit to the shape of the tree, and the claws on his toes provided extra leverage. He made it to the branch Rorrik was on, his tail swinging to maintain his balance.

Rorrik nudged him a tad too hard, and Valen gripped at the tree in panic. "Hey!"

"Good job! You'll be scaling buildings in no time," the felidaren laughed. Before Valen could reply, Rorrik was scurrying up to the next branch, making it look easy.

Valen set off after him, making it look considerably less easy.

Rorrik sat down four branches up and scooted over to make room for Valen. The demorinkin cautiously lowered himself onto the branch and leaned up against the tree for further support.

The day had passed by both too slowly and too quickly; one moment Valen longed for the waiting to be over, then the next he wanted it to never end. He was both nervous to face the Fangs but also ill from the apprehension of it looming over him. The anticipation of it all was torturous, but luckily Rorrik had kept him occupied in both mind and body for a large chunk of the day. The tabby had found the demorinkin sulking before suggesting they play target practice. "It'll be good training, *and* it's fun!"

Thus, a game of chase not unlike what they had played several times before had begun, but instead of a cramped basement, an entire building was at their disposal. Valen had wielded his training slinger, attempting to blast Rorrik as the felidaren hid and ran and climbed about the shrine, proving more than ever a difficult target to hit. The demorinkin had no illusions to help him, as he had to save as much of his magical reserves as he could for the attack. Despite it, Valen had tasted a few bursts of triumph as he finally landed some shots, encouraging him.

Following that, Rorrik had led them out into the forest, where they proceeded to explore and presently climb.

Vivid, orange sunshine from the setting sun was filtering through the canopy, bathing them both in a hue of gold. Rorrik's fur was haloed by the light, a sight that Valen admired shortly before glancing away, yesterday and all its embarrassment and confusion fresh in his memory.

"So... are you still mad?" Rorrik asked after a brief silence, almost tentatively.

Valen frowned, his eyes on the canopy. "I... I don't know..." For the entire day, his gut had been chewing on working with Vallika and all its corresponding frustration. As he had weighed on it further, the fire of his anger had lost much of its heat, despite a pettier part of him that demanded it to remain hot. Mrs. Catty had a point when she had mentioned setting aside pride to complete the job. At first, he was loath to understand that part of his anger came from pride, but as he dissected his feelings, he found the root of his offense to be in ego, indeed. He did not want to work with Vallika merely because she was a Fang, despite her turning on the organization and providing means to finish the conflict.

That did not change the fact she had a hand in taking his parents away. That thought still stung woefully, but the consensus of his heart had decided on acceptance. His parents were gone, and now because of Vallika, he could finish what they had started. He would never feel completely fine with the idea of working with his parents' murderer, but the opportunity to stop the Fangs of Hellbane outweighed his discomfort.

"I guess not..." Valen mumbled, his ears heavy. "I just... I just want this all to be finished."

Rorrik draped an arm across Valen's shoulder. "Good thing it will be soon!"

370

Valen's apprehension was riled by the reminder. It hit him harder than ever that in only a handful of hours he would be facing the Fangs of Hellbane, finishing what his parents started. "I'm..." He let go of a shuddery breath and leaned into the felidaren for comfort, tears pooling rapidly. "I'm scared..."

Rorrik's grip on his shoulder tightened. "I'm... I'm scared, too," the tabby admitted. "But, remember we're doing this together."

The words touched the demorinkin, riling the coming rain of tears further. The family, Miss Porte, Pepperglow — they had all sacrificed so much for him. He could never have come so far without them; he could never truly thank them all enough.

That would not stop him from trying. "Th-thank you..." the demorinkin whispered, his voice strained with emotion.

Rorrik's chest began to bubble with a purr, vibrating pleasantly in Valen's ears. "Don't mention it."

■　■　■

They had leaned on each other until the sky was more blue than orange. They climbed down from the tree, Valen slow and cautious, Rorrik fast and practiced.

A simple meal of soup and bread awaited them when they arrived at camp. Even though anxiety had stolen his appetite, Valen still ate, knowing full well he needed every ounce of energy.

Following dinner, Valen noticed that Mrs. Catty, Miss Porte, and Pepperglow were chatting inside a large tent, its flap open to show them sitting at a table. Valen lingered in the doorway and cleared his throat, earning their attention as they each looked over and greeted him with a nod.

"Yes, Valen, what is it?" Mrs. Catty asked, pleasant.

"I... just wanted to say thank you," Valen said, humbled. "To all of you. For everything."

Mrs. Catty regarded him with a soft smile. "You are so very welcome, kit."

"Not a problem, youngster!" Pepperglow punctuated with a chuckle.

Miss Porte dipped her head in a nod. "We are merely doing our job."

"So, how have you been doing?" Mrs. Catty then wondered.

Valen's gaze found the ground, and his shoulders lifted in a drawn-out shrug. "Nervous..."

"Just remember we've got the upper hand," the felidaren encouraged. "Even if it turns out to be a trap, we outnumber the Fangs and are well armed to incapacitate them."

Valen's anxiety worsened, and his stomach threatened to reject his dinner. "Trap?"

"We have to entertain the possibility," Miss Porte said. "Although Fatecry's story adds up, we can never be too careful."

"If it takes a turn for the worse, I'll be right there with you to help," Pepperglow promised. "Don't you worry."

Valen tried not to, but his paranoia had already latched onto the possibility.

Mrs. Catty stood up to put a hand on his shoulder. "We've got this under control, Valen. We're going to finish this, one way or another."

■ ■ ■

Kyla

The moon told it was close to ten o'clock, signaling that it was time to prepare. They collapsed camp, and Kyla moved her people into the shrine while Avalene led hers into the woods. Vallika was brought up to the second floor, where she would continue to be chained until it was time for her to interrupt the meeting. She revealed the guards' post would be on the second floor facing the clearing, and it was agreed Bluebird and Gavin would take them out.

They all began to take their positions, but Kyla stopped Rorrik and Valen before they could head up the stairs.

"Please be careful, you two. Watch each other's backs and don't stray from Pepperglow," she told them.

They both gave a nod.

"Yes, ma'am," Valen answered.

"We'll be fine, Mom!" Rorrik assured.

She stared at them both, unable to stifle her worry. For a brief moment, she wondered if they were ready, but she tried not to let herself linger on it. They had shown to be capable; she had to believe in them.

"I'll look after them, Spot. Don't sweat it," Pepperglow added, another nail in her doubt's coffin.

"Well, get up there, then," she ordered.

They nodded once again before hurrying up the stairwell to the fourth floor, Pepperglow right behind them.

With that, Kyla took her own position on the second floor, and the waiting game began.

・・・

Valen

The fourth story was the smallest of the floors, as it had no wings framing the courtyard like the others. Archways spanned along the walls facing the courtyard and the clearing, unguarded by a railing.

The room had a few stone benches dotted about, and there was an altar flanked by life-sized statues of Korinthis and Nathalia adorning one of the walls. The statues had their heads dipped and their swords sheathed, contrasting the lively poses of the sculptures in the courtyard. Valen noticed an inscription on the altar in a language he did not recognize. Underneath it was a statement written in common, much smaller.

'May we remember that our sword does not solve all conflicts. We must not forget restraint in our passion.' – Korinthis, wielder of the shining light.

Valen's brow wrinkled with a frown. Yet another statement said by Korinthis himself that contradicted the Fangs' purpose and ideals, as he had understood in *The Light that Pierces.*

"Hey! Check out my crossbow, Valen!"

Valen turned to look, seeing Rorrik heft his weapon.

"You really know how to use that?" Valen asked through a nervous grin.

"Well, yeah!" Rorrik laughed as he loaded a tranquilizer dart. "It's not too hard. You just aim, squeeze the trigger, then reload." He aimed the weapon out into the courtyard, squinting through the scope. "Of course, practicing since I was a kit helps, too."

Valen was ready to be surprised but realized it wasn't far-fetched when remembering the family's line of work.

"So, what do you think? It's pretty cool, right?"

Valen had to admit it was neat. He nodded, spurring a smile out of the felidaren.

From there, silence followed, time feeling distorted as it dragged by. Valen gazed out into the clearing, his nerves frayed, his heartbeat thumping to the beat of his anxiety.

"Sooo, what are you thinking about?" Rorrik asked eventually, breaking the quiet.

Valen sighed and bowed his head. "What if she... turns on us?"

"We already discussed that, youngster," Pepperglow reminded, seated on a nearby bench.

"I know, but..." Valen stared out into the clearing, his expression knotting. "I can't stop worrying about it..."

"Remember what Spot said. Even if she does, we outnumber the Fangs and have the advantage. Trust in us and your own resolve, youngster."

Valen finally allowed himself to accept that, and his resolve bested apprehension. Awash in fresh confidence, the demorinkin directed his attention back onto the clearing...

...just in time to witness a portal ripping open, its roar throbbing across the field.

Rorrik gasped audibly. "Whoa!"

Dread and awe overcame Valen as he beheld the portal's shimmering, jagged opening, watching as cloaked individuals in familiar garbs passed through it: The Fangs of Hellbane.

Apprehension resurged tenfold, casting a shadow of fear over his determination, threatening it.

"Remember, youngster, let your fear become resolve," Pepperglow whispered to him. "You've done it before; you can do it again."

Pepperglow was right. *'I'm afraid... but I can fight!'* He called upon his parents for strength. *'I want to fight!'*

■ ■ ■

Kyla

Kyla gazed out from her hiding place as the Fangs arrived in lines of five across, ten groups total. Following behind were two figures clad in blue garbs akin to Vallika's, but one had a reflective gold fabric decorating the hood and chest, styled in the image of a bright light. *'That must be Cloudhook.'* The other blue figure had to be Nathian.

Kyla's adrenaline coursed as the Fangs steadily drew closer to the shrine, their faces ominously covered by the gloom of their hoods. They filed into the tunnel, and the felidaren moved to get a visual of them entering the courtyard. Two of the group split off and started up the steps, presumably the guards. Kyla dodged their detection as they passed and took their posts, precisely where Vallika advised them they would be.

The rest of the Fangs massed in the grass, leaving the masonry path open for their superiors to walk along. The leaders stepped onto the stage, and Nathian lit a candle on the altar before bowing.

He began to call out a prayer, his voice rich and powerful. As he spoke, the rest of the Fangs bowed along with him. "Exalted Korinthis and Nathalia, look down on us now with forgiveness and bless us with zeal anew, for we gather under your swords and holy light humbled and battered. We are in desperate need for your guidance and favor, oh glorious

374

ones, you who were esteemed by Xerstelle above, holy is his name and great is his judgment. By your shining light and piercing sword, bestow us the discernment and power to continue your legacy."

Nathian rose and so did the mass. Kyla looked behind her and saw that Gavin and Bluebird were already successful in taking out the guards by the grace of a silence spell and tranquilizer. The guards were cuffed and gagged, officially marking them out of the way.

"Avalene, your group is good to go," Kyla signaled over the radio in a whisper.

"Moving forward now," Avalene's voice buzzed in her earpiece.

"And why should they bless us?!" Cloudhook's voice boomed across the courtyard. "How pathetic must we look to Korinthis and Nathalia?! We have repeatedly failed our mission! We should be above this!" He pounded his fist against the altar, the candle casting a shadow of his fist on the cliff side behind them. "We should be above this!"

The mass took his scolding with silence, pulsing with shame.

Kyla approached Vallika, who was watching the meeting with disgust, her gaze seething and her lips tight. She noticed Kyla, and they shared an intense look with one another. Vallika jerked her head in a nod, and Kyla returned the gesture. The tortoiseshell swallowed hard and freed the leader from her binds, releasing whatever plan Vallika had in store.

"My sword," the celestborn said expectantly. Kyla resisted for a moment before nodding to the guard. He handed the weapon over to Vallika, and Kyla braced herself for betrayal. Instead, the celestborn stomped to the edge of the building and hung in the threshold of the archway, glaring down below.

"You are correct, Cloudhook," Vallika shouted, the mass reacting with a jump and turning to face her. "We *should* be above this."

Kyla watched, waiting with bated breath for what Vallika would say and do.

"*Vallika*?!" Cloudhook barked, stupefied.

"You escaped?" Nathian presumed.

The celestborn leapt down from the second story and landed with force. "Why is it, then, that we have sunken below what we *should* be?!" She began to march forward on the masonry path and jabbed a finger at Cloudhook. "I see the reason standing before me, calling himself our arch!"

Cloudhook's features convoluted with a snarl. "Are you doubting my authority, Vallika?"

"I am doing more than just doubting it!" Vallika cried. "I am challenging it!"

An eruption of gasps and murmuring from the mass responded.

"You dare disregard Levaris' wishes in naming me arch?!" Cloudhook spat.

"Levaris' wishes were disregarded when you began soiling all he stood for!" Vallika shot back. "You disrespect his name and title! You spit on his legacy!"

Nathian stood silent glancing between the two of them, his expression still and displaying no clear emotion.

"How dare you!" Cloudhook bellowed. "You wretched bitch!"

"All Levaris stood for is in ruins!" Vallika turned towards the crowd. "Look around you! Look at *yourselves*! We are but a husk of what we used to be! It is shameful! *Despicable*! Ask yourselves why we still fight and you will have no answer — your eyes betray your hearts!"

The mass shuffled and looked amongst themselves, defeated and ashamed.

Vallika set her attention back on Cloudhook and pointed her sword at him, the length of the blade glinting in the moonlight. "The Fangs of Hellbane is unfit to exist any longer. Both its arch and its members have sullied its name beyond repair. For Levaris and all our fore-archs, I will not stand for it any longer! The Fangs of Hellbane are *finished*!" In an instant, she was charging forward, her sword swinging towards Cloudhook.

The arch parried her strike with his own blade, the clang of their steel echoing throughout the shrine. "You crazed fool! You think you can stop us?!"

Kyla decided the time was ideal. "Now!" she ordered over the radio.

■ ■ ■

Valen

"That's our cue!" Pepperglow said before crying out an incantation. A brief flash of light enveloped the courtyard, followed by an ear-splitting bang. When the light faded, the Fangs in the courtyard stood startled and dazed.

"That ought to make them an easy target!" Pepperglow laughed before shouldering her crossbow.

Rorrik readied his own weapon, peering through the scope as he took aim. He fired in unison with several others, creating a volley of darts that rained down on the Fangs. Several shots connected with the demorin hunters, about ten, a successful first strike.

"Traitorous infidel!" Cloudhook screeched at Vallika, to which she took another swing at him, only to be parried yet again.

"You are the true traitor!" Vallika accused with another spirited swing.

The members in the yard came to and ran for cover in the surrounding wings, crying out curses as they fled. They took shelter behind the pillars while their leaders clashed on the stage, both in sword and in insults.

'We need to draw them out!' An idea struck him, and he focused on an illusion, picturing a spitting, roaring flame and its powerful, sweltering heat. He let that image boil in his mind until it was envisioned with clarity, and he manifested the spell, casting the illusion in the back of the left wing. The roar of a flame bursting into life started behind the pillars, joined with the imagery of a spreading fire, and the Fangs were chased out with screams and more curses.

"Great thinking, youngster!" Pepperglow complimented.

About twenty of the Fangs began running for the exit, a chunk of them being promptly shot. Although they continued running, it would not take long for the sedative to take effect. They disappeared into the tunnel, where Miss Porte's people waited beyond.

"I got one!" Rorrik cheered.

"Keep it up, both of you!" the gnome encouraged.

Valen took a moment to recover, sucking in a deep breath. He exhaled and manifested the same spell on the right wing, driving out the other side. Five more of them ran for the exit, and they suffered the same fate as the others who attempted to flee.

The remaining Fangs clustered by the fountain, set their attention above them, and then belted out incantations, summoning beams of magic towards their aggressors. Valen and Rorrik had to duck behind one of the pillars to dodge a wicked bolt of lightning, its static tickling as it fired past. It collided with the ceiling, blackening the stone and leaving a sprawling crack.

Valen gaped at the damage, his heart in his throat.

"Careful, youngsters!" Pepperglow shouted. "Let me put up some defenses!"

The mage cast a spell, and a transparent wall assembled in front of them, a solid ten feet across, its mass shimmering as though a flame were distorting the air.

"That can take a few strikes before shattering!" Pepperglow told them. "It's oneway, keep shooting!"

Another beam of lightning struck, but it was stopped short by the barrier with a clamoring bang. Rorrik shuffled back into position, his tail all frizz. Valen followed his example and forced himself to look back out into the courtyard, his heartbeat impossibly fast.

The Fangs proceeded to propel spells, effectively stunting the assault. With a quick glance around, Valen noticed more damage the spells had caused, from cracked pillars to crumbling archways. Pepperglow proceed to cast more walls, but there was a lot of space to cover, and the Fangs would likely keep firing.

'I have to distract them from shooting!' He glanced around, spotting a compromised pillar, and another idea popped into his mind.

He pictured the pillar beneath them crumbling, the rock cracking and groaning as it failed. He imagined it falling forward and spiraling towards the ground below, right where the fountain sat in the courtyard.

He manifested the spell and the illusion was birthed. The pillar beneath them was suddenly falling apart, tipping forward, headed right for the fountain.

The Fangs panicked and leapt out of the way, most of them falling prone. The barrage of spells ceased, and another volley of arrows rained down, striking another five or so of the Fangs.

The Fangs scrambled back to their feet and noticed the fountain remained untouched, despite the pillar that should have fallen on it.

"It was an illusion!" one of them cried. They glanced at the wings and noticed the lack of fire. "Split up and take cover behind the pillars! Don't be tricked!" They fled for shelter, a couple of them being shot as they ran.

From the Fangs' newfound cover the spells started up again. Another blast of magic crashed against their barrier, and the wall began to waver.

"That's some strong magic!" Pepperglow hooted. "I can't keep generating barriers left and right! Spot! Perhaps we should move Porte's people in to directly engage them?"

"I was thinking the same!" Mrs. Catty replied over the radio.

Valen winced as another shot of magic struck the wall, finally dispelling the barrier. He hid behind a pillar for cover, unable to do much else. Avalene's people would have to take it from there!

■ ■ ■

Avalene

Her people had incapacitated every Fang that had come running out of the shrine, sedated or not. They had cuffed and rounded up about thirty of them when she heard Pepperglow and Kyla suggesting that she move her people inside.

"I'm on it," she answered.

"There's about ten left hiding in the wings, and they're not buying any more illusions!" Kyla reported. "They're also firing spells, be careful!"

"Got it." The vigilante began to march forward into the tunnel. "Fifteen of you, come with me! The rest of you hang back — do not let *anyone* past!"

They arrived at the end of the tunnel and Avalene assessed the situation.

The Fangs had split so that they were hiding in both wings, while Vallika and Cloudhook still looked to be fighting on the stage. Nathian was nowhere to be spotted.

"Seven of you, head down the right wing! The rest, come with me!" Avalene hissed in a whisper. "They're distracted! Try to sneak up on them!"

They moved forward into the entrances framing the tunnel and sneaked towards their targets. They slipped past the paintings on the walls and came along the Fangs, whose attention was still on the upper floors.

Her people tiptoed so they stood directly behind the demorin hunters, and Avalene prepared her stun blaster, the device awakening with a whine of energy. The Fang she was targeting turned around and desperately slashed with their sword, catching Avalene along the shoulder. She grunted in pain but managed to fire the weapon, tasing the Fang into submission. Her shoulder oozing blood, she knelt and cuffed the celestborn with expert speed. With a glance, she saw the rest of her team was successful. The spells quit firing across the field, suggesting the others were also victorious.

"Get them rounded up!" Avalene barked to her men.

"That's all of them!" Kyla exclaimed from across the radio. "That went better than we could have hoped for!"

Avalene moved out into the courtyard, trying not to mind her shoulder. She began to handcuff the passed-out Fangs that dotted the yard, moving quickly.

"I'll be right down!" Kyla said. A few moments passed. "Wait," the felidaren gasped. "Where's Vallika?!"

Dread slammed into Avalene as she looked towards the stage. Cloudhook was bloody and lifeless, draped over the altar, Vallika nowhere to be seen.

∎ ∎ ∎

Valen

"We did it!" Valen shouted in utter exuberance, high from adrenaline. He lifted Rorrik off the ground and squeezed him as tight as he could. "I-I can't believe we did that! That was— we— it—" He wildly shook his head as no coherent thought could filter through his excitement. "We did it!"

"I know!" Rorrik guffawed. Valen dropped him, and the felidaren bounced up and down, his emerald eyes huge and sparkling.

"We were so cool!" the tabby gushed. "They didn't stand a chance!"

Valen began to pace around, unable to keep still as his mind and heart raced. "I can't believe we did that! I can't believe it!" The plan could not have gone more perfectly. Vallika had not turned on them, after all! The Fangs of Hellbane were finally defeated, they had finished what his parents had started!

Valen proceeded to pace. "I just can't believe—" he started to repeat, but then a thud landed on the roof, shaking the ceiling above. Valen froze with confusion.

Rorrik's ears pressed back. "What was that?!"

"Wait," Mrs. Catty then gasped from over the radio. "Where's Vallika?!"

To answer both questions, a figure dropped in from the roof, their sword drawn, the steel slathered in blood.

Valen's world slowed. Vallika.

Chapter 45

Valen

Vallika's abdomen was bloody from a fresh wound on her stomach, but she still stood tall and unwavering, her golden glare menacing. Her gaze burned into Pepperglow, and a spell released from the demorin hunter's palm, delivering a blast of wind that barreled into the gnome. Pepperglow was pushed back and tossed over the edge of the building.

Valen started forward in a desperate run. "No!"

Vallika cast the same spell again, and this time it connected with Rorrik. Valen's stomach plunged with dread as the felidaren was blown across the ledge with a yowl.

"Rorrik!" the demorinkin cried out, diving forward to grab him, but it was too late. Rorrik was tumbling towards the ground from four stories up, helpless.

Valen screamed out in a sob, his hand still outstretched. 'No! *No!*' A pressure rapidly built in his palm, and the familiar sensation of a spell manifesting shot through his blood. The pressure released, and Rorrik's plummet slowed to a crawl, taking both the felidaren and the demorinkin by surprise.

"Nice Slow Fall spell, youngster!" Pepperglow hollered. Valen followed her voice in alarm but saw that the mage was gently falling in a similar manner. Her eyes then went wide. "Behind you!"

Valen had no time to react before a hand gripped at his back and yanked him upwards. He was spun around and met with Vallika's smirking face.

Valen gawked at her, stricken with terror as Mrs. Catty shouted his name over the radio in a panic.

"I finally have you!" the celestborn sneered. She gestured to a glistening barrier that spanned across the arches and blocked off the stairs. "None of your meddling accomplices can help you now!"

She readied her sword to strike, her amber eyes glinting wildly. "I will honor Levaris and all my fore-archs by spilling your cursed blood, Vaaskiir! In killing you, I will uphold my vow and restore my dignity. Watch and bless me now, Korinthis and Nathalia, as I glorify your name!"

She thrust the sword towards his chest, but then the blade froze in place, the steel kissing his shirt, his innate constrict spell once again saving his life.

The demorinkin fought to hang on to the spell as he struggled out of Vallika's grasp and fell to the ground ungracefully. He scrambled to his feet, wobbly from panic and magical exertion, unable to maintain it any longer.

He surrendered control, and Vallika immediately swung at him again, shrieking with determination. He leapt out of the way, narrowly dodging her bloodied blade. He drew his spell slinger and aimed it towards the celestborn, poised to shoot, but laden with hesitation. She turned on him to strike once more and his instincts won out. He fired the spell slinger, and she was pushed back several feet with a grunt, the wound on her abdomen exacerbated.

She bellowed with laughter. "I should have foreseen that you would put up a fight! You *are* your father's son!" She readied her blade. "It is in vain, Vaaskiir. I have the blessing of the exalted Korinthis and Nathalia on my side."

Valen balked as injustice overcame him. "You're wrong! You don't follow their teachings correctly! You offend everything they stood for!"

Vallika's smirk morphed into a grimace. "What do *you* know about Korinthis and Nathalia, hellspawn?!"

"Enough to know that Korinthis *himself* said one's heritage doesn't define them!" Valen shot back. "That just because I'm a demorin, it doesn't make me evil!"

"You misunderstand and twist his words to befit you!" Vallika spat. "How dare you pervert his message?!"

"No, that's exactly what *you're* doing!" Valen proclaimed. "*You're* the one perverting his message!"

"Enough of this!" Vallika screeched. "You understand nothing — I will put you in your place, Vaaskiir!"

Valen scowled at the demorin hunter, his features taut with indignation. "You understand only what you want to understand!"

The celestborn charged forward, coming towards him alarmingly fast. Valen activated his bracers in a burst of urgency, augmenting the armor's strength. Vallika's sword found his chest, but the mage-armor deflected the strike. He stumbled back from the impact of the blow, and Vallika once again attempted to drive her sword into him, the mage armor denying her. However, the forcefield reached its limit and was promptly dispelled, expelling a wave of pressure that startled Vallika back a foot.

Valen's brow wet with sweat, he readied his spell slinger and shot, the impact forcing Vallika back another several feet, right into the statues. She took the impact with a roar of frustration and pushed off yet again, rushing right for him.

He desperately jumped out of the way, but she could follow his movements. He once again activated the bracers, but a much weaker spell responded, his magical reserves exhausted. Her sword caught his side, and the mage armor could not ward off the entire strike. The blade sliced through his shirt, finding skin. He cried out in pain before firing his spell slinger once more, its force push proving weaker as it sent Vallika back.

'*I can't keep this up!*' Panic blared through Valen's body, white hot and persuasive. Vallika braced herself to charge at him again, her abdomen battered and gory, but doing little to slow her down. '*She's just not stopping!*'

Vallika once again shot forward, and Valen was forced to retreat. He ran around the floor, crazed with fear. Vallika's pace proved slower but that did little to comfort him.

'*I can't just keep running forever!*' Valen regarded the shimmering walls that kept him trapped. '*She's going to kill me! I'm going to die!*'

"We both know how this is going to end!" Vallika shouted at his back. "Accept the same fate as your father, Vaaskiir!"

'*My father...*' His parents' final stand flashed through his mind, how they had rejected complacency and collapsed the temple on the Fangs of Hellbane. Yet another idea struck him. '*The damage from the lightning bolt!*'

His eyes scanned the ceiling, and it was not hard to find the crack it had left. He ran towards it, Vallika still giving him chase.

He stopped about ten feet past the crack and swung around, breathing hard.

"History tends to repeat itself, doesn't it?" he asked, his question spurring laughter out of Vallika.

The demorin hunter drew closer, her golden eyes shining with moisture. "That you are correct on."

Valen waited for her to pass underneath the crack, his heart thumping impossibly loud. She was a step away when he aimed the spell slinger at the ceiling and summoned everything he had left in him to shoot. A thunderous shot left the weapon, yanking Valen back as it fired. It connected with the crack, and the ceiling surrounding it crumbled, vomiting stone onto the floor below. The rubble slammed into Vallika, knocking her to the ground as it bombarded her.

Valen scooted back as the ceiling proceeded to cave, burying the demorin hunter. A cough of dust and grumble of stone signaled the end of the collapse.

Valen's vision was blurry as he gawked at the damage. He could barely make out Vallika lying there through the veil of dust, still struggling to stand and fight. She groaned and growled but it was to no avail. The demorin hunter succumbed, her body going limp, the barrier around the place dissipating as she lost consciousness.

Valen struggled to breathe, overstimulated and dizzy. He gasped and coughed and lay down, the world around him slurring and contorting. His ears were ringing, and he could not move his arms or legs. He closed his eyes, flashes of color dancing around the blackness of his vision.

"Valen! *Valen!*" In a far-off corner of his mind he recognized the voice as Mrs. Catty's. He was suddenly being shaken, but he could not open his eyes or move.

"He's losing consciousness!" he thought he heard Pepperglow say. "He strained himself too hard magically. He needs immediate attention. I'll get him out of here!"

The color in his vision surged with utmost brightness, and then it was rapidly fading, only the blackness remaining.

■ ■ ■

Rorrik

Rorrik kept vigil at Valen's bedside, drowsy but too anxious to rest. The felidaren had his upper body sprawled over the mattress, his head lying close to Valen's non-injured side. A weak purr sputtered in his chest, both to hopefully comfort the demorinkin and himself.

Valen lay sleeping, his breathing strained and his skin beaded with sweat. His ribcage was bundled in gauze that was pink with blood, courtesy of the wound Vallika had inflicted. The cut was not terribly deep, but its location hampered Valen's breathing as his chest struggled to lift against the injury.

He was being treated at a private clinic Pepperglow had teleported him to the night before. The demorinkin had substantially exhausted his runa reserves, and thus his body had suffered heavy physical strain. The medic had since then kept him stable as he slowly recovered his energy.

"He needs lots of rest as his body recovers," the medic, a young male terran dotted with round, opaque, pastel-blue stones, had said. "He'll be asleep for some time; anywhere between a couple of hours to over a day."

It was currently the following night; Valen had been asleep for almost an entire twenty-four hours. It had been a tortuously long wait, despite the reassurance both the doctor and his family offered.

"He'll be fine, kit," his mother had told him several times. "He'll wake up soon."

Rorrik lifted his head and stared up at his friend, his lips jutted with a frown. '*How soon is soon?*'

The medic walked into the room. "He's still snoozing, huh?" he observed, coming up to the bedside to check the demorinkin's vitals.

Rorrik nodded before stuffing his face back into the sheets.

"Hmm, looks like his fever broke! That's good news," the medic noted. He dabbed the sweat from Valen's brow with a cloth and inspected the bandages on his side. "It shouldn't be much longer now."

Rorrik hoped so. He yawned and nestled into the demorinkin's side, sleepy. While Valen had done nothing but rest, the felidaren had gotten

384

scarce sleep; he was simply too antsy for Valen to wake up to get any solid slumber.

After all, he still had to thank the demorinkin for rescuing him. If it had not been for Valen's slow fall spell, he could have gotten seriously injured or worse. He was impatient to convey his gratitude.

Regardless, he would have to keep waiting. Valen slept on, his example lulling Rorrik into closing his own eyes. The tabby groggily sighed and finally succumbed to sleep.

■ ■ ■

Valen

A gigantic stone was crushing him, making every breath a struggle. He tried to escape the rubble, but his limbs were too heavy to move.

"Crushed just like your parents," Vallika's voice sneered right into his ear, aggravating the headache that pounded in his skull. "History does repeat itself, indeed, hellspawn!"

His ribs began to throb more intensely and he moaned with pain. He was desperate to remove the stone from his chest as it pressed further into him, goading his agony. He fought harder to wiggle free, gasping for breath.

"Valen!" Rorrik's voice suddenly called.

The rock was so heavy; he just couldn't move it.

"Help me!" he tried to say, but the words were mute as they left his mouth. He desperately tried again, but it was no use.

"Valen! Hey, wake up!" Rorrik said, much too loudly.

The headache felt like it was going to split his skull. He groaned, and the stone on his chest dug even deeper. He gasped as his eyes shot open, a mess of blurry brightness overtaking his vision. The stone on top of him was gone, but not the pain from its burden.

He winced against the light as it harassed his headache. He looked around, disoriented, his head heavy as he struggled to calibrate himself with his surroundings.

"Valen!" Rorrik repeated.

Valen turned towards the tabby's voice, and two Rorriks were sitting next to the bed the demorinkin was apparently lying on. The Rorriks teetered towards each other before sloppily forming into one. "You're awake!"

Valen was overwhelmed and confused. He closed his eyes with another moan, his ribs hurting terribly.

"Medic!" Rorrik yelled, exacerbating the pain throbbing in Valen's skull. "He's awake!"

Valen's eyes cracked open to see a terran hurry into the room, which was cramped and windowless. There was a beeping coming from behind him in a fast rhythm.

"Try to settle down," the terran calmly suggested. "You're fine, you're safe."

Valen attempted to calm down, but his ribs prevented any satisfying breaths.

"How's your pain?"

"Terrible," Valen croaked.

The medic fiddled with something at Valen's bedside; when he turned to look, he noticed it was an IV drip. "That should help. Give it a minute or two."

The minutes passed and relief arrived, nullifying the edge of his pain. The beeping behind him slowed to an occasional blip.

Mrs. Catty then entered the room and hurried up to his bedside, beaming. "Valen, it's so good to see you awake!"

Valen weakly grinned and glanced between the tortoiseshell and her son. "Uh, how long was I out?"

"For about twenty-six hours," the medic informed him. "You were unconscious due to magical exertion."

Valen was abruptly struck with realization. "Wait! What happened to Vallika?!"

Rorrik and his mother shared a brief wince.

"Well…" Mrs. Catty began, taking a seat in a chair by the wall. "Her injuries *had* been stabilized and she was in recovery… but not long after she was found dead. The autopsy revealed her heart had ruptured. We can assume it was from a spell." The felidaren shook her head. "She had warned us that she knew a spell to end her own life… I guess that proves she wasn't bluffing."

Valen processed the news with a flip of his stomach. '*So, that means…*' His gaze found his knees as relief and hesitation clashed within his heart. "So… it's… over, then?"

"Thanks to the map Rorrik had brought back, yes." Mrs. Catty answered. "Nathian *had* escaped, but we were able to track him down to one of the map's marked locations, an estate north of the city. Porte's people were able to arrest him and get him behind bars." The mother's lips parted with a smile. "So, yes; it's over. The Fangs of Hellbane have been defeated."

"We did it!" Rorrik exclaimed, jumping to his feet.

Valen's hesitation gave one last surge before finally surrendering to relief. It came in sparse drops at first, like a sprinkle of coming rain. Then, it was rapidly pouring down, drenching him. His eyes grew glossy, and his chest threatened to burst.

It was finally over; he had finished what his parents had started.

But, he could have never done it alone.

"I cannot thank you all enough..." Valen said, his voice thick with emotion. "Thank you. *Thank you.*"

"No, thank *you!*" Rorrik then guffawed. "You saved me back there! I would have been a furry pancake if it wasn't for you!"

Valen was reminded of the slow fall spell he had apparently cast. His cheeks warmed with a light blush, and he grinned at his friend. "I'm glad I could help."

Rorrik's fangs shown in a toothy smile. "Me, too!"

"I am sorry to interrupt, but am I to magically heal his injury?" the medic redirected conversation.

Mrs. Catty gestured to the demorinkin. "That's up to him."

Valen tilted his head with a tickling of apprehension. "What?"

The medic regarded Valen with a pleasant grin. "If you are so willing, I can accelerate the healing of your wound with a spell. Are you aware of the risks of the procedure?"

Valen grimaced and his shoulders meagerly lifted in a shrug. "Well, my father's leg didn't heal right because of a healing potion..."

"I am sorry to hear that. However, it would not be a potion. Whereas a potion is unguided which may lead to complications, my spell is carefully performed with precision. It is unlikely complications would arise, due to the minimal intensity of your injury. Since the wound is light, you would not be completely put under, rather put on a mild sedative and a strong painkiller. Your wound would be healed within minutes, although you can expect some pain as I work, even with the painkiller. That, and magical healing always leaves an extraordinary scar."

Valen digested his words, afflicted with uncertainty. "I'm not sure..."

"What gives you pause?"

Valen thought back to his father's crippled leg. "You said it's unlikely complications would arise?"

The medic dipped his head in a nod. "Indeed. The procedure is far less risky than a potion, if that is what you're worried about."

"But... isn't magical healing really expensive?" Valen worried.

"Don't worry about that, cub," Mrs. Catty excused.

Guilt added to Valen's apprehension. "You've already done so much for me..."

"And this is one more thing we would like to do," the mother pushed. "It's important you get better as fast as possible. We insist."

"A scar would be so cool!" Rorrik contributed.

Valen wasn't quite sure what to think of a scar.

"Mundane healing will likely take four to six weeks. I'd give you painkillers to manage the pain," the medic said.

'*Four to six weeks is a long time...*' Valen tried to sigh but the pain in his ribs prevented him, an argument for the procedure within itself. His mind was made up. "Okay... I'll do it."

• • •

The drugs had him dopey and drowsy as the medic strapped him to the bed on his back. The beep of the machine behind them chirped slowly, like a bored bird. That comparison made Valen snicker.

"It's important you don't struggle as I work," the healer told him, his voice sounding far away. "Less chance of complications that way."

Valen giggled as he finished restraining him. "Okey-dokey…"

"Are you comfortable?"

Valen's giggling turned to laughter. "As comfortable as I can be in binds."

The terran gave a single chuckle and took a seat next to the bed. He lifted his hands and hovered them above the demorinkin's wound, which was exposed and free of gauze, glistening with medicine.

"I'll start slow," the medic said. "You're going to feel some discomfort."

Valen flopped his head in a nod, his skull feeling heavy. "Gotcha…"

A light blue aura enveloped the medic's hands and then the wound. A pressure rapidly began building in Valen's torso and painful stimuli followed it, spreading across his ribcage like a wave striking the shore. He cried out and tried to arch away from the pain, but the binds restricted his movement. The beeping of the machine turned frantic.

"Easy…" the medic cooed. The aura shimmered on, and the pain grew worse and worse. The wound became white-hot and alive with static as he worked, Valen's ribcage pulsing with agony all the while.

This painstakingly dragged on. Valen was wet with sweat and whimpering when the blue aura finally faded, the pain vanishing along with it.

"That should do it," the medic said. He began to unstrap him, Valen still recovering from the procedure. "How does it feel?"

Valen craned his neck to look down at the injury, seeing a scar laced with a faint, silvery sheen. His drugged mind stumbled for words. "…Better."

"The procedure was a success, then," the medic chimed. "You're all healed."

• • •

Valen collapsed in Rorrik's bed facedown with a grunt, his muscles throbbing with exhaustion. Although his wound was healed, the strain of his magical exertion still endured. He groaned as his muscles complained even with him lying completely still.

Rorrik climbed up into the loft bed and plopped down with similar enthusiasm. "Man, I'm going to sleep forever…"

"You and me both…" Valen grumbled into the sheets.

Valen had been discharged following the procedure after the drugs had worn off.

"Drink plenty of fluids and perform no magic for at least a few days," the medic had told him. "Take it easy for the next week."

Mrs. Catty had then taken him back to the hideout, a short drive. Considering the late hour, Valen had headed straight for bed, Rorrik in agreement with that plan.

However, as Valen lay there, tremendously sore and aching, sleep dodged him despite his exhaustion. His mind was busy with thoughts of the Fangs of Hellbane and the realization of their defeat. Relief punctuated his musings, but a feeling of restlessness persisted, despite it.

The Fangs' reasons for hunting his bloodline still held too many wonders; Vallika's explanation had left him with more questions than answers. Who were Approphas and Kaliina? What was the ancient artifact they had sealed away? Why had his ancestor forsaken demorinkind? He felt foolish for not asking Vallika follow-up questions, for now there was no way to sate the wonders burning in his mind.

…Or was there?

Chapter 46

Valen

"We should check out the scholar's library," Valen suggested the morning after a day of regaining his strength.

Rorrik tilted his head. "What, why?"

"Vallika mentioned something that I want to look into," the demorinkin revealed.

Rorrik seemed instantly intrigued as his eyes went large. "The thing about those celestelles who sealed away the artifact?!"

Confusion rippled across Valen's face; Rorrik definitely wasn't there for that conversation. "How do you know about that?"

The tabby smirked and rolled his shoulders in an exaggerated shrug. "I have my ways."

"I told him," Gavin then contributed from the kitchen table, smug.

Valen was certain he didn't see Gavin at the exchange, either...

Rorrik squinted over at his brother before rolling his eyes.

The demorinkin dismissed his puzzlement with a shake of his head. "Anyway, yes, that's what I want to research."

"Do you remember the celestelles' names?" Gavin questioned.

Valen's confidence in his memory was suddenly shaken. "Uh, well—"

The felidaren was already pulling out a sheet of paper from a small notebook in front of him. He scribbled something down before folding the paper and holding it out. "Blue thinks that's the correct spelling."

"Show-off..." Rorrik jested with a scoff.

Valen received the paper and glanced at the writing. 'Approphas and Kaliina', it read.

The demorinkin stuffed the note into the pocket of his sweat pants. "Thank you!"

Gavin got to his feet with a nod. "I can drive you both there, if you want."

"That would be great, thank you!" Valen agreed.

Rorrik once again rolled his eyes, but did not complain.

Valen scooted into the backseat of the vehicle with a tingle of paranoia, the fear that had been conditioned into him stubborn to fade, despite the fact the Fangs of Hellbane were finished.

Rorrik gracelessly flopped into the passenger seat. "Can I drive?"

"Pffft, no," Gavin sneered through a smirk as he adjusted the mirrors.

"Wait, you can drive?" Valen questioned, his eyebrows shooting up.

"Of course!" Rorrik claimed. "Since I was like, ten!"

Valen thought of a ten-year-old driving and his head spun. "That's so young!"

Rorrik gave a wink. "Just all a part of training!"

Valen was still snagged on the oddity of it. "Isn't that illegal?"

Both brothers had a laugh.

Valen's lips sunk with a frown. "How do you not get in trouble?"

"Cops always seem to be a little lazier when we're out and about," Rorrik giggled.

"And plump with cash," Gavin added.

"Sooo, you bribe them?"

Rorrik turned to smile at Valen. "You're getting it!"

Valen didn't return the smile as he dropped his gaze to his feet; he wasn't sure he wanted to get it.

Gavin pulled out of the garage and merged onto the road. Valen's curiosity finally emerged victorious over his anxiety as he spared a peek out the window, allowing himself a look at Sengard for the first time. The architecture of the area was old and compiled of cobblestone of cool gray and maroon hues, a contrast to Akarth's warmer colors of yellow and red. The buildings only rose to a few stories, but Valen knew that giants could be found elsewhere in the city, towering and massive.

The car drove along to an ambiance of beeping and commotion, a sound Valen had grown accustomed to in Akarth. He remembered how assaulted his ears had first felt as he desperately searched for slumber on those first long, torturous nights, his mind already bombarded enough by the noise of his thoughts. The clock tower had offered some respite from the ruckus of the city, but it was still always a distant clamor.

He sighed away the memories of Akarth and put his chin in his hand. He tried not to linger on the clock tower, his heart too tired to dwell on all he lost there. His heart still panged and his chest flinched accordingly, albeit with exhausted regard.

"I can't wait to show you around the city!" Rorrik then chirped, his excitement shooting through the demorinkin's melancholy like an arrow. "We should do that tomorrow! Oh, um, if you're feeling good enough, that is."

Both intrigue and apprehension arose at the prospect, but curiosity was able to shine the brighter. "I'd like that."

Rorrik perked up. "Really?!"

Valen nodded and offered a gentle smile.

"You're not too tired or anything?"

"I'm actually feeling a lot better," Valen replied, truthful. Much of his muscle soreness still lingered, but the heaviness in his limbs and general fatigue had lessened dramatically since spending the prior day resting. He had awoken that morning feeling zealous to discover the answers of the questions that had harassed him in his recovery.

"If you say so!" Rorrik accepted happily enough. "I can't wait!"

■ ■ ■

They parked on the side of the street, the library awaiting atop a shallow hill with carved out steps. Gorgeous windows of stained glass decorated the walls of the building, which spanned an impressive three stories. Valen marveled at the sight as he scooted out of the vehicle and stepped out onto the sidewalk.

Rorrik emerged from the car and then Gavin.

"Wait, I thought you were just driving us?" Rorrik remarked through a squint.

Gavin's lips twitched in a grin. "You could use my help with research."

"We can research just *fine*, Gavin!"

Gavin started up the steps with a flick of his tail. "We'll see."

"You just want to snoop!" Rorrik accused with a flattening of his ears.

Gavin turned around, a smile breaking. "Guilty as charged."

Rorrik hissed a sharp sigh, and Valen weakly grinned at his friend.

"It's fine, Rorrik. He's right, we could use the help," the demorinkin tried.

Rorrik shook his head and set towards the building, Valen following alongside of him.

Gavin paused at the entrance, his back to them as his tail ticked. "That's inopportune…"

"What?" Valen came up next to the tabby and his spirit plummeted as he noticed a sign on the door. 'Closed until the Autumnal Equinox', it read. *'No! That's weeks and weeks away!'*

Valen didn't hide his disappointment as he gaped at the sign.

Rorrik placed a hand on his shoulder. "Hey, it's okay! It doesn't *have* to be closed for us."

Valen's brow knotted. "What do you mean?"

Rorrik smirked at him, and his meaning clicked for Valen. "No — we shouldn't steal!"

"It's not stealing if we plan to give it back," Rorrik argued. "Come on, do you really want to wait *weeks*?"

"I—" Valen bit at his lip before thrashing his head. "We don't have to do that! Just let me try something!"

Both Rorrik and Gavin raised their brow at him.

"Like what?" Rorrik inquired.

Valen gave a harsh rap on the door, letting that be his answer.

They all stared at the door as no reply came from within.

Valen knocked again and then again, more urgently each time. "Hello?" he called out hopefully, only to be disappointed.

"Well, thanks for confirming that no one is home," the oldest brother snorted.

Valen dipped his head in defeat, crestfallen.

"You can wait here. We'll be back," Gavin said before slinking into the bushes running parallel to the building, Rorrik joining him.

Valen extended out a hand to stop them, but it fell short, stunted by indecision. His conscience threw a conniption, disgusted that he was complacent with the plan, but it was not enough. He let them sneak off without a word of protest. *'I'm going to give back anything they take. It's fine. It's not stealing!'*

He leaned against the railing that lined the stairs, his guilt like acid as it soured his stomach. *'It's not stealing... it's not—'*

There was a loud creak of a door opening, and he turned to see a girl around his age with remarkable silver eyes and platinum blonde hair standing in the frame. Her sharp features were bent in a peeved grimace.

"Can't you read?" she questioned him, her voice crisp with a celestine accent. "The sign says we're *closed*."

Valen gawked at the girl, startled someone had finally answered the door. Instincts that had not been called upon for several weeks birthed a pleasant smile on his face as she regarded him with crossed arms.

And thus, he fell into an old routine. "I'm very sorry to bother you, but I was hoping you could help me," he said, his voice rich with charm.

The girl raised an eyebrow, failing to look impressed, let alone charmed. "The library is *closed*. The scholar is out."

"She's still recovering, then?" Valen guessed. "I hope she is doing well. She helped us so much, after all."

The girl narrowed her eyes. "Helped? With what?"

Valen grinned. "We're getting ahead of ourselves. I'm Valen Vaaskiir, and you are...?"

"*Vaaskiir*?!" the girl gasped. "Wait, so you—" She crimped her face, and her milky skin colored with a blush. "What are you doing here now?"

"There is a legend I am wanting to research. The tale of..." He retrieved the paper from his pocket in a seamless gesture. "Approphas and Kaliina." He handed the paper over, and the girl took it with a jutted lip.

Her silvery gaze scanned the sheet for a lengthy moment, and then she was shaking her head. "But the library is closed..." She didn't meet his eyes.

Valen nodded, slow and cool. "I understand that. I just thought that since we had helped the scholar, perhaps it would be alright if I had a quick look around even though the place is closed?"

The girl appeared torn at that. "I'm really not supposed to—"

"I promise not to be long or get in your way," Valen pressed. He flashed a playful smile. "Unless you want to help me look, that is."

The girl found his eyes, and her cheeks darkened in rose. "It's just... uh..." She just as quickly glanced away. "...demorins... aren't... allowed inside."

Valen's confidence was considerably shaken at the statement, but he still managed to bluff a grin. "Oh? Why's that?"

"Uh, well..." The red of her cheeks went darker still. "It's just... the rules."

"So, I can't go in just because I'm demorinkin?" Valen wondered, dubious but patient.

The girl appeared embarrassed as she craned her neck away from him, her diamond eyes guilty.

Valen thought for a second. "You know, that strikes me as an odd rule. Have you ever heard of Korinthis and Nathalia?"

She looked back at him, her expression incredulous. "Of course I have."

"Well, do you agree with what they stood for?"

The girl's nose wrinkled with puzzlement. "...Yes."

"Really? Because not allowing demorins in your library on the account that they're demorins seems to contradict their message."

Her brow darkened. "That makes zero sense. The Piercing Light *hunted* demorins."

"That is correct. However, if you read their book, you'd find that they said that one's heritage does not make them evil; paraphrasing, of course."

The girl's embarrassment turned to confusion. "I don't remember reading that."

"Well, I do! And, I'm willing to bet on it!" Valen smiled wide. "If you look in the *Light That Pierces* and find that what I'm saying is true, then you will let me do my research. However, if it is not there, I will leave you alone and not come back. Do we have an agreement?" He did his best to channel all his charm into a warm smile.

And the girl was charmed; at least, enough so. "Alright, fine. Follow me."

■ ■ ■

Rorrik

Rorrik was several feet away navigating through the snagging branches of the bushes, when he heard talking back where Valen was left waiting.

Gavin turned to look behind them, noticing it, too.

They paused to listen in, hearing a Valen they had never witnessed before. This Valen was sure-spoken and confident, a far cry from the meek and nervous demorinkin they knew.

Eventually Valen and the girl wandered off inside, and the brothers took the opportunity to escape from the foliage.

The fur on Rorrik's cheeks tingled with heat and a smile stretched his cheeks. Valen had been so charming; he had no idea that the demorinkin could talk like that!

Gavin chuckled from next to him. "That was impressive, huh?"

Rorrik hurriedly nodded, his eyes large with excitement and curiosity. "Tell me about it!"

Gavin smirked at him before opening the door and walking inside.

One of Rorrik's ears tilted, and he followed his brother with a sideways look. "What?"

Gavin only had another chuckle to offer him.

■ ■ ■

Valen

The library certainly looked like it should be closed. There were several toppled shelves and many books massed in piles about the floor. Blackened blemishes marked the walls and ceiling, what Valen assumed to be the aftermath of the battle Miss Porte had stepped in on.

Other than that, the place was beautiful. The floor of the main room was a stone of bleached white and the stained-glass windows offered a vivid aura of color where their light touched, livening the neutral colors of the space. Several rock pillars boasting intricate patterns dotted the floor, holding up a ceiling that towered three stories above. A loft ran along each floor, accessed by metallic ladders that sparkled in the sunlight. In the middle of the ceiling was a small section that raised another story, its top composed of stained glass.

A few tables were dotted about, one looking mighty disheveled. It did little to distract from the place's beauty.

"It's gorgeous in here…" Valen complimented, gazing around in admiration.

The girl scoffed. "More like a mess…"

She led them up to an intact shelf and scanned its contents before pulling out the *The Light That Pierces*. Valen looked on, unable to contain a grin.

"It's near the back," he instructed. "Around page three hundred, if I remember correctly."

The girl flipped to the spot, and Valen waited for the picture of the bested celestelle Mrs. Catty had described to pop up. It did before long and Valen pointed. "There! Read that and the next page."

She did so, her eyes shooting to and fro as she hastily read. Bewilderment splashed across her face, worsening as she turned the page and saw the image of the demorin in between Korinthis and Nathalia, conflict free. Her cheeks blared red, and she was silent as she read the passage again.

"...I..." she murmured, her voice humbled. "I guess... you're right."

"So, does that mean I get to do my research?" Valen asked, wanting to smirk but refraining.

She sighed and closed the book. "Yeah..." She returned it to the shelf and hugged her sides, her skin still pink with a blush.

"Would you mind directing me on where to start?" Valen said, friendly.

She nodded, but then her eyes widened as she looked past Valen. "Hey! The library is closed! Doesn't anybody read signs?!"

Valen turned to look and saw Rorrik and Gavin standing there, both giving little waves.

"They're with me, don't worry!" Valen eased with a nervous chuckle.

"We were just parking the car!" Rorrik excused.

"Sorry to startle you," Gavin added.

The girl looked unimpressed but did not question it further. She rolled her eyes and started walking towards another shelf, Valen following.

"You never did introduce yourself," Valen mentioned as they walked.

"Nadelyn Windsong," she told without turning around.

"Nadelyn is a lovely name," the demorinkin schmoozed.

"I prefer Lyn," Nadelyn, rather Lyn, said.

"Lyn it is, then," Valen agreed. "It's a pleasure to meet you."

She brought them up the ladder and gestured to a shelf. "This row here is all we have on the Legend of the Twin Roses."

Valen counted nine sizable, thick books total. "Great, thank you so much!"

Lyn nodded before walking off, her platinum hair gliding behind her. "If you have any questions, just let me know."

■ ■ ■

Valen scanned through the book for the third time, his expression tired and demoralized.

"I'm still not finding anything…" he mumbled, his tone defeated.

"Yeah, me neither," Rorrik shared.

"No mention in this book, either," Gavin, too.

Valen could not understand. They had checked five different books, all of them talking in great length about Approphas and Kaliina, but nothing about Vaaskiir ever came up, not even a brief mention or hint.

It made no sense. Vallika would not have lied to him about the legend, why would she have? It was obvious *something* had happened with his ancestor that bothered the Fangs enough to hunt his bloodline, yet there was no evidence of the deeds they swore Vaaskiir committed.

The story, called the Legend of the Twin Roses, was about two elemental celestelles, an ice celestelle called Approphas and a fire celestelle named Kaliina. They set out on a quest to do good, and in their travels came across the plot of a powerful demorin named Norox. Norox sought to steal an artifact called the Hand of Judgment from a deity's temple in the outer realms. The Hand of Judgment was said to be a tool used by divinity itself: it had the power to create and destroy anything. Norox succeeded in stealing the artifact, but Approphas and Kaliina were able to stop him from following through with his plan to overtake Azyria. To ensure no one would ever be able to use the tool again, the two of them locked the artifact away in a seal bound by their very blood and life essence, an act that resulted in their death. In their sacrifice, they ascended as celesteons.

The page Valen currently had open depicted Approphas and Kaliina intimately entwined with one another in a pool of their own blood. Apparently, a romance had resulted from their journey, hence the usage of roses in the legend's name.

Valen scooted out of his chair and went to find Lyn, discovering her sorting through one of the many piles of books on the ground.

"I don't understand," he said with quickly failing calm. "Vallika Fatecry said my ancestor was involved in that legend, but we've looked through several books and haven't found anything!"

Lyn peered up at him from the floor and regarded him with a sideways look. "Um, the only demorin in that legend is Norox."

"She said Vaaskiir helped Approphas and Kaliina! That he tried to do good!" Valen explained hurriedly.

Lyn had no recognition in her eyes. "Uh, sorry, that's not true."

"It has to be!" Valen cried. "Why would she have lied to me?!"

"Maybe she just had her facts wrong?"

"What did Vaaskiir *do* then?!" Valen demanded, his tone raw with desperation.

Lyn frowned at him, the gesture awkward. "I don't know. I only recognize that name because of the Fangs of Hellbane."

Valen felt like screaming with frustration. He ran a hand through his hair and clutched at his scalp.

"There has to be more to this!" the demorinkin fretted. "It just — makes no sense!"

"The Fangs of Hellbane were lunatics," Lyn bitterly remarked. "They probably had no good reason for hunting you."

"Vallika herself told me they did!"

Lyn raised her brow at him, doubtful. "And you believed her?"

"She had no reason to lie!"

Lyn shrugged and dropped her attention back down onto the pile of books. "Sounds like she just wanted to drive you crazy."

Valen froze at that, struck by the potential truth of it. Could that be the case; did Vallika just stir up falsehoods to torture him?

'She planned to kill me...' Valen remembered. *'She didn't think I would have the chance to look into it!'*

"No..." Valen decided. "There's definitely more to this."

Lyn shrugged. "You can read every book in this library, but you're not going to find anything."

Valen gazed around the collection of shelves, thousands and thousands of books staring back at him.

"Maybe," he mumbled. "But I have to try."

■ ■ ■

The light shining through the stained glass eventually grew blue with night, suggesting it was time to head back to the hideout. Valen hesitantly closed the book in front of him, yet another adaptation of the Twin Roses that left out his ancestor.

"Ready to go?" Gavin gently asked him.

Valen left his chair, too bummed to reply.

Rorrik gently headbutted him on the shoulder. "I'm sorry we didn't find anything."

"You can always look another time," Lyn's voice then came from behind them. Valen turned to look at her, but she didn't meet his eyes. She shrugged and tossed back her hair. "I mean, if you really plan to read every book, you're definitely going to need more than a day."

Valen's expression softened into a weak grin. "Thank you, Lyn."

The celestborn stepped up to gather the books on the table. "I'll put these back. You're free to go."

■ ■ ■

Valen sat in the car, hypnotized by the beams of streetlights as the vehicle drove underneath them. He was groggy, disappointed, and more than ready for bed.

"So!" Rorrik then started from the front seat. "Who *was* that earlier?!"

Valen wasn't following. "Lyn?"

"No! *You*, silly!" Rorrik guffawed.

Valen tilted his head. "What do you mean?"

"You were incredible back there — talking all suave, getting Lyn to agree to let you in..." Rorrik turned to look at him, his emerald eyes beaming. "You were so *charming*!"

Valen's cheeks instantly heated with a deep blush. 'Charming?' He thought back to the conversation and his chest nearly burst with revelation. He had reverted back to his old self and was able to use charisma to his aid. Which meant —

"You're right!" he exclaimed, his cheeks straining with a smile.

Rorrik excitedly nodded, albeit with a hint of confusion.

"Do you know what that means?!" Valen went on, his heart singing. "It wasn't just the vest, after all! I'm *charming*!" A priorly insurmountable weight was lifted, leaving a lake of relief in its crater. 'I'm charming! I'm charming!'

Rorrik matched his smile and laughed. "I told you so!"

Valen was never happier to be proven wrong.

Chapter 47

Valen

The hideout's halls were still dim when Valen awoke the next morning, restless. Despite the early hour, he decided he was up for the day.

A quick sniff told him he could use a bath, and so he approached the dresser to grab a change of clothes. His attention found the vest, the garment still neatly sitting upon the outfit Rorrik had bought for him.

Valen mindfully stared at the article, as he had several times before, his chest tightening. In times prior, he would consider wearing it before rejecting the idea in the name of bleeding confidence, but now those wounds were patched and healing. He had established that his charisma was not a sole product of the vest, thus the hurt of the accusation was steadily fading.

He did not have to consider for long. Instead of leaving the vest behind with sunken pride, he grabbed it with fresh confidence, finally ready to wear it.

■ ■ ■

The bath instilled him with a contradicting mixture of relaxation and discomfort, his nakedness never failing to spark memories that haunted both his mind and body. Despite the therapy of cleansing away filth, he could not shake the traumatic recollection of shame and molestation, ice and pain. Bathing brought him back to a place that he hated to visit, thus he felt robbed of an activity that had always previously brought him peace and satisfaction.

A stubborn part of him still endeavored to enjoy the refreshing scent of shampoo and embrace of warm, sudsy water, but the discomfort spoke the loudest. Therefore, the bath was over quickly.

As he had hastily scrubbed himself, he noticed the sheen of his new scar and his thoughts found the Fangs of Hellbane. Much of him still failed to process the fact the Fangs of Hellbane were finished, let alone by his help. He wondered if his parents were proud of him, but the question brought more worry than comfort. How could they be, after he broke his promise? He stuffed those worries away, unwilling to face them.

Anticipation vibrated within Valen as he dried off from his bath and set his focus on his clothes. He stepped into the rich brown pants and donned the charcoal shirt, his fingers clumsy with excitement as he fiddled with each button.

Finally, he took up the vest and carefully shrugged into its familiar embrace. He fastened the buttons and turned to regard his reflection, his breath catching as he saw a familiar sight in the mirror.

His reflection brought him back to the clock tower, inciting a powerful surge of emotion. For a moment, it felt like he was just getting ready for another day in Akarth, but it was only a feeling. Akarth and the clock tower were gone; *Karreo* was gone.

All the feelings he had avoided were suddenly cornering him, forcing acknowledgment. Helpless, he gaped at his reflection as remorse and longing rocked him, like a boat on a raged sea. The guilt crashed over him in gnarly waves, drenching him.

It was all gone, and it was all *his* fault.

He gawked down at the vest, suddenly feeling utterly undeserving to wear it. Beside himself with self-contempt, he was starting to unbutton it when a stirring of grace froze his hand.

Mrs. Catty's advice echoed in his mind. *"We cannot forever regret what we did or did not do. There's no way to go back and change what happened. The only thing we can do is move on."*

Valen's hands shook, and he hung his head. How *could* he move on? The guilt was too heavy; he couldn't possibly carry it forward; it would weigh him down forever.

…Unless he let it go. His conscience balked and rejected the notion, offended at the mere idea of it. By letting go, it meant he accepted what happened; it meant that he had to forgive himself. Neither of those things were reasonable; he surely deserved to trudge through self-loathing forever.

…But he couldn't. Deep down he knew he shouldn't, either.

"I'm so sorry…" he mumbled out to Karreo, to his father, to himself. "I broke my promise… I-I ruined everything."

"You're so young, Valen. It was so much to ask of you, and he knew that. He would want you to forgive yourself," Mrs. Catty's prior words softly assured.

Would he want Valen to forgive himself, truly? He thought of his father, ever patient and caring, warm and gentle. Valen remembered his even temperament and understanding nature, how he had always been fair and reasonable. All signs pointed that he would forgive Valen, indeed, yet Valen still could not picture it.

After all, he had dated Siena even though he knew the risks. He had failed his shift and led terrible people to their home. He had broken his promise, and Karreo had been subjected to the consequences.

"Why *should* he forgive me?!" the demorinkin snapped hoarsely, wanting to scream but unable. "Why should I forgive myself?!"

He wanted to yank the vest off his back, but the grace within him surged and disallowed him. Valen leaned forward with a dry sob, feeling torn in two.

Mrs. Catty's wisdom echoed on. *"Forgiving ourselves doesn't come easily. It's a choice we have to make."*

Valen briefly regarded his reflection as conflict warred within him. *'I have to make the choice…'* His eyes squeezed shut, turning his face into a mess of wrinkles. *'I have to choose to forgive myself.'*

He did not want to; it spat on fairness and justice. It betrayed Karreo, his father, himself; he deserved to stay in the muck of his self-loathing.

"He would want you to forgive yourself," Mrs. Catty's words yet again reminded, piercing his argument.

The demorinkin buckled under the pressure of his emotions as he accepted Mrs. Catty was right. His father would not want him to wallow. His father would understand.

His father would want the best for him, and that meant moving on.

'I can't…' Valen slammed a fist against the mirror, despondent. *'I can't…'*

"It may take a long time to fully accept it, but the journey will never get started until we put a foot forward. I know it's hard, kit, but you have to move on."

He cracked his eyes open, his chest tight enough to choke him. He once again faced his reflection, his fist still braced against the glass.

He had to make the choice. He would keep sinking in muck, crushed under the impossible weight of self-hatred, until he made an effort to let go.

As impossible as it felt, he had to try.

He stared at himself, tears welling. All his mistakes stared back, all his loathing and shame and hopelessness. He forced himself to keep eye contact, his lip shuddering and his brow sunken.

His fist uncurled, and his hand pressed up against the glass. *'I forgive you…'*

His reflection began to shift, the red hue of his skin giving way to an olive tone. The sclera of his eyes brightened into white, and the yellow of his irises shown green. His horns melded into his head, and his tail retracted.

Sphinx stared back at him now, guilty and meek.

Valen's hand squeezed against the glass, and he touched his forehead against the mirror. "I… I forgive you…"

His shift did not fade away like it had several times before, remaining by the mercy of his forgiveness.

Valen stayed up against the mirror for a time, his heart and mind swirling with emotion. The miserable half of him endeavored to reject his apology, but the grace flowing through him encouraged otherwise. The fight ended in a draw as no obvious victor emerged.

The demorinkin finally stepped back from the mirror to size himself with a long look. Although he knew there was a long journey ahead, he had finally taken the first step in moving on.

…The next step would be brushing his hair. He fetched a comb and got to it, eager to see the knots sorted through.

. . .

Sphinx

His shift held even beyond his self-reconciliation in the mirror, filling him with a wonder on how long it would keep. Perhaps he was finally over the block that had prevented stability before.

He would only know if he put himself to the test. He decided he would be Sphinx for the day.

The clock showed it was five in the morning, still incredibly early. Sphinx had a couple of hours before the family would be awake. He *could* rest or study or read, but a different idea popped into his mind instead.

He walked into the kitchen and searched for an apron, finding one hanging on a hook next to the fridge. He adorned it so that his clothes would stay pristine as he prepared the family a hearty breakfast. Making a meal for the family would be a, however small, token of his appreciation for all they had done for him.

Sphinx had spent much too long out of a kitchen; the prospect of working with actual supplies and ingredients again filled him with anticipation.

He was mindful over what meal to prepare. It would be nice to share a piece of Akarth with the family; the area was known for its masterful cuisine, after all. A quiche with a side of fruit-stuffed crepes would show off his culture perfectly. He made a quick check for the supplies he needed and was thrilled to see they were all there.

The quiche would be stuffed with vegetables, onion, garlic, and spinach, along with shredded chicken and cheddar cheese. The crepes would have a sliced strawberry filling complete with fresh, hand-whipped cream. A dusting of powdered sugar on top for extra sweetness would complement the salty cheese of the quiche, while the tang of the strawberries would round out the pallet nicely.

He got to preparing the dough of the quiche, adhering to a recipe he had followed several times in the past. He beat together oil and water before combining it with a mixture of flour, salt, and pepper. He pressed the ingredients into a dough, pleasantly minding the feel of flour squishing past his fingers. He patted the dough until it was flat and then lifted it into a floured circular pan, pressing it against the sides to create a pie crust, then storing it in the fridge to chill.

404

Next came cutting an onion and mincing a clove of garlic, Sphinx feeling bubbly with nostalgia as he worked the familiar motions of chopping. He sautéed the vegetables until they were crispy and golden and then added a generous a handful of spinach. The aroma of the ingredients danced about the kitchen as he worked, a scent he had longed to breathe in again. When the mixture was cooked enough, he set it aside in a separate bowl.

Using the same skillet, he browned some chicken before shredding it into stringy pieces with a knife and fork. As the meat sizzled, he separated a yolk from an egg, saving only the white. He noted with satisfaction that he hadn't lost even a drop of the egg to the counter. A quick nibble told the meat was well seasoned. He pulled out the crust from the fridge, brushed the egg white onto it, then layered on a generous handful of cheese crumbles, the vegetables and chicken.

Sphinx then whisked several eggs in a large bowl, completing the mixture with milk and a pinch of seasoning. He watched with satisfaction as the ingredients meshed together, forming into an ideal shade of pale yellow. He then slowly and patiently poured it into the crust, allowing the liquid to drain into the nooks of the chicken and vegetables.

He topped the quiche with more cheese crumbles and then stuffed it into the oven to cook, where it would stay for the next forty minutes or so. He wiped his brow and broke into a smile; it felt wonderful to be able to cook again, to create.

"Who are you?" a familiar voice then came from directly behind him, causing Sphinx to start with a jump.

The disguised human swung around and saw Talis standing there, the youngest felidaren's eyes large and curious, as they often were.

Sphinx could not fend off a smirk as he regarded the child. He gave a little bow, cheeky.

"You can call me Sphinx," he introduced, indulging in the fun of his persona. Surely Talis could tell it was actually Valen, but still he played.

"Okay, Sphinx!" Talis chirped. He then peeked at the oven behind Sphinx, his head dramatically tilting. "Sooo, what're you doing?"

"Why, I'm preparing breakfast!" Sphinx answered with a giggle. "Would you want to help?"

Talis' ears perked, and his expression burst with excitement. "Yeah, yeah!"

Sphinx laughed at his enthusiasm. "Alright, you can help me make the crepes!"

"Grapes?" Talis incorrectly echoed, perplexed.

Sphinx chuckled. "No, no, *crepes*. They're almost like pancakes."

"Oooh!" Talis bounced up and down. "I love pancakes!"

"You should like these, then," Sphinx told him through a smile. "First, we need to combine the wet ingredients. Do you know how to crack eggs?"

"Yeah, yeah!" Talis assured, still bouncing.

Sphinx gestured to the carton of eggs. "You can help me crack them, then! We will be putting in three eggs total."

Talis fetched an egg and cracked it with surprising dexterity, clean and efficient.

Sphinx was impressed. "Wow, great job!" he guffawed and began measuring the milk. "Why don't you crack all of them, actually?"

"Okay!" Talis accepted with glee. He hastily made work of all three eggs, each crack as solid as the last.

Sphinx poured in the milk, the eggs morphing into a yellow and white marble as the ingredients collided. He then added water, Talis watching with bated attention.

"We need to melt down butter," Sphinx mentioned before dropping a brick of such into a glass dish. He focused for a moment on a spell, and the butter responded by rapidly melting. He felt a pulse of fatigue as he did so, a sour reminder of his prior strain. *'Right, not supposed to perform magic for a week...'*

Talis sounded in a thrilled squeal. "You can do magic?!"

Sphinx chuckled and dripped the liquid butter into the bowl. "If you're impressed by that, wait until you taste these. That'll be the real magic."

He added a pinch of salt to the mixture and then a few spoonfuls of sugar. With that, he handed Talis a whisk. "Go ahead and whisk that up."

Talis followed orders, giddy as he stirred.

Sphinx kept a close eye. "Try doing this motion instead," he offered advice, demonstrating with his hands.

Talis giggled and matched his example to near perfection. *'Wow! He's a fast learner!'*

Once the mixture was adequately beaten, Sphinx measured some flour before adding it in all at once as to not thin out the batter. "Keep stirring!"

Talis seemed more than willing to continue.

The batter gobbled up the flour before long, and Sphinx nodded with approval. "That's good; looks fantastic!" He held out a hand for a high five and Talis reciprocated, punctuating with a giggle.

"What now?!" the youngest brother questioned, ever enthusiastic.

"Now we get to cook them," Sphinx answered with a chuckle. He started a flame under a fresh skillet and let it grow hot before dropping butter on its surface, the action resulting in a satisfying sizzle.

"Watch me closely, alright?" Sphinx told the felidaren. He scooped out some batter and poured it over the skillet, simultaneously tilting the pan so the batter completely spread across the surface in a thin layer.

"Whoa! That's a really big pancake!"

Sphinx chuckled at that. "It's so you can fold them up, like an omelet."

"Ooooh," Talis hummed.

When bubbles began to dot the side of the batter, Sphinx gingerly lifted the side of the crepe to check its progress and noted an approving shade of gold. He then flipped the crepe with practiced skill and let the other side cook.

Talis looked on, his tail ticking. "It's so skinny!"

"That's a crepe for you," Sphinx replied with a twitch of his lip. Once the crepe was fully cooked, he moved it to a plate to cool. "Since you're so good at whisking, why don't you start making the whipped cream?"

"How do I do that?" Talis wondered, his kitten eyes round with intrigue.

Sphinx turned around to pour some cream into another sizable bowl and added a couple spoonfuls of sugar. "Just whisk that until it becomes fluffy." He handed the tabby a clean whisk.

"That's easy!" Talis didn't spare a second.

"It takes a while, but you can do it!" Sphinx encouraged. He returned to the stove and got to preparing another crepe, and then another. The scraping of fervent mixing and perfume of cooking batter filled him with warmth; it felt wonderful to cook again.

He was more than a few crepes in when he turned to check up on Talis' progress, seeing that the cream was nearly done as it raised up in airy peaks. When the mountains went stiff, he nodded at the tabby. "There you go, it's done!"

Talis quit whisking and stuck a finger into the whipped cream, stealing a taste. He laughed and danced, leading Sphinx to assume it tasted exceptional.

"Leave some for the crepes!" the disguised human joked.

Once the batter was exhausted, he got right to slicing the strawberries. Upon finishing, he rained a light kiss of sugar over the slices and offered Talis a broad smile. "Well, it's time to stuff them!"

■ ■ ■

Rorrik

A homey waft of bread and eggs greeted Rorrik as he dragged himself out of slumber. With a stretch and a yawn, he groggily rolled off the loft bed and to the floor below, landing cleanly despite his sleepiness.

He spared a look at the queen bed, seeing it was empty; Valen must have already woken up for the day.

Enticed by the aroma of breakfast, he made his way to the kitchen after a quick stop to the bathroom. He stepped into the room, overtaken by a powerful scent of onions and garlic. He expected to see his mother standing in front of the stove, but a stranger was there instead, immediately jolting him awake. There weren't supposed to be any guests at the hideout!

He was about to be alarmed when he noticed Talis was calmly standing next to the stranger, helping him stuff some kind of… pancake?

"Talis! Who is this?" Rorrik questioned sharply, his brow furrowed.

"This is Sphinx!" Talis answered, normal enough.

The stranger, an olive-skinned human with charcoal black hair that was parted handsomely down the middle, lifted his head and regarded Rorrik with forest green eyes. He looked stunningly familiar, but…

"Hello there," the human greeted, his voice rich with an Akarthi accent. "As he said, I am Sphinx."

Rorrik gawked at the stranger as his voice incited the same sense of familiarity. It then clicked. "Valen?!"

Valen tilted his head with a polite smile. "Who?"

"What— you—" What happened to his red skin and horns and tail?! The memory of walking in on Valen changing his form answered that wonder. *'He must have shifted!'*

"Wait, you're Valen?!" Talis gasped. "Whoa!"

"No, no, I am Sphinx," Valen chuckled. "You are mistaken."

"You shifted!" Rorrik said.

Valen's chuckling turned to fledged laughter. "That I did!"

Rorrik cocked his head. "Aren't you not supposed to be doing magic?"

"This is different," Valen excused. "Shifting is a natural ability, not a spell, so it doesn't take any runa expenditure. My dad once explained it that my body is always under the effect of a spell of sorts, therefore that runa has already been spent."

Rorrik didn't claim to understand that, but took his word for it. He went on to look Valen up and down, seeing that the demorinkin was wearing his mother's apron. His attention fell on the food and he raised his brow.

"Did you make these?"

"With help of Talis, yes!" Valen replied with a smile.

"I whisked and stuff!" Talis proclaimed, puffing his chest with pride.

"Wait, so you can cook?"

"I like to think I can." Valen shrugged, still smiling. "I've been doing it since I was a kid."

"He's really good!" Talis vouched.

Valen returned to stuffing the pancake-like dish with strawberries and whipped cream. "Would you like to help us, Rorrik?"

Rorrik stepped up with a nod. "Sure!"

"You can help stuff. Talis, you can start sprinkling the wrapped ones with powdered sugar."

Talis bounced eagerly. "Yeah, yeah!"

■ ■ ■

The rest of his brothers had a similar reaction when they first walked into the kitchen and mistook Valen as a stranger. For whatever reason, Valen still insisted his name was Sphinx each time, confusing Rorrik. They knew he was Valen, he could drop the act!

A timer went off, and Valen retrieved a pie-like dish from the oven that smelt of eggs, chicken, vegetables, and cheese.

"Whoa! You made a pie?!" Talis cried, thrilled.

Valen laughed as he placed it on a cooling rack. "It's a quiche. It's a dish we like to make in Akarth."

"Akarth is so cool!" Talis gushed. "You have pie for breakfast!"

His mother then walked into the room, her eyes narrow but her lips spread in a smile. "Who made breakfast?"

"Valen did!" Rorrik answered.

"And me!" Talis pitched in.

Valen's disguised olive skin went pink with a blush and he smiled. "I wanted to show my gratitude for... everything. I know it's not much, but—"

"Don't be silly!" his mother assured. "This is wonderful!" She then looked the demorinkin, rather human, over. "I see you shifted!"

Valen nodded.

"...and you're wearing my apron!" the tortoiseshell laughed.

Valen nervously grinned. "I hope that's not a problem!"

"Not at all!"

"Sooo, is it all done, then?" Jate asked from the table.

"After the quiche cools, yes," Valen replied. "The crepes are ready, though."

"Crepes? Is that what these are?" Quinn wondered, inspecting one of the pancake-like treats.

"They're huuuge pancakes!" Talis exclaimed, spreading his arms to describe his point.

Valen giggled. "Kind of. They're pastries that you can stuff with anything. These are filled with strawberries and whipped cream."

"Sounds delicious!" Jate said.

"I'll say!" Quinn agreed.

"This stuff is weird..." Calvin whined.

"Give it a chance, kit. Valen worked very hard on it," their mother said.

"I made the whipped cream!" Talis pointed out.

Their parent ruffled the youngest's hair. "You did a great job, cub."

When the quiche was cooled, they all grabbed a piece along with a crepe and gathered around the table to eat. Valen sat down next to Rorrik, still shifted.

Rorrik took his first bite of the quiche and tasted an explosion of salty flavor. He eagerly swallowed the bite and took another. "This is really good!"

The rest of his family dug in before expressing their own approval.

Calvin was the slowest as he pecked at his slice of quiche before taking a tentative bite. He chewed it for a long second and then scooped up another mouthful. He shrugged, letting that be his blessing.

Valen sat straighter and dipped his head in a nod. "I'm so glad!"

"Hope you don't mind cooking more often!" Jate jested.

"It would be my pleasure."

Rorrik bit into the crepes and was met with the tang of strawberries and fluff of whipped cream, accompanied by the mildly sweet dough of the crepes, made sweeter still by the powdered sugar. It was *delicious*!

"Oh, wow," he gushed before swallowing. "That is *awesome*."

The others took a bite of the crepes and mirrored his reaction.

"It's so tasty!" Talis shouted.

"You're truly an exceptional chef," Quinn told Valen.

Rorrik nodded and bumped his shoulder into his friend. "You really are!"

Valen was beaming, his smile strikingly handsome. "You're all too kind, thank you."

"And thank *you* for doing this," their mother said. "It's very appreciated."

"You're quite welcome," the demorinkin replied. "It's the least I could do."

■ ■ ■

"So, do you still want to go out on the town today?" Rorrik asked Valen after breakfast.

Valen met his eyes with a grin, nodding. "Yeah, let's do it!"

Rorrik was thrilled. "Really?!"

Valen assured him with another nod.

"You're going to love it — I know just the place to bring you! You can see the city really well from it!"

Valen laughed. "I can't wait!"

"I have to say, that's an interesting wardrobe choice, Valen," Jate then commented in a snicker.

Valen glanced down at himself and saw that he was still wearing the apron. "Ha! Whoops!" He began to unstring it and pulled the article away, revealing...

"The vest!" Rorrik gasped, taken aback. Underneath it was the outfit he had bought for Valen.

Valen looked down at himself. "Oh, right!" He shifted back into his demorinkin self and struck a pose. "What do you think?"

Valen looked more handsome than ever in his new clothes. Rorrik couldn't pull his eyes away, enthralled by the shapely look of the vest and snug fit of the pants.

"You look amazing!" the tabby complimented, still mid-stare.

As he proceeded to admire, his lower abdomen responded with stimulation, and he flushed with surprise and confusion. He yanked his eyes to the floor and blinked, stunned.

"It's so nice to wear it again..." Valen sighed, evident with relief.

Rorrik forced himself to look up and saw the demorinkin's attention was still on his clothes.

'Thankfully...'

Valen then faced him, his smile bright and warm. "Thank you so much, again."

Rorrik's fur caught fire as he stared directly into Valen's eyes, enchanted by the demorinkin's charm. "I—" he stammered, but no words followed. Embarrassment added to Rorrik's flush. 'What's wrong with me?!'

"Whoa-ho-ho!" Jate then interrupted, turning around from doing the dishes. "Looking good there, Valen!"

"Indeed! Very dapper!" Quinn added from wiping the table.

Gavin poked his head in from the living room. "Red is definitely your color."

Valen absorbed the praise with a little bow. "Why, thank you!"

Rorrik swallowed hard and began a fast trot to his bedroom. "I'm going to get dressed, then we can go!"

■ ■ ■

Rorrik had never taken so long to put together an outfit. Everything he tried seemed to clash or was silly or just flat-out bad. He had finally made his mind up on a two-toned purple shirt accompanied by black capris, but he was still far from satisfied. He worried if he looked good or not, but he had already kept Valen waiting for far too long.

He returned to the kitchen to find Valen, but he was turned back into a human again.

"Why are you shifted?" Rorrik asked, confused.

Valen's disguised green eyes found him. "Now that I can shift again, I want to see if I can hold it all day long. I need to prove to myself that I can, you know?"

Rorrik couldn't help but prefer his natural form. The tabby battled with disappointment and bluffed a grin. "Oh, okay! That makes sense!"

Valen nodded before looking the felidaren up and down. "I like your shirt! Purple is a fantastic color on you!"

Rorrik's fur was reignited and he sloppily dropped his attention to his outfit. "Uh, um— thanks!" He winced as he yet again stuttered.

"You're welcome!" Valen replied. "So, where are we going?"

Rorrik walked towards the stairs, attempting to recover from his social blunder. He felt a tad more confident with his back to Valen. "You'll see!"

▪ ▪ ▪

Sphinx

For the first time, he was brought out of the hideout via the steps instead of a secret passage. Rorrik leading the way, they headed up the stairs and stepped into what appeared to be a storage room, as there were bins and boxes strewn about.

Rorrik didn't dawdle. They kept walking out into a hall and then through double doors that opened into a sizable lobby.

Sphinx spared a captivated look around. A pallet of relaxed browns and reds decorated the room, which spanned two stories in the center of the space, framed by a loft. A stairwell allowed access to the second floor, and a fireplace joined by a cozy seating area spanned the front wall, complete with tall windows. A bar was tucked away in the back where they had stepped out, a seating area with booths to the front of it. Several tables occupied the floor, housing a handful of patrons.

A burly human man with a crown of auburn hair was standing behind the bar. "'Morning, Rorrik. Who's your friend?"

"Hey, Walter!" Rorrik greeted before gesturing to Sphinx. "This is Valen!"

"It's a pleasure to meet you, sir," the disguised human said, offering his hand out.

The man accepted his shake with a stiff grip. "And you as well, lad. Name's Walter Felle."

"Walter is the innkeeper," Rorrik explained.

Sphinx smiled politely. "You have a lovely inn, Mr. Felle."

Mr. Felle snorted at that. "Perhaps after she's had a scrub! Rorrik, I could use a paw with that."

"No can do, we've got plans!" Rorrik rejected with a pinch of sass.

"Oh? And what's more important than scrubbing your pads raw?" Mr. Felle pried, his tone snarky.

"I'm showing Valen the city!"

Mr. Felle chortled before punctuating with a smirk. "That'll do. Best get to it, then."

412

Chapter 48

Sphinx

They sat on a bus, Sphinx glancing around with a sense of wary curiosity. The vehicle was packed with a copious cast of different individuals, some dressed for business, others adorned for performing, and others still in mundane get-ups.

The disguised human felt naked and paranoid being in the company of so many others. He endeavored to remember that the worst of his worries were behind him, that he no longer had to fret over the Fangs of Hellbane hunting him down. The faces of strangers no longer held threat of murder or ill intentions; he had nothing to fear. Despite knowing this, his anxiety was not so easily swayed, as the past still cast a long, influencing shadow.

And so, he set his attention instead on the window, watching buildings of striking gray pass by, the cool colors of the architecture livened by a cheerfully blue sky. It was mild and sunny outside, with an active breeze gifted by the lakefront; a perfect summer day.

Rorrik leaned over him and pointed out the window. "So, right now we are close to Farpoint," the tabby mentioned. "It's a huge shopping district in the city. It's close to Downton, which is the main hub of the city — lots of skyscrapers and businesses. Pretty much like The Ring in Akarth."

The Ring was the most famous downtown area in central Akarth. It was named such for a man-made canal that branched off the river on opposing sides and looped into the city, forming a circle. The most famous buildings made up the skyline there.

Sphinx had vaguely heard of Downton; he knew that Sengard's skyline was famous for it, at least.

"We'll stop by Farpoint and I can show you around there. Then, we can walk to Downton. After that, there's a place there I can't wait to show you!"

Sphinx accepted the plan with a nod. "Sounds great!"

. . .

Rorrik told him they were close to their destination when Sphinx began to see towering skyscrapers on the horizon. *'That must be Downton!'*

The bus ride was a solid half hour as the route weaved through dense traffic to the ambiance of constant honking, leaving no doubt that they were heading deeper into the city.

They exited the bus at a stop with a good chunk of the patrons, mostly the performers and mundane. The businessmen were likely headed to Downton, to one of the several skyscrapers that lined the horizon ahead.

A crowded street greeted them upon arrival, instantly overstimulating Sphinx. He stood closer to Rorrik for support, focusing on his desire to explore rather than his worry. He was there to have fun, not long for another quiet day in the hideout.

Rorrik gave him an encouraging smile and started forward, moving with the crowd seamlessly. Sphinx struggled to keep up, bombarded by the rush.

Rorrik noted his difficulty and reached for the disguised human's hand with a snicker, the felidaren's paw pads curiously smooth as they pressed into his palm. "This way, come on!"

Sphinx followed Rorrik's lead as the tabby shuffled through the crowd, never letting go of his hand. They walked faster than most of the mass, which meant lots of weaving and gentle pushing.

As they went, Sphinx couldn't help but notice them receiving a collection of dirty looks, leading him to assume that many were less than happy about their urgency. Rorrik didn't seem to mind, but Sphinx kept his head low, feeling rude.

They moved with the crowd until they found themselves at the edge of a massive plaza, an impressive fountain at the heart of it. Sphinx gaped all around, seeing stall after stall and a plethora of different businesses bordering the street.

"So, this is Farpoint Plaza!" Rorrik said with a sweeping gesture.

"It's huge!" Sphinx gawked.

Rorrik responded with a laugh. "This is only the beginning! There's a lot more to see!"

■ ■ ■

They spent the entire morning and start of afternoon exploring about Farpoint. Several streets stretched out from the plaza, all offering their own unique shops and stalls. Between clothing stores, trinket shops, and furniture warehouses, it seemed there was nothing left to be desired and everything to browse.

Street performers enticed onlookers with displays of artistry, athletics, and skill, earning Sphinx's attention on more than one occasion. One performer could create stunning paintings with a mere smudging of their fingers, while another danced in an outfit that fanned out in a brilliant circle when they spun. Rorrik had lent Sphinx some coinage to tip the performers, to his delight.

They still had one more street to head down before they journeyed towards Downton. Sphinx had his attention on the shops as they strolled along, watchful for which place to browse next.

A sign in the shape of a treble clef demanded his attention. 'Trouble Clef', it read on a musical staff next to it.

Sphinx was instantly intrigued. "Let's go there!"

Rorrik followed his gaze. "The music store?"

"Yes!"

The felidaren seemed eager. "Alright!"

They walked into the business and a jovial bell dinged on their arrival. The shop was crammed with a stunning collection of instruments, from clarinets to drums to violins to...

'Guitars!' An entire wall of them!

Sphinx hurried up to have a closer look, Rorrik at his side. He gaped up at the instruments with a mixture of longing and excitement, his thoughts on his old guitar.

"Can I help you boys?" a clerk asked, a clay-skinned orc with smooth hair pulled back in a neat half ponytail. His tusks were thick and rounded rather than sharp.

"No, thank you! We're just browsing!" Sphinx dismissed.

"Very well. If you wish, you may pull a guitar off the wall and have a strum." With that, the clerk walked off to stand behind a counter.

Sphinx was tempted to take up that offer. He only needed to stare at the wall for a short second, quick to decide. He gingerly retrieved an acoustic guitar of reddened wood, the body giving a sheen as he lowered it.

He glided his fingers along the strings, the instrument responding with a rich hum. Sphinx's heart swelled at the sound, a bittersweet sensation. He again strummed the guitar, this time in a chord.

Rorrik watched him with a tilted head, appearing curious.

Sphinx was incredibly rusty, but that did not discourage him from playing a simple melody. By the grace of muscle memory, his fingers fell into form without difficulty, taking him by surprise. He recited a song he had always liked to play when warming up, the notes familiar and warm.

Rorrik gasped before flashing a thrilled smile. "You can play?!"

Sphinx shrugged modestly as he continued to strum. "I used to."

"That's so cool!" Rorrik gushed. "Why don't you anym—" the felidaren cut off and his ears pressed back. "Oh, right, sorry..."

Sphinx shook his head and offered a weak grin. "It's okay."

"You sound wonderful!" the clerk then contributed from the counter. "You picked out a wonderful guitar, there. Felkrith mahogany, very dignified."

Sphinx glanced at the price tag, reading a very dignified eight hundred Pines. He could not help but wince.

That made the clerk chuckle. "Worth every copper, I assure you."

Sphinx returned the guitar to its spot on the wall. "I have no doubt!"

They proceeded to look around the shop, spending a lengthy time browsing and fiddling with other instruments. Eventually, they had to leave the music shop behind, Sphinx mindful over the guitar. He already missed the slight resistance of strings as they slipped past his fingers and the soothing resonance of the instrument's voice.

However, it was all but a memory. His guitar was gone, left buried in the rubble of his old life.

"Are you hungry?" Rorrik then asked, interrupting Sphinx's sulking.

The question brought a hollow feeling in Sphinx's stomach to the forefront of his mind. The disguised human simply nodded.

"I know a place we can get great sandwiches!" Rorrik said. "It's just up ahead!"

■ ■ ■

Following lunch, they made the hike towards Downton. Before long, they were standing between buildings that stretched impossibly high in majestic stature, a marvel of architecture.

"There's a building with a great view," Rorrik brought up eventually. "It... takes a bit of a climb to get to it, though."

"Climb?" Sphinx echoed.

Rorrik nodded before flashing a smirk. "Think you can handle it?"

Sphinx wasn't certain. "When you say... climb...?"

Rorrik snorted. "Don't worry, there's stairs."

■ ■ ■

The felidaren laughed at him from the next floor. "Come on! It's not that much longer!"

"You said that five floors ago!" Sphinx whined, his chest heaving with a heavy pant.

Rorrik hooted. "I really mean it this time! Don't worry!"

They were escalating a fire escape that spanned up many, *many* floors. Sphinx hoped the view was worth the ascent, let alone the eventual descent!

Fortunately, Rorrik wasn't lying. Only three floors later they were finally stepping onto a roof, the hustle of the streets below a distant clamor.

Sphinx had to compose himself as he leaned over, attempting to catch his breath. Rorrik seemed hardly fazed by the trek.

"You're lucky we took the easy way!" the tabby teased.

Sphinx shot him an incredulous look. "And what's the hard way, then?"

Rorrik smirked and gave a wink. "Minus the stairs!"

Surely he had to be joking. Sphinx shook his head and let another huff go before gasping in a deep breath.

"Man, you're really winded!" the tabby commented.

"Well, I *am* still recovering from magical exhaustion," Sphinx reminded.

"Oooh yeah, right. Sorry!" Rorrik's amusement faded from his face. "Are you okay?"

"Yeah, yeah, don't worry!" Sphinx dispelled. "I just… need a second."

"Well, when you're ready…" Rorrik walked up to the edge of the building and leaned over a stone railing, his tail swishing. "The view is waiting."

Sphinx decided he was well enough to at least make his way over to the edge. He came up next to Rorrik and spared a look down, the sight stealing away the breath he was gasping for.

They were at least fifteen stories above the streets, their vantage offering a sightly view of the city. Sphinx gawked at the streets below and the high-rise buildings that still rose straight ahead, unsure of what to focus on.

Rorrik pointed west. "If you look over that way you can see part of Northstone Park!"

Sphinx followed his finger and saw treetops and an expanse of grass instead of cobblestone. It stretched on behind what their viewpoint could cover.

"It's really big — I'll have to take you there another day!"

Sphinx smiled at the tabby. "I'd like that."

Rorrik returned his smile and gazed back out to the city, his brunette hair dancing in the breeze and his emerald eyes vivid. Sphinx found himself staring, caught by the sight of him.

"So, that's Uptop Bank." Rorrik gestured to a building northeast of them. "And that's Connection Trade. That over there is Arlin Suites, and that's…"

Each building name blended into the other as Rorrik pointed out one after another. Sphinx still nodded, however, overwhelmed.

"Well, if you want to get going, there's one last place I want to bring you!" Rorrik said after they marveled at the view for a while longer.

Sphinx internally winced at the idea of going down the stairs. "Yeah, let's go."

Instead of heading back to the fire escape, Rorrik walked to a door that lead into the building they stood on. The tabby inserted a key and opened the passage, beckoning Sphinx inside. "I only imagine you want to take the elevator this time."

Sphinx flinched with indignant shock. "There's an elevator?!"

Rorrik smiled innocently. "Well, yeah!"

"Then why did we take the fire escape?!" Sphinx fretted.

Rorrik laughed at him before slipping inside. "Come on, let's go!"

■ ■ ■

They took a taxi to wherever Rorrik had in store next in order to preserve Sphinx's energy.

The lake came into view, so big it looked more like an ocean. Lake Conigan was one of the most expansive lakes in all the realm of Azyria, larger even than several seas. Sengard was its crowning gem, a shining beacon of the trade route along the lake.

Sphinx watched the horizon, seeing docks and several boats ahead. Then, something more striking caught his eye: a massive pier that stretched on and on, complete with a roller coaster and a ferris wheel!

Rorrik nudged him, his fangs showing in a thrilled smile. "That's where we're going! Gard Pier!"

The taxi dropped them off on the lake's edge, next to a path that led along the water. A thick swarm of people trudged along it, Sphinx anxious to join them.

After paying the driver, Rorrik brought them forward. "It's a short walk from here!"

They moved with the mass of people, Rorrik not as fast and pushy this time around. Regardless, Sphinx still noticed people giving them dirty looks.

For a moment, he suspected his shift might have failed, but when he checked his hands he saw olive skin, and when he turned to look behind him he spotted no tail. *'But, then why...?'*

He noticed a person reposition their bag to their front, and Sphinx watched as they glared specifically at Rorrik, not Sphinx.

The disguised human furrowed his brow as his lips sunk in a frown. Why were they looking at Rorrik that way?

They arrived in front of sizable building, a lit, gigantic sign sprawling across the front of it: 'Gard Pier'.

They headed inside with the crowd, entering a multistoried room with a glass ceiling. Vendor carts were scattered all around, a river of people coursing throughout the space. Multiple doors beckoned ahead, huge windows revealing what lay beyond their passage: a fairground.

Rorrik grabbed his hand and tugged him forward. "We've done enough browsing today! Let's go on some rides!"

■ ■ ■

They spent the next couple of hours doing just that. From a modest roller coaster to a spinning pendulum, they had ridden all there was to ride.

All, that is, but the ferris wheel.

"We'll wait until it's getting dark for that one!" Rorrik had excused. "The city looks its best then!"

There was still another hour or so until then, but Rorrik promised he had a great way to spend the time: fair games.

"Aren't these rigged?" Sphinx whispered as they stood in line for a dart toss.

Rorrik snorted. "Yep!"

Sphinx slowly raised a brow. "So, you're just going to throw money at it?"

"No, silly," Rorrik smirked. "I'm going to throw the darts."

Sphinx shook his head and offered his own smirk. "You seem confident."

"For good reason!" Rorrik boasted. "I win these things all the time."

"Oh yeah?"

"Yeah!"

"This ought to be good, then!" Sphinx teased.

Rorrik's turn came and he gave Sphinx a wink before tossing the first dart.

It clanked to the ground prior to flirting with a balloon.

Rorrik's ears began to press back, but then he smiled. "Just warming up!"

He threw another…

…only to have similar results.

Yet another toss yielded the same, and so on.

Sphinx couldn't stop himself from snickering. "What was that about winning these things all the time?"

Rorrik rolled his eyes at him.

"It's a shame. I was really wanting that griffon." Sphinx pointed up to the largest prize the game awarded.

Rorrik looked up, his expression hardening with resolve. "…I'm going to win it. Just watch!"

Rorrik placed money for a second round, only to fail again. He gave it another try, still coming out a griffon short. Sphinx began to feel bad after the fourth try.

"Rorrik, I was just kidding…" he attempted to dissuade, but the felidaren wasn't having it.

"I've got it down now," Rorrik promised.

A few popped balloons vouched for that claim. However, two out of five of the darts still missed.

The attendant handed over the medium prize, a serpentine dragon. "Have to pop all five for the biggest prize," they reminded.

"The dragon is good enough—" Sphinx tried, but Rorrik slammed down another payment.

The tabby then took a deep breath and relaxed, his eyes closing. He spent a few seconds in that pose before snapping back to attention, determined.

He threw the first dart. *Pop.*

He tossed the second. *Pop.*

Yet another. *Pop.*

"Three in a row!" Sphinx cheered, impressed.

Rorrik didn't respond as he chucked another dart. *Pop.*

Sphinx was stunned. "Only one more!"

Rorrik once again relaxed before sending off the last dart.

Pop.

"You did it!" Sphinx shouted in a mixture of amazement and disbelief.

Clapping sounded, and Sphinx turned to see that a modest crowd had gathered. They cheered as Rorrik was handed the griffon plush, the tabby giving a bow.

He then offered it to Sphinx.

The disguised human shook his head. "Rorrik, I was just kidding!"

"I won it for you!" Rorrik pushed. "It's yours!"

Sphinx's cheeks warmed with a blush as the crowd cooed with awws. He took the griffon, touched. "Well, thank you!"

Rorrik beamed at him. "I told you I can win these!"

Sphinx smiled back. "You certainly showed me, huh?"

■　■　■

The pier was alit with vibrant lights of playful colors, courtesy of the games and streamers. The sky was finally purple with dusk, the perfect time to ride the ferris wheel, as Rorrik had argued.

They currently were in the queue for the ride, both munching on the hotdogs and milkshakes they had purchased for dinner. The line moved at a decent pace until finally it was their turn to board.

Sphinx looked out as the ride raised them upwards, slow and steady. His gaze eagerly took in the sight of the city, the buildings bright and alive with dazzling lights. It contrasted the gloom of dusk with beautiful starkness, the city taking on an even more majestic persona than its daytime alter ego.

As they rose higher and higher, the view became more and more lovely, Sphinx enchanted by the glow of the city.

Rorrik was right; it was worth waiting, after all.

Rorrik

Rorrik's attention was not on the city, but instead on Valen. The tabby's heart sung at the wonder in his friend's eyes, at how happy he was. The felidaren felt an encompassing wave of pride and relief; it was so rewarding to see Valen having fun.

The disguised human gaped out into the horizon, utterly enamored. Rorrik gazed at him in admiration all the while, appreciating the way his hair framed his face and the lights danced in his widened eyes. He looked so handsome, so—

Valen turned to look at him. "This is fantastic!"

Rorrik flushed as they locked eyes. "Y-yeah! Isn't it?"

"It really is!" Valen went back to regarding the city. "It's so beautiful!"

Rorrik peered out to finally have a gander of his own. 'Yeah... yeah it is.'

. . .

They stepped down the stairs to the hideout, both tired but still in high spirits. They reached the basement and Valen gave a relieved sigh before his form abruptly began to shift. His human disguise melted away, revealing his true form.

"That feels sooo much better," the demorinkin said, stretching.

"Looks better, too!" Rorrik added with a nudge, excited to see the real Valen again.

Valen turned to look at him and warmly grinned. The demorinkin then wrapped his arms around Rorrik in a tight hug, taking the tabby by surprise. "Thanks..."

Rorrik returned the embrace with a nuzzle. "Any time..."

The hug dissipated, and Rorrik fought a yawn, not wanting to go to bed just yet.

"So... what do you want to do now?" the tabby questioned, somewhat hesitant.

Valen grinned at him, almost knowingly. "Well, we never did have that sleepover, huh?"

Rorrik leapt with excitement. "No, no we didn't!"

Valen retrieved the cupcakes from the oven, splashing the room with a chocolatey aroma. "They look done!"

"Finally!" Rorrik cheered.

The demorinkin placed the cupcakes on a cooling rack. "Now, to wait for them to cool."

The two had been up talking for a couple of hours before the demorinkin got the idea to bake cupcakes. Despite the late hour (and partly because of it), Rorrik had immediately taken to the plan.

Valen had prepared the batter from scratch, Rorrik intrigued by the demorinkin's culinary prowess. They had joked and goofed off throughout the process, trying to keep quiet but mostly failing.

Rorrik was sat up on a counter, his gaze on the cupcakes. "They came out great!"

He turned his attention back on Valen, seeing that the demorinkin was suddenly staring at his feet, his brow furrowed.

Worry struck Rorrik. "What's wrong?"

"I couldn't help but notice…" Valen began, his voice serious. "People kept… looking at you weird when we were out. Why… why is that?"

Rorrik blinked at him, taken off balance by the switch of topic. His shoulders lifted in an exaggerated shrug. "Uh… probably thought I was going to pickpocket them or something."

Valen squinted at him. "What? Why? Do they… know what you do?"

Rorrik scoffed. "Pffft, no. They just assume."

Valen kept his narrowed gaze on him. "…Assume what, exactly?"

He gave another shrug and tried to smirk. "…That because I'm felidaren, I'm out to rob or scam them or something."

Valen dropped his gaze to the floor, and his lips went tight. He was quiet for a lengthy moment. "So, all this time you've been telling me not to worry about prejudice even though you *face it yourself*?" The demorinkin appeared troubled as his words were strained.

Rorrik frowned. "Well, uh, I *guess* so…"

"It's not 'I guess so'! That's prejudice, Rorrik!" Valen snapped.

Rorrik held up his hands defensively. "Valen, I mean, come on. They aren't wrong!"

"What's that supposed to mean?!"

"Well, I've done those things!" Rorrik awkwardly admitted. "So, they're not wr—"

"They *are* wrong! They *assumed*, Rorrik! Just because you're felidaren! That's wrong!"

The two of them stared at each other, the room tense.

Valen then looked away, and the intensity in his expression softened. "I… I'm sorry. I shouldn't… I just…" He squeezed his eyes shut. "It… bothers me that you… that you have to deal with it, too."

422

Rorrik wasn't sure how to react. He eventually grinned weakly. "It's okay! I'm used to it."

Valen sighed, his eyes still clamped shut. "That's the problem."

. . .

Impatience had them frosting the cupcakes before they were fully cooled. The tension from earlier had mostly dissolved, but Valen was much quieter.

Rorrik eyed the cupcake in his hand as he guided the frosting on it upwards in a swirl, just as Valen had taught him to. The tabby then smiled. "Isn't it funny that this was the first thing we did after we met?"

Valen looked over with a blink. "That's right, isn't it?"

Rorrik nodded. "Yep!"

Valen chuckled as he frosted his own cupcake. "We'll see if it ends a lot less sticky this time."

Rorrik laughed. "I think your vest hopes so."

"And what about your nose?"

Rorrik was turning to say something just as a glob of frosting hit him square in the nose.

The tabby recoiled and saw Valen standing there in false innocence, his coyness foiled by a sprawling grin.

"Are we doing this?" Rorrik laughed, readying his utensil.

Valen answered by flinging another glob of frosting.

. . .

"It looks like it washed out," Valen said, inspecting his vest. They were upstairs in the Den's laundry room, wet from washing up and in fresh clothes. Their prior frosting-covered outfits had been tossed in the washer, which had rendered them clean and sugarless.

"Great! We can hang up the clothes downstairs!" Rorrik said with a yawn. Despite his desire to stay awake, his exhaustion was becoming more and more persistent.

Valen mirrored his yawn and gave a groggy nod.

. . .

Valen was down on the queen bed and Rorrik was up in the loft bed. It had been quiet for a while, as they were drifting off to sleep.

"...Rorrik," Valen then mumbled, instantly waking Rorrik.

"Hm?"

"Thanks for today. It was... really fun," the demorinkin said.

Rorrik looked over the edge and met the demorinkin's eyes. "You're welcome," the felidaren replied warmly. "I had a lot of fun, too."

Chapter 49

Kyla

"Now that the dust has settled with the Fangs situation, it's paramount we find you a home," Avalene began, frank but gentle.

Valen flinched, worry striking his expression. "…home?"

The vigilante pushed a pile of papers across the meeting table. "These three families are a willing and suitable match. Go ahead and give them a look."

Valen bowed his head, quiet as he glanced over the papers with weak regard. He said nothing after looking at the sheets for a handful of seconds, never lifting his head.

"…I understand that everything feels like it's moving too fast — that you've only just recently had a moment to relax. However, the sooner we get you situated, the sooner your life will return to a sense of normalcy," Avalene reasoned. "I know it's difficult, but please, we're only trying to help you."

Valen still said nothing, his eyes glued to the papers. Kyla was brought back to the first time the three of them had talked in that very meeting room, the demorinkin unresponsive as they attempted to coax replies out of him.

Following a tense silence, Valen grabbed the pile and finally lifted his head, his expression strained. "Can I at least look them over for a while?"

Avalene nodded. "Of course. This is not a decision to be made on a whim"

"…Can I be excused, then?"

Avalene gestured towards the door with another nod. "We have covered all we need to."

Valen scooted out of his chair and made for the exit, his head once again dropping as he left. The door clicked closed, leaving Kyla and Avalene alone.

Kyla bit at her lip as her chest squeezed and her stomach flipped. She thought of the families on the papers, of Valen leaving, and her heart thrashed in protest.

"Avalene…" the tortoiseshell started, her brow knotting. "Is there any way—"

"You want him to stay here, don't you?" Avalene immediately guessed.

Kyla raised a brow at her old friend. "...Is it that obvious?"

"History tends to repeat itself," Avalene said through one of her rare smirks. "Knowing that, you can assume what I'm going to tell you."

Kyla mirrored the human's smirk. "...Run it by Niem and the boys?"

Avalene gave a nod. "If everyone is on board, including Valen, I can get everything arranged."

Kyla flashed a smile. "Better start filling out the paperwork, then."

■ ■ ■

Niem was up on the roof, hunched over a cup of tea on the railing. His ears flicked in greeting, but his attention stayed on the horizon ahead. There was a mild breeze in the air, gently caressing his jet-black fur.

"Thanks for meeting me here," Kyla spoke upon coming up next to him. "I know you're busy."

Niem's only reply was a stiff nod. He took a sip of his tea; dewstar petal and catmint, her nose told her. She knew the cup to be a favorite of Niem's when he was seeking relaxation; Kyla wondered if that was a good or bad sign.

"Well... I was just speaking with Avalene..." Kyla paused to search for words. "We are trying to find Valen a home, and..."

Niem scoffed. "Took you long enough." Another sip of his dewstar tea. "The answer is yes."

Kyla flinched at her mate's words, taken off guard. "Wha—"

"You want him to stay here," Niem correctly assumed. "You have my answer."

"...You're honestly alright with this?" Kyla asked with a hint of skepticism, hesitant but hopeful.

Niem finally met her eyes. "I've been expecting it since our last conversation on the matter." His lips then twitched with a faint smirk. "I am fine with it; it will make the boy's training easier."

Kyla's ears pressed back, and her gaze found the railing. "You're still expecting that out of him, then?"

Niem let go of a single chuckle. "Of course," another gulp of his tea. "It's what *we* agreed."

'*But not Valen...*' Guilt flooded into her thoughts, like a leaking faucet left unchecked. Her chest tightened, and she closed her eyes, unable to escape her shame. '*He is right... it is what we agreed.*' She had to live with that choice.

"I'll talk to him," Niem then offered after downing the rest of his mug. "You can talk to our sons in the meantime."

"What are you going to tell him?" Kyla worried.

Niem turned around to head back down into the Den. "What's expected of him."

. . .

Valen

Valen couldn't stomach looking at the names and faces of strangers for long. He placed the papers on an end table in the living room, too bothered to entertain the idea of his life once again being uprooted, any comfort he had built up being yanked from right beneath his feet.

He lay on the couch, dejected as he scanned the room, his stomach contorting into knots. He didn't want to leave the hideout — the family; he despaired at the idea of starting all over again.

After a while of sulking, he heard someone clear their throat. Valen shot into sitting up with a startled yelp, seeing Niem in front of the couch, the felidaren's stark yellow eyes searing into him.

Valen forced down a nervous swallow. He was opening his mouth to speak, but Niem beat him to it.

"We have something to discuss." The black-furred felidaren gestured his chin towards the kitchen, heading there without waiting for a reply.

Valen hurriedly followed him into the kitchen where the felidaren had already taken a seat. The demorinkin sat down, his heartbeat in a gallop.

Niem stared at him for a tortuously tense second. "We helped get rid of your enemies and gave you a safe spot to stay, all at extreme risk to us. It is time you helped us in return."

Valen processed his words with guilt and alarm. "W-what can I do?" he stuttered the words out, nervous enough to sweat.

"Work for us," Niem answered simply.

"W-work?" As in, be a criminal?!" Valen's alarm augmented tenfold. "But—"

"You *owe* us." Niem told, his tone even, but powerful. "It's only fair."

Valen opened his mouth to protest, but the felidaren's point resonated deep. Niem was right. The family *had* sacrificed a lot for him; it was only right—*fair*—to help them in return. He had been wanting to repay them, after all. *'But not... not like that...'*

"You have access to magic and the ability to shift your form," Niem went on. "I expect you to put those skills to apt use."

Valen dropped his gaze, his conscience bombarded on both fronts. He did not want to be a criminal, but he did not want to take advantage of the family, either!

An earlier realization then hit him. '...I already am a criminal.' His illegal magic, his existence outside official paperwork, his involvement with Miss Porte and the family...

That ship had already sailed.

...What was stopping him, then?

"...O-okay..." Valen hesitantly accepted with a twist of his guts. "B-but, there's just one thing I want to know first..."

Niem waited.

"...What... what is it that you do, exactly?" Valen asked, curious for the answer but dreading it equally.

"We gather sensitive intelligence and products of value, whether by the wish of our clients or our own goals," Niem replied. "Bluntly, we're spies, infiltrators, and thieves."

And there it was; Valen was forced to acknowledge the truth. They did not just steal or live outside the law for necessity; it was their job.

The fact manifested as an unwieldy stone in his guts. He tried to swallow but was unable. "Do you... do you ever," he stammered, dizzy with anxiety.

Niem raised an eyebrow.

"...Kill... people?" Valen forced out, his voice small.

Niem shook his head. "No. That is outside our line of work."

Unexpected relief washed over the demorinkin at that. At least he wouldn't be a murderer. 'I can... live with that.'

Another question burned on his tongue. "...What will I do, then?"

"There are many uses for your skills. Acting as a distraction or taking on a different identity to infiltrate a premises will be amongst your most common roles."

Valen slowly nodded, attempting to come to peace with it all. 'It's... it's the fair thing to do. I owe them.'

"Do you agree, then?" Niem said, his yellow glare intense.

Valen's expression crinkled with one last surge of uncertainty, but it was short-lived. He lifted his attention and stared at the felidaren, his lips tight.

The demorinkin nodded, spurring the felidaren into doing something Valen had never seen him do: grin.

. . .

Rorrik

Rorrik and his brothers had been called home from their duties in the city, in the name of a family meeting. They mustered in the meeting room where their mother was waiting.

"I called you all here to discuss something very important," she instantly got to it when they had all taken a seat. "…What do you all think about Valen staying here? As in, for good?"

Rorrik burst out of his chair with excitement. "What?! Like, living here?!"

His mother was all smiles. "Your father has already approved. All we need now is all of your blessing and Valen's."

"Yes!" Rorrik shouted, exuberant.

"He's already basically a member of the family!" Quinn pointed out in a chuckle.

Gavin nodded, grinning. "I see no issue with it."

Calvin shrugged, attempting to look indifferent, but Rorrik spotted a threatening smile.

"It will be great having him around!" Jate agreed, too.

"So, we get a new brother?!" Talis exclaimed, his tail frizzing with excitement.

The tortoiseshell nodded. "He would be a part of the family, yes."

"Yay!" the youngest whooped.

Their mother laughed. "Remember, though, Valen has to agree first!"

"Then what are we waiting for?" Rorrik wondered. "Let's go ask him!"

■ ■ ■

Kyla

"Let me talk to him alone for right now," she told her children. "We don't want him to feel pressured."

A reception of hurriedly bobbing heads answered her.

She found Valen in the kitchen, looking deep in thought as he sat by himself at the table.

She took a seat next to him, gaining the demorinkin's attention.

"Hey there," she greeted. "How are you holding up?"

Valen broke eye contact, and his shoulders bumped in a weak shrug.

"Have you looked over the families?"

The demorinkin frowned and dropped his gaze down to the table. "I… uh, well…"

"I understand." Her hand gently wrapped around the demorinkin's.

A short silence followed, Kyla spending it mindful on how to approach the next subject.

"Well," the felidaren finally started, a smile begging to stretch her lips. "I had a word with Miss Porte and my family, and there is something I want to run by you."

Valen lifted his head, appearing curious. "What is it...?"

"We were wondering if..." She paused for weight. "Instead of trying to find you another family, you would just want to stay here... with us?"

Valen gaped at her before a smile exploded across his features. "What — really?!"

Kyla's own smile broke free. "We would all love to have you. What do you say?"

"Y-yes! Of course!" The demorinkin threw his arms around her, and the mother returned the embrace, kissing the side of his head.

With that, her children poured into the room, cheering and laughing. They joined the hug, forming a huddle of love, of family.

"Thank you!" Valen sniffled. "Thank you!"

Kyla broke the hug, and Rorrik swept Valen up next, squeezing tight. He nuzzled the demorinkin with fervor, them both laughing.

The other brothers then had their own turn embracing their newest family member, Kyla stepping back to call Avalene on her corresponder.

"I hope you started that paperwork," the queen said when the vigilante picked up.

Avalene had a chuckle. "It's already finished. All it needs is your signature."

Chapter 50

Valen

Rorrik was nestled into Valen's back when the demorinkin awoke the next morning. It came as no surprise, considering the entire collection of brothers had crammed themselves on the bed the night before to cuddle. None but Rorrik remained, the others having left one by one throughout the night.

Valen was much too awake and restless to fall back asleep. He gingerly scooted away from Rorrik and grabbed his clothes for the day. He donned them in the bathroom, sparing his reflection a long glance, the vivid red of his vest brilliant as ever. After brushing his hair and teeth, he set out towards the kitchen.

He noticed that the lights in the hall were still dim, meaning the hour was early. The clock in the kitchen said it was almost five; he was up early again.

He thought about cooking but ended up walking up the stairs to the inn's roof instead. Rorrik had shown him the way when they had explored the city before.

He reached the roof, stepping outside into the moist and crisp air of night. The sky was dark with a rich purple, but a stunning display of pink and yellow were piercing the bottom of the horizon, the first inkling of the sun.

Dawn was approaching.

Valen draped across the railing, emotional as he beheld the tapestry of evolving color before him. The sun, framed between a skyline of buildings across the water, inched higher and higher, the sky intensifying in saturation as it climbed. As the light transformed the world, Valen couldn't help but notice the symbolism.

It was remarkable how, despite the blackest of nights, the sun would always shine the brighter. The light and warmth of dawn would always come, a promise of a new day.

Valen thought of the terrible night he had been suffering through, all the pain and shame and despair. He realized that his own dawn was finally approaching, by the light of a new family, friends, and surroundings. The cold moisture of the night would persist as dew, indeed, but the warmth of the sun would eventually undo the drops. As such, there was still healing to be had, struggles to surmount, but the presence of the sun, of hope, made it all achievable.

Valen heeded the sky with relief and wonder, his expression warm and bright with light. Night was behind him; he had finally arrived at dawn.

■ ■ ■

Valen walked down the steps to the hideout, mindful over which meal to cook for the family. He could try potato pancakes, or perhaps omelets, or maybe—

He was suddenly drenched in water as he passed through the entry door, yelping out in shock. A bucket clattered to the floor, and laughter from multiple voices erupted as he spun around in consternation.

"We got you!" Talis screeched with glee.

"That was *way* too easy!" Calvin hooted.

Valen spotted all the brothers in the entry hall, bent over as they guffawed.

The demorinkin gaped in confusion, slow to process just what had occurred. "What was that?!"

"A prank, silly!" Jate snorted.

"You're going to need to be more alert if you don't want to fall for that one again," Gavin snickered.

"Indeed! They only get cleverer from here on out, too!" Quinn warned.

Valen still stared, his hair and shoulders sopping wet. Then, the laughter finally came, a concoction of surprise, humility, and humor.

Rorrik draped an arm around the demorinkin and gave a wink. "Welcome to the family, Valen!"

Epilogue

Valen

The waiting room was charged with anticipation as Valen gazed about with a smile, watching as the felidaren brothers shared eager looks and animated chatter. The demorinkin was mutually excited; they were about to get a new family member, after all!

Mrs. Catty had gone into labor hours before, Rorrik and he getting the news as they were out on a watch. They had hurriedly met up with Gavin and Quinn and drove to the private clinic the family typically did medical business with. Jate and the two youngest had already arrived, greeting them with jests over their lateness.

The energy of the room kept high despite the lengthy wait. Conversation of what color of fur Aylan would have, and if he would beat the prior record for heaviest brother (Jate was the current record holder at 8 pounds) buzzed on and on. Valen was an amused audience as the family indulged in their enthusiastic guessing games and musing.

"Hey, you two. Want to go on a walk?" Jate eventually asked the two youngest.

"Okay!" Talis leapt up from his chair, frizzy tailed.

"I guess," Calvin complied.

The three of them left, and a different energy very abruptly swept across the room, taking Valen off guard.

"Dad said Mom is having a hard time," Gavin informed, serious. "She and Aylan are stable, but she's struggling."

Valen was slammed with worry. "What do you mean?"

The brothers shared a glance with each other, their ears pressing back.

"She's been... sick for a while," Quinn shared.

"You haven't noticed?" Rorrik mumbled, his eyes dropping to the floor.

Valen had noted that Mrs. Catty seemed particularly drained and required longer periods of rest, but he had chalked that up to her pregnancy.

"Is she going to be alright?" Valen worried, struck by the brother's sudden solemnness.

"The doctors aren't sure," Gavin replied. "But she's stable for now, so that's good."

"What is she sick with?" the demorinkin asked, hesitant.

"Vetroxis," Quinn answered. "It's a virus that inhibits organ function. Its intensity comes and goes."

"She had been doing a lot better, but the pregnancy has been tough on her," Gavin contributed.

Rorrik was quiet, his expression tight as he kept his attention on the floor.

Valen looked between all the siblings, the news slow to process. He put a hand to his forehead, feeling distant and dizzy.

In the coming minutes, silence followed, Valen struggling to accept what he had just heard. He didn't want to believe it. What if Mrs. Catty—

The doors abruptly burst open, a beaming nurse standing in the doorway. "The baby is here! Mom and baby are doing fine!"

All four of them snapped to attention.

"I'll go get them," Gavin volunteered before hurrying out the exit.

Rorrik pulled Valen in a hug, the demorinkin feeling moisture where the felidaren buried his face. Valen returned the embrace, awash with relief.

Quinn draped an arm over them both. "She's okay, it's okay."

It was only a few more moments until Gavin returned with the others and they rushed inside to meet the newest family member.

■ ■ ■

They filed into the room, hushed and anxious. Mrs. Catty was sitting up in a bed, her brunette hair damp with sweat and pushed every which way, but doing little to detract from her beauty. She was visibly exhausted but still glowing with maternal pride, her attention on the little bundle in her arms: Aylan.

The sight incited a powerful memory of his own mother when she had given birth to Karreo. Valen teared up as his emotions surged, utterly moved.

Niem was at Mrs. Catty's side, his typical intense stare instead soft as he beheld his newest child. The parents glanced up as they all arrived, Mrs. Catty smiling and Niem nodding.

They approached the bed, Aylan coming into view as they drew closer. Instead of tabby or pure black fur, speckles of brown and white dotted the baby's charcoal cheeks, joined by a mask of copper: tortoiseshell, just like Mrs. Catty.

The brothers all gasped as they stared at their new sibling, taken aback.

"Hold on!" Jate whispered, shocked.

"Does that mean—" Quinn stammered, just as surprised.

"No way!" Rorrik added.

Valen glanced between them, feeling as though he were missing something.

Mrs. Catty chuckled, strained but amused. She hefted Aylan in her arms and the baby's eyes cracked open to reveal a stark yellow instead of green. "Boys, meet your new *sister*, Aylee."

About the Author

Heather Kannianen is one of two authors for the Adventures of Azyria book collection. Her collaborator is her husband, Jared Kannianen, who goes by the penname J.K. Lore.

Heather lives in the northern suburbs of Illinois, accompanied by her husband, four boisterous cats, and many fish. Heather has always enjoyed creating, which naturally bred a passion for storytelling both in writing and in tabletop roleplay.

Her books all take place in the expansive world of Azyria, a universe of magic, gods, and fantastical races. Azyria has been technologically advanced by its magic, painting a setting that is pseudo-modern and familiar, yet still enchanting and peculiar. Each novel employs a wide arrangement of characters who take part in emotional, character-driven narratives.

Heather and Jared Kannianen have many plans for the Adventures of Azyria book collection. You can keep up with them on social media.

Facebook: facebook.com/AoAzyria
Twitter: twitter.com/AoAzyria
Tumblr: azyria.tumblr.com

www.ingramcontent.com/pod-product-compliance
Lightning Source LLC
Chambersburg PA
CBHW051538250626
47157CB00001B/98